*Emma Caldridge went to sleep in first class on
a British Airlines flight from Miami to Bogotá,
and woke sixty seconds before the plane
was downed in the Colombian jungle . . .*

*Emma was on a mission to reclaim her life.
Dying in a plane crash would be a cruel twist
of fate, but only one of the many cruel twists
she'd endured this year . . .*

RUNNING FROM THE DEVIL

"Freveletti skillfully keeps *Running from the Devil*
realistic and tense with believable characters
worth caring about and action that never stops. . . .
[She] never gives her characters—or the reader—
a moment's rest. Tense action is packed into the plot
from the first page to *Running from the Devil's*
explosive end. . . . Freveletti sets high standards."
South Florida Sun-Sentinel

"Ten pages in, my heart was pounding—
and the tension only grew from there."
Tess Gerritsen, *New York Times*
bestselling author of *The Keepsake*

"Full of thrills and tradecraft,
pace and peril. An outstanding debut."
Lee Child, *New York Times*
bestselling author of *Nothing to Lose*

By Jamie Freveletti

RUNNING FROM THE DEVIL

Coming Soon in Hardcover
RUNNING DARK

JAMIE FREVELETTI

RUNNING
FROM THE
DEVIL

HARPER

An Imprint of HarperCollinsPublishers

This book was originally published in hardcover May 2009 by William Morrow, an Imprint of HarperCollins Publishers.

HARPER

An Imprint of HarperCollinsPublishers
10 East 53rd Street
New York, New York 10022-5299

Copyright © 2009 by Jamie Freveletti
Excerpt from *Running Dark* copyright © 2010 by Jamie Freveletti
ISBN 978-0-06-168423-4

First Harper paperback printing: June 2010
First William Morrow hardcover printing: May 2009

HarperCollins ® and Harper ® are registered trademarks of Harper-Collins Publishers.

Printed in the United States of America

Visit Harper paperbacks on the World Wide Web at
www.harpercollins.com

10 9 8 7 6 5 4 3 2 1

For my mother, Judy Clayton,
jazz singer, actress, inspiration,
who sings "Angel Eyes" like no other

With love, J

ACKNOWLEDGMENTS

This book would not have been possible without the support and assistance of an entire army of people.

To my agent, Barbara Poelle at the Irene Goodman Literary Agency, whose great advice and good humor set me on the right track, kept me laughing, and helped me through the publishing gauntlet.

To everyone at HarperCollins/William Morrow who was willing to take a chance on a debut thriller writer.

To my initial editor, Carolyn Marino, whose editorial expertise was so good that reading her suggestions was like taking a condensed writing class. Two years ago I created a short "wish" list of thriller editors for the book and Carolyn was on it. When Barbara called to tell me whom I'd be working with at Harper, I was speechless. I was also ski-less, as I was just getting on a lift when the call came through and in my excitement forgot to strap on the skis.

To my second editor, Lyssa Keusch, who caught the pass from Carolyn Marino without missing a beat and who guided me through the next stages in editing the manuscript.

To Wendy Lee and Johnathan Wilber, who helped me with the myriad of details required in preparing the manuscript.

To Angela Swafford, Colombian author, journalist, and intrepid adventurer, who obtained clearance to ride with the

Colombian army and tour the Cano-Limón-Covenas pipeline and generously shared her experiences with me.

To the professionals and friends who gave advice on technical matters, some mentioned in the Author's Note at the end of this book. Any errors are mine. George E. Boos, retired commercial airline pilot; Ronald A. Sherman, MD, MSc, Dtm&H, Department of Pathology, University of California, Irvine; Jess T. Ford, director, International Affairs and Trade, United States Government Accountability Office; Sergeant Brandon Verstat, United States Marine Corps; Bill Edler and his wife, Carolina Diaz Osorio; and the woman scientist on the other end of the line at the University of Chicago Department of Molecular Genetics and Cell Biology who didn't treat me like a nut when I called out of the blue and asked how to genetically reconstitute burned plants.

To Robert Thorson, Jill Griffiths, and Darwyn Jones, who taught me how to write copy, helped me create the perfect pitch, and edited my query letter.

To the other writers willing to give me their feedback: Lisa Rosenthal and the writers in her "Dig in" revision workshops, the Bucktown Library Writers' Group, and the "Chicago Contingent."

To Dana Kaye, Darwyn Jones, and Marcus Sakey, who invited me to join the Contingent.

To my father, who enthusiastically read anything I mailed to him.

To my mother, who was willing to drop everything to read drafts of troublesome chapters, and who raised me to follow my dreams.

To my children, Alex and Claudia, who helped me run off the ski lift in my boots and still weren't embarrassed to be seen with me.

And to my husband, Klaus, whose ultramarathon running

inspired part of the book's premise. Klaus encouraged me to write and didn't flinch when I told him I was going to take a sabbatical from my law practice to do it. His love, support, and willingness to travel to questionable areas to help research my settings make life a blast. Thank you, my love, for driving the getaway car.

RUNNING
FROM THE
DEVIL

EMMA CALDRIDGE WENT TO SLEEP IN FIRST CLASS on a British Airlines flight from Miami to Bogotá, and woke sixty seconds before the plane was downed in the Colombian jungle.

It was the middle of the week in early August, and the half-empty plane contained business travelers, a few tourists, and Emma. A chemist and endurance racer, Emma was on a mission to reclaim her life. Dying in a plane crash would be a cruel twist of fate, but only one of the many cruel twists she'd endured this year.

She listened as the pilot's voice came over the intercom, warning them that the airstrip he'd been ordered to use was too small for the jet and asking the passengers to assume crash position. Emma pulled her backpack out from under the seat in front of her and curled over it.

The plane pointed downward at an angle so extreme that Emma slid forward in her seat. The walls vibrated as the jet picked up speed. The engines whined while the plane tilted from side to side, as if the pilot and the copilot were in a battle for the controls. The other passengers started screaming.

The cabin depressurized and the temperature dropped so fast that ice formed on the windows right before Emma's eyes. She tried to breathe, but her lungs felt like they were collapsing from the inside. The screaming passengers went silent, as if they no longer had enough breath to shriek. The ceiling opened up and the air masks dropped down, swaying on their rubber tubes. Emma snatched at her mask, yanking it once before sucking greedily into the yellow cup.

They hit the ground with a huge bang, still catapulting forward. The lights went out, plunging them into darkness. Only the tiny row of exit lights running along the floor remained on, illuminating their path to nowhere. Emma's seat pulled away from the floor and she flew into the black.

2

EDWARD BANNER STOOD IN THE COMMUNICATIONS
center of the United States Southern Command in Miami
and watched as a breathless CNN correspondent broke the
news about Flight 689 to the world. Carol Stromeyer, his
company's vice president, stood next to him.

"Did you brief CNN?" Banner said.

"I left that to the State Department. They're trying to control the information flow."

"Do we have a manifest?"

"British Airlines is faxing it now."

"Was a marshal on board?"

"We don't think so."

Banner pulled a hand through his salt-and-pepper hair.
His blue suit fit to perfection, and his tie formed a faultless
knot at the neck of his custom-made shirt. Former military
and current CEO of Darkview, a company that provided
special forces personnel under contract to the Department
of Defense, Banner brooked no wrinkles, slackers, or untidy
Windsor knots. Despite his current age of forty-five, he could
still shoot a rifle with deadly aim, dispatch an assailant with
a well-placed kick, and outdrive the best of them behind the
wheel of an armored Mercedes. Only he knew that his con-

tact lenses were bifocals, his right hand sometimes shook from a bullet-wound injury he'd sustained fifteen years ago, and his left rotator cuff throbbed every time it rained.

"Any idea how this happened?"

Stromeyer sighed. "None. The pilot's last communication was a routine check with the control tower. After that, silence."

"Then why do we think it was hijacked?"

"It was a flight to Bogotá, but it turned long before and headed to the mountains."

"Any chance that the instruments failed and sent the pilot off course?"

"Not likely."

"Did it veer toward Venezuela?"

Stromeyer shook her head. "Don't know. The hijacker turned off the tracking transponder. It could be anywhere."

"Has anyone contacted the Colombian government?"

"*Everyone* has contacted the Colombian government. They claim to know nothing more than we do."

"They're lying. A jet that size doesn't change its flight plan unannounced without someone noticing something. At the very least, land-based radar would paint the jet as it flew by."

"They think it was downed in the northwestern mountains, near the Venezuelan border."

"That's the Freedom Fighters of Colombia territory."

"And the drug cartels."

"And way too close to Venezuela," Banner said.

Stromeyer nodded. "Intelligence is trying to determine if anyone from that country had a hand in the incident. If they did, the press will go into a frenzy. It'll take their focus off the Middle East."

"What time do we brief the president?"

"In ten minutes," Stromeyer said. "I'll check for the fax and meet you there."

Banner watched her leave. At forty, Carol Stromeyer was one of the best officers he'd ever met. She was as well trained as he in the fighting arts, but had never employed her skills in the field. She'd spent her early years in the administrative and noncombat roles routinely relegated to women in the army. She'd risen through the ranks by virtue of her almost uncanny ability to find any piece of information within five minutes, and her detailed knowledge of all things, and forms, bureaucratic. If a new unit needed commissioning, money needed assigning, or a whole army brigade needed moving, Stromeyer knew who to contact to get it done and what forms to file in triplicate to grease the wheels. When Banner left the special forces to start Darkview, she was the first person he'd recruited.

Banner figured she'd have the manifest in three minutes and detailed information on every passenger listed in under twenty-four hours.

He grabbed a notepad from his desk and headed to the meeting.

EMMA LANDED ON HER BACK IN SOME BUSHES, STILL strapped into the seat. Her arms flung outward, and the backpack flew off her lap. An explosion ripped through the air, sending a wave of heat washing over her. She struggled to remove her seat belt, rolled off the seat, and staggered to her feet.

What she saw was Dante's Inferno.

Emma stood to the right of the wreckage. The plane's nose and what was left of the first- and business-class cabins lay in front of her about one hundred yards. The remaining debris sat farther back and at a forty-five-degree angle to the makeshift runway, with a gaping hole where the plane had ripped in half.

People swarmed at the hole in the fore section. The lucky ones jumped to the ground. The unlucky ones fell when they were pushed from behind by the stampeding passengers.

The people from the aft section of the plane were not as fortunate, because the rear of the plane was on fire. Heavy black smoke poured from the twisted metal. The passengers jumped from this section of the plane as well, but some were already burning. They dropped and rolled, but as they did the flames increased. The ruptured fuel tanks sprayed fuel everywhere, and the people were rolling in it and reigniting themselves. Several trees caught fire. Emma watched as the spewing fuel leaped out to meet them. When the fuel reached the burning trees, they exploded, sending a huge fireball into the air. The force kicked Emma's feet from under her and threw her several feet. Her back hit a tree and she slid down it. Her legs didn't seem to work. She slumped at the base of the tree and watched the carnage. Huge tongues of fire shot straight upward, turning the sky an orange-red color.

A large group of men, all armed and dressed in fatigues, stood at the beginning of the runway next to the plane's tail. Their faces glowed red and black in the eerie blaze of the fires. The men watched in fascination as the passengers jumped from the airplane. They roared with laughter each time a passenger rolled and caught on fire. Light flickered off the bottles of liquor they passed from man to man.

Hell comes complete with its own army, Emma thought.

The lead soldier barked an order, and the soldiers fanned out. They walked toward the plane, collecting any surviving passengers as they did.

Emma tried to stand, but the world spun around her. She dropped to the ground and crawled away from the landing strip. When she reached her backpack, she grabbed the strap and dragged it with her. Her fingers clutched at the earth as she pulled herself forward. She gasped for breath and shivered in what she supposed was some sort of shock reaction. She couldn't control the shaking. The blood from a cut on her head had congealed into a sticky mass from her temple to her jaw. When she moved, the mess cracked, like dried mud. Her head pounded with an unholy sharp, stabbing pain. She stole a quick glance behind her. The men in fatigues were busy collecting the survivors. They didn't look Emma's way.

She focused on reaching the safety of the tree line. Once there, she scrambled into the forest and collapsed behind a fat bush. She rifled through her backpack, looking for her cell phone. She found it, flipped it open, and waited while it searched for service. After a minute, the screen displayed NO SERVICE. She felt blind panic rise in her, swamping her. She willed herself to calm.

"Screw it," Emma whispered.

She typed a text message anyway. She knew that the text system often worked even when the phone service did not. Her fingers shook as she dialed her boss's number and typed:

Am alive, plane downed, in jungle, army men taking hostages. Help.

Emma hit send and waited while the phone displayed a little hourglass that spun as it searched for service. After a minute the display read UNABLE TO SEND.

"You worthless piece of shit!" Emma hissed out loud at the phone. She turned it off and snapped it shut. She slumped back down and stared at the burning treetops. Her eyes grew heavy, her head ached. She felt a strange languor wash over her. She worried that a concussion was causing her drowsiness, but she no sooner had that thought than she slipped into unconsciousness. The orange flames blurred as her mind shut down.

4

BANNER SAT IN SOUTHERN COMMAND'S CONFER-
ence room and gazed at a large screen that contained a
PowerPoint satellite photo of a black mushroom cloud. He
wasn't sure of the significance of the picture, but he figured
it didn't bode well.

Department of Defense, State Department, NORAD, and
Department of Transportation personnel filled the room, as
well as a soldier named Miguel Gonzalez, who'd been ap-
pointed to run a possible special operations first response
force. About thirty, he was a slender five foot ten, and Banner
guessed he was of Cuban descent. The others referred to
him as "Major." Banner didn't know Miguel's background,
and no one offered the information. Presumably Stromeyer
knew the details, but she hadn't volunteered them, either.

The group in the room consisted of some of the best military and political minds in the country. The highest-ranking
members of the army, navy, air force, and marines fiddled
with legal pads, flipped pencils in the air, and sipped coffee
from china cups that they held like mugs, ignoring the el-
egant, curved handles.

Jordan Whitter represented the political branch. Whitter's

reputation for maneuverability within the State Department was legendary. As a result, his career had already outlasted two presidents. Whitter had shrewd eyes and a lifelong bureaucrat's aversion to sticking his neck out. He wore a dark suit and a striped tie that he kept adjusting.

Banner watched Whitter fidget with his tie and wondered why he'd chosen that particular combination. He'd bet a week's salary that the stripes on the tie matched Whitter's college colors.

Banner's own participation in the meeting wasn't clear, even to him. He attended at the request of an old friend, Brigadier General Robert Corvan. Corvan asked Banner to moderate the meeting, but made no mention of hiring Darkview for a mission.

When Darkview provided the military with highly qualified special operations personnel, Banner flew the men into extremely volatile situations—wars, guerrilla insurgencies, and genocidal civil conflicts. Although they often fought alongside the regular army, they were technically not a part of the United States military machine, and so their deployment could not be considered by the "host" country as a formal act of war.

The men's unique status conferred some equally unique benefits. They were not required to follow military protocol, they had state-of-the-art equipment, and their pay was much better than their regular army counterparts. Their status conferred some negative consequences as well. Although they died in battle, their deaths were not included in official war tallies, no one hailed them as war heroes, nor did anyone present their widows with posthumous medals acknowledging their sacrifice. The unkind called them mercenaries.

Recovering a hijacked plane, even by force, could be handled by regular military search-and-rescue teams sent openly into the target area. Banner's crew generally implemented covert missions, and so Banner wondered what the collected men in the room knew about this situation that he did not.

Miguel fiddled with a laptop computer, replaced the mushroom-cloud photo with a large satellite map of Colombia, and began his presentation.

"The first thing we did was look for any distress signals emitting from where we believe the plane landed. A satellite passing over Colombia returned a report of a cell-phone-based GPS transmission in this part of the country." Miguel pointed to the northwestern mountains near the Colombia-Venezuela border.

"Unfortunately, the satellite passed again approximately one hundred minutes later, and the ping was gone."

"Could it have been from a passenger's phone?" the undersecretary of the navy said.

Miguel nodded. "The GPS transmission code was registered to a phone owned by a passenger named Emma Caldridge. And Ms. Caldridge was kind enough to send us a note." The photo behind Miguel shifted to a copy of Emma's text message. The words *army men taking hostages* were highlighted.

Whitter groaned. "This is awful."

Banner couldn't agree more, but he was surprised at Whitter's empathetic response. Perhaps the man had a heart after all.

"I agree, sir. But at least we know that some people survived the crash. Better to be a hostage than dead," Miguel said.

Whitter slapped his hand on the table. "Hostages are a political nightmare! How many? There were two hundred and sixteen people on that jet. This administration cannot have such a breach of security under its watch."

What an asshole, Banner thought.

Miguel shook his head. "Tough to know how many survived. Once the cell-phone ping disappeared, we looked for any other anomalies that could indicate a downed jet, and we found this."

The mushroom-cloud photo reappeared. Miguel pointed at it with a laser pointer.

"We believe it was a large explosion that caused this actual cloud. If this is the plane, either it exploded on landing, or it was deliberately exploded."

"How long will it take to get a small troop to the location pinpointed by the cell phone transmission?" Banner said.

"It's done already," Miguel said.

"Excellent." Whitter smiled for the first time that day.

Miguel grimaced. "We requested that the Colombian military send a helicopter to verify that it was the crash site and assist in a search-and-rescue mission. They did, and they say that no crash exists at those coordinates."

Whitter's face fell. "Could she have sent the message while the plane was still flying? Perhaps the plane continued on for a while?"

Miguel shook his head. "I doubt it."

Whitter pointed at the screen. "What about your satellite? You got a picture of the mushroom cloud. How about a picture of the crash?"

Miguel shook his head again. "This area is mountainous and covered by dense foliage. Once the mushroom cloud dispersed, all we saw was green."

"That's FFOC territory, isn't it?" Banner said.

"Not just FFOC. Every guerrilla and paramilitary group in Colombia keeps a satellite force here. It's one of the most dangerous areas in Colombia, if not the world."

"Why there?" Stromeyer said.

"The Oriental gas pipeline is there. The pipeline pumps fifty thousand tons of oil a day. The groups bomb it regularly and then extort protection money from Oriental and the nearby municipal authorities."

Banner snorted. "I hope Oriental's executives aren't stupid enough to pay. They'll never make a penny."

"They did pay, until six months ago, when the United States sent a special operations force of five hundred men to protect the pipeline."

Banner sat up straighter. "Why is the United States Army protecting a private corporation's pipeline? Shouldn't the corporation hire its own force to guard its property?"

"You mean like your guys?" Whitter's disdain for Banner's men rang in the room.

Banner stared Whitter down. He allowed no one to disrespect his men, especially a career politico in his college colors who had never fired a gun in his life.

"I mean exactly that," Banner said. "Deploying regular army to protect a corporation, even an *oil* corporation, is a waste of the taxpayers' dollars."

"Mr. Banner, since 9/11 our new mission is to eradicate terrorism wherever it may exist in the world. If that means we send the military to protect an American corporation, then that's what we'll do," Whitter said. Banner and Whitter glared at each other. Several people shifted uncomfortably in their seats as they watched the two men square off. The undersecretary of the army broke the stalemate.

"We're there for training purposes only," he said. He raised an eyebrow at Banner.

Miguel cleared his throat. "That mission, however, actually increased terrorism."

Whitter shot a look at Miguel. "Explain that statement."

"The special forces have been in a pitched battle with the FFOC and the cartels since they landed. We've been dropping tons of herbicide on their coca fields and intercepting their saboteurs on the pipeline almost nightly."

"Who's winning?" Whitter said.

"It was a stalemate. While the attacks on the pipeline diminished and some coca fields decreased, the cartels adjusted quickly. They've ordered the farmers to begin moving their crop to the base of the mountains, where the planes can't spray, and this hijacking could be payback." Miguel turned to Stromeyer. "Major Stromeyer, do you have any information on Emma Caldridge? Is she on your manifest?"

Stromeyer riffled through her many sheets of paper. She pulled one out with a passport picture at the top. A pretty young woman with brown hair and vivid green eyes gazed at the camera with a hint of a smile.

"Here she is!" Stromeyer waved the page at the others. "Emma Caldridge. Thirty years old. She's a chemist working for Pure Chemistry, a laboratory specializing in formulating products for some of the top cosmetic companies in the world. Her supervisors say she's one of the best chemists they've ever hired. She has an expertise in plants and herbs. She studies them for any special properties they may have in a cosmetic application."

"You've spoken to her supervisors?" Whitter looked impressed.

Banner could have told Whitter that speaking to a key target's supervisor would be the minimum Stromeyer would do. She had been working so long at her manifest lists that he suspected she had each person's shoe size and preference in wine cataloged as well.

"A good dossier requires contact with someone with personal knowledge of the target," Stromeyer said, sounding every bit the bureaucrat.

"All right," Banner said. "What about boyfriends, husbands, lovers? Anyone she could have teamed up with to assist in this hijacking?"

Stromeyer looked startled. "You think she's a player?"

Banner shrugged. "She survived and sent a text message, didn't she? I wouldn't rule anything out."

Stromeyer nodded. "I see your point. She's single, lives in Miami Beach, and travels for business. She was going to Bogotá to meet with a local scientist, and then was headed to Patagonia for an endurance race. No current boyfriend, although a secretary at the lab had heard a rumor that she'd previously been engaged to marry a man who died suddenly. I'm still working on that, as well as her family connections."

"What does she do with her time? Does she belong to any questionable activist groups or have political affiliations?"

"Not at all. She works. And when she isn't working, she runs ultramarathons."

"What the hell is an ultramarathon?" Banner said.

"A marathon of thirty-five miles up to over one hundred."

Banner couldn't quite believe his ears. "Are we talking one hundred miles or one hundred kilometers?"

"Miles. I know it sounds crazy, but she literally runs one hundred miles at a time."

Banner ran five miles every other day at five in the morning. He used a treadmill and watched the *Early, Early* show. It took him an hour and he was always happy to be finished.

"Hell of a way to spend your time," Banner said.

"It is. And Ms. Caldridge ran the Badwater 135, one of the most grueling runs in the world."

Miguel looked intrigued. "Why so?"

"It's also known as the Death Valley run. The competitors run one hundred thirty-five miles through Death Valley. When Ms. Caldridge ran it last year, it was so hot that the rubber on the bottom of the competitors' shoes melted to the pavement."

Banner whistled. "Tough lady."

"She had better be," Miguel said, "because she's going

to have to outrun this man." The photo behind him shifted again and a picture of a ferret-faced man in faded army fatigues filled the screen.

Miguel placed a laser dot on the man's forehead. "This is Luis Rodrigo, head of a small band of paramilitary losers whose home base is in the mountains near where the mushroom cloud occurred."

"What's their role in all of this?" Banner could see from the picture that Rodrigo looked like a rodent and had the brains of a single-celled creature.

"We're not sure, but his group camps in the vicinity of the mushroom cloud, and the location alone suggests he's a player in the hijacking. If he is, we are dealing with a very bad guy."

"Worse than your average guerrilla leader?"

Miguel nodded. "Much worse. Rodrigo is insane. He makes the leaders of the drug cartels look respectable by comparison. He governs a band of outcasts that have all been ousted from the more established organizations. Rodrigo, though, is able to control them. When one messes up he simply maims or kills the offender. He cuts off ears, tongues, and plucks out eyes. The really incompetent assholes he shoots. Lately he's been said to have taken a page from the Afghan playbook and beheaded two particularly stupid soldiers."

"If they're so stupid, how did they plan and execute this hijacking?"

Miguel shook his head. "There is no way he did it alone. He must have had help. Either from the cartels or the FFOC, or both."

"Do you think this man has control of the passengers?" Whitter said. He looked appalled.

"Anybody wandering around that location will have to deal with him eventually, so we need to extract any survivors quickly. This man is volatile and could kill them all in a fit of rage."

"Suggestions?" Banner said.

Miguel nodded. "Wait until they make contact and then send them whatever ransom they demand. It's the best plan for getting those people out alive, and the price demanded will pale in comparison to the cost of a rescue mission."

Whitter shook his head. "Absolutely not. The United States does not negotiate with terrorists."

"Actually, we already have negotiated. There's a tacit agreement between the United States and Colombia to allow the far-right guerrilla leaders immunity from extradition to the U.S. if they agree to lay down their arms. If that's not negotiating with them, I don't know what is."

Whitter bristled like a porcupine under attack. "That deal was not cut by the United States. It was cut by the president of Colombia with the guerrilla leaders."

"And the United States didn't argue with it."

"It's still not the same as negotiating with kidnappers."

Banner put a hand in the air to silence the men. "Miguel, help me out here. Did these paramilitary groups take the Colombian president up on his offer and lay down their arms?"

"Thousands did," Miguel said.

"Then why do you think we're dealing with a paramilitary group in this hijacking?"

"Because the president has been negotiating only with the far-right paramilitary groups. The far-left guerrillas, the FFOC, have not been approached by the Colombian government."

"So you think this kidnapping is a bid to force the president of Colombia to begin negotiations with the far left," Banner said.

Miguel paused. "Perhaps. It could also be an attempt to derail the peace process entirely. The process requires that the paramilitary groups return control of the country to the government. These guys may not be too keen on giving up that kind of power."

"Or it could be unrelated and we are drawing the wrong conclusions." Whitter stabbed a finger at Miguel as he said this.

"That is also correct," Miguel said.

Banner liked that Miguel conceded the point to Whitter. It showed him that the man would not proceed on assumptions blindly.

"Alternative suggestions to negotiating?" Banner said.

"Pull twenty special forces personnel off the pipeline detail and gather them for a reconnaissance mission to find the crash site. From there try to determine the location of the passengers. Track them through the jungle, if that's what's required." Miguel sounded determined.

Whitter shook his head. "No. It's a waste of resources. Why go to an area that the Colombian military has already canvassed?"

"Because I don't believe them," Miguel said.

The undersecretary of the air force snorted. "You think these guys are lying?"

"There are those who say that the Colombian army has been hand in glove with the paramilitary groups for years. Even Colombia's own special forces unit in charge of rescue operations has been implicated in a massacre of the Colombian police. I don't think we can take anything for granted in an area as rife with corruption as this one."

"I won't go along with this," Whitter said. He turned to Banner. "If we go there anyway, it looks as though we don't trust the Colombian government. This country is an ally."

For the first time, Miguel looked aggravated. "Mr. Whitter, that's why I suggest that we use the men already posted in the area. We save valuable time and we avoid the questions that would arise from sending a wave of new military manpower."

So that's why I'm here, Banner thought, to provide unofficial muscle if Miguel's plan fails. He glanced at Miguel and kept his voice mild. "Did General Corvan approve the mission?"

"He did, pending your input. He said that no one knew better than you how to run a search-and-rescue mission in hostile territory."

"I'm flattered." Banner and General Corvan went back to the early days, when they had taken turns saving each other's hide.

"Who would be in charge of the mission?" Banner asked the question, but he figured he could guess the answer.

"I am. I leave tonight," Miguel said.

5

LUIS RODRIGO STOOD IN THE BAKING SUN ON THE scorched airstrip and watched his soldiers shove the airline passengers into a small circle. One man moved too slowly, and a guerrilla hammered him with the butt of his gun. The man dropped like a stone. Rodrigo's first lieutenant, Alvarado, came to stand next to him.

"They are stupid and slow," Alvarado said.

"Each is worth more money than you'll see in ten years. You tell Jorge I see him hit another without my permission and I'll cut off the hand he used at the wrist."

Alvarado stepped back. "They are arrogant Americans. They need to know who is in charge."

"*I* am in charge. I will decide who lives and who dies."

"We made more money with the coca. This"—Alvarado swept his arm to take in the passengers—"this does not pay the same, and the risks are large."

"Coca is dying every day. I don't need to remind you of this, Alvarado. You see the herbicide-dusting planes flown by the Americans. The fields are withering. In two years coca won't pay enough to cover the plane fuel to transport it."

"Coca will always be profitable," Alvarado said.

"For the cartels, yes, but not for us. We need to show the cartels that we can be profitable partners for them."

Alvarado stared at the passengers. He pulled a cigarette out of a pack rolled in his sleeve and lit it.

Luis analyzed the hostages as he watched the plane get stripped. Most had the soft, obese, and overcivilized look of Americans. One drew Luis's eye. He stood six feet three inches and weighed about one hundred eighty pounds. Seven inches taller and thirty pounds heavier than Luis, he had dark hair and an athlete's body. He moved easily, sweating in the heat, his mouth set in a grim line. This man smelled like danger to Luis. He made a mental note to watch him.

Luis swept his gaze over his men. Alvarado looked hung over, Juan's pupils were the size of quarters, and Manzillo gulped from a bottle of *aguardiente* and stumbled over something that only he could see. The mental state of the rest was always suspect. If they weren't armed, they couldn't have subdued a fly. Armed, they were ticking time bombs waiting to explode.

"How many do we have?" Luis said to Alvarado.

Alvarado shrugged. "Fifty. Maybe sixty. Is this enough for the FFOC?"

Luis counted sixty-eight. "They expected more. Especially given the risk."

"Then they should have let us land on a longer strip. I don't like it, Luis. The gringos won't take this lying down."

Luis felt his irritation rise. Alvarado was right, but lately he'd been sounding like a broken record, always negative, always warning. This job was a joint effort of the FFOC and the northern drug cartels, and the first time they'd given Luis any role in one of their operations. The FFOC provided the expertise and detailed planning needed to hijack the jet, and the drug cartel provided the planes within the country that would transport the passengers to the exchange location once they were ransomed.

Luis's role was to deliver the hostages and any valuables to a secure location in the mountains to await ransom. The FFOC and the drug cartels considered Luis's small group of paramilitary losers to be expendable, and so gave them the most grueling and dangerous job.

Luis knew the majority of his men were morons, long past stupid and incapable of any thought beyond their daily hit. Still, he was proud that he had been able to turn them into some semblance of a military group. The FFOC had finally responded to his repeated requests to be given a job that would prove his value as a leader. He intended to make the most of it.

"By the time the Americans find the crash site, we'll be deep in the mountains. No gringo knows these hills like we do. It will take them months to search for them. By then, the ransoms will have been paid."

Alvarado sucked on his cigarette, his eyes never moving from the passengers. "It would be easier if we could load them on the trucks and use the road."

Luis let his irritation show. "That would also be easier for the Americans to find us. No trucks, Alvarado. We make a trail through the jungle to the first checkpoint. We'll get them on trucks at that point."

"We'll lose at least ten more from the land mines as we march," Alvarado said.

"We march them in front of us. Better one of them step on a paw-breaker than one of us, eh?" Luis grinned at Alvarado. "And put the fat ones in the front. I want to keep the fit ones for working."

"And the women?"

"The women we reserve for other things."

Alvarado laughed.

6

EMMA CAME TO SOME TIME LATER. THE TREES STILL
burned. Heat reflected off the landing strip, creating waves
that looked like transparent streamers undulating upward.
She disentangled herself from the bush and moved farther
up the mountain to get a better view of the landing strip.

The surviving passengers sat huddled in a circle at the
beginning of the runway. Some leaned against their neigh-
bors, while others curled forward with their heads on their
knees. Emma recognized several from the plane. An older
gentleman, with a full head of white hair, sat tall, despite
his age. All but four had their hands tied behind their
backs.

Thirty guerrillas, armed with assault rifles, guarded them.
They all wore the same dirty green fatigues with lace-up
boots. Some drank from canteens that they kept in holders
attached to their belts, some smoked cigarettes, and others
sucked on hand-rolled brown sticks that looked like joints.
All were armed.

One guerrilla stood out from the others. Lean, wiry, with
an unshaven, rat-thin face and crazy pinball eyes, he shouted
orders and marched back and forth in front of the circle of
survivors. The others jumped to obey him.

They'd landed on a dirt airstrip the size of a football field backed on one side by a mountain, on the other by dense foliage. Several trees and jet parts still smoldered, sending thin ribbons of gray smoke into the air. The jungle threatened to encroach on all sides. Stately trees fought with smaller palms for every inch of available space and light. Tropical vines coiled around everything upright and ran along the ground, searching for their next host. The foliage formed a living wall.

Huge potholes dotted the dirt strip, creating a hazard for the landing gear of any plane forced to use it. A deep gash ran the length of it. The end of the gash disappeared under the aft section of the jet. Sun beat down on the strip. Charred bodies, still smoking, littered the dirt around the aft section. Emma gritted her teeth to stop the nausea that rose at the sight of the dead.

The guerrillas barked orders at several male passengers as they worked to pull blackened suitcases from the remains of the cargo hold. Emma recognized one of the passengers who'd sat in the third row. About thirty, tall and slender, with thick dark hair and dressed in a polo shirt and khakis, he had spent the entire flight typing furiously on a laptop computer, stopping only to stare around the first-class cabin with a hyperalert demeanor. On the plane Emma had pegged him either as an overworked oil executive or a paranoid coke addict. She had dubbed him "Wary Man" and hadn't thought about him again. Now soot covered his face and his polo shirt was in tatters, but he still exuded an air of silent intensity.

A surprising amount of cargo survived the plane's ill-fated landing. Four guerrillas went to work emptying the suitcases, removing anything valuable. They took laptop computers, jewelry cases, and cameras, but left most of the contents scattered on the ground. Clothing, toiletries, shoes, and hair dryers littered the runway.

One passenger fell to his knees from heat and exhaustion. Rat Face pushed off the Jeep he leaned against and sauntered over. He barked an order in Spanish to a nearby comrade. The soldier grabbed the passenger by the arm and dragged him back to the circle, dumping him facedown in the dirt. The other passengers stayed frozen, staring at the prone man, fear on their faces.

The guerrillas pointed to another passenger sitting in the circle. They untied his hands and pushed him toward the discarded cargo. He joined the others, which Emma now dubbed the "work crew." At one point, she watched Wary Man push a suitcase and a silver metal briefcase behind some wreckage when the guerrillas weren't looking.

The noise of engines accompanied by a cloud of dust came from a road that ran up a hill next to the airstrip. Two flatbed pickup trucks appeared only twenty-five feet below Emma's perch. They ground to a halt at the edge of the airstrip, the doors flew open, and three men stepped out.

The first man out of the trucks wore green twill pants and a collared shirt, the sleeves rolled to his elbows. His hair was dark and full, but his face was etched with wrinkles. Emma held her breath as he scanned the foliage in her direction. His eyes held a dead look that frightened Emma with its intensity. She shivered in the heat.

He pulled on a cigarette as he scrutinized the smoldering airplane. Two men surrounded him. These wore fatigues like the rest of the guerrillas on the airstrip, but theirs looked cleaner, and their shirts were sleeved. They dogged the smoking man's steps while holding machine guns at the ready.

Smoking Man strolled to the back of one flatbed, lowered the hatch, and flipped open a laptop computer. Next to the computer sat two large field phones, each in its own individual bag. Both the phones and the computer had some sort of satellite uplink. The man dialed a number and chatted on the phone, stopping every few minutes to consult the computer screen.

The second phone sat in the corner of the flatbed, next to a mesh bag of apples and a liter bottle of seltzer water. Emma focused on the apples. Her mouth watered at the thought of them. Her stomach growled and her throat burned. She was so thirsty that each swallow felt painful. If she could reach the flatbed undetected, she could take both the field phone and an apple. There were so many in the bag, she doubted the man would notice one less. She would wait until dark to make her move.

Smoking Man finished with his phone call and waved Rat Face over. Smoking Man pointed to something on the computer screen before indicating the passengers huddled on the airstrip. Smoking Man, Rat Face, and the bodyguards spread out, walking through the people, looking at faces. If a passenger stared downward, the men snapped out an order. The passenger looked up.

When they reached the end of the huddled group, Smoking Man shook his head at Rat Face. He tossed his cigarette on the ground and strolled over to him. Another conference. This time there was a lot of yelling on both sides. Rat Face indicated the bodies gathered around the plane's aft section. He walked over and kicked one of the burned corpses. He put his hands in the air and shrugged.

Emma gasped. That a human being could treat another in such a fashion, even after death, was a matter beyond her comprehension.

Smoking Man barked an order. The guerrillas jumped up and started unloading metal disks from the back of the truck. They carried each disk gingerly, as if it were fine china, not a hunk of steel. Emma watched as they hid these disks on the side of the dirt road, alternating sides in a zigzag pattern.

Her heart dropped once she realized that the only road to the wreckage would be booby-trapped with land mines. The entire hijacking now appeared to have been planned with an almost military efficiency. Her hopes of a quick search-and-rescue mission were fast disappearing. The enormity of her situation was sinking in, and along with the realization came anger. She settled back in to watch the proceedings with an eye toward disrupting their plans.

While the guerrillas unloaded the disks from the first truck, Smoking Man's bodyguard climbed into the second truck. Emma scrambled to her feet. Her fear of losing the phone and food was so great that, for a brief moment, she almost ran straight to the truck. She caught herself and slid behind the trunk of a large palm. She watched while the truck drove away. Emma closed her eyes and put her cheek against the tree. After a minute she slumped back down to the ground.

Ten minutes later, the flatbed truck reappeared and resumed its spot at the edge of the strip. The bodyguard jumped out. There sat the second field phone, the mesh bag of apples, and the bottle of water.

The passengers worked in the heat, the discarded cargo grew to a mountain, and Smoking Man inhaled his cigarettes. Sweat soaked through Emma's clothes, causing her to itch, and her arms and legs started to ache as her body emerged from the shock of the crash. Her hunger grew, becoming a living thing that she found harder and harder to ignore. Her stomach growled and her head pounded. A fly buzzed in her ear and she batted it away.

The guerrillas stopped to eat. They fed the passengers, handing them reddish brown strips of some sort of smoked meat and flattened bread made out of corn or maize. Emma closed her eyes while the group on the airstrip ate. She was so hungry that watching them made her weak. The entire crew was massed on the far side of the strip, concentrating on eating. Emma decided to make her move.

She shoved her pack under the bush. She crouched over and worked her way through the trees, keeping low. She focused on her feet in order to avoid stepping on twigs. The thick bed of rotted leaves and soft earth served to muffle her footsteps. While she was grateful for the soundproofing, the sheer density of the jungle made it difficult to move without slapping through branches or rustling through plants, and the leaves were slick underfoot.

She crab-walked for almost a hundred yards, taking pains to move up the side of the mountain. She twisted her body sideways to slide between branches of a palm, and placed each foot down toe-first to minimize sound. She stopped thirty feet above and to the right of the vehicles. The truck with the apples sat on the other side of the truck that contained the tarp. They were lined up next to each other, five feet from the edge of the tree line. To reach them, Emma would need to step out into the open, climb over the first truck's flatbed into the second's, grab the apples and phone, and retreat back the way she came.

Rivulets of sweat poured off her. It ran down her face and soaked under her arms. Her heart raced. She took several deep breaths to try to regain some composure. She cast a glance at the guerrilla group. Rat Face, his men, Smoking Man, and the bodyguards, all stood in a semicircle with their backs to Emma. She could hear the sounds of their voices rising and falling. Emma needed to get to the truck before they finished with their conference.

She plunged down toward the flatbeds. While she tried to move as quietly as she could, she didn't want to spend the time it would take to move through the brush in silence. Her world coalesced into one goal: reach the truck.

She slipped on the wet leaves, but was able to catch her

balance at the last minute. She was twenty feet from the flatbed, then ten feet. Now she didn't bother watching for sticks. Her need for speed trumped any concern about noise. She closed the gap to the tree line. She reached the edge. Now she was five feet from the truck. No time to waste. She lowered to the ground. Took a deep breath and crawled into the open.

The sun hit her back full blast. Within seconds she began overheating. Her heart raced, the pounding blood sounding loud in her ears. She worked her way to the first truck's rear. She crouched behind the wheel well. She cast a glance at the airstrip. The passengers remained huddled in a large group, between her and the now-conferencing guerrillas. They stayed in the same position they were in two minutes ago. Only one looked at her.

Wary Man stared, a look of astonishment on his face. They locked eyes. He turned his head to look at the guerrillas, still in a circle. He turned back to Emma, shook his head slightly, then cocked it to the side, as if to tell her to get back into the trees. But Emma wasn't about to quit now. She frowned at him, shook her head, and mouthed the word *no*. Wary Man frowned back at her with a look full of frustration.

She rose until she could see over the side of the first flat-bed's walls. It contained only the tarp, and the sides matched that of the flatbed containing the prize. She needed only to scurry across the first flatbed to the second. The unused field phone sat in the corner farthest from her along with the apples. She'd have to crawl into the bed to reach them.

She stepped onto the wheel well and swung a leg over the side. She stepped onto the truck's bed and lowered herself back into a crouch. She crawled to the opposite side on all fours. Her foot hit the large rolled tarp. It moved.

Emma nearly screamed her surprise. The tarp wriggled again and the edge fell away to reveal the frightened face of a boy. He had a bandanna gag in his mouth, and his dark eyes were wild with fear. The tarp fell farther away to reveal that he wore the same faded T-shirt and camouflage pants as the other guerrillas. He appeared to be no more than sixteen years old. Emma took a quick look over her shoulder. Smoking Man yelled at Rat Face, jabbing a finger at him for emphasis. All of the guerrillas watched the argument raging between the two men.

The boy pulled his hands out of the tarp. They were tied with a rope. He made frantic noises while he shoved his hands at her.

"Shh!" Emma hissed at him. The noises stopped. Emma reached around his head to yank at the bandanna's knot. The old, dried cloth resisted. Emma's blood pressure shot up even higher. She could feel her panic rising. She took another look back at the guerrillas. Now they were nodding, as if they'd reached an agreement. The conference wouldn't last much longer. She took a quick look at Wary Man. He craned his neck to see over the truck's hatch. This time he shot her an urgent, questioning look. He swung his head around to check on the guerrillas.

Emma switched her attention from the bandanna to the rope tying the boy's hands. He didn't need to speak, he just needed to be able to get away. The rope knot came free quickly.

The second his hands were free, the boy swung his legs out of the tarp and began working on yet another rope wrapped around his ankles. Emma helped him. She glanced sideways at the guerrillas. She wanted to see what they were doing but was unwilling to take her eyes off the task at hand. The guerrillas stepped back, and two turned. Their conference was over.

"Faster!" Emma said.

The boy nodded, never removing his gaze from the rope.

Tears ran out of his eyes and fell on the rope as he and Emma scrabbled at the knot. Emma cast one long look at the field phone and apples sitting in the second truck. They were only a few feet away, but they might as well have been a mile. She would never reach them and get back into the trees undetected. She returned her attention to the knot binding the boy's feet. It came free. In an instant the boy was up. He leaped over the truck's side. Emma leaped after him. She thudded onto the dirt and pitched forward onto her hands. The boy ran into the tree line. Once in the shadows, his camouflage pants made it appear as if he'd disappeared, like smoke.

Emma ran forward to follow him just as a capybara burst from the foliage three feet in front of her. It ran straight at her. She pivoted to avoid it, and her feet flew out from under her. She landed on the ground, hard. She watched in horror as the small animal shot toward the circle of passengers.

The capybara barreled past Wary Man. A woman shrieked at the sight of the flat-faced rodent about the size of a small dog. The bodyguards spun around at her screams. They raised their assault weapons into firing position. Wary Man shot to his feet and stepped between the men and Emma on the ground, using his body to block their view. He pointed at the animal shooting toward the tree line. The bodyguards trained their rifles on the little beast, tracking it across the strip. Emma scrambled backward on her seat, fighting her way back into the safety of the trees, all the while keeping her eyes on the guerrillas.

The capybara veered sideways, making a play for the forest and safety. One bodyguard took aim and fired. The capybara flew into the air before landing on its side. It twitched once and then stilled.

The guerrillas applauded the shot. The second bodyguard slapped the first on the shoulder. Emma inched backward until she was once again far enough in the trees to work her way around to her backpack. She sat down next to it and buried her face in her hands.

Smoking Man barked an order and his entourage climbed into the pickups. The engines kicked to life, and Emma watched the trucks as they drove up the road, zigzagging to avoid the scattered metal disks. Emma wanted to cry as she watched her only possible link to the outside world inch slowly away.

The rat-faced guerrilla blew a whistle. His soldiers lined the passengers up, front to back. They marched into the forest, led by two passengers who hacked at the dense foliage with machetes. Wary Man glanced once at the place where Emma had fallen before he turned to follow the others.

They left the clothing, airplane, corpses, and Emma behind.

EMMA LAY FACEDOWN IN THE DIRT AND LET THE
tears flow. She cried for Patrick, for her, and for the dead
people that lay all around her. The familiar feeling of despair washed over her. For the last year, since Patrick's
death, raging anger and debilitating despair had been her
constant companions, sucking her will to live.

She lay on the ground and thought about Patrick. The way
he read the *Financial Times* on the train to work, his brow
furrowed in thought, and dropped a dollar in the guitar case
of the blind musician playing on the subway platform. How
he kept his apartment stocked with the tea she liked even
though it cost a fortune and he thought it tasted like grass.
How he'd keep an eye out for unusual plants when he traveled
on business and once even carried them home to her, pressed
between the pages of a book, only to be stopped at O'Hare
Airport by the Department of Agriculture when their sniff-
ing beagles sat next to his briefcase.

His death had sent her into a tailspin with an intensity that
shocked her. Her anger knew no bounds. As far as she was
concerned, God had let Patrick down, and her rage threatened to consume her. Some days were so gray that she wondered if the fog would ever lift. Even her move to sunny

Miami Beach, with its sparkling sea and bright Art Deco colors, had failed to revive her love of life.

The only way she found to quiet her mind was running. In this, she excelled. While Emma's daily life was marred with a depression so deep that the antidepressants prescribed by her doctor were rendered useless, she found she could channel the despair into her running. When Emma ran, she focused on her muscles, the path, her heart rate, her hydration, her caloric intake, and her distance. With these concerns foremost in her mind, the despair stayed at bay. Emma channeled her rage and used it to fuel her legs to greater speeds. Her single-minded focus allowed her to breeze past others who had collapsed in the dark hours of the night on the eightieth mile of a hundred-mile race. Emma threw away the pills and trained more and more each week.

But now she was having periodic bouts of uncontrolled crying. It was just like the first days after Patrick's death, when she cried for two days without stopping. She felt as though all the small gains she had managed these past months had been wiped away in one horrifying minute.

An hour ticked by before Emma felt the darkness lift. It took another half hour after that for her to feel brave enough to leave the safety of her hiding place. She hauled herself upright, wiped her face on her sleeve, and started to move. She skirted around the nose of the plane, cowering in the shadows it provided. A glance showed her that nothing remained of the first-class cabin but wreckage and twisted metal. She avoided looking in the cockpit. She didn't want to know what happened to the pilot with the smooth voice that never shook, professional to the end.

She rooted around the tree line by the nose and found useless debris and charred bodies, many still strapped into their seats. The stench of the dead permeated the air. It was a good thing that she hadn't eaten in a day, because she would have thrown up at the sight of the dead. As it was, acid saliva was all she tasted.

A food cart, blackened and bent, lay on its side about thirty feet from the edge of the landing strip. Dead bodies surrounded it. The bodies created a macabre maze that Emma would have to navigate to reach the prize. Once there, she would have to work on the cart while the bodies kept her company. She forced herself to think about survival.

Emma took careful steps over the bodies of three passengers. She turned her eyes from their faces and did her best to focus on the goal of reaching the cart. Two more bodies lay on either side of the metal box. She stepped over one's leg, and this step brought her flush up against the box. She had no room to maneuver, however, without moving the other body out of the way.

It looked to be a man, badly burned. She nudged it with her toe. It rocked but didn't move far enough to give her any room. She tried to push it again, but it again rocked and fell back into position against the cart. In a fit of exasperation and gnawing hunger, Emma bent her knees, leaned the small of her back on the cart, bracing herself against it, and put one foot on the corpse. She shoved it as hard as she could. It rolled over one complete rotation before stopping a foot away.

Emma grabbed the door of the cart and yanked it open. Food packets tumbled out. She pounced on them. Her hands shook as she sorted through the scorched packets. She fought with one, trying to pry the aluminum lid off the shallow plastic container that acted as a plate. She ripped it open and looked inside.

The plastic plate had melted onto the food and then hardened into one congealed mess once it cooled. Emma couldn't tell where the plastic ended and the food began.

Oh no. I need this food, Emma thought.

She tossed the ruined plate and grabbed the next one. Same congealed mess. She grabbed a third, also inedible. She clawed at a fourth. This time when she removed the foil she found an intact filet mignon, side salad, and baby carrots, all nestled in their own little sections.

Emma grabbed the filet and shoved it in her mouth, ripping off a section with her teeth. It tasted like heaven. She couldn't chew it fast enough. She swallowed a large portion whole and ripped at the filet again. She chewed twice before raising her eyes.

She glanced at a nearby corpse. It was a woman. Her eyes gazed at Emma in an unblinking stare. Emma stopped chewing and felt her stomach start to rebel. She closed her eyes and took slow, deep breaths. Keeping the food down was imperative. After her stomach settled, she opened her eyes and looked at the dead woman.

"I'm so sorry." Emma whispered the words.

An overwhelming sadness settled over her. She got up, still clutching the food plate, and stumbled away from the body and the woman's lifeless eyes. She sank down near her pack and finished the filet, all the while doing her best to keep her gaze off the destruction all around her.

When she was finished she made her way back to the cart and fished through the plates. Out of fifty or sixty packets, she found ten still intact. She grabbed them and carried them to her backpack.

She sat at the end of the runway and stacked the few precious food plates next to her pack along with a small parcel of airline napkins. She'd brought the pack, a compass, compact tent, bedroll, and a portable Coleman stove. Only the pack went with her as a carry-on. The other items she had checked into cargo.

She assessed the backpack's contents. It contained a paperback book, her passport, wallet, a reflective sheet that collected heat, a pillow that could be blown up to act as a neck rest on the long flight, her telephone, notepad with attached pen, and tester tubes of the new Engine Red lipstick that she'd created for a cosmetic customer's elite makeup line. Their development was shrouded in secrecy. She tossed the book, the pillow, and stared at the lipstick testers. There were two. Their cases were different, but the color was the same. She shoved them into a side pocket with the useless cell phone.

She continued rooting through the discarded remnants of the passengers' things. She found a traveler's first-aid kit, several airline bottles of scotch, and one small bottle of wine. She also found a beautiful silver lighter with the initials *AEG* engraved on the side.

She reached the area where Wary Man had hidden his luggage and the briefcase. A brass bag tag on the luggage held a business card that read *Cameron Sumner, Southern Hemisphere Drug Defense Agency* and listed an address in Key West, Florida.

Emma sat back on her heels. So Wary Man has a name and a job fighting drugs, she thought. She opened the suitcase. It contained nothing of interest. Just all the normal items packed by any business traveler.

She turned her attention to the metal briefcase. The words UNITED STATES ARMY were stenciled on the top in black script. Emma pried it open. It contained two handguns and some spare ammunition. She nearly wept when she saw them, partly from joy and partly because she didn't know how to fire them.

Emma's bags weren't among the looted luggage that lay all around. She didn't care much about the clothes she'd brought, what she really wanted was the bag that held all her hiking material and the separate duffel that contained her compass and the special hiking tent. The compass was crucial to her survival. Without it she could wander in circles until the food ran out or the guerrillas captured her.

The tent was far less important. Designed to be worn on a hiker's back, it weighed only four pounds but opened to accommodate two people. The manufacturer claimed that it was rugged enough for an expedition to Everest. When collapsed, it didn't look like much, and she hoped the guerrillas hadn't recognized it for what it was.

Half an hour later she found the duffel. It was ripped in half, and empty. Emma rifled through it before tossing it down. She searched in a circular pattern but didn't find any pieces. Her precious compass was gone. She tried to ignore the sudden rush of panic that accompanied this realization.

"Get a grip, Emma. It's not like it was food or anything." She spoke out loud. Her voice sounded strained, but surprisingly normal. Just hearing herself helped. It confirmed that she was alive, and not a wraith wandering among the dead.

She found her luggage twenty-five yards into the trees, blackened, but otherwise in perfect condition.

"Louis Vuitton, god of luggage design," Emma said. "Why the hell didn't I put the compass in here?" She started laughing like a hyena. She sank to her knees. The laughter morphed into tears and then panic.

Emma forced herself to take deep breaths to halt the riot of emotion that overwhelmed her. She dragged herself upright, took an extra pair of socks from her luggage, and half-heartedly resumed her search. She found the tent under a heap of discarded clothing. The black outer nylon carry bag had melted at the corners, but the tent itself was undamaged. Her joy at finding it far outstripped its value to her, she knew, but she felt as though fate had thrown her a bone. She attached the tent to the flat side of the backpack. It acted as a frame, and made the load a bit more bearable. She finished rummaging through the luggage but found nothing useful.

She went back to her pack and filled it with the food and alcohol. She shoved one pistol into the pack and put the other on top. She took out the notepad, dated the first sheet, and hesitated. While Emma itched to leave the airstrip, she knew she should stay with the wreckage. The authorities would search for the plane first. Staying near it would give her the best chance for rescue. Her only other options would be to run down the dirt road Smoking Man used, or follow the passengers into the forest. Emma wanted to avoid Smoking Man and his soldiers at any cost, and the guerrillas holding the passengers were no less frightening.

She wrote, *I'm still alive. The guerrillas took passengers into the jungle. About seventy. Cameron Sumner is one of them. The others I don't know by name. I will stay near this crash site unless forced to leave.*

She signed the note, ripped it out of the pad, and placed it in her bags on top of the clothes. She stashed Sumner's luggage under a palm and shoved her own next to it.

The sky clouded over and an afternoon rainstorm began. Emma moved into the tree line. She sat with her back against a tree and watched the fat raindrops hit the dirt, making little puffs of smoke with each hit. The airplane sides sizzled. The charred bodies simply smoked.

Emma sank into a torpor. She watched the rain pummel the earth in a hypnotic trance. She gazed at nothing, letting her mind wander. Once she was in the trees, the air felt thick with humidity and smelled like warm earth and green leaves. After the stench on the runway, Emma thought it was one of the sweetest smells she could imagine. She didn't want to go back near the jet's wreckage. She shrugged off her pack and lay down, using it as a pillow.

8

BANNER'S MEETING ENTERED ITS FIFTH HOUR.
Miguel and the members of the military were gone, and
Whitter was slumped in his chair and had untied his tie
completely. On the wall a flat-screen television, set to CNN
and muted, flashed a map of Colombia and some photos of
people that Banner assumed were Colombian. It was the
tenth time they'd seen the stock footage.

Dispatching Miguel solved the immediate problem of
search and rescue, and the meeting turned to intelligence
gathering. The remaining attendees aired the information
they knew about the flight, and now it was Stromeyer's turn.

"I've analyzed the data from the manifest. There are
two or three interesting characters among the passengers."
Stromeyer handed around a copy of the plane's manifest.
Four names were highlighted.

"First. Manuel Cordova Sanchez is listed as the copilot.
He is a Colombian-trained pilot, his license is up-to-date,
and his credentials more than adequate."

"So what's the problem?" Banner said.

"He is not, and never has been, an employee of British
Airlines. He boarded the plane in Miami, using false identi-

fication and claiming that the real copilot was ill. He was ill all right. The police found him in his hotel room, dead."

"So he gets into the cockpit, threatens the pilot, and flies the plane into the mountains."

Stromeyer nodded. "That's the current theory."

"Wouldn't the pilot resist? He's got a whole plane to assist him," Whitter said.

Stromeyer shrugged. "Depends on what was used to threaten him. He's in charge of the plane, and perhaps he felt that the passengers stood a better chance to live if he didn't resist."

"Isn't there some action he could take?" Whitter said.

"Yes, but nothing that would help if the hijacker has already made it to the cockpit. One protocol suggests he put on his mask and send the plane into a deep dive, which causes rapid depressurization and renders the passengers and any hijackers in the main cabin unconscious. But the copilot has his own mask and could use it to stay alert. Honestly, if there are any survivors, then whatever the pilot did was correct."

Whitter sighed. "I see what you mean."

"And the others?" Banner pointed to another highlighted name. "What about these two, Carlos and Consuelo Rivera?"

"Let's talk about them last. The next, very interesting, name is Cameron Sumner."

"Why does that ring a bell?" Banner said.

Stromeyer nodded. "I'd heard it before, too. He's a licensed jet pilot. He flew private jets—Gulfstreams, Lears, like that—for various corporations located in Florida. One of the corporations paid for him to train in bodyguard techniques and weapons with us at Darkview."

"Do you have a picture of him?" Banner said.

Stromeyer slid a passport photo at Banner.

Sumner's face was only vaguely familiar. "Did we send him to Iraq?"

Stromeyer shook her head. "No. His Darkview evaluation sheet says that he was focused, intelligent, extremely proficient in firearms, and damn near unflappable. We made an offer to him, but he chose to continue flying for the suits. That is, until last year. Last year he became a trainer and monitor at the Southern Hemisphere Drug Defense Agency. He was stationed in Key West, where he oversaw training of personnel for the Air Tunnel Denial program."

"The what?"

"The Air Tunnel Denial program, or ATD. It's a joint program administered by the United States and Colombia designed to identify and intercept drug running aircraft that enter into U.S. or Colombian airspace."

Banner stared at Stromeyer. "Are you telling me that the United States has an *entire program* set up to review suspicious aircraft entering Colombian airspace, and they are still unable to locate a commercial airliner downed in Colombia?"

Stromeyer shrugged. "It's not as crazy as it sounds. The ATD program is administered from various air bases in both the United States and Colombia, and concentrates its attention on smaller aircraft that fly at low levels. Its mission is to identify the suspicious plane, establish visual and radio contact with it, and order it to land if it appears to be a drug transport. The planes used for drug transport are small private planes that can land in the remote areas using short runways. There was no reason for ATD personnel to be suspicious of a large commercial jet."

Whitter groaned. "Reason won't come into it. The press will eat us alive for funding a program that is supposed to spot suspicious aircraft activity and yet doesn't even notice a huge jet lumbering off its course."

Much as he hated to, Banner agreed with Whitter. The mistakes were piling up in this disaster.

The gentleman from the Department of Transportation spoke up. He looked to Banner like either an accountant or an engineer. He wrote on a pad lined with tiny grids that he'd brought himself, and he carried a sheaf of papers with him.

"Mr. Whitter, I think you need to be prepared for the eventuality that we may never find this jet. Especially since it landed in a mountainous region with significant jungle coverage. In the last ten years in the United States alone, fifty-three plane crashes have never been recovered."

"In what type of terrain?" Banner said.

The man shrugged. "All types. One involved a Learjet that crashed only a few miles from a regional airport. Hundreds of searchers on foot and multiple helicopters were deployed for three weeks. That plane, all eight tons of it, has never been found."

"Where did it crash? Alaska?" Whitter said.

"New Hampshire."

"You have a missing plane in *New Hampshire*?" Whitter's voice registered shock.

The DOT official looked pained. "We do. Of course some UFO enthusiasts have added it to their roster of unexplained events. But their claims are grounded in ignorance. They don't know, or don't believe, the statistics."

Banner rubbed his forehead, where a headache began forming.

Stromeyer reached below the table into a briefcase and pulled out a small tin. She slid it across the desk to Banner while she turned to Whitter.

"Mr. Whitter, wait until you hear the rest of my report. The ATD program isn't the only one the press is going to excoriate us for," she said.

The tin contained aspirin. Banner opened it and chugged two down.

Whitter held his hand up to stop Stromeyer. "Great, Ms. Stromeyer—"

Both Banner and Stromeyer interrupted him. "Major Stromeyer," they said in unison.

Whitter took a breath. "*Major* Stromeyer, let's talk about the other problem areas last. Right now, tell me why was this guy flying to Bogotá?"

"He was scheduled to give a quarterly report to Colombian authorities about the Air Tunnel Denial program. What's interesting is that he requested and received clearance for two pistols to be transported in the cargo hold."

"Did he now?" Banner said. He circled Sumner's name over and over again.

"That does seem like an odd request," Whitter said. "Why would he need guns for a speech about monitoring radar? Do you think he was involved with the hijacking?"

Stromeyer shook her head. "Doubtful, but the request is odd and we can't overlook the possibility."

"What about these other two?" Whitter pointed at the manifest list.

"Ah, yes, the Riveras. Both Colombian nationals flying home after a two-week stay in Miami. The Colombian government reports that Carlos used to be a midlevel operative in the terrorist Colombian National Self-Defense paramilitary group, or the CSD, before he was captured by the Colombian army. Now that the CSD has agreed to peace talks, he is one of the first of the former terrorists to claim benefits under the funds set aside by the U.S. and Colombia to aid in repatriating former CSD. Problem is, he was seen outside the real copilot's door the morning before the flight. He appears to have aided the terrorists by killing the real copilot. So the first beneficiary of our new program to end terrorism ends up using the funds we paid him to expand it."

"Shit," Whitter said. He pointed to the tin still on the desk. "Is that aspirin?"

"Be my guest," Stromeyer said. She slid the tin toward Whitter.

9

THREE HOURS AFTER LEAVING THE AIRSTRIP, ROD-
rigo and the passengers detonated their first land mine. The
lead passenger never knew what hit him. One moment he had
stopped to hack at the foliage, and the next he blew up, his
body thrown several feet into the air with the blast. Shrapnel
hit the two passengers next to him, cutting their faces.

The passengers screamed and charged backward. The
panicked people ran right into the guerrillas, pushing them
aside in the chaos. They poured back down the path like rats
fleeing a fire.

Alvarado heard Luis roar from the middle of the pack.
"Stop, you stupid fools!" He shot his machine gun into
the air.

The people kept running. Several other guerrillas followed Luis's lead and peppered the sky with bullets in an
attempt to slow the stampede. Alvarado used his gun as a
club and clubbed the people who pushed past him. Alvarado
saw Luis, now standing in the middle of the path, hammering the trees with shot. Low-lying branches cracked and tree
branches and bits of bark and leaves flew onto the people,
frightening them even more.

Luis roared threats. "Stop running or the next round will kill you all!"

The passengers kept moving. They clawed at one another, each trying to get ahead of his neighbor. They flowed off the path and into the tree line.

"Stop moving! Stay on the path! The mines are laid in patterns. You keep running and you will hit another!" Alvarado screamed.

Tall Man yanked one of the passengers back onto the path just as another plunged off it and triggered a second land mine. The resulting explosion blew off the passenger's arm from the elbow down.

The passengers froze. A woman sank to her knees and put her hands over her eyes.

Luis stormed up to the injured man, who lay groaning in the leaves next to the path. Luis shot him in the head.

The shot echoed through the mountains. The people left remained still. Only the sound of Luis's heavy breathing, and a woman gasping, could be heard. Everyone else stood like statues, unmoving.

Rodrigo marched over to the gasping woman. About sixty, with graying hair, she sat on the path, her body heaving in its attempt to get air.

Luis yelled at her. "What is wrong with you?"

The woman spoke between gasps. "Heart condition. I lost my medication in the crash. I need a hospital. I can't continue." Luis pointed his gun at her. She sat up as straight as she could and looked him in the eye.

"May God have mercy on your soul," she said. She pulled a rosary out of her pocket. She clutched it in her hand while she stared Rodrigo down. He looked at the cross, then at her.

"If you can't continue, you stay here." Rodrigo turned to the passengers. "Now get back in line. All of you!" The passengers formed back into a line along the path, stepping carefully. All evidence of the last minute's panic was gone. They huddled next to one another as if afraid to move.

"You." Luis pointed to a male passenger. "My English is not so good. You understand Spanish?"

The man nodded.

"Good." Luis switched to Spanish. "Retrieve the machete. You will be the new leader. Only this time, if you see a piece of nylon line strung across the path, you do not disturb it. You understand me?"

The man nodded again.

"And watch for a cone-shaped object. These mines are called Chinese hats and they are more powerful than the ones that were just detonated. Translate this for the passengers."

The passengers listened to the man and nodded as a group. They waited while the new leader retrieved the machete. Tall Man braced a passenger, holding him up by his arm. They proceeded forward, leaving the dead to the mountain.

THE SOUND OF AN ENGINE crashing through the brush made Emma lift her head. The noise grew closer. She grabbed the pack with one hand and retreated deeper into the jungle. She fought through the trees, moving up the side of the mountain. She stopped one hundred yards above the airstrip, lowered herself to the ground, and peered through a break in the trees. From her new location she could see the strip but was hidden enough to be safe. Below her, the motor's noise grew louder and louder. She watched a jeep as it burst from the tree line onto the strip.

The jeep circled the wreckage once and then stopped. Three guerrillas stepped out, each carrying cone-shaped devices. They placed the first device at one end of the wreckage. One guerrilla attached a nylon string to it. He ran the string along the ground, at a height of about six inches. Fifty feet later, the man attached another cone-shaped device to the string, and then moved fifty feet again. Soon the cone-shaped devices formed a rough triangular pattern around the main part of the wreckage.

Two of the guerrillas drove the jeep up the dirt road until it was out of Emma's sight. She heard it stop, but couldn't see it. The guerrillas reappeared on foot. They stopped at each metal disk and attached string to it. They unwound the string as they walked across the road, stopping only to attach the string to a bush or tree on the other side. When they were finished, several strings spanned the road at various heights. They stepped over each line and waited at the top of the hill for the last guerrilla to finish.

The last guerrilla left on the strip bent over the final cone. He reached into the bag that sat next to him and removed an old-fashioned oven timer. Emma could see the familiar white shape and the large dial on the front. The guerrilla bent forward again over the last cone, blocking Emma's view, while he worked with the timer. After thirty seconds the man gave a yell and started running. He slowed at each line of string, taking care to step over. When he reached his two buddies they all fled up the road. Emma heard the sound of the jeep's engine fade as it drove away.

The timer sat on the dusty earth, ticking downward.

"Oh, God, they're going to blow it up," Emma said.

She grabbed her pack, which felt like it was filled with lead, and tried to fling it over her shoulders as she ran straight up, into the trees.

She didn't get very far. The heavy foliage slapped at her face, and the ground-cover vines grabbed at her ankles. The pack caught on a nearby tree branch, and no sooner had she wrenched it free than it caught on another two steps later. She'd wasted twenty seconds fighting the jungle. She'd never get far enough away unless she chose an existing trail.

Emma spun around and ran down toward the strip. She skidded and slid down the side of the mountain until she reached the bottom. She took a quick glance around before she stepped out into the sun and the heat. The glare from the light reflecting off the plane's metal body made her squint. The wreckage lay in front of her. It looked like a disjointed piece of metal sculpture. The smell of decay, burned hair, and the still-smoldering rubber was so strong that she was forced to put a hand over her nose and breathe through her mouth.

The path the passengers had forged lay on the other side of the piled wreckage. To cross the airstrip required a run of one hundred yards over dead bodies, discarded clothing, and jagged metal pieces sheared off the jet's body. Emma could skirt the deadly triangle, or she could cut straight across. Straight across saved time.

She took a deep breath, stepped over the nylon line and ran. She dodged the metal jet pieces and bloated bodies, disturbing the flies that fed off them. The insects rose up in a cloud, buzzing in protest.

Emma focused on the far side of the strip and the narrow path cut by the passengers. She could hear the ticking noise of the oven timer as it counted down. A bumblebee flew in front of her, diving at her face and then swooping away. Sweat poured down her face and into her eyes, making them sting. She wiped her face as she jogged, not missing a beat. She reached the second line marking the far end and stepped over it. She lunged onto the trail, running for all she was worth. The pack banged against her back in a rhythmic cadence.

At one hundred yards in, the strip behind her blew.

The blast knocked Emma flat. The ground shook. She stayed down, flinging her hands over her head. After ten seconds she struggled back to her feet to run again. She took two steps, and the second bomb blew. This blast felt even stronger than the first. Black smoke boiled into the sky. Emma ran a few more yards and the third detonated. This one sent metal shrapnel catapulting upward. The pieces rained down on the trees, each one sharp and deadly. Emma threw herself back down and once again covered her head. A huge burning chunk of metal fell onto the path behind her. A woman's hairbrush hit her back and rolled off.

Emma heard the fire before she could see it. Panic engulfed her. She imagined the fire was shooting toward her, burning everything in its path. She pulled herself upright, took a final deep breath, and plunged down the path to follow the passengers.

10

MIGUEL STOOD IN APIAY, COLOMBIA, IN THE SMALL
offices that housed the Air Tunnel Denial program. He listened as Señor Lopez, a skinny man with a face like a hound and a personality to match, nattered on about the myriad small runways that littered the countryside.

"We cannot possibly monitor them all, can we?" he said.

Miguel decided Lopez was a whiner. "It's your job to monitor them all."

"With inadequate equipment and no help from the police!"

"These are your problems, sir, not mine. My problem is finding a large jet downed on one of those runways. My commander in the U.S. suggested that you could help pinpoint the location of the airstrip the hijackers may have used. Now, with all this radar equipment at your disposal, are you telling me you didn't see this jet when it entered your airspace?"

Señor Lopez chattered on some more, and Miguel tuned out. All he caught was something about "procedure," "trajectories," and "mushroom clouds." The last comment caught his attention.

"What do you mean, 'mushroom clouds'?" he said.

Señor Lopez shrugged. "We heard that a mushroom cloud was seen somewhere around here." He pointed to a map of Colombia that hung on a wall next to the radar equipment.

"That's where we noted it, as well as a cell-phone transmission. However, when we sent the Colombian military there, they said no flight had landed. Should I believe them?"

Señor Lopez pursed his lips. "What town did the military embark from for this mission?"

Miguel named a small town. "It was closest to the cell-phone transmission."

"That town is controlled by the paramilitary."

"Controlled? How?"

"Some say they are blackmailing the mayor."

Miguel felt his irritation rise. "I do not care about money, and neither should the mayor. Is it possible that he lied to us?"

"That is entirely possible."

"Perhaps he should care more about innocent lives being taken," Miguel said.

Señor Lopez nodded. "He does. The paramilitary group threatens that if he does not cooperate, they will kill his wife and children. He is a father of four. So he cooperates."

Miguel didn't know what to say for a moment.

"What about the airstrips? Do you map those?"

Señor Lopez nodded. "There are hundreds. The drug runners' airstrips will be no easier to find than your jet—perhaps harder." The man waved at the map on the wall. "Here are the ones that we have been able to locate. Each red line is a strip."

Miguel counted forty such lines. The map also had a large circle, drawn in red, with Apiay marked as a dot on the circle's edge. The mushroom cloud occurred outside the circle.

"What is that circle?"

"That is the distance that our surveillance airplanes can fly before they must turn around and come back to refuel. Our planes are small. They can fly to the edge of the circle, but they have only ten minutes to find the airstrip used by the drug transport. After that time, they must turn back or they will run out of fuel before they're able to land. If we fly to your mushroom cloud, then the plane doesn't have enough fuel to return."

Miguel studied the map. There were tiny pins stuck on what appeared to be random points. The majority of the pins were scattered in an area along the Colombian-Venezuelan border. All fell outside of the red circle.

"What do the pins mean?" Miguel said.

"All are suspicious flights and landings," Señor Lopez said.

"As in drug flights?"

"Yes. But you see, most of these so-called suspicious flights landed outside our interference capabilities."

"So the drug runners know how far you are able to fly," Miguel said.

"And they have adjusted their operations accordingly, yes."

"Do you know Cameron Sumner? He works as a trainer with the American organization charged to help you find and intercept these drug flights."

Señor Lopez nodded. "I do know him. He is a quiet, efficient man."

"Is he a survivor?" Miguel said.

"I will answer that by telling you a story about an incident that occurred here eight months ago. Mr. Sumner was here to review our policies and determine whether we were acting in accordance with the terms of the joint cooperation between his agency and mine. While he was here, we spotted a suspicious flight. Mr. Sumner insisted on flying the intercept plane himself."

"I understand that he is a good pilot," Miguel said.

"He is an excellent pilot. He chased the plane and determined it was a drug transport. When the pilot refused to land, Mr. Sumner followed it outside of the red circle."

"And?" Miguel said.

"He shot the plane down."

Miguel was shocked. "Is that protocol?"

"Absolutely, and Mr. Sumner followed it to the letter. With the exception that his flight tracked beyond the area where the plane could safely return, however."

"How did he get back?"

"He turned around, flew as far as he could, and landed on a drug runners' airstrip ten miles from his origination point. He hiked back to us through the night."

"Determined man."

"Very much so," Lopez said.

Miguel poked a finger at the map where the mushroom cloud was seen. "He was on the plane that created the cloud."

Señor Lopez looked even sadder than his usual sad expression. "Then I am truly sorry for him, because a man that goes into that area without additional security does not come out alive."

"He came out alive before." Miguel felt compelled to voice an optimism that he didn't feel.

"But that time he flew back very far and was armed. This time I presume he is unarmed and on foot."

Miguel nodded. "If you were Sumner, what would you do?"

"I would tell the guerrillas that my relatives are wealthy Americans and will pay any amount to ransom me."

"Would you tell them you were with the Southern Hemisphere Drug Defense Agency?" Miguel asked.

Señor Lopez looked horrified. "Absolutely not! If they discover this, they will kill him on the spot."

Miguel stared at the map.

Señor Lopez sighed. "I will miss Mr. Sumner."

11

THE HOWLER MONKEYS BEGAN THEIR EERIE HOWL-
ing at dawn. The noise started low, then rose to a bass-toned
roar before ending in a full-throated howl. The sound echoed
through the forest. It sounded like a thousand lions roaring
in a cave. As others took up the call, the jungle came alive
with sound. The mournful howl set Emma's teeth on edge,
and chills ran up her spine.

No sooner had the howler monkeys completed their morning chorus than the parrots started screeching. By the time
they finished, the sun was up. Emma dragged herself out of
the tent, broke it down, and began to run.

Stinging insects plagued her and the oppressive heat dehy-
drated her. The passengers moved so slowly that she doubted
they had completed fifteen miles. She'd caught up with them
without any trouble and adjusted her pace to match theirs.
She trudged behind them, close enough to be able to hear
their progress but not so close as to be discovered.

She was losing weight at an alarming rate, because she
sweated profusely, but she rationed the drinking water.
Every day, when the rains came, she set out the small plate
from the airline food to catch what she could. Finding water
was the second item on her mental list. The first was staying
hidden from the guerrillas.

* * *

THE TORRENTIAL RAINS DRENCHED her clothes and turned the path to mud. At times the water pounded so hard on the leaves above her that it sounded like drumbeats. The only positive thing about the rain was that it kept the bugs from biting.

At dusk, Emma heard a whistle blow. She took it as a signal that the day's march was over. She set up her tent and crawled into it. She removed her shoes and peeled off the soaking-wet, sweat-drenched running socks. She flicked on the lighter to look at her feet. They were bone white, with red patches on the edges of her toes where blisters were forming. The shriveled skin had a cheesy texture. She'd switch to her second pair of socks, but if she didn't find a way to dry them soon, the blisters would never heal. Then each step would be agony, and she would start bargaining with the devil: If I take off the shoes, will you promise not to have my feet swell to balloons? She propped her feet up on the backpack and hung her socks out to dry. Without the benefit of sunlight, the humidity ensured they never would.

She sat in the tent and thought about her situation. She'd already eaten one whole packet of food last night, her first night after running away from the airstrip. She had nine packets left. If she ate one half a day, she had, at most, eighteen days to eat. She reached out and fingered a packet. The meat was cooked, so it wouldn't spoil immediately, but she doubted the packets would stay fresh enough to eat for as long as eighteen days. The heat would rot it in three, maybe four. She revised her food intake downward. She'd eat one full packet a day. She'd continue to eat it once it rotted. Nine days. She needed to reach safety in that time.

She turned her thoughts to her third agenda, which was summoning help. She still clung to the hope that the authorities would find the jet. If they knew better than to take the booby-trapped road, they might see the crudely hacked path. Emma decided to leave clues along the path.

The next morning, she began her march with a clearer purpose. She located a stone and etched an *X* into the trunk of a nearby tree. She had a difficult time adjusting to the passengers' slow pace. One minute she would think she was far behind them, the next she would hear them only a few feet away around a bend in the trail. While the slow pace wasn't taxing, the feeling they were getting nowhere was.

Emma stepped around a group of trees and found herself looking at the back of a lagging guerrilla. She froze. She held her breath and willed the man not to turn around. He stood ten feet in front of her. Close enough that she could see the grime on his gray T-shirt. He stopped, exhaled a cloud of smoke, and rubbed the back of his neck. A minute later the man sighed and started forward once again.

After her close encounter, Emma took one of the pistols out of her bag and put it in her pocket. She didn't bother to load it; the guerrillas would empty an entire clip into her before she'd squeezed off one shot, plus she was afraid that it would discharge accidentally and shoot her in the thigh. She reasoned that if confronted, she could wave it around to buy a little time. No one need know it was empty.

She also kept her eyes peeled for any sticks stout enough to be used as both a walking stick and a weapon. In the afternoon, during the obligatory downpour, she huddled in the tent and used a stone to hack at one end of the stick, fashioning a crude spear. When it was finished, she gazed at it with pride. She couldn't remember the last time she'd felt such a sense of accomplishment in her work.

THE AIR PULSED WITH the scratching sounds of thousands of insects. Emma hated the bugs. They tormented her before she entered the tent, and swarmed at the tent's mesh opening when she was inside. She plunged her hands into the soft earth at the base of a tree, pulling up fistfuls of the soft loam. She smeared the mud on her arms and face. It smelled fresh and the coating provided some relief from the biting bugs.

As the next night deepened, she fell into a fitful sleep. She started awake, momentarily disoriented by the dark. She fumbled for the illumination button on her watch. The numbers glowed three in the morning. Emma huddled in the dark, her heart thumping. She couldn't pinpoint why she'd awoken, but her whole body tingled with some primitive instinct. An eerie quiet settled over the forest. She heard a soft footfall a few feet away from the tent's walls.

Something stepped out onto the makeshift path hacked by the passengers. Emma saw its shape through the mesh door. The animal turned its head to her, and its eyes glowed like the face of her watch. It slunk away, as quietly as it came. After a minute the scratching sounds of the forest resumed, as if the lesser animals were celebrating their near miss from the predator.

At four in the morning, Emma woke again. She hovered in the twilight between waking and sleeping. She'd been dreaming she was on a life raft and she'd just spotted land.

A twig snapped. Fear surged through her, but she managed to stay motionless, hoping it was another animal that would slink away. Another twig broke, closer. Emma slid her hand along the tent's nylon floor until her fingers reached her spear. She closed her fist around it.

Now whatever, or whoever, was coming toward her was moving fast. Sticks cracked under its feet, and she heard stones crunching. The footfalls came faster and faster, closer and closer. She heaved herself to her knees, holding the spear at her side, ready to attack whatever came through the tent's mesh door.

The moonlight broke through the clouds, sending shafts of light through the foliage. The light revealed a man's shape, standing five feet from the tent's entrance. He swung a rifle off his back by the strap and in a few seconds closed the distance. He shoved the rifle into the tent's entrance.

The man's head followed his rifle into the tent and he locked eyes with Emma. He smelled like rancid meat and old smoke. His face registered shock and fear. His gaze swept across the spear. He got a crazy, wide-eyed look, like he was seeing a monster.

Emma lunged forward, burying the spear tip deep into the man's shoulder. He shrieked and fell backward, out of the tent. Emma pulled the spear out of him, feeling the drag as it yanked at the man's flesh. The man rolled to his knees and grabbed at his rifle. Emma heard his fingernails scratch across the metal. She tumbled out of the tent after him. He flipped the rifle up to aim.

"No!" Emma screamed at the man. She took the spear and swung it like a bat, catching him across the side of his head. The spear connected to bone and then splintered with an explosive, cracking sound. The man swayed, then toppled over, blood spurting from his temple. He fell over like a stone.

Emma stood over the prone man, breathing hard. She struggled for control, but she felt the tears gathering in her eyes.

Shit, Emma, this is no time for a crying jag, she thought, but the utter hopelessness of her situation was once again upon her, blocking out all logical thought. She took three cautious steps backward.

Emma jumped behind a tree and listened for signs that the other guerrillas had heard her yell or the spear break. The injured man didn't move. After a few minutes, Emma went back to the man, grabbed his arm, and checked for a pulse. His heart beat in a strong rhythm. She searched his pockets and found a folding knife and a large rag that smelled of gunpowder and grease. She took both.

She knew she should kill him. If she let him live he'd return to camp and set the other guerrillas on her trail. She'd have to do it quietly. She looked at his knife in her hand. She could slit his throat. She opened the wicked-looking five-inch-long blade and lowered herself to one knee next to him.

The sounds of the night intruded on her. The wind rustled the leaves in a soothing sound and a tree frog croaked nearby. The man breathed softly in and out as he lay in front of her, defenseless. He looked like he was sleeping.

Emma felt as though some wide chasm had opened before her. The years of her Catholic-school upbringing crowded into her head and she thought of the Ten Commandments, "Thou shall not kill" being the foremost among them. She could have killed him in the heat of the moment in self-defense, but now, with the immediate danger over, what she contemplated felt like murder.

Emma closed the knife with a sigh. She lifted him under the arms and dragged him down the trail. He weighed too much for her to drag very far. She put him on the side of the path and covered him with branches.

When she was finished, she checked the trail. A long smear ran in a straight line from the path to the brush where she'd hidden the guerrilla. Emma used a tree branch to sweep away the telltale signs of dragging. She broke down her tent and put it and the pack on her back. She swung the man's rifle onto a shoulder. More firepower that she didn't know how to use. She'd analyze it later. When she was done she took one last look around, turned, and ran back the way she came.

BANNER GAVE HIS FIRST NEWS CONFERENCE THIRTY-
six hours after Flight 689 went down. He wore a bespoke suit
made in Hong Kong and a silk tie, also from Hong Kong,
and his French cuffs hit his wrist with precision. He stood in
a borrowed conference room in a Miami hotel and tried to
tell himself that he'd faced much worse in his career. It was
true, but the thought didn't help calm his nerves.

Stromeyer raised an eyebrow when she saw him in all his
sartorial splendor. "Feeling a little vulnerable, are we?"

Banner grimaced. "Wouldn't you? I have to report to the
most rapacious wolves in the industrial world that not only
did we allow a plane to get hijacked, but this time we can't
even locate it or the people on board."

"Why isn't a State Department spokesperson giving this
conference?"

"No one wants to face the tough questions about how airport security was compromised. As the Department of Defense's leading search-and-rescue consultant, they figure I
can take the heat when they can't."

"They're right. I've never seen you sweat before."

"Stromeyer, those were field operations. I'd much rather

be in the jungle tracking a hostile force. This media stuff always gets to me."

"Don't you think your reaction's a little extreme? At least the media can't kill you." Stromeyer peeked at the computer monitor that showed an interior view of the rapidly filling conference room. "That jerk TV reporter O'Connor is here."

"Least of my problems. The guys from MSNBC are the really worrisome ones. They know their stuff."

The last hours had been hell. Banner had dealt with the various agencies assigned to handle the crisis, while Stromeyer drew the unenviable job of "Victim Relative Liaison." She fielded hundreds of frantic calls from distraught relatives of the plane's passengers. All received the same news: That it was too early to tell if there were any survivors, but that the United States Army had boots on the ground searching for the plane.

The only relative that would have heard different news was someone related to Emma Caldridge. However, no one called about the woman. When Stromeyer contacted Caldridge's employer to ask for next-of-kin information, the receptionist transferred the call to the vice president of research and development for the company.

"Gerald White." The man's hearty voice boomed through the phone.

Stromeyer introduced herself. "I understand that you were the one Ms. Caldridge sent her text message to after the plane went down."

Mr. White cleared his throat. "Yes, I head up her department. I gave the message to someone from the Department of Transportation."

"Yes, thank you, but I'm not calling about that. I've been trying to track down her next of kin. No one has asked for her. Do you have any information?"

"It's not my area. I think you'll need to speak to human resources for that."

Stromeyer bit her tongue to quell a retort. "Mr. White, if our suspicions are correct, Ms. Caldridge survived the jet's landing. If there are any next of kin worried about her, I need to know that. Surely she left instructions with the firm about who to call if there is an emergency."

"Perhaps she did. I'll be happy to look into it and get back to you."

"I'm in a press conference that should last about an hour. Is that enough time? I can drive over to your offices after."

Mr. White cleared his throat. "Yes, that would be fine."

Now Stromeyer drew circles around Mr. White's name while she waited for the press conference to begin. She heard Banner cough.

"You look preoccupied. What's up?" he asked.

Stromeyer frowned. "Something about Emma Caldridge is bothering me. I think she has family in Florida, or at least a man named Caldridge lives near her in Miami Beach, but when the plane went down she sent a text message to her boss asking for help."

Banner took his eyes off the computer screen. "Maybe she isn't close to her family."

Stromeyer nodded. "Maybe. But in such an extreme circumstance wouldn't you text your family first?"

Banner shook his head. "I'd text you first. You're the one I know could manage the situation to my best advantage."

Stromeyer smiled. "Thanks for the vote of confidence, but she's not a covert operator, she's a civilian. I would think they'd text the person they love the most."

Before Banner could reply, the door swung open and Whitter strode into the room. From the look on his face it was clear that he did not have good news.

"Banner, I just spoke to the secretary of defense. There's

been a strategy reversal. You are to tell the press that we already have five hundred special forces personnel in place in Colombia whose sole mission it is to find and free these people."

Banner snorted. "Sole mission? Five hundred? Miguel said he's working with twenty." Banner pointed at Stromeyer's computer. "Is Rubenstein there? The smart one from that cable channel?"

She checked the computer monitor. "You betcha."

"And," Whitter continued, "you are to tell them that we flew these men down within twelve hours of learning of the trouble. You are to let them know that we had fighter planes scrambling in one hour and ready to go within three."

"What a crock of shit," Banner said.

Whitter bristled, pulling himself up like a private on roll call. "It's not shit. We do have five hundred men in Colombia."

"There to protect some private corporation's precious pipeline."

"There to fight terrorism whenever and wherever it may be found!"

Banner grabbed a clipboard that contained his notes and headed to the door.

"Do you hear me, Banner?"

Banner was gone. Stromeyer made herself busy with her ever-present manifest lists. Whitter slammed out of the room.

The news conference went fine for twenty minutes and slid south at twenty-two, when O'Connor threw the first mud ball.

"Major Banner, isn't it true that this breach of security would never have happened if the liberals in Congress had approved additional spending for Homeland Security?"

Banner gave O'Connor his patented military stare, a look that had quelled greater men than the soft reporter. In his relentlessly perfect suit, with his erect military carriage, and with his reputation as a former military man who'd seen battle, even the jaded media guys in the room felt a certain respect.

"Mr. O'Connor, save the spin for your television show. We don't have the time for it here."

The other reporters snickered.

"Isn't it true that this administration had fighter pilots in the air within two hours of learning of the event and over five hundred special forces personnel on their way in three?" O'Connor said.

Banner glanced at Whitter, who leaned against a wall in the back of the room. The smirk on his face was enough to tell Banner that he intended to get the ridiculous story out one way or another.

Banner knew if he confirmed the lie, then he would be the one in the hot seat when Congress convened a committee to review the events. Whitter leaned against the back wall and looked very pleased with himself while he waited for Banner to take the fall.

Over my dead body, Banner thought.

"There are five hundred special forces personnel in the area and available to assist should we need to call on them," Banner said. At least that much was true. Banner figured a guy with O'Connor's simplistic thought processes would never see the difference in the two assertions. He was right. O'Connor gave a supercilious nod, as if Banner had confirmed what he already knew.

Banner wasn't out of the woods, though. While O'Connor wasn't bright enough to see the fine distinction Banner had drawn, Rubenstein was.

"What were they there for, if not to assist in this operation?" Rubenstein said.

Banner watched an alarmed look wash over Whitter's face. Serves you right, asshole, Banner thought.

"There are several projects proceeding in Colombia that require a U.S. military presence," Banner said. He eyed Whitter, who seemed to hold his breath.

"Like the joint effort between Colombia and the U.S. to spray herbicide on the coca plants to reduce cocaine production?" Rubenstein said.

"Like that," Banner said. "Now, ladies and gentlemen, that's all I can tell you right now. I'm needed back at headquarters to continue managing the situation. We will attempt to keep the press, and the public, informed as much as is reasonably possible as this unfolds." He strode out of the room while the press corps screeched questions at him like a flock of magpies.

"Good job," Stromeyer said. "But a little short. You didn't give them much to report."

Whitter slammed into the conference room before Banner could respond. Today's tie was a hideous gray with yellow vines running up and down in a trellis pattern. Banner would rather have taken a bullet than wear such a tie.

"That was damn close," Whitter said. "You didn't tell them what I told you to."

Banner handed Stromeyer his clipboard. "If you want to tell them something, tell them yourself."

Whitter pursed his lips. Banner glanced at Stromeyer, who flicked a glance at Whitter and then winked at Banner. Her lighthearted response to Whitter's aggression made the muscles in Banner's neck relax. She had a way of making the worst situations bearable.

"Meet me at Southern Command offices. We're having a conference call with the American embassy in Bogotá in twenty minutes." Whitter snapped out the information and stalked out of the room.

The Miami sun felt like a blowtorch. Banner and Stromeyer strolled along the downtown streets, taking a short break before heading to Southern Command's offices. It was their first quiet moment since the hijacking, and the constant meetings and conferences were taking their toll on both of them. The sunlight and fresh air revived them. A limousine prowled behind, waiting to whisk them away when necessary. Banner began overheating within seconds. He searched for shade, while Stromeyer turned her face up and let the sun wash over her.

"You like the heat?" Banner said.

She nodded. "I love it. I grew up in Iowa, and this kind of weather came only in August. I lived for August."

The sun warmed Banner's shoulder, and he realized it hadn't pained him once since his arrival in Miami. Darkview's offices were in Arlington, Virginia, close to the powers that be in the military. Arlington was home, but Miami had a certain flair.

"We could open a satellite office here," Banner said.

Stromeyer laughed. "I'd love the weather, but I don't know if I could stand the vibe. It feels like a banana republic, all glitter and too laid-back for type As like me."

Banner grinned. "Maybe they've got it right and the poor working stiffs like us have it wrong."

Stromeyer smiled at him. "I love my work."

The Southern Command building was new and, to Banner's mind, much more inviting than most army headquarters. Waving palm trees and ample parking surrounded the two-story building. Built less than ten years ago, the facility boasted state-of-the-art technology, and its location near Miami International Airport made commuting convenient. One thousand people worked there. Banner thought the pink exterior color a little strange and whimsical for a building with such a serious purpose, but it tended to blend with the other construction in the area.

They passed through security in silence. Stromeyer's mood darkened the minute she stepped out of the sunlight.

She said, apropos of nothing, "I hate talking to the relatives. I hope Miguel rescues the hostages soon. This situation is breaking my heart."

They stepped into the main conference room. Whitter, two aides, and another man sat there. Whitter introduced the others as embassy personnel. He waved at the flat-screen television that showed a man in a suit sitting at a table. The man sipped from a coffee cup and looked at them as if he could see them.

"We're on closed-circuit television," Whitter said. He clicked on the speaker phone.

"Mr. Montoya, can you see us?"

Montoya nodded. "I can, Mr. Whitter."

"Good. Then perhaps you tell us how the Colombian government views this situation."

Mr. Montoya shook his head sadly. "I am afraid they are as puzzled as the rest of us. They believe that the disarmament program with the guerrillas is progressing well. They do not view this situation as a result of a hostile act against Americans. In twenty minutes the Colombian president is going to give a press conference in which he will tell the world that the plane was not hijacked." Banner and Stromeyer looked at each other, stunned. Whitter closed his eyes.

Banner recovered first. "If the plane wasn't hijacked, then what accounts for the text message we received from one of the passengers that said army men were taking hostages?"

Montoya gave a small sigh. "Major Banner, the last plane that was downed in the Colombian jungle landed there due to an equipment malfunction. Five American bank executives survived. They were taken hostage by some guerrillas in the area shortly after the crash. It was not a planned kidnapping, merely a crime of opportunity. The men landed in the wrong place at the wrong time."

"When was this?" Banner said.

"Three years ago."

"Where are they now?" Banner prepared to note their names.

"They are still hostages."

Banner sat forward. "No one's gotten them out? Have you gone there?"

Montoya shook his head. "Absolutely not! Major Banner, I don't think you understand the extent of the problem here. Embassy personnel are forbidden to travel to these areas. For our own safety we are not allowed to use the roads or public transportation. We fly over these areas, if we go there at all."

"But these men are American citizens. Surely the embassy could assist in negotiations, or search and rescue," Stromeyer said. Banner knew her well enough to hear the underlying layer of anger in her voice.

"Ms. Stromeyer—"

"It's Major Stromeyer," Whitter said. Banner did his best to hide his surprise at Whitter's correction. Stromeyer raised an eyebrow, but said nothing.

"I apologize," Mr. Montoya continued. "*Major* Stromeyer, the embassy has a strict policy of noninterference. We have no jurisdiction. We tell all Americans that they assume the risk when they come here, and if something happens they must appeal to the Colombian government and to the Colombian forces in charge of kidnap rescue."

"How is their success rate?" Stromeyer said.

"Good, but this is a big job and the hostages are deep in the jungle."

Whitter and Banner exchanged glances. For a brief moment, Banner saw a flicker of pain in Whitter's eyes.

"Did you know the bank executives?" Banner said.

Whitter gave a curt nod. "One. He was an acquaintance. His family lives in D.C. My wife sees them occasionally." He turned to the image of Mr. Montoya. "Mr. Montoya, what do you think is behind this extraordinary decision? Is the Colombian president aware that the American government believes the plane was hijacked in a manner consistent with terrorist action?"

Mr. Montoya sighed. "Mr. Whitter, I think the Colombian president is concerned that if he acknowledges the plane was hijacked by forces that could be defined as terrorists, then America will overreact. He is frightened that the aid will stop and the United States military will be sent in to wreak havoc on his country."

"Good thing I didn't tell the press that we'd flown five hundred soldiers into the country." Banner spoke to Whitter under his breath.

Whitter shot him a dirty look before turning back to Mr. Montoya.

"Mr. Montoya, has the Colombian government told the embassy what it intends to do to find these passengers?"

"I understand they have sent a search team," Mr. Montoya said.

"That found nothing," Banner said. "Do you believe them?"

Mr. Montoya sighed. "I don't believe anything until I can confirm it through trusted sources. The corruption here is staggering. But understand that these people may have been long gone before the search team flew over. However, the Colombian president is also aware of the statistics regarding missing planes. He intends to mention these statistics in his defense of the Colombian special forces, and to defer any claims of corruption."

Banner leaned toward the television. "Mr. Montoya, I need to hear from someone in the administration. I want to know the steps they are taking to locate these people. If they are not adequate, then I will form an alternate plan."

Mr. Montoya held out his hands. "I understand and I'll arrange a liaison with the proper authorities. There are over sixty political prisoners held in Colombia. The Colombian president is right now negotiating their release as part of the disarmament. Perhaps he should add this latest group to that list and then *all* the hostages will be released once the deal is finalized."

"And if the deal falls through? Then what?" Banner said.

"Then I think we need to have faith that the Colombian government will put all its resources behind the search. That's all we can do right now."

"I'll assume that the Colombian government will do its job, but if it does not, then I intend to do mine," Banner said.

EMMA TRUDGED ALONG, NOT LOOKING RIGHT OR
left, when she nearly stumbled over the hand of a woman
lying on the side of the path. The woman lay sprawled on her
back. Her brown flowered polyester dress was covered with
bits of nettles from various plants that she must have brushed
against and her heavy legs were covered in bug bites. Emma
squatted down next to her. The woman's gray hair flowed
over her face, obscuring her features. Emma moved it away.
The woman looked to be about sixty-five, with the heavily
lined face of a smoker. Her skin had a pasty white color.
She gasped in short breaths, like a fish gulping air. Emma
slid her arm under the woman's shoulders to lift her up. The
woman's eyes fluttered and then opened.

"Please help me," she said.

"Are you from Flight 689?"

The woman nodded. "I'm Gladys Sullivan. I lost my heart
medication in the crash. I can feel my heart is failing. I need
my medication."

The woman struggled to sit up. Emma moved behind her
to support her back.

"What were you taking?" she asked. The woman mentioned a pill that Emma knew worked to regulate heart rate.

"My heart's been getting worse every day. I kept telling them I needed a doctor, but they didn't care. They left me here to die." The woman's eyes shone with tears. Emma took the woman's pulse. The beat was erratic, and it was clear she wouldn't last much longer without her medication.

"I'm a chemist. I can't replicate your medication, but I did see some foxglove back on the path about an hour ago." The woman seized in Emma's arms, her whole body shaking. The convulsion passed and she grabbed at Emma's hand.

"Foxglove? Will it help?"

Emma hesitated. She hated to give the woman too much hope. When properly distilled, foxglove became digitalis, one of the most effective heart medications for the past two hundred years. Problem was, it was also highly toxic.

"It's the plant that makes digitalis, but—"

"Oh, yes! Please. You must get some for me." The woman choked out the words between gasps.

Emma shook her head. "It's highly poisonous. I wouldn't know the right amount to give you, and it could veer into toxicity too quickly for you to survive."

"What's your name?" Ms. Sullivan said.

"Emma Caldridge."

"Well, Ms. Caldridge, does it look as though I'll survive much longer without it? I think it's worth the chance." Emma couldn't argue with the woman. She looked dreadful. Emma shrugged off her pack and set up her tent. The woman's eyes widened.

"Will you look at that," she said.

"Let me help you inside. You can rest in there while I run back for the foxglove."

The woman clutched Emma's arm. "Promise me you'll return."

"Of course I will. Let me help you into the tent." Emma wanted nothing more than to get moving. The light was fading. Soon the path would be too dark to navigate and they'd have to wait for dawn. Emma didn't think Ms. Sullivan would last that long. She helped the woman shift into the tent and then patted her hand.

"Just rest here. I'll go get it." Ms. Sullivan closed her eyes and let her head fall.

Emma bolted out of the tent and ran down the path. She moved more freely without the pack. It was almost a joy to have the weight off her. She sped back, her head swinging from side to side. Perhaps she'd missed some more foxglove that was closer? Forty-five minutes later she spotted the tall plant with its white flowers surrounded by what looked like dried grass. She carefully removed the leaves and placed them in the leg pocket of her cargo pants. She spun around to return to Ms. Sullivan.

By the time she reached the tent, the sky had deepened to a red glow. A minute later, the jungle plunged into full dark. Ms. Sullivan lay on her side in the tent, still gasping. Emma flicked on her lighter. The woman's face held a white sheen and her breath was even more labored. She opened her eyes but seemed to look right through Emma. Emma pulled out leaves, ripped one in half, and gave the other half to the woman.

"Here, chew on this. I don't know if it's enough or if it's too much." Ms. Sullivan nodded. She took the leaf in her shaking hand and put it in her mouth.

No hesitation there, Emma thought. She watched as the woman grimaced.

"Tastes bad?" Emma said.

"Awful," Ms. Sullivan managed to whisper. "Do you have any water?"

"I'm sorry, no. I collect it in a small plate when it rains, but there is no way to transport it, so I have to drink it all and wait until I can collect more."

Ms. Sullivan waved a hand in the air. "Don't worry," she said. "When will we know if I swallowed too much?"

Emma felt helpless. "I have no idea. It should take at least twenty minutes to start entering your system."

Ms. Sullivan lay back down and closed her eyes. Her chest still heaved with each breath, and her face stayed pale. Emma switched off the lighter.

After ten minutes, she switched it back on. Ms. Sullivan's face looked pinker, and her breaths came in the longer, slower rhythm of sleep. Emma lay next to the tent's wall and fell asleep.

The next morning, Ms. Sullivan's breathing was once again labored, but not as much as it had been. She opened her eyes, looking around the tent before spying Emma.

"So you weren't a hallucination," she said.

"Not at all. How do you feel?" Emma checked the woman's pulse at her wrist.

"How is it?"

"Erratic. But better than before, I think," Emma said.

"Help me out of this tent, will you? It's as hot as Hades in here."

Emma helped her slide out of the tent, where she sat on the ground to catch her breath.

"Do you have any food?" Ms. Sullivan said.

Emma handed her a food package. Ms. Sullivan opened it and wrinkled her nose.

"This is turning."

"I know. But it's all I have."

Ms. Sullivan handed it back. "Is it your last? Here, you take it."

"Not at all. I have six more. You might as well eat it. They'll all turn soon."

Ms. Sullivan nodded. "I guess you're right." She tore into the filet and closed her eyes.

"Tastes like heaven, though. Much better than that dried beef jerky they're feeding us." She waved a finger at Emma. "I know. You're thinking I should lose some weight."

Emma patted her on the shoulder. "I am thinking no such thing, Ms. Sullivan." She looked thoughtful. "Come to think of it, how *are* they carrying all that food? I only see a small backpack like mine on each."

"They handed it out to us the first day. From the trucks that were parked on the side of the road. We carry our own."

Emma looked at Ms. Sullivan's empty pockets. "If that's true, where's yours?"

"They took it from me when they left me there to die. Call me Gladys, dear." She stuck out a hand for Emma to shake. "I'm from Chicago. South Side Irish. I was heading to Bogotá to meet my sister, who moved there fifteen years ago."

Emma shook her hand. "Call me Emma. Why Bogotá?"

"A man. Why else would an Irish woman from Chicago go to Bogotá?"

"What does he do?"

"Did. He died two months ago. I was heading down to help my sister pack to leave. He was a Christian missionary. He worked for a nonprofit that was dedicated to eradicating child soldiers and to bringing Jesus to the indigenous peoples."

"They use child soldiers here." Emma thought about the boy tied up on the back of the truck.

Gladys nodded. "Usually teenagers. They recruit them much like the gangs recruit in the States."

"Do they force them?" Emma said.

Gladys shook her head. "They don't have to. In parts of Colombia joining a paramilitary group is like joining the army in the States. The kids often have little schooling and fewer job opportunities, so the guerrilla groups offer a place to go." She finished the entire plate of food and put it down.

Emma felt a pang of panic. If Gladys continued to eat at that pace, they'd be out of food by tomorrow.

"I saw you on the plane. 'Course then you looked different. Right now you look like a heathen. What in the world have you rubbed all over your body?"

"Mud. It stops the mosquitoes."

"Ah," Gladys said. "They are horrible, aren't they? They sure do torment a soul. Have you been following us? Wouldn't it have been safer to stay with the wreckage?" Emma was having a little trouble keeping up with Gladys's stream-of-consciousness conversation, so she answered the last question she heard.

"After you marched out they came back and blew it sky-high. I ran before it exploded. I followed you because I didn't know what else to do, and I was afraid of that man in the truck."

"The one in the shirtsleeves? He was a bad one, for sure. But the skinny one is crazy. He beats someone every day. Oh! That reminds me." Gladys reached into a pocket of her dress and pulled out a rosary. "I've said a prayer every day since we've been captured."

Emma eyed the rosary. It was made of heavy beads that looked like onyx. A large silver engraved cross hung from the bottom. "Your rosary is beautiful."

Gladys held it up for Emma to see. "It was a gift from Charlie, my sister's husband. One of the guerrillas tried to take it, but I told him God would curse him if he did."

"And he stopped? Didn't he realize what he's doing to all the hostages is far worse than stealing a rosary?"

"You're in Latin America now. Christianity is strong here, and it coexists with shamanism, santería voodoo, you name it. Guerrillas can be very superstitious. He didn't want to mess with such a powerful symbol." Gladys fingered the rosary and sighed. "Charlie was a good man. I pray for him, too."

"Then I'll leave you to it. I want to head down the path a little. Perhaps there's a stream nearby and we can get some water." Gladys nodded and closed her eyes. Her fingers ran over the beads, one by one, and Emma watched as her lips moved in the silent ritual prayers assigned to each.

Emma ran for half an hour. No water anywhere. No food, either, at least nothing that she could identify as edible. She eyed a few caterpillars hanging out on a tree. If worse came to worst, she supposed she could eat them. She would have preferred some plants first.

She spun around and ran back to Gladys. She found her lying in the same spot next to the tent, sweating profusely and gasping again. Emma grabbed some more foxglove out of her pocket. Tore the leaf in half and handed it over. Gladys chewed, this time without grimacing. After fifteen minutes, her breathing took on a more regular rhythm.

"That was a close one," Gladys said.

Emma didn't know what to say. Gladys needed a hospital, and soon. The foxglove wouldn't work for long. Eventually Emma would overdose her by mistake, or the combination of a lack of food and water coupled with her heart condition would stress her body to the breaking point. These problems weren't immediate, however.

Their immediate problem was one of logistics. Gladys couldn't walk far, Emma needed to leave her if she was to forage for food, and each hour that passed meant that Gladys's condition would worsen. Emma warred with the idea of pushing Gladys to rise and walk with her, or to leave her there with the tent and her remaining packets of food while she herself continued to trail the passengers in the hopes of coming upon a village.

"What are you thinking about?" Gladys's shrewd eyes were on her again.

"What to do next. We need food and water, and we'll get neither by sitting here."

Gladys shifted. She waved Emma over. "Help me up."

"Are you sure you should move? Perhaps we should rest."

Gladys waved Emma off. "I'm feeling better now. We should move while I can. Sitting here gets us nowhere."

Emma collapsed the tent. She took Gladys's elbow to steer her down the path. They slogged forward. Emma found the slow pace excruciating. Gladys leaned heavily on her arm. She'd put the rosary in her pocket, but every so often she removed the beads and worried them about with her fingers. They stopped every half an hour to allow Gladys to rest.

The rains came in the afternoon. Emma hurried to place her tray out before scurrying underneath the leaves of a palm tree. She sat next to Gladys. They both stared at the plate as it filled.

"Is the tall man with the dark hair still alive?" Emma said.

Gladys frowned in thought. "You mean the handsome one? Shredded navy polo shirt?"

"That's the one. I think his name is Cameron Sumner."

Gladys nodded. "He's an interesting man. He helps the weaker ones when he can, but he doesn't say much. Seems he's always thinking. You can almost see the gears turning in his head. And the skinny one hates him."

"How do you know?"

"The skinny one spends a lot of time staring hate at him. Hate flows from the skinny one like a waterfall." Gladys shook her head. "He's the devil, that's for sure."

When the rain ended, the plate was half full. Emma let Gladys drink first.

"That was wonderful," Gladys said. "I'd kill for a cigarette just now."

Emma laughed. "I'd kill for a helicopter to come and take us away."

"That, too," Gladys said. She grew serious. "Emma, you need to leave me behind." Emma started to protest, but Gladys put up a hand. "I'm slowing you down. It doesn't do either of us any good if you continue to drag me along. Eventually you will run across a village. Those kidnappers are headed somewhere safe for them, but there's a good chance they will pass through a village on their way."

Emma sighed. "I know. They must be marching the passengers to a ransom point with some sort of modern communication and food. They need to eat just like the rest of us, and their packs are getting emptier each day, right along with mine."

Gladys nodded. "That's right. You're not afraid?" Her warm eyes filled a little.

Emma patted her on the arm. "I won't lie to you, I've been a mess this past year, but I'm not about to give up. I'm going to dog their tracks, leave markings all over the trail, and with any luck get both of us out of this situation."

Gladys clapped her hands. "Good girl! I like a woman who knows what she wants."

Emma smiled. "Come on. Back on your feet. A village could be right around the corner. You should walk as far as you can. It'll be good for you."

Gladys heaved to her feet. "You sound just like my doctor. 'Gladys, quit smoking, Gladys, quit eating.' "

"Gladys, start walking," Emma said.

Gladys rolled her eyes and started to move.

The path opened up into a green expanse at the base of the mountain. Emma gasped at the beauty of the little field, surrounded on three edges by jungle, with the mountain rising from the far end. Neat rows of bushes that looked like vines in a vineyard stretched almost a quarter mile on the small, flat expanse. The cultivated rows of crop ran in perfect parallel lines. The plants rippled in a slight breeze, and flashes of sunlight sparkled off the green leaves.

"Emma, look at this crop. There must be a farmer somewhere nearby. We've been saved!" Gladys clutched Emma's arm in a death grip. Her breathing hitched.

"Calm down. You're going to make yourself sick. Sit a moment." Emma lowered her down onto a nearby boulder next to a tree. She bent down and checked the crop.

Coca. The narrow leaves looked like any other wild weed. Emma found it hard to believe that such a harmless and unassuming-looking plant could cause such misery and heartache the world over.

She straightened up and shaded her eyes against the sun. No farmer worked the fields, for which she was thankful. Whoever owned this field would not be the sort that Emma would want to meet up close and personal.

"Gladys, this is coca," Emma said.

Gladys's face turned grim. "So not a *nice* farmer."

"No," Emma said. She saw a glint of light off to her right. A tin roof flashed in the sun. She pulled the remaining foxglove out of her pocket.

"Take these. There's a hut off to the right. I'm going to check it out."

Gladys shoved the leaves into her pocket. "Be careful. Don't let them see you. Oh, dear." She pulled her rosary out of her other pocket and started rubbing the beads like mad.

"Saying a prayer for me, are you?" Emma said.

Gladys nodded. "Always, dear girl."

Emma gave her a swift kiss on the cheek. "Just stay put," she said. She patted Gladys on the arm and moved away. She skirted the tree line, doing her best to stay in cover.

The field showed signs of being newly plowed. A cash crop, lovingly tended. The sound of a truck engine shattered the peace. Emma jogged back to the tree line and made her way over to Gladys. The sound of the approaching engine grew louder. She ran faster, stumbling over roots jutting out of the earth near the tree line. She'd left Gladys all alone, and the engine sounds were coming from that direction.

She was too late. At thirty feet from the little area where Gladys sat, two men, both dressed in gray T-shirts and both carrying assault weapons, stood next to a battered truck with wooden slats for sidewalls on the bed. Gladys stood facing them. She stood at an angle from where Emma hid, which gave Emma a good view of her profile. She talked to the men, punctuating her words with elaborate hand gestures. She mimed smoking a cigarette.

One of the men snorted, grinned at the other, and pulled a crushed pack of Marlboros from his front pocket. He shook out a cigarette and offered the box to Gladys. She snagged it and wasted no time placing it between her lips. The other man stepped forward with a cheap plastic lighter and lit the cigarette. Gladys inhaled, deep. Emma moved closer.

"Thank you, boys, you have no idea how much better that makes me feel," Gladys said.

The man with the cigarettes chattered at Gladys in Spanish. Gladys gave an elaborate shrug.

"Bogotá? I'll pay *mucho dinero*," Gladys said.

The cigarette man shook his head. "No Bogotá." He barked out a name. Gladys cocked her head. "I know about that town. It's one dangerous place, señor. *Mucho dangeroso!*" Gladys's Spanish was a disaster, but the man seemed to understand her. He pointed his weapon at her.

"Whoa!" Gladys said. She bent forward in a fit of coughing.

Gladys, stay calm. Emma almost said the words out loud. She could tell that Gladys's heart was racing. Nevertheless, the woman finished with her coughing fit and took another huge drag off the cigarette.

"Hospital?" Gladys said.

The man shook his head. He pointed to the truck's bed. It was clear he wanted Gladys to get in. He grabbed her arm. Gladys yanked out of his grasp.

"Okay!" She held up her hands in surrender. The cigarette jutted out from her index and middle fingers. Emma watched the smoke rise into the air. Gladys never relinquished her grasp on the cigarette. She turned her head in the direction of the field and dropped to her knees. She clasped her hands together, as if to pray. Instead, she threw her head back and yelled to the sky.

"Emma, if you can hear me, I'm going with them, but you stay put. The second man here was at the airstrip with the killer in shirtsleeves. He's taking me to a town controlled by the paramilitary. But I need to ride, I just can't walk anymore."

The man yelled at Gladys and grabbed her by the arm. This time he didn't let go until she was directly in front of the flatbed. He shoved her toward it.

"Okay, keep your shirt on," Gladys said. She waved at the back and mimed opening the hatch. "Can you lower it?"

The man made an irritated sound and lowered the back door. Gladys heaved her bulk onto the flatbed, never relinquishing her hold on the cigarette. The man slammed the hatch closed, waved at his buddy, and crawled into the truck's cab.

Emma heard the gears grind as the engine turned over. She felt tears gather in her eyes. Gladys leaned out of the back of the flatbed. In her hand was her beloved rosary. The truck wheels spun on the soft earth. The rosary swung in the sudden movement. Gladys dropped it on the ground.

"For you, Emma!" she yelled into the air. "It will give you the strength to continue. Don't give up, dear girl. I'll pray for you every day." Gladys waved, and Emma waved back, even though she knew Gladys couldn't see her. Emma watched the truck disappear in a swirl of dust and smoke. Gladys continued to wave as it drove out of sight.

Emma wiped her eyes, walked over, and retrieved the rosary. The cross sparkled in the sun as it swung from side to side. Despite her anger at the omnipotent being the rosary represented, she felt like it was a talisman. She shoved it in the cargo pocket of her pants and started across the field.

Emma plodded down the rows, keeping her eyes lowered, taking care not to smash the plants with her feet. The ever-present sun beat on her head, and little puffs of dirt rose around her feet with each step. She heard the distant roar of a small airplane. She craned her neck to look into the sky. The roar got louder. The plane was flying low.

Drug plane or rescue team? she thought. The plane came into view. In one second she heard the roar but saw nothing. In the next the plane was upon her. It flew so low that it seemed to touch the treetops. As soon as it cleared the jungle it descended even lower, while a mass of black dust poured from a tank in back.

Emma's heart did a flip. "Hey! Over here!"

She screamed and waved her arms. The plane flew right at her. She threw herself down as it roared over her head. The chemicals landed on her in a huge, choking cloud. Her throat closed in protest and water streamed from her eyes. She heaved a breath and then started to cough. The chemical scorched her mucous membranes, and the inside of her mouth was on fire. It sprinkled into her hair and layered over the cut that she'd gotten on her head during the plane crash. The cut burned as the chemical chewed into her skin.

The plane turned around and flew back at her. The dust

poured again, covering the entire coca field in black sediment. It passed over Emma, once again enveloping her in a cloud of chemicals. Her lungs burned. She opened her mouth to breathe. She sucked in the harsh chemical, and her stomach rebelled. She retched, but nothing came up, thanks to the meager rations she'd eaten. She dry-heaved over and over.

The plane flew away.

The dust cloud cleared. The field of coca, previously so green, now looked black. Emma sat up and shook the black granules off her skin. She plucked a leaf off a nearby coca plant. She shook some of the herbicide off the leaves onto her palm, and took a closer look at it.

The granules looked like glyphosate, a typical herbicide used in agricultural applications, but it was mixed with a surfactant of some sort. Emma couldn't identify it. The surfactant would assist the herbicide to penetrate the waxy surface of the leaves. It would also turn the EPA-approved herbicide into a concoction deadly to humans, plants, and animals. The coca would die, but so would everything else in the jungle.

"Asshole!" Emma yelled into the air. "Kill everything, why don't you?"

Emma staggered into the jungle. She needed to get the herbicide off her skin before it entered her system through her pores. The mud she'd spread all over would act as a temporary barrier, but the surfactant would eat its way through it soon enough. She watched the sky. It had rained daily since her ordeal began, so she hoped that it would again, and soon. She felt her panic rising as she used a stick to scrape the mud off her. She felt terrible dropping the herbicide on the ground where it would poison the dirt, but she had no choice.

An hour later, the rain came. Emma stood naked in the

pounding water, and washed the mud and chemical off her skin and hair. Her clothes were draped on a nearby boulder. The rain pummeled everything, including the coca field. The herbicide sluiced off the plants and mingled into the muddy dirt below, turning the ground into a chemical wasteland. When everything was soaked, she collected her things and hiked back to the trail.

Emma felt clean for the first time in days. She hated to replace the mud. She decided to get away from the herbicide area before reapplying it. She hiked for half an hour but couldn't take much more. The mosquitoes feasted on her fresh skin as if it were a gourmet meal. She sat on a boulder and counted her bites. One hundred twenty. Sixty on each arm. She sighed. She found some wet earth at the base of a tree and smeared the mud on.

14

LUIS GNAWED ON A PIECE OF BONE-DRY BEEF AND barked orders at the guerrillas. He washed the beef down with a swig of burned coffee. He'd woken up in a very bad mood. One of his sentries was missing. Desertions were common, but each time it happened it set Luis on edge. He viewed each as a failure of his ability to frighten the men into total obedience.

Alvarado snapped out orders as well. Luis heard his voice grow hoarse with the yelling. Only the passengers were quiet. Most had entered the depressed, somnolent state that Luis knew was a sign of despair. He kept them hungry and tired, and made sure that one was beaten every day while the others watched. Nothing commanded more obedience than the fear of pain.

Luis sipped his coffee and eyed the tall man. He'd hollowed out some in the last days due to dehydration, but he still maintained a watchful stillness that bothered Luis. He'd proven invaluable, however, helping to lift fallen logs or other obstacles that needed to be moved as the group progressed, and he still walked with a fluid stride. Luis decided that the man would be the one beaten today. Perhaps then he would see the fear in the man's eyes that signaled respect.

A small group of soldiers stood next to the tied passengers. They waved their arms excitedly and gathered in a semicircle at the edge of the clearing.

"Shit," Luis said. He spit the coffee onto the ground.

Alvarado stepped out of the circle of guerrillas and waved him over.

"We found Juan." Alvarado's eyes held a grim look.

Luis grabbed a machete and strolled over to the circle of men. They moved aside as he approached. Luis enjoyed the anticipation of the moments before he would come eye to eye with the man he intended to kill.

In the center sat Juan. His head bled from a huge gash above his ear and his clothes were soaked with blood. Luis noted that his eyes, always red from the crack he smoked, looked like two neon lights.

"Where have you been?" Luis spoke in a conversational tone of voice that belied the ticking time bomb of rage that was building in him.

"I was attacked in the forest! By El Chupacabra!"

The circle of men fell silent. Two made a rapid sign of the cross.

Luis did his best to hide his surprise. He'd expected a long tale of woe from Juan, but not this. The men peered around them with uneasy expressions on their faces. Luis stared hard at Juan, trying to buy time while he decided how to deal with the wild claim. The last thing he needed was a bunch of drug-addicted, drunken men believing they were seeing bloodsucking creatures with red eyes, green skin, and spines running up and down their backs.

Luis snorted. "El Chupacabra is a myth. There is no such thing." He waved a hand in the air, as if such myths were not worth mentioning.

One of the guerrillas, a farmer named Manzillo, stepped forward. "No, Rodrigo, it is not a myth. I have seen one with my own eyes. It killed three of my goats and six chickens. It sucked the blood right out of their bodies." The men all muttered to one another and several eyed the trees worriedly. Manzillo's insistence surprised Luis. He was a farmer forced into service by the FFOC. He'd never shown a spine as long as Luis had known him.

"We have been in these hills for years, Manzillo. Why would the animal be attacking us now?" Luis spoke in what he hoped was a calm, reasonable voice. It was not a voice he usually employed, so he was not sure if he sounded convincing. Especially when what he really wanted to do was grab both Juan and Manzillo and shake the shit out of them.

"Because of the herbicide. The gringos are killing the coca fields and the farmers are taking their goats and chickens to other places. Without the chickens to eat, it is forced to be bold to get food."

The other guerrillas were struck silent. Luis knew it was because none of them was smart enough to come up with such a logical reason for a mythical animal to attack them. Manzillo's reasoning sounded like rocket science to them.

"This is ridiculous, Manzillo." Luis's anger had always been enough to control the men. But this time, it didn't work.

"It is not, Luis. We must have a plan for tomorrow night, or someone else will be next." Manzillo drew himself up to his full height, which was not tall, but such a move from a mouse like Manzillo made him appear heroic.

Luis felt the blood rush to his face as his anger rose. He glanced at the tall man, who stood three feet from Luis at the edge of the group of passengers. Luis saw a flicker of amusement in the man's eyes, which stoked his rage. He focused again on Juan.

"How much rock did you smoke before you saw this Chupacabra, eh?"

A couple of the guerrillas snickered. Luis chalked their reaction up as a hit.

Juan shook his head. "No more than usual, huh? And look at me. How do you think I got these wounds? I tell you, I was attacked by El Chupacabra!"

"You. Were. *Not!*" Luis grabbed the machete tighter and spun around. The steel glinted in the early morning light as he slashed the blade down, aiming at the tall man's neck. A woman passenger screamed; a scream cut short by a male passenger clapping his hand over her mouth.

Luis timed the attack to match the moment the tall man looked away, but the man spun around at the sound of the scream and dodged the blade. The machete sank into his upper shoulder, slicing the skin, but missed his neck, which was Luis's real target. The tall man staggered but didn't go down.

The tall man faced Luis, his eyes clouded with anger and pain. He said nothing as his blood soaked through his shredded shirt. After a minute, he took several slow steps backward, still standing upright, stopping when he reached the circle of passengers.

Luis threw the machete on the ground. "That is what will happen to you, Juan, if you talk about green monsters again. And, Manzillo, you will stand sentry tonight."

Luis stalked back to his coffeepot and dry-meat breakfast. Alvarado resumed yelling, and the camp prepared once again to march.

MIGUEL STOOD IN A DOUBLE-WIDE TRAILER THAT
served as a command post and looked at the twenty special forces men assigned to assist in the airplane reconnaissance. Most had been stationed in Colombia for the past six
months. All had seen some sort of action. Three had minor
injuries, and one was newly recovered from a nasty bout of
dengue fever, the scourge of hot-weather locales the world
over.

Miguel had arrived by helicopter, flying over the area he
would traverse on foot. Nothing but trees and mountains for
miles. The beauty stunned him; the complete isolation worried him. The Colombian police force refused to join him in
the search.

"That is for the Colombian special forces. We do not have
the additional men to spare for such an endeavor," one official had said.

"This is how the Colombian government treats its allies?"
Miguel said.

The official nodded. "Your government has not suf-
ficiently provisioned you for the mission you are about to
undertake. You have no dogs to sniff for the mines, and no
army backup. You will be dead in a few days unless you take

additional precautions. I will not send my men on a suicide mission."

"Any suggestions?" Miguel hadn't bothered to keep the sarcasm from his voice.

"Fly over the area. Do not attempt to go there on foot. The forest is heavily mined and bandits are everywhere. You can find the wreckage just as easily from the air, perhaps more so, and your odds of dying while looking will be drastically reduced."

"We will begin with air review, of course, but once we spot the crash site, we will drop men into it. They will canvass the vicinity for survivors."

"A very bad idea, sir. They are bound to step on a land mine." The government official looked sad.

"Perhaps I'll arrange for a bomb-sniffing dog," Miguel said.

"I'd suggest you get one for every soldier. If you do not, the paw-breakers will get them."

"Paw-breakers?" Miguel said.

The man nodded. "Small mines designed to blow off limbs. They are homemade and activated by hypodermic syringes or mousetraps."

"Wonderful," Miguel said.

"Welcome to Colombia." The man had shrugged as he said this.

Miguel was heartened when he saw the soldiers assigned to the mission. He had been forced to accept fewer men than he'd wanted, but the ones he did have seemed solid and ready for the jungle trek. Most looked fit enough for the hiking that would be required, but none looked very eager to begin. Worse, they all wore light, sand-colored camouflage pants. They might as well have been wearing white, for all the good the light camos would do for them.

Miguel introduced himself. "I'm your commander for this search-and-rescue operation. We're planning on heading deep into the jungle, so can anyone explain to me why you're all wearing camouflage used for desert missions?"

"We were scheduled to go to Iraq, but they pulled us off at the last minute and sent us here instead." One of the soldiers in the back row offered the clarification.

Miguel sighed. The Colombian officer's comment about the lack of preparation for the mission appeared to be right on target.

"Anything I need to know that may be useful in this mission?" Miguel's question opened the floodgates.

"The paramilitary groups are worse than the cartels, by far." A soldier in the front row piped up with this not-so-helpful comment.

"Worse than drug dealers? Hard to believe," Miguel said.

"Believe it, sir. They care less about life than the drug dealers. The drug dealers want to keep their clients alive. Dead clients don't buy drugs, after all. But the paramilitary guys don't give a damn about civilian life because they don't make all their money from the drug trade."

"What's your name and how do you know so much about the paramilitary guys?"

The soldier stood up and saluted. "Private Gabriel Kohl, and I've been here the longest."

"Well, Private, then how do the guerrillas make money?"

"They siphon gas from the pipeline and sell it on the black market. Those that aren't siphoning bomb it, and extort protection money from the local government. Those that don't siphon or bomb, kidnap."

"So I've heard. And the government pays extortion money? Why?"

"Hell, half the paramilitary guys we're dealing with are

the relatives of the governmental officials, so in many cases the government has no real incentive to shut them down."

"Sounds just like Miami." Miguel's voice was dry. He handed out copies of a picture of Emma.

"This is a passenger from Flight 689. Name of Emma Caldridge."

Kohl whistled. "Man, she's pretty!"

Miguel frowned at Kohl.

"Uh, sorry, sir, just an observation," Kohl said.

Miguel glanced at the picture. "She is pretty, but that's not why I gave you the picture. She's an extreme runner and chemist who somehow managed to send a text message from her telephone after the crash." He handed out copies of Emma's text message. "There are several guerrilla organizations operating in the area from where we received the message, but we have reason to believe that the group that collected the passengers was headed by one Luis Rodrigo."

Several men groaned.

"Exactly," Miguel said. "We need to find the passengers before Rodrigo annihilates them all. And we'll need some way to locate the mines. I understand he's famous for them. Kohl, do you have any idea where we might obtain a bomb-sniffing dog?"

Private Kohl thought for a moment. "The Colombian army guys have a couple of German shepherds that they use for mine clearing."

"Take me to them. Let's see if we can borrow them."

Within a couple of hours, Miguel arranged to take two German shepherds, named Boris and Natasha, with them on their journey. After securing the shepherds, Miguel called Carol Stromeyer.

"Major Stromeyer, I've got twenty special forces men dressed for the Iraqi desert instead of the Colombian jungle.

Any chance you can get the DOD to spring for the proper clothing?"

"No problem. Get me their names. I'll look into it and get back to you."

Three hours after that, the first search helicopters took off.

16

STROMEYER STOOD BEFORE A YOUNG RECEPTION-
ist sitting behind a mahogany desk in the Pure Chemistry
lobby. The company's success was manifested in its corpo-
rate offices. Housed in a glass building with green-tinted
windows, the facility occupied half a city block. A brochure
placed in the reception area boasted that Pure Chemistry
contained a state-of-the-art laboratory.

Stromeyer introduced herself. After a few minutes, a large
man dressed in khaki pants and a short-sleeved white shirt
walked up to her. He sported a bad comb-over, a polyester tie that was askew, and a plastic pocket protector in the
shirt's breast pocket. Stromeyer couldn't begin to imagine
the thoughts Banner would have if he saw Mr. White. He
smiled a grin that exposed miles of gums, and stuck his
hand out.

"I'm Gerald White. Nice to meet you. I've got the additional information on Emma Caldridge that you need."

Stromeyer shook his hand. "I appreciate it."

White led her past the receptionist into a carpeted hallway
lined with doors. They reached one in the back.

"Here's my office. Would you like some coffee?" He
opened the door.

Mr. White's office bore the stamp of a professional decorator. It was the antithesis of the man himself. The square-shaped room had a bank of windows on one side with a view of a small grassy area next to the building. A sleek cherry-wood desk held a laptop in a docking station, a manila folder, and nothing else. Bookshelves lined the walls. Stromeyer saw a *Grey's Anatomy* along with several volumes of scientific journals. A book titled *Nostradamus, the Predictions* caught her eye.

"Interesting choice, Nostradamus," she said.

White gave her a sheepish look. "He was a sort of scientist, you know. I've always been fascinated by him." White grabbed the manila folder. He perched on the edge of the desk.

"I have Ms. Caldridge's personnel file here. As you know, it's confidential, but I can tell you some information without the need for a subpoena. Like how long she's been employed by us, her job description, et cetera."

"How long has she been employed here?"

"Eighteen months. She transferred here from a job at a prestigious lab in the Midwest. We were very excited to get her, because she already had quite a reputation for her knowledge of plants."

"I've read an article about her in *Science* magazine. Something about adding artificial chromosomes to plants," Stromeyer said.

Mr. White nodded, a look of excitement in his eyes. "Yes, that work is truly groundbreaking. The Mondrian Chemical Company is looking to license her technology."

"Is she continuing that research here?"

Mr. White shifted, as if nervous. "Not exactly. We do cosmetic chemistry. However, some of her work complements our needs. For example, we know that vitamin C liquid acts as a powerful antioxidant, but a serum containing it degrades quickly into a useless liquid. Ms. Caldridge helped create the technology that allows the ingredient to retain its potency for consumer use."

"Why did she leave her last job?"

"Her fiancé died. She decided to move here to be near her father. He had retired to Florida."

"I'd heard something about the fiancé. How did he die?"

"Car accident. He was hit by a drunk driver who veered into oncoming traffic."

"How tragic."

White nodded. "She doesn't talk about it much, but I bumped into some of her former colleagues at a seminar and they say she was devastated." He handed Stromeyer a piece of paper from the folder.

"She gave her father's name and address as her emergency contact. George Caldridge, 2370 Poinsettia Place, Miami Beach. Here's the phone number."

"Do you think he knows that she was on Flight 689?"

White nodded. "I imagine not the exact flight, but he knew she was headed to Bogotá. Ms. Caldridge mentioned to her secretary that she'd informed her family of her trip."

Stromeyer couldn't help but be shocked. What kind of father didn't call after his daughter when he knew she was on a flight from the same American city, to the same region, on the same day, that a jet went down?

"Has he been in contact with Pure Chemistry?"

White shook his head. "Not at all. In fact, we tried to contact him, but there's no answer, and the machine is set to take no messages."

"Ms. Caldridge sent a text to you after the plane went down. Are you very close?"

Mr. White looked pleased. His face turned pink in the beginnings of a blush. "We are. She's brilliant, but easy to work with. Not the usual combination in our business. A lot of scientists are eccentric, to say the least." It was clear Mr. White had a crush on Ms. Caldridge.

Stromeyer stood up. "Could I see her office? It would give me a feel for her."

"Of course. Most of her time here is spent in the lab, which is off-limits to visitors, but her office is right down the hall." Stromeyer followed White, who led her two doors down the hallway. He opened the door and waved her in.

The office benefited from the same professional decoration as White's. It, too, had windows that looked out onto the same grassy area, a bookshelf built into a wall, and a cherrywood desk that was identical to White's. Her desk contained a notepad engraved at the top with the words *From the desk of Emma Caldridge,* an empty laptop docking station, and a framed photograph of Emma with her arms wrapped around the waist of a man. Stromeyer picked up the picture.

"Is this the fiancé?" she said.

White nodded. "His name was Patrick McBain."

Both Emma and the man smiled into the camera. They looked happy and carefree. Stromeyer replaced the frame on the desk.

"Do you know if she took her laptop with her?"

White shook his head. "Doubtful. We have strict controls on how much information our scientists can cart around. We'd hate for a competitor to get their hands on some of our work, and laptops can be easily stolen. When not in use, they're locked in a secure room."

Stromeyer was surprised. "Is the information that valuable?"

White smiled. "The cosmetics industry is based on fast-paced innovation. Once a product is on the market, generics will re-create it within months. Next thing you know, your expensive face cream is shelved next to the drugstore's cheaper house brand. Our clients expect to be copied once they launch, but they insist that we maintain tight security during the research-and-development phase."

Stromeyer eyed the bookshelf. A volume entitled *The Indigenous People of Colombia* caught her eye. She pulled it off the shelf and showed it to White.

"Had she been to Colombia before?"

White wiped his hands on his thighs. Stromeyer thought he once again looked nervous.

"She went to the Ciudad Perdida last year."

"I beg your pardon?"

"The Lost City. Ancient ruins, like Peru's Machu Picchu, located in the Colombian Sierra Nevada Mountains not far from the coast. The site remained hidden until the 1970s, when grave robbers discovered it. Of course the indigenous people always knew it was there. To get there requires a grueling six-day trek through jungle and paramilitary-controlled coca fields. Not too many people attempt it. Emma took the trek last year."

"Looking for plants?"

"Yes."

"Did she find any?"

White shook his head. "She'd hoped that the indigenous people would utilize the local plants in a new, useful way, but all they used was the coca plant."

Stromeyer was surprised. "Really?"

White chuckled. "Really. They think it's a sacred plant that confers strength and fertility on those who ingest it. They chew it for energy. Needless to say, we couldn't utilize that particular plant."

"You win some, you lose some." Stromeyer smiled at White.

White laughed. "You've got that right."

Stromeyer replaced the book and held out her hand. "Thanks for your help. I'll drive by Mr. Caldridge's house and check it out."

"Of course. As I told you on the phone, Ms. Caldridge is one of my best researchers. She's one of the few people I know who are completely unafraid of new situations. She'd fly to the most dangerous places in the world if it meant discovering something new and exciting."

"Does Pure Chemistry have kidnap insurance for her?" The thought just popped into Stromeyer's head.

"No. We only take out 'kidnap' and 'key man' insurance for our CEO. The rest of us are stuck flying without a net, so to speak. Perhaps her family will offer a ransom."

"Not likely, Mr. White. They haven't bothered to check on her."

Mr. White looked glum. "I know. Not what I'd expect, frankly. She's a nice woman. Seems like she'd come from a nice family."

After leaving Pure Chemistry, Stromeyer drove over the MacArthur Causeway to Miami Beach. She found Poinsettia Place in a small, gated community on a strip of land flanked by water. The houses were solid brick with shingle roofs, unusual for Miami, with its emphasis on Spanish tile and Mediterranean architecture. These houses could have been in New Hampshire or Connecticut.

The Caldridge house was a ranch style with a red brick exterior and a dark shingle roof. Solid and prosperous-looking, it sat on a corner, with trimmed bushes surrounding the perimeter, red bougainvillea climbing up the side walls, and orange hibiscus and crocus plants lining a brick sidewalk.

Stromeyer rang the bell and waited. Four minutes later, she rang again. She checked her watch. Five minutes later, she rang again. Nothing. The curtains on a front picture window remained closed. Whether against the noonday sun or because the owner was gone, Stromeyer couldn't tell. She walked around the house. Two large air-conditioning units sat on one side. Silent. This told Stromeyer everything she needed to know. As far as she could tell, these were the only air conditioners in the entire state of Florida that were switched off. Florida's streets baked in oppressive heat, while every interior Stromeyer visited remained ice-cold. If George Caldridge's air was turned off, he wasn't home and wasn't planning on being home for a while; it was as simple as that. She climbed back into her government-issued sedan and ruminated on the missing-in-action senior Caldridge all the way back to Southern Command.

She located Banner pacing in the conference room, a coffee cup in his hand. His eyes lit up when he saw her.

"Good news, I hope? I need some."

Stromeyer sank into a swivel chair. "Emma Caldridge put her father down as her emergency contact. But he's gone, flew the coop."

Banner stopped pacing. "Are you sure?"

"I went to his house. The machine doesn't accept messages, no answer at the door, and his air-conditioning is turned off."

"Any idea where he worked? Maybe he's on vacation."

"He's retired. Maybe he's traveling, but I doubt it. Even if he was, you'd think he'd check in on his daughter when he saw the CNN footage. Unless he's in some extremely remote area, he's bound to have seen it."

"Have we checked her house?"

"Not yet. Honestly, I didn't think it would be necessary. I'll contact the FBI, get a warrant, and head over there right away. I did get one piece of interesting information, though. Seems that last year she visited a remote area of Colombia looking for plants. She found nothing Pure Chemistry could use, but was supposedly headed back there for work purposes. It's a little odd."

Banner took a sip of his coffee. "I had a feeling she was a player," he said.

EMMA CAUGHT UP WITH THE PASSENGERS TWO
hours after washing the herbicide off her skin. She trudged
behind the line, her spear gripped in her hand and the guerrilla's rifle over her shoulder. The path in front of her curved
right. The trees were less dense than before, which allowed
sun to filter between them. Grass grew knee-high in the
patches of light. Emma could see the line of passengers between the breaks in the trees. Two guerrillas held up the
rear. She dodged behind a tree to let them regain their lead.

A snorting, huffing sound came from the jungle, somewhere between Emma and the line of passengers. The
guerrillas called a halt. The snorting sounds continued,
along with rustling sounds made by whatever was in the
tall grass as it moved through. The soldiers holding up the
rear became agitated. They kept spinning around to look
behind them. Two turned around and walked backward,
their eyes scanning the jungle. The snuffling sounds intensified.

"Pigs!" one of the lagging soldiers yelled. He yelled it
in Spanish, but Emma recognized the word. At least she
thought she did, until she saw the others guerrillas turn to
peer into the grass. The fear on their faces was unnerving.

Why in the world are they so afraid of pigs? Emma wondered. She kneeled behind the tree and watched the men.

The rat-faced guerrilla pushed back through the line of passengers. He crouched next to the path and aimed his rifle toward the snorting sounds. Emma was thirty feet away and directly in his line of fire.

Emma froze. She warred with herself. Should she move slowly away? What if he heard her? Stay behind the tree? Take the risk that he'd spot her? Or stay frozen and let him shoot, taking the risk that a stray bullet would hit her?

Before she could decide to do either, the rat-faced guerrilla fired. He sprayed the area with shot. Emma heaved herself backward as the bullets landed all around her. She dropped to the ground and curled into a ball to make herself as small a target as possible.

The guerrilla let off another round. This time, loud squeals accompanied the noise of the gunfire. Emma watched as the low-growing palms and grasses moved in waves. When the waves were twenty feet away from her, she saw the wild pigs.

They were unlike any pigs she'd ever seen before. The size and shape of small pit bulls, they were muscled and hairless. The lead pig had two large tusks that grew from his lips, like a wild boar, except these tusks stuck straight out in front of his snout. He squealed in rage and ran at her. Six others fell in behind him.

Emma grabbed her spear, pulled herself upright, and took off back down the path. She ran as fast as she dared, dodging tree branches and avoiding small ruts. The spear flashed in her peripheral vision each time it moved with the pumping action of her arms. Her feet slipped and flew out from under her. She stumbled forward and landed face-first in the mud. She could still hear the pigs running and grunting behind her.

She got up and took two steps, and on the third, pain shot

through her left shin. It felt like someone had driven a nail through it. It flared with each bone-jarring step. Emma's brain registered the injury that she recognized as a shin splint, a tiny fracture of the shinbone, while the rest of her strained to continue running. She looked back.

The lead pig gained on her. She heard its hooves scrabbling on some loose stones. It moved with a speed that Emma did not think possible in an animal that size, and it showed no signs of slowing. The other animals fanned out behind it.

Emma's injury made outrunning the beast impossible. She would have to stand and fight. She turned to face the charging animal, gripped her spear, and prepared to attack.

The lead pig was six feet away and barreling toward her. Emma planted her feet, and when the animal came close enough, she jammed the spear into it with all the energy in her. The beast ran right onto the point. The spear vibrated on impact and penetrated straight through the pig's body. The force of the hit made Emma stagger, and the spear's shaft slid through her palms, scraping the skin. The spear entered at the pig's flank and exited on the other side near the animal's tail. The pig squealed a death squeal, twitched once, and stilled.

The other pigs were on Emma in a flash. Emma swung the spear around in an arc, with the pig still impaled on it. She clubbed the second pig with the body of the first, and whipped the stick back the other way to swipe at the third. The fourth pig's tusks scraped her arm, but Emma managed to club it before it could sink the tusk home.

The lead pig's corpse spun off the weapon and flew sideways. It landed four feet to the right of Emma. The other pigs turned in unison and descended on the body of their leader. They attacked it in a frenzy, snorting and stabbing at it, tearing it to pieces with their tusks. The pigs ignored Emma while they ravaged the dead animal.

Emma got up and limped her way back to the path where she had last seen the guerrilla shoot. When she found it, she kept moving. As she walked, she shook with fear. Her shaking lasted long after the noise of the maddened pigs receded in the distance.

That evening, Emma set up the tent a football-field length down the trail from the guerrilla campsite. She could smell smoke from fires and the pungent aroma of cooking meat made her mouth water. For a brief moment, she regretted leaving the dead pig behind. It would have made a decent supper. She considered going back the next morning to see if anything was left of it, when reason prevailed. By the next day it would be decaying in the heat and covered with flies. She settled into her tent, the folding knife she'd taken from the guerrilla open at her side.

18

MIGUEL, HIS PILOT, KOHL, AND BORIS HAD BEEN
flying over endless stands of beautiful trees and lush green
foliage for two days. The terrain conspired against them.
The thick cover could hide something as big as a jet with
ease. Miguel doubted that they'd find the jet at all if it had
landed in the denser parts of the jungle. While in the beginning Miguel had sat in awe of the beauty laid out before him,
now, after two days of flying, he watched without interest
as the terrain below them flashed by. He started the search
close to the coordinates for the cell phone, and expanded it a
little more each day, flying in concentric circles.

Kohl and Boris the dog sat behind Miguel. Kohl held binoculars that he used to look out the window, scanning the
ground. Every so often he'd reach over to give Boris a pat.
For his part, Boris looked miserable. It seemed to Miguel
that the dog didn't like the noise of the rotors.

"There it is!" Kohl yelled over the noise and gestured at
the ground. The pilot leaned his head to the side and then
nodded.

Miguel looked down. A huge crater sat in the middle of
what looked like a thin road carved into the trees.

"Looks like a huge hole," the pilot said to Miguel.

Miguel spun his hand in a circle. "Take us back around."

The pilot swung the helicopter around for a second pass. The jet body itself was missing, but a huge crater indicated where explosives had been detonated. Miguel tapped the pilot on the shoulder.

"Can you get closer?"

The pilot nodded and lowered the copter.

"See the long straight gouge in the earth that disappears into the crater?" Miguel said to Kohl and the pilot as he pointed to the earth.

"That's a runway they blasted," the pilot said.

"What's the line on the road? Plane dragged something that created it?" Kohl said.

Miguel shook his head. "Not likely. Maybe the landing gear didn't retract."

"No way that runway is long enough for a jet." The pilot yelled this information to Miguel. "My guess is she broke up on landing."

"Take us down," Miguel said.

"Hold on." The pilot pulled on the collective, and the helicopter heaved to one side. Boris slid across the floor and knocked into Kohl, who threw his arms around the dog to steady him. The pilot hauled the helicopter back the other way and then spun in a circle and dropped downward. Miguel felt his stomach drop with it.

"What the hell are you doing?" he yelled at the pilot while he braced himself against the wall.

"Evasive maneuvers. Below three thousand feet and we're in sniper range. We never go straight down. Not if we want to survive the landing."

"Yeah, boy!" Kohl yelled while the helicopter swung from side to side and spun around.

Miguel felt like he was on a Tilt-a-Whirl ride at a carnival.

He hated that ride. He watched the ground approach. When the copter landed, he was the first one out.

Miguel stood on the remains of the runway and looked around. Debris was everywhere, but very little of it was recognizable. He walked around the area, kicking at broken tree limbs, pieces of luggage, mounds of dirt, bits of shoes, and sections of steel that had survived both the landing and the explosion.

Kohl and Boris searched the fringes. After a minute, Kohl burst from the trees, Boris jogging along next to him. Miguel watched him stop and vomit.

"Let me guess, you've found the bodies," Miguel said.

Kohl took a deep breath before answering. "Not bodies, *pieces* of bodies. There are a couple of heads and a torso back there."

"Are they burned? Or are they blasted apart?"

Kohl gave Miguel an incredulous look. "Sir, no disrespect meant, but does it matter? They're sure enough dead, I can tell you that. I didn't hang around long enough to analyze the manner of death."

"Manner of death counts. Burned means that the plane caught on fire and our chances of finding survivors are few. Blasted means that they were blown apart by whatever caused this crater, and perhaps there are other survivors who avoided the explosion."

"What about burned *and* blasted?" Kohl said.

"Means that God and the devil fought and the devil won. But don't worry, God may lose a battle or two, but He always wins the war."

"I sure hope you're right about that," Kohl said.

Miguel marched to the perimeter and looked at the casualties. It was a ghastly sight, and he himself had to repress an urge to retch. He kneeled, said a short prayer, and made the sign of the cross when he was done. His years as a soldier killing the enemy had not taken the conviction from him that the dead needed a prayer said for them. At least the innocent dead. The killers he wouldn't give the time of day. He waved Kohl over.

"Burned *and* blasted. You have to wonder what kind of assholes kill people twice. Is once not good enough for them?" Miguel sighed. "You take Boris and search the area from here in about one hundred yards. I'll canvass the perimeter."

Twenty minutes later, Miguel found the crudely hacked path. That it was fresh was obvious from the still-green leaves that lay on the ground. They hadn't had time to yellow after having been cut off. Miguel bent down to get a closer look at the dirt. The marks of shoes were so numerous that they overlapped one another. Miguel felt a little hope rise in him. If the tracks were any indication, quite a few passengers may have survived the landing.

"Kohl, get over here."

Kohl jogged over, Boris at his heels.

Miguel showed him the path. "That's where we start hunting. Looks like a bunch of passengers made it."

"Why would they leave the area?" Kohl said.

"Their guerrilla welcoming committee must be moving them to a secure location." He pointed to the jagged branches that stuck out, about shoulder height. "These cuts were made by a machete hacking at the branch. While the TSA misses a lot of contraband at airport screening, Transit Security is a lot better than that."

"What next?" Kohl said.

"Let's head back to camp and get the others. Tomorrow we come back and take this path."

THE NEXT MORNING, MIGUEL, KOHL, AND TEN OTHER special forces personnel swarmed over the bomb site. They'd found several bodies in the surrounding forest, but the bulk of their finds were body parts, not intact bodies. They collected them all, however. DNA would help identify the dead. Miguel led Boris the dog into the tree line. After a few minutes, he found the hidden luggage.

"What do we have here?" Miguel patted Boris on the head. He checked out the bags. The first black roller was good quality, but utilitarian. The kind of inconspicuous bag that Miguel would buy if he ever needed to travel out of uniform. He flipped over the tag.

"Mr. Sumner's bag survived, if not the man himself," Miguel said to Boris, who stood next to him, panting. He opened the suitcase and sifted through it. Nothing useful jumped out at him. He turned to the neighboring bag, which was covered in some sort of fancy designer logo. Miguel forgot the guy's name. This luggage was also high quality.

"Too flashy, hey, Boris? What do you bet these are a woman's bags?"

Boris flapped his dripping tongue once, and sat down.

Miguel unzipped the bag and looked at Emma's note on top of the clothes.

"Kohl, come over here," Miguel said. Miguel handed him the note. "Ms. Caldridge left us another clue. And Mr. Sumner of the Air Tunnel Denial program survived the crash."

Kohl read the note and gave a low whistle.

"Seventy alive. Excellent. You were right about that path. Do you think she's still around?"

"My concern is that she was hiding and got caught up in the blast." Miguel stood up and gazed around.

"I sure hope not," Kohl said.

"Me, too. But my guess is that she's alive. Call back to Banner and let him know that Ms. Caldridge survived after she sent the text message." Miguel paused, thinking. "I just wish I knew what she decided to do."

"What would you do?" Kohl said.

"I'm a trained soldier, so I don't think what I would do applies in this case," Miguel said.

"Didn't you say she was some sort of extreme runner through tough terrain? Doesn't sound like the kind of person who would fall apart at the sight of a jungle. Even one like this." Kohl waved his hand to indicate the thick foliage. "Hell, she could run her way out of here."

Miguel nodded slowly. "You've got a point. But she needs food, water, and some idea of direction, or she'll end up running in circles."

"Could she use the stars?" Kohl said.

"Could you? I mean, before you joined the special forces."

Kohl's grin was a little sheepish. "No way. The only star I could identify was the Big Dipper."

Miguel laughed. "Don't feel bad. I couldn't, either. No, I think she would do something easier, more obvious. She wouldn't have a machete, so cutting her own path is out."

Kohl shrugged. "Then her only option is to use the trail or the road. If the road, that means she split from the passengers. The guerrillas must be cutting the trail to avoid being seen from the sky."

Miguel nodded absentmindedly.

"How about I go up the road a bit? See if she left any more clues for us to find?" Kohl said.

Miguel shook his head. "No! That road is probably loaded with mines. We follow the trail. The footprints all over it lead me to believe the guerrillas are herding the passengers that way."

"But what about Ms. Caldridge? We just can't leave her." Kohl's voice held a note of shock.

Miguel stood up and dusted off his hands. "She's on her own."

Kohl made a noise in protest, and Miguel waved him off.

"While I'm pleased that Ms. Caldridge survived, my job is to rescue all of the passengers, not just her."

Kohl looked stricken. "But if we find her, she could tell us how much of a head start the passengers got and how far ahead she thinks they are."

"I doubt we'd catch Ms. Caldridge, even if we wanted to," Miguel said.

"Why?"

"She's able to move a hell of a lot faster than we are, I can tell you that."

"She's got to be tired, too. She's only human," Kohl pointed out.

"Kohl, her brand of tired is completely different from ours. She's conditioned to run in the heat for miles on end. What she does can only be done by a handful of people in the world. It's like trying to chase a Formula One race car in a golf cart."

"I hate to leave her out there."

Miguel sighed. "I know, but we can't spare the time look-ing in different directions. We need to focus our efforts in a way that is likely to find the most passengers. And who knows? Maybe she's following the guerrillas, too. Come on, let's move out."

Kohl turned away, a dejected look on his face.

Within fifteen minutes, they were jogging down the trail. Boris and Natasha ran in front; Miguel, Kohl, and the rest followed. Within an hour, Miguel was drenched. His clothes clung to his body. Thirty minutes later, he reduced his pace to a brisk walk. After thirty minutes more, he was walking even slower.

Miguel called a halt. He sat on a nearby tree stump and drank from his canteen. The wet heat felt like a blanket set-tling on him. The minute they'd stopped walking, the mos-quitoes began forming into clouds. Miguel pulled out some bug spray and sprayed his arms. The unique chemical smell floated in the air. His arms felt sticky and he smelled like a chemical processing plant.

Great, he thought. He waved Kohl over. "What happened to the odorless bug spray?"

"We never had any that I know of."

"Now my scent can be detected a hundred yards ahead."

Kohl laughed. "Not by the guerrillas. They all smoke like fiends. Their sense of smell shut down years ago."

"I hope the same can be said of the cartel guys." Miguel's voice was dry.

"They're worse. They smoke weed. That smell will cover anything in its path." Miguel stood up and ran a bandanna over his face. Kohl shuffled his feet and studied the foliage all around them.

"Well, look at that," Kohl sounded excited.

Miguel rubbed the sticky chemical deeper into his skin before glancing up to see what interested Kohl so much.

That's when he saw the large *X* carved into the trunk of a tree. He gave a low whistle.

"Wonderful," he said.

"It's her!" Kohl's voice was filled with excitement, and way too loud.

"Kohl, pipe down," Miguel said. He walked over to the *X*. Ran a finger in the grooves. He didn't care who carved it, he was just thankful that they did. He spun around. Kohl grinned a crooked grin and batted at a cloud of mosquitoes. "Time to go," Miguel said.

They started forward again; this time, no one jogged, except Kohl, who seemed to have a new lease on life since seeing the *X*. Miguel figured they had four hours of light left before the men would need to eat. Each soldier carried a pack that contained food, water, a hammock, and mosquito netting.

Boris came to a dead halt. He stopped so quickly that Miguel stumbled over him. He landed on his knees next to the dog. It was then that he saw the thin nylon wire strung across the path. It disappeared into the tree line. Miguel couldn't see where it stopped, but he assumed it ended on a spring-loaded mine.

"Everyone stop!" Miguel yelled to the men. They froze in place. Kohl inched forward and squat down next to Miguel. He eyed the line.

"Don't you just love that dog?"

THE DAY AFTER JUAN APPEARED BABBLING ABOUT
El Chupacabra, Luis awoke to discover that three men had
deserted during the night.

"We have a very big problem," Alvarado said.

Luis was boiling with rage. He focused on the tall man.

"It is this man who causes us trouble," he told Alvarado.

Alvarado gave Luis an incredulous look. "Luis, forget that
man, will you? How could he be the problem? He is here the
entire time, while these sentries see monsters in the dark."

Luis swung toward Alvarado and poked a finger in his
chest. "Or do you believe it is El Chupacabra, too?"

Alvarado shook his head. "I think it is some sort of animal
that stalks us. A *real* animal, not a legendary beast."

"How do we kill it?" Luis kept his gaze on the tall man,
who was kneeling next to a passenger.

Alvarado shook his head. "I do not know."

Luis watched the tall man talk to the passenger.

"Luis, focus," Alvarado said.

"No more sentry duty. Everyone sleeps in camp today. If
the beast comes, it will have to enter the circle to attack, and
when it does, we will kill it." Luis continued to stare at the
tall man, then spun on his heel and walked away.

Alvarado stayed in the rear, brooding. Luis's single-minded determination to complete this project and show the cartels his leadership abilities worried him. Luis was a man of little complexity and great, explosive anger. While he was known for leading the small band of losers well, Alvarado did not think he was up to the task of running any type of real organization. His anger always ended up creating a disaster.

Like his unprovoked attack on the tall man, whose machete wound had become infected. It oozed yellow pus. He still managed to walk with an easy motion, but Alvarado saw how his mouth was pinched with the pain. His hair hung in greasy clumps and his eyes were bloodshot. Alvarado thought the man looked slightly mad. He expected him to die from the infection, and this meant less money for all.

The loss of the tall man wouldn't be their only loss, by far. Three other passengers were already sick. Two diabetics had lost their insulin in the crash, and their moods were fluctuating wildly as their blood sugar rose and plunged. One passenger had broken his arm and the swelling refused to lessen. The man kept it wrapped and held it close to his body. Alvarado wasn't sure how long the man would survive if the swelling didn't go down. He figured all these would die before they could be ransomed.

At three o'clock in the afternoon, Luis and his entourage reached the first checkpoint on their journey. Three flatbed trucks and two jeeps, covered with leaves and tree branches for camouflage, were parked at the beginning of a crude dirt path.

"Thank God," Alvarado said. "We can ride for a while."

Luis waved at the soldiers. "Get everyone into the trucks." He turned to Alvarado. "At least we move the cows faster now, eh? I was ready to kill them all just so we could get here."

Alvarado shook his head. "Fifty miles, and only a little bit faster. This road is a mess. Then more walking."

"Fifty miles in a vehicle. Who cares how fast? It's still much better than fifty miles on foot," Luis pointed out.

Alvarado nodded. "True, but this part is dangerous. The gringos can follow the road from their Harpies." Alvarado scanned the sky above him, looking for helicopters.

Luis watched, too. He slapped Alvarado on the back. "What goes up must come down, Alvarado. I've yet to see a Harpy you couldn't shoot on descent." Alvarado looked pleased at the compliment.

"But we throw out the sick ones here. We don't have the room to carry them all," Luis said. "Take that diabetic man out of here and shoot him." He pointed at the weaker of the two diabetics. "The tall man, too. His infection will kill him in the next few days, and I am tired of looking at him."

Alvarado frowned in disapproval.

"You have a problem with this order, Alvarado?" Luis glared at his lieutenant.

Alvarado pursed his lips, then shrugged. "The diabetic man will be in a coma soon." He said nothing to Luis about the tall man. He thought the chances of him beating the infection were slim, but he'd survived this long, a near miracle. Alvarado snapped his fingers at a group of guerrillas that lounged against a jeep. "Take those two back on the path and kill them," he said.

EMMA ROUNDED A CORNER AND SKIDDED TO A
halt. A small group stood on the path thirty feet ahead. Foliage obscured her view, but she caught glimpses of the men
between the swaying branches.

Three guerrillas stood in a semicircle around Sumner
and another passenger. The extent of Sumner's deterioration
shocked Emma. He was unshaven, with five days' growth
of beard and a long red, swollen cut on his shoulder blade
that oozed a yellow substance. He was naked from the waist
up, his back was covered in bug bites, and his pants hung on
his frame.

The other man was not much better off. His ashen face
gleamed with an unnatural sheen, and he swayed a little.
Sumner reached out and clutched the man's forearm, lending what support he could.

The guerrillas passed a joint between them in silence. The
pungent marijuana aroma wafted toward Emma. Each carried a rifle slung over his shoulder by a strap, one wore ammunition belts crisscrossed over his chest, and the third held
a plastic water bottle.

They ignored the two passengers while they took their
time smoking. The executioners, rather than offering a last

smoke to the condemned, were taking one themselves. It was as if Sumner and the other man didn't exist. As if the guerrillas thought the men were already ghosts. Emma felt a sense of dread just watching the silent group. She found herself staring at the guerrilla with the ammunition belts as he put the joint to his lips, inhaled with closed eyes, and then took it away in a slow motion. She knew that when his joint was over, something awful was going to happen.

The smoke curled into the air in slow patterns. The two guerrillas without ammunition belts sat down on the ground to roll another. The guerrilla with the ammo stayed standing, and continued smoking. Sumner and the injured man waited, swaying in silence.

Emma slid the pack off her back. She lowered it to the ground and carefully pulled out one of the pistols and a tiny bottle of scotch. She shoved the gun into her waistband, cracked open the scotch, drank half of it, and poured the remaining alcohol over the grease-soaked rag that she still had from her encounter with the guerrilla. She placed the neck of the bottle under her foot. The top broke with a satisfying crunch, leaving a jagged tip and a wider opening. She shoved the piece of cloth in the bottle and picked up the lighter. She crept toward them, until she was only fifteen feet behind the group.

The ashen man's eyes glazed over, and he sank into unconsciousness, falling quietly onto the thick bed of rotted leaves that covered the trail. The smoking guerrilla removed the joint from his mouth, pointed his rifle at the prone man, and blew his head off. Bits of bone and brains splattered against the thick foliage. The blast set a group of monkeys screaming in the trees.

Emma gasped in horror and fumbled with the lighter, flicking it at the soaked piece of rag. While she did, the guerrilla raised the gun and pointed it at Sumner, who stared at it with a resigned look on his face.

The rag lit. A tongue of flame whooshed upward. Emma moved into position behind the guerrilla aiming the rifle. She shoved the barrel of her gun into the back of his head.

"Don't even think about it," she whispered in his ear.

She felt his body freeze. The other two leaped up with almost comical speed.

"Get down!" Emma yelled at the top of her lungs and threw the flaming bottle of scotch at them. They dove back onto the ground to avoid it. Sumner jumped over and yanked the rifle from the standing guerrilla's hands. He trained it on the others. Everyone froze, like some grotesque sculpture.

Emma grabbed the rifles away from the other two, still lying on their stomachs. She now had four guns that she didn't know how to use, three guerrillas she didn't know what to do with, and one man with wild, bloodshot eyes on the verge of a nervous breakdown.

And a corpse.

Emma's hands shook as she held the pistol.

"Take off your clothes," she said.

The guerrillas didn't move.

"I said take off your clothes!"

This time she punctuated her statement with a kick to one man's shoulder. He babbled at her in Spanish, clearly not understanding her.

"What in the hell am I going to do now?" Emma said, frustrated.

Sumner gave her a reddened stare before he turned to the guerrillas. He barked an order in Spanish, his voice hoarse. The men looked at him in surprise. He said the same words again, then knelt down and shoved the rifle into the face of one of the guerrillas.

Emma noted that whatever he said worked, because all three began to rip their clothes off. Sumner shot Emma a questioning look but said nothing as the pile of clothes grew.

"Keep the guns on them," Emma said.

Sumner nodded. He still stared at her as if she was a creature from outer space. Then she remembered the mud that covered her body. She must have looked a fright.

"It's mud. It stops the bugs from biting."

Sumner said nothing.

Emma grabbed one man's pants and took the pocketknife to them, cutting the pants into strips. She tied the arms and legs of each, shoved pieces of the cotton into their mouths, and wrapped another strip of cloth around to hold the gag in place. She grabbed the water bottle the guerrilla had dropped in his surprise. She held it up for Sumner to see.

"This is precious." She shoved it in her backpack. She handed one of the T-shirts to Sumner.

"For you to wear. Your back's a mess of mosquito bites." Sumner took the shirt but made no move to put it on.

"Help me carry them off the path," Emma said.

Sumner didn't move. He continued staring at her. Emma felt her anger rise. Why didn't he speak? Had he gone off the deep end?

"Help me carry them into the trees!" Emma made her voice sharp. "While I can't kill them in cold blood, I would like to stop them from chasing us for long enough to get away!"

Sumner swung the rifle over his good shoulder, stuck the tail of the T-shirt into his waistband, and grabbed the nearest soldier by the armpits. Emma pulled on the man's ankles, and she and Sumner carried him into the brush. When they were done, Emma stood over the corpse. She didn't like to look at it.

"Should we move him?" she asked.

Sumner shook his head.

Emma hesitated. She didn't want to touch the man, and she rebelled at the idea of leaving a human being sprawled on the path without any type of proper burial, but she would leave him if it meant extra time to get away. The anger she carried around with her flared, bringing with it a feeling of despair. She shoved the emotion aside. Most of the passengers on the plane were dead, this man was dead, and if she didn't make a decision about moving him soon, another guerrilla would appear and then she'd be dead.

"Perhaps the body will reassure any tracking guerrillas that their buddies had completed their mission," Emma said. "We'll leave him here. Let's get the hell out of here before someone comes."

Sumner shrugged on the shirt. Then he nodded.

Emma shot him a glance. Perhaps he didn't speak English? Well, she didn't speak Spanish, so he'd have to do his best to understand her.

"I hate to go back toward the airplane, but following the rest is no longer an option. Once the others realize these guys are missing, they're going to double back. I saw a small trail that branched off a few miles back. Let's take that and hope for the best."

Sumner looked at her but again said nothing.

"Come on." She waved him forward.

He fell in behind her.

Emma thought that what they needed the most they didn't have—a machete. She stepped gingerly over what was left of the dead man and started down the path at a slow jog.

Two hours later, shooting pains arced from her feet through her overworked calves and through her already fractured shin. Emma swore under her breath. The microscopic fracture hurt like hell, and the only way to cure it was to lay off running until it healed.

That's not going to happen anytime soon, Emma thought. She grimaced and kept going, maintaining a grueling pace despite the stabbing pain in her legs and the load on her back. She noticed how Sumner struggled to keep up. His shoes were cut in several places and he winced with each step. He stumbled. He needed a rest, but they had at least four hours of light left, and Emma intended to use every minute of it to get some distance between them and the guerrillas. They passed a huge palm tree, and she stopped to stare at it.

"I'm a little surprised to see one of these," she said.

Sumner stood on the path, his chest heaving. He leaned back to view the palm.

"It's called a traveler's palm. I didn't think they grew wild in this part of the world." Three more of the trees were scattered around in a semicircle, looking as if they'd been planted. "It's pretty distinctive; see how the fronds are fan shaped and stick right up into the sky?"

Sumner nodded.

"When I tell you, put your mouth at the base," she told him.

Emma walked to the first tree's trunk, which was twenty inches in diameter. The fronds wrapped around it and over-lapped one another at the base. Emma followed along the edge of a frond with her fingers.

"Put your mouth at the place where this frond meets the trunk."

Sumner raised an eyebrow at her.

"Trust me. You'll like this," Emma said.

He kneeled and lowered his mouth to the frond.

Emma gently pulled the base of the frond from the trunk, and as she did, clear water poured from a channel between the frond and the trunk.

Sumner drank greedily.

When he was finished, he sat back on his heels. A small smile played around his lips.

"Pretty neat, huh?" Emma said.

Sumner nodded, still looking at her with a whisper of a smile.

"All traveler's palms collect water in their base. They got the name because travelers used them to drink. Pull another frond back for me, will you?"

Sumner repeated the procedure and Emma drank from the tree. She wiped her arm across her mouth.

"Let's go."

Emma started out at a brisk walk, and they kept that pace until sundown. She left Sumner sitting on the trail, collecting his breath, as she walked in a semicircle to look for a place to camp.

They should have kept going, but Emma didn't think Sumner could make it. He still hadn't said anything, nor did she. She preferred to focus on putting one foot in front of the other at a speed that would keep her ahead of any possible pursuers. Emma retrieved Sumner after she'd set up the tent and cleared a place to sit. He sank down with a sigh.

"Food," she said as she handed him an airline package.

He barked a soft laugh when he saw the package but wasted no time ripping it open. The rancid smell of spoiling meat wafted from the tray, but Sumner didn't seem to notice. He ripped at the meat with gusto. While he did, Emma pulled out the first-aid kit and walked over to inspect his infected shoulder. She lit the lighter in the darkness to have a look. The cut was eight inches long and filled with yellow pus.

"What caused this?" she said, although she already knew.

"Machete," he said in perfect, unaccented English.

"I need to lance this and pour alcohol on it as a disinfectant," she said. He stopped eating and stared at her, his eyes gleaming in the lighter's glow.

"Can you hold the lighter? I don't want to start a fire that would attract them."

His hands closed over hers in the dark. His palm felt wet and clammy. Too clammy. He was working on a fever.

Emma dropped the lighter into his palm. He tried to flick the lighter on, but his slick fingers slid off the starter twice. On the third try he managed to light it. He held the flame while she used it to heat the knife. When it cooled, she pushed the blade into the oozing blister. He groaned, but didn't move as she used the airline napkins to soak up the infection.

"Incoming alcohol," Emma said. She poured a small amount over the wound. He groaned again. She covered the mess with a bandage and patted his arm when she was done. She sat next to him to eat her own filet.

Emma waved at the tent. "It's supposed to hold two, and we'll sweat to death, but it's a lot better than being eaten alive by mosquitoes all night. You're welcome to join me."

He nodded again; his eyes flashed as they caught a shaft of moonlight. Emma crossed her fingers that he hadn't gone over the deep end, and crawled into the tent. Sumner joined her a minute later. Their bodies lay against each other from shoulder to ankle. Emma moved as far away as possible, which in that closed space meant about two inches. She lay awake a long time, sweating, with the sounds of the night pressing down on her.

22

THEY WOKE AT DAWN AND ATE A LITTLE BEFORE
heading out. Two bright red circles on Sumner's cheeks indicated that he was feverish.

"Can you walk today? You look like you have a fever,"
Emma said.

"Yes," he said.

It was the last thing he said for the next eight hours.

The only bright spot in the day was when they found a
stream.

"Oh, thank God, water." Emma's relief was profound.
"We need to stay along this stream. If there are any villages
in these mountains, they will be near it, you can bet."

They spent the rest of the day following the river. As good
as finding it was finding the cattails that grew alongside.
Emma collected them as they appeared.

"We can eat these. What a great day!" Sumner raised an
eyebrow but said nothing. Emma used a vine to attach them
to the outside of her pack. Sumner watched her without interest. That his mind was elsewhere was obvious. Emma
didn't bother to try to snap him back to the present. Perhaps
his thoughts consisted of things more pleasant than their
current circumstances. Far be it from her to force him back

to the grim reality they faced. It seemed they were to be forever silent.

By late afternoon, Sumner's eyes burned bright, and the two spots on his cheeks expanded to cover his face and neck. Emma continued to march him through the jungle despite his rising fever. Each hour his cheeks grew more flushed and his eyes more glazed. The only thing that kept him going seemed to be sheer determination. Emma was familiar with the type. Endurance runners have the same undivided drive to push themselves against all reason. Except Sumner had a reason, a very good one. They could hear chopping sounds.

Emma knew from her many trips to search for medicinal plants that while the jungle foliage made it impossible to see more than a few feet ahead, it also magnified, rather than dampened, sound. It was a paradox she never could figure out. The chopping sounded close, but in reality the person making the sound could be miles away. While Emma knew this intellectually, she was having a hard time accepting it. Her adrenaline surged every time a sound echoed through the forest. Her mental state was deteriorating with each hour in the jungle.

Sumner stumbled, and this time he stayed down. He rolled onto his back and waved her off.

"I need a break," he said.

Emma squatted next to him to wait. He had lapsed into his usual silence, but she felt compelled, finally, to break it.

"Your name *is* Cameron Sumner, isn't it?"

He shot her his signature wary look.

"Yes," he said after a long minute.

"Don't worry, I'm not psychic or anything. I saw you hide your luggage from the guerrillas. When you left I retrieved it and read your business card. Southern Hemisphere Drug Defense."

"I saw you at the airstrip. Why were you trying to get into the truck?"

"The Smoking Man had a spare field phone. I was trying to steal it."

Sumner shook his head. "That was an incredibly risky move."

"Thanks for diverting their attention to the capybara. I thought I was done for when that thing shot out of the forest and the woman screamed."

"How did you manage to avoid capture in the first place?"

"The crash catapulted me out of the plane, free of the fuel."

"Lucky you. That was a scene from hell."

"Where were you thrown?"

"To the rear. I landed right in the group of guerrillas."

"You didn't have a chance," Emma said.

"I was a damn sight better off than most of the others. I'm alive."

Emma couldn't argue with that.

"I'm Emma Caldridge."

She didn't give the usual smile that accompanied an introduction. Under the circumstances, smiling was unnecessary.

Thirty minutes later, Sumner dragged himself to a sitting position. After a few minutes sitting, he hauled himself up to standing.

They started again. A sheen of sweat covered him. Emma warred with herself over whether she should ask him to wade into the stream to lower his temperature, or whether she should continue to drive him forward, away from any pursuers. She chose to drive him forward. When he collapsed there would be time enough to work on bringing down the fever.

The heat rose to over ninety degrees. The path alternated

between oozing mud and wet leaves. Emma plunged into a spiderweb, its sticky gossamer threads clinging to her face and hair. She saw the web's maker, lurking at the edge. It was almost three inches across, black, and hairy.

"Ugh. Sumner. A spiderweb. I hate spiders!" Emma spoke louder than she'd intended, a mistake, because noise carried far in the jungle. She clawed at the web with her fingers. Her frantic movements alerted the spider. It scuttled sideways toward her.

"Oh, no, you don't." Emma plunged forward so fast that she tripped over a root. She jogged another couple of feet, all the while brushing at the web that clung to her arms and face, and then hauled up short just inches from another web stretched in front of her.

Sumner banged into her back. He grunted.

"Sorry," Emma said. "We'll have to go around this one."

She turned and came face to chest with Sumner. She looked up, and it took all her control not to gasp. It was as if Emma was staring into a death skull. Sumner's face was gray. Drops of perspiration dotted his forehead, and rivulets of sweat ran down the sides of his face. His eyes had sunk into his head and dark, black circles ringed them. His lips were cracked and dry, strange because the air was filled with humidity and nothing in the entire jungle was dry, and when he exhaled Emma could smell the excess ketone bodies in his breath. She recognized all the symptoms of infection, dehydration, and malnutrition. Starvation and infection were causing his liver to oxidize his body's fatty acids, a process accelerated by the strenuous pace she had set.

"Sumner, can you continue?" Emma whispered the question. He looked at her through eyes that were glassy with fever.

He nodded. Once. And then swayed a little. He straightened slowly. Emma turned and continued on, but now at a drastically reduced pace.

An hour later, his legs gave out. Fever consumed him. Emma dropped the backpack and set up the tent. They'd gone only about an additional six miles the whole day due to the lack of a machete. At around noon gunshots had echoed through the forest a lot closer than Emma had hoped. Sumner's collapse couldn't have come at a worse time. Tears ran down her face, and her hands shook. Having company had felt better at first, but now she couldn't leave him, and she suspected that the guerrillas were close.

Emma stripped his shirt off and peered at the machete wound. The skin around the slice was swollen like a balloon and a dark, angry, red color. Pus dripped out of the slash. The wound smelled sweet, putrid, and thick, like decaying flesh. It was clear to her that Sumner would die unless she could find a way to draw the infection from the wound and hold his fever down while she did.

Emma stripped Sumner's remaining clothes off and carried them to the stream. She submerged them in the water, wrung them out, and placed them over the branches of a bush in the sun. She wanted the sun's rays to burn off any infection that remained on the clothing. She heard a loud buzzing noise. A nearby bush seemed to vibrate with the sound. Emma took a cautious step toward it. The sound intensified. When she reached the bush, she saw the sound's source. A dead capybara lay next to the bush. Hundreds of blowflies covered the corpse. The black mass stayed in constant motion, the flies moving and battling one another for position. New flies hovered over the body, plunging into the heaving mess and flinging themselves back into the air. Several buzzed around Emma's head, dive-bombing close to her face.

Emma batted at the disgusting insects. She waved her hand to knock them off the capybara's body. It was then that she saw the maggots. The tiny, flesh-colored larvae writhed on the dead corpse, creating an illusion that the animal moved.

"Perfect," she whispered. "You guys are coming with me." She rooted around for a stiff leaf and a stick. She found both a few feet from the capybara corpse. She scraped the stick across the body, using the leaf to catch the maggots that fell off. The flies buzzed at her angrily, hitting her in the face as she worked. Her hands were full, so she resorted to shaking her head, making her hair flick at the angry insects in an attempt to keep them at bay. Sweat ran down her face and into her eyes. A horsefly bit her on the arm and she yelped at the sharp, pointed sting. She gagged at the smell that rose in a gaseous cloud from the animal, the same smell attracting the flies and maggots that she viewed as worth more than their weight in gold. When the leaf was full of maggots she bent the edges together to form a pocket, grabbed the wet clothes, and jogged back to Sumner.

He hadn't moved since she left him, but his face had taken on an even darker red hue. Emma rolled him over gently. She took the first-aid kit from her backpack and unrolled the gauze bandage. She carefully opened her leaf over the machete wound. She knocked the maggots onto the wound, taking care to gently push them deep into the seeping slash. They attached almost immediately, sucking onto the inflamed flesh. She made sure that the youngest, smallest ones were the ones she inserted. She carefully wrapped the writhing mass in the gauze, loose enough to let air in, but tight enough to hold the wriggling worms against the cut. She knelt back to get a look at her work. The gauze undulated, but the maggots stayed in place.

She made a small fire, burning the neem-seed pods that

she'd collected when she'd gathered the leaves. They smoldered, creating an antiseptic-smelling smoke that repelled the mosquitoes. Emma now viewed them as a secondary problem. Mosquitoes carried dengue fever and malaria, two diseases that posed the biggest risk to humans in the jungle, but Emma felt they created the most damage with their bites that itched like crazy.

Sumner tossed and turned and mumbled in his delirium. Emma found herself getting desperate again. She didn't want to be left in the jungle alone, and she didn't want to watch another human being die.

She laid the wet clothes over him, focusing on his forehead and the area around the wound. When she was done she sat next to him and stared at the fire. She stayed that way for hours, watching the flames lick upward. Thinking about Patrick. God hadn't spared him, and it looked as though He wouldn't spare Sumner, either. She wondered if she would be next to die, or if He would allow her to complete the important thing she'd come to Colombia to do. She needed to set right the tremendous wrong she had done. She didn't want to die before she did.

The flame colors mesmerized her. The dancing shadows created by the light lent an eerie feeling to the night. She dozed, sitting up.

Emma jerked awake when she heard Sumner start to moan. He began thrashing on the ground. She leaped up to stop his violent movements, which threatened to dislodge the maggots. Even feverish, Sumner surprised her with his strength. She tried to pin his arms to the ground to stop him from flipping over onto his bad shoulder. He pushed himself off his stomach with his arms. He looked around wildly, then lowered himself back down and rolled over onto his back.

"Sumner, stop. You're running a terrible fever from the machete cut."

Sumner gazed at her, glassy-eyed.

"Where are they?" His voice was a whisper.

"I don't know. Near, I think." Emma found herself whispering back.

Sumner closed his eyes. He opened them again. "My shoulder burns."

"It's horribly infected. I'm treating it."

"We need to keep moving." Sumner sat up. The clothes fell off his chest onto the ground. He looked down at them, as if he didn't understand what they were.

Emma placed her hands on his chest. "Lie down. On your stomach or the side opposite your shoulder."

He put a hand on her face. "Thank you for saving me back there."

"Lie down," Emma repeated, keeping her voice soft. "I'll take watch while you sleep." Sumner lay back down. Within minutes he slept again. This time Emma dragged him into the tent.

The morning came too soon for Emma. She'd slept next to Sumner. A shaft of sunlight shot through a slit in the tent door and bored straight into her eyes.

She awoke with a groan. Every muscle ached. Her mouth felt woolly, and her lids were crusted with sleep. She scrubbed her fists into her eyes and focused on Sumner. He was awake, lying on his back, his head turned to stare at her.

"Good morning." His voice was reedy thin.

"How long have you been awake?" Emma moved next to him and checked his forehead for heat. He was much cooler than the night before.

Sumner tried to shrug. He inhaled sharply. "My shoulder feels like it's being stabbed with a million little knives."

"The infection nearly killed you. I'm treating it."

Sumner raised his eyebrows. "How?"

Emma hesitated.

Sumner's gaze sharpened. "How?"

"Maggots. They'll suck out the infection, eat the dead skin, leave the healthy skin alone."

Sumner stared at her. He shifted slightly. "Did you say maggots?"

Emma nodded.

Sumner blanched. "I'm afraid to look."

Emma smiled. "It's covered by a bandage. You won't see them."

Sumner took a deep breath and turned his head. Emma watched him take in the gauze, which still undulated from the writhing bodies. He groaned.

"Ah, God, that's disgusting," he said.

"But it must be working. Your fever is much better."

"It hurts."

"That's perplexing. I'm not sure why it would hurt. Maggots don't bite, they only attach and suck. Perhaps the wound rests across a bundle of nerves."

"How long?"

"Forty-eight hours. But trust me, they're all that is between you and a massive, systemic infection. If they do their job, you should be infection-free soon."

Sumner closed his eyes. "I do trust you." In a few minutes, he was asleep again.

THREE HOURS AFTER HIS MEN LEFT TO KILL THE
tall man and the diabetic passenger, Luis knew something
had gone wrong. The three he'd sent were his best men,
reliable in a way none of the other losers on his team could
ever be.

He waved over Alvarado. "The men have not returned and
it's almost noon. You go in and find them. The tall man has
done something!"

Alvarado's reaction was quick. "Me? No! I have to watch
sixty prisoners and thirty guerrillas, all without one brain
between them. The tall man is dead by now, Luis. The men
will return soon."

Luis advanced on Alvarado. "I said go. What are you
afraid of—El Chupacabra?"

"You know I am not. But who will watch these men when
I am gone?"

Luis pounded his chest. "I will."

Alvarado glared at Luis. "Fine. I will go. Just make sure
that Manzillo doesn't hear about me having to track more
missing men. Last thing I need is more deserters."

An hour later, Alvarado found the diabetic man's corpse

and a pile of discarded clothes. Thirty minutes after that, he found the naked, bound men in the forest.

He kicked each one in the head. They groaned through their gags. Alvarado yanked the piece of rag out of the nearest one's mouth.

"Tell me what happened. And spare me from the El Chupacabra bullshit."

"We were attacked—" The man's explanation was cut short by Alvarado's boot hitting him yet again.

"Not by El Chupacabra. Alvarado, wait!" Alvarado had wound up for another kick. "It was a woman. English speaking. She had a gun and ambushed us."

"Was she United States Army?"

The man nodded. "She may have been. She was covered in mud and issued orders in English. The man translated to Spanish."

"Where is the tall man?"

"He left with her."

Alvarado stood over the naked man, breathing heavily, while a feeling of dread flowed into the pit of his stomach. He'd had a bad premonition about this job from the start, and now the unraveling had begun. He didn't want to tell Luis that the tall man he obsessed over had escaped. Luis was perfectly capable of killing the messenger.

He untied the men and threw their clothes at them. "You fools will tell Rodrigo that you were incapable of killing an unarmed man and a woman. I'm not taking the fall for this."

The men climbed to their feet. They stood there, eyeing one another.

"Let's go. Rodrigo is waiting." Alvarado turned around to return to the camp.

The lead man, without a shirt and dressed in pants that

sported one leg ripped off to the thigh, grabbed a stick and swung it, hard, at Alvarado's head. It hit with a loud, thudding sound. Alvarado dropped like a stone.

"Jorge, why did you do that?" The second guerrilla, this one lucky enough to be fully dressed, bent down to check for Alvarado's pulse.

"You want to tell Rodrigo you failed? He'll kill you in the last two seconds of the story. I'm not that stupid. I'm leaving here. Alvarado will be fine. When he comes to, he can talk to his buddy Rodrigo. Perhaps he'll survive the conversation."

"And where will you go, eh? That trail leads to the airplane, which by now will be crawling with American soldiers."

Jorge wagged a finger in the air. "I will take the cutoff to the second encampment. From there I go to Cali, where I have friends." He jogged off down the trail. After ten seconds, the other two followed. They knew that Rodrigo was not an option.

SUMNER'S FEVER BROKE AT DAWN THE NEXT DAY.
He slept peacefully for the first time in eight hours. Emma
dragged herself out of the tent to make her way to the stream.
She was dizzy with sleep deprivation and hunger. She rinsed
Sumner's clothes in the stream and laid them on the space-
age sheet in the sun to dry.

She filled the empty water bottle and laid it on the sheet
as well. She'd once read in a scientific journal that the sun
could kill all the bacteria in water if the water was in a clear
container, placed in full light, and left for three hours. The
writer had suggested the technique be taught to inhabitants
of third-world countries. Emma had never dreamed she'd be
using it for her own drinking supply. She rose to head back
to the tent when a silver flash caught her eye. She made her
way to it.

It was a discarded hubcap, half buried in the silt on the
side of the stream. She pounced on it, pulling it out of the
dirt. After a quick rinse in the water, it looked as good as
new, albeit with a little rust on the edges. Emma scouted
around for medium-size stones. She flipped the hubcap over
and used it as a tray to hold the stones.

The heat sucked all the energy from her body. Emma's

own clothes were soaked through with sweat. She couldn't remember what it felt like to be cool and dry. She grabbed a palm leaf, stripped, and waded into the stream. She used the leaf to rub the worst of the dirt and sweat from her skin. She used a stick from the neem tree to brush her teeth, pulled her clothes back on, and jogged to camp. She put the stones from the hubcap into the banked fire she'd made the night before and crawled into the tent to sleep.

Emma woke in the afternoon. Sumner was on his side, his face resting on his arm, looking at her. For the first time it seemed as though he was present, back from the remote place he'd inhabited in the clearing and the delirium from last night.

"How are you feeling?" Emma said.

"Thirsty." His voice was a whisper, and reedy thin.

She reached out of the tent and retrieved the last of the water. "Drink it all. I have a new supply soaking in the sun."

He emptied the plate and handed it back to her.

"Are the maggots still on me?"

Emma cut a glance at the bandage. It bulged, not from the slice, but from the maggots, which had grown to twice their size in the last hours. The bigger ones were working their way out of the gauze, probing through the webbed cotton with their heads. Emma did her best to act nonchalant.

"Still there," she said in as cheery a voice as she could muster under the circumstances.

Sumner glanced at the bandage at the precise moment that a plump, fully grown maggot pushed its head through the cotton and wriggled free. It dropped off his shoulder onto the tent floor.

"Just when I thought it couldn't get any more revolting," he said. Emma chuckled as she picked up the maggot and tossed it out of the tent.

"They're making a run for it. Once they're big enough to

work their way out, they'll fight to reach the surface, in this case through the bandage. When they drop to the ground they'll search for a good hiding place, where they'll move into the next stage of development. Eventually they'll emerge as fully grown blowflies."

"And the cut?" Sumner said.

"They'll take the infection with them. It's the pus that they ate that makes them so plump." Emma ignored Sumner's groan of disgust. "If we keep it clean with the alcohol, you should be okay. Can I have a look?"

He nodded and rolled onto his stomach. Emma inched the bandage up a bit. She could see pink skin under the nearest maggot. She replaced the gauze and patted Sumner's arm.

"Looks good."

Sumner gave her a bemused glance. "I've never met a woman who would willingly touch maggots."

"I was a tomboy growing up. I loved bugs. I used to collect the discarded shells of cicadas. They looked just like the live bugs: wings, legs, eyes, you name it. I kept them in a box. My favorite I named Fred."

Sumner smiled a small smile. "Your pet was a dead cicada named Fred?"

Emma nodded. "Fred was great. He was the only shell I ever found that even had the membrane that covered his eyes left over."

"I can see how that would win over a girl," Sumner said.

Emma laughed.

Sumner turned serious. "What time is it?"

"I don't know. Afternoon, I guess."

"How long have we been here?"

"Two days. You were sleeping, and I needed some rest, too."

"We need to move." Sumner struggled to rise. He pulled himself upon his arms, then dropped back down on the tent floor.

"Sumner, you should rest. You nearly died. I'm going to make an astringent tea that will help you fight infection."

She flipped over the hubcap, filled it with water, and fished out the stones from the fire. Once they were added she hunkered down to wait. Within twenty minutes the water was steaming. She added cattails. After a few minutes she fished them out and placed them on her backpack to cool. Then she placed several neem leaves in the water and let them steep. She poured the resulting tea into the airline tray.

"Sumner, sit up a minute."

Sumner struggled to sit, never opening his eyes. Emma braced his back. She put the airline tray to his lips.

"Drink," she said.

He drank. He jerked his head back when he tasted the bitter liquid.

"What is this?" His voice was still hoarse.

"Antiseptic tea made from the leaves of the neem tree. It's an amazing tree. The oil from it is like tea-tree oil."

"Tastes like engine oil."

"It will help bring down the fever." Emma mentally crossed her fingers. She hoped her crude tea would help. Generally she would have waited to dry the leaves before steeping them.

Sumner lowered his head to the tent floor and closed his eyes. Within minutes he was sleeping again.

Three hours later, Emma ate a cattail and stared at the last food carton. The final filet. Sumner sat against a tree, munching on his own cattail and two baby carrots, which was the sum total of his lunch and dinner.

"You're El Chupacabra," he said.

"I beg your pardon?"

"The sentries kept running back into the camp with various wounds and babbling that they'd been attacked by 'El Chupacabra.' "

"What is an El Chupacabra?" Emma could barely pronounce the word.

"A mythical being that is routinely sighted in Mexico, Texas, and South America, but is never caught. Kind of like the Big Foot sightings. El Chupacabra has green skin, is scaly, and its long claws and teeth can rip livestock apart. It sucks the blood from its prey."

Emma shook with laughter. "Oh my God, that sentry I speared thought I was a green beast with scales?"

"Don't laugh. When you burst out of the trees covered in mud and shrieking, you even had me thinking that you were a beast."

"I don't know who was more frightened, him or me."

"They are drug addicts and ignorant peasants. I imagine in the dark, and through a hashish-induced haze, you could be mistaken for a beast."

"And here I thought he was racing back to the camp to tell everyone that a passenger had escaped. I expected a posse to come after me every minute."

"No, but I'll bet the posse is coming now. The guerrilla leader told his soldiers to take me out and kill me on the trail. He wants me dead, and he won't rest until I am."

"Is that the skinny one? I call him Rat Face."

Sumner snorted. "Good name. His actual name is Luis Rodrigo."

"Do you two know each other?"

"Not before the crash, no. But in my job I had to learn the names and techniques of most of the better-known paramilitary organizations in Colombia. Rodrigo's was mentioned as a particularly vicious, loose affiliation of maniacs. From what I saw, the reputation is deserved."

Emma fought against the depression that was settling over her.

"I left the clothes drying in the sun. I'll go get them."

She left the tent and headed to the stream. On her way, she passed some jimsonweed, a common plant that grows in abundance in the jungle. The trumpet-shaped white flowers made the bush look beautiful against the green leaves. Emma ignored the flowers, however, and collected the spiny seedpods. She shoved several into her cargo pants pockets.

The clothes had dried, thanks to the hot sun and the added reflective abilities of the silver sheet. Emma held them to her cheek, relishing the dry warmth. She grabbed everything and turned back. She heard the sound of engines somewhere close. She jogged up a small rise and looked down.

A Range Rover sat at the side of the road that ran along the trail. Two men stepped out. They wore cargo pants tucked into steel-toed boots. The first man wore a shirt with the words LOUISIANA STATE on it. The second man sauntered to the back of the Rover, flung open the hatch. Two bloodhounds jumped down. They ran in circles, happy to be released. One relieved himself on the Range Rover's tire. The men slung packs over their backs and added assault weapons on their shoulders.

"Hotter than a bitch here, ain't it?" the second man said.

The first shrugged. "Like Louisiana. Used to it. Got the scent?" His voice carried to Emma. He spoke with a drawl that wasn't quite southern.

The second man nodded. He reached back into the Range Rover and retrieved a piece of white cotton with a name embroidered in blue stitching on the pocket. He balled it in his fist and shoved it under the dogs' noses. Emma recognized the cotton.

It was her lab coat.

She shot back on the trail, running for all she was worth. When she got to the camp, Sumner was standing in the clearing, stark naked, holding a rifle. He looked like a feral man. He put a finger to his lips and waved at the trail behind them. Emma listened. Between the scratching of insects and the twittering of the birds came a chopping sound.

"Jesus, they're close."

Sumner nodded.

"But they're not our worst problem." The sound of barking dogs drifted toward them. Sumner frowned.

"What the hell is that?"

"They're bloodhounds, and they're after me."

Sumner raised an eyebrow. "Care to fill me in?"

Emma shoved the clean clothes at him. "I was headed to Colombia to accomplish a specific goal. Somebody must want to stop me. I don't want to say more. The less you know, the better for you if they catch us."

Sumner took the clothes and dressed in silence. He paused for a moment, as if deciding whether or not to speak. The baying hounds echoed through the jungle. He shook his head.

"I've got a maniac after me, and you have bloodhounds after you. We're quite a pair. Let's get out of here," he said.

They collapsed the tent. Emma slung it onto her back. They hit the trail. Emma ran like she'd never run before. Sumner stayed with her, moving with surprising agility for someone so newly recovered. The hounds bayed behind them. Emma now knew what a fox felt like when it was hunted. The baying was loud, insistent, magnified by the jungle's echo. The howls ignited an age-old, primitive fear in her. The hairs on the back of her neck rose.

They ran until the night came. The baying quieted only once. Emma supposed the dogs were given a break. Sumner was drenched in sweat and stumbling after two hours. Emma braced him with her shoulder when it appeared he'd collapse.

Sumner's fever returned that evening. He lay in the tent, barely moving.

"You pushed too hard, too soon," Emma said. "We'll stay put tomorrow so you can rest."

"We can't. They'll be upon us by midday." Sumner's voice was a whisper.

"We'll have to risk it."

"No risk is worth them catching us. They'll tear us to shreds."

Emma didn't reply. There was nothing to say.

25

BANNER KNEW THE DAY WAS SHOT WHEN HE HAD
a call from Whitter at eight o'clock sharp. Whitter's message
was succinct. He expected to see Banner at 0830 hours in
the war room. There was news.

Banner walked into a room filled with DOD personnel,
various aides and interns of congressmen assigned to the
endless committees that sprouted like weeds in Congress,
and the secretary of defense, Carl Margate.

Banner considered Margate to be one of that breed of
men who love all things military, but who never joined any
military branch. They were the men who debated the Battle
of Waterloo, who questioned the decisions of generals like
MacArthur, but who did it from the safe distance of their
leather chairs in their paneled libraries under the roofs of
their quiet and restful mansions.

Margate was all these things, but took it one better, because not only did he imagine himself a brilliant strategist,
but he hadn't a shred of human decency. To him the soldiers
enlisted to protect the country meant nothing more than the
plastic toy soldiers he used to plot moves and countermoves.
He didn't care how many died as long as his political and
personal agenda was met.

Banner took one look at Margate and he just knew that the man was going to lay a bomb on him. When everyone got seated, the secretary opened his mouth, and the explosion issued forth.

"We conveyed to the Colombian president that unless the passengers are freed in the next twenty-four hours, the United States will suspend aid to Colombia and demand the immediate extradition of all drug and paramilitary leaders suspected in the manufacture and import of cocaine into America."

Banner glanced at Whitter. Whitter's expression didn't change, but Banner had spent quite a bit of time with him in these past few days, and he could tell that Whitter was shocked. Whitter's face rarely froze.

No one spoke. The interns scribbled furiously on their pads of paper.

Banner was no expert on Colombian matters, but he knew that the one thing the paramilitary and cartel leaders feared most was extradition to the United States. Once they were extradited, their fortunes would be confiscated and they would be tried for their crimes in a country where their influence and ability to ensure a favorable outcome were gone. Convictions and life sentences would follow. They would enter a United States prison on their feet, and leave it in a coffin.

Margate's ultimatum, if carried out, would put the Colombian president between a rock and a hard place. If he agreed to extradition, the paramilitary groups would once again pick up their arms; and if he did not, the United States would cut off $1 billion in aid to his country. Since no one in the room saw fit to speak their mind on the issue, Banner decided to throw in his objection.

"Secretary Margate, just why do you think such an ultimatum will help this situation?" He asked the question in a mild voice.

Everyone in the room shifted in their seats.

"We're trying to bring pressure on the government down there to clean house. What that man is doing is offering sweet deals to murderers, kidnappers, and thieves."

"A deal that this administration turned a blind eye to until just now."

"Well, now we don't like it. Why should we send aid to a country that kidnaps our citizens?"

As a general proposition, Banner agreed with Margate. But as a military strategist, he believed that the ultimatum, like all ultimatums, would backfire. He struggled to find a way to convey his opinion without alienating the other man.

"I don't see the value in punishing the Colombian president by cutting off his aid. He is no more responsible for this reprehensible act than you are for the gangbangers in every city in this country who kill with impunity."

"That he is devastated by the turn of events is obvious," Whitter said. "We just learned that he called a prayer meeting over the incident. He and his staff said the rosary and prayed to Our Lady of Chinquinquira, a Virgin Mary figure." Margate looked at Whitter as if he'd grown three heads.

"That will get the job done." Margate's voice was loaded with sarcasm.

"Pull all five hundred of those special forces men off the pipeline detail and put them on the hunt for the passengers. Without them, we *will* need divine intervention to pull off this rescue," Banner said.

Margate slammed his hand on the tabletop. Now Banner knew where Whitter had learned the mannerism. He considered it a piece of dramatic theater, nothing more. The interns and Whitter jumped. Banner and the other officers didn't react.

"We take those men off the pipeline and the paramilitary groups will blow it to kingdom come just for spite."

"Maybe. But what makes you think they won't bomb it once they hear about the extradition demand?"

"I agree that they will bomb it. And that pipeline supplies a big portion of the gas that the average American citizen demands for his SUV. *That's* why the special forces stay where they are and we cut off aid if nothing gets done."

"Your ultimatum makes my military plan that much harder. Why would the Colombian president help us in our search once his aid is gone? That aid goes directly to support his army. And the threat of extradition will kill the disarmament deal and send the paramilitary groups on a rampage. The threat is a foolish move that can only hurt our relationship with Colombia, while putting the passengers at greater risk."

Margate frowned. "You've heard my decision."

Banner saw the futility in arguing further. "I'll put my objections to the current approach in writing and send it through the proper channels."

Margate narrowed his eyes. "I'd prefer it if we would simply 'agree to disagree.' "

Banner shook his head. "It's not that simple. I believe strongly that pressuring the Colombian president at this time is the absolute worst thing you can do. I will not have my name attached to the decision."

"If I remove you from any position of authority regarding the mission, then you won't have to issue your memo, will you?" Banner had expected this threat from Margate.

"Be my guest, but the media is bound to notice such a move. They'll question me as to the cause, and I'd be forced to say that my plan for saving the passengers and yours didn't match. Then you could explain why you thought yours was better, and we can let the talking heads on CNN, NBC, and Fox, your personal favorite, decide who had the better plan. Frankly, I think an internal memo is much less damaging than that, don't you?"

Banner heard everyone in the room inhale and hold. It was as if they had sucked all the air out of the space. Whitter's face was ashen. The navy commander across the table from Banner had a twinkle in his eye, relishing the moment.

Margate pushed away from the desk and stood up. "Write your memo, but my decision stands. We deliver the message to the Colombian government. You have twenty-four hours to bring this matter to a successful conclusion, Major Banner."

Margate marched out of the room, followed by two shaking interns.

"Jesus, Banner." Whitter took a huge gulp of water. "Why did you take him on?"

Banner was furious. "His administration's tenure is over in two years, but I intend to keep my company going long after that. I'd lose all credibility if I approved such a half-assed plan. Besides, I've stood opposite an enemy at ten feet with an assault rifle pointed at my heart. You think a politician in an ill-fitting suit is going to worry me?"

"I'll bet his suit was expensive," Whitter said.

"All the money in the world doesn't buy class, Mr. Whitter."

"Don't I know it," Whitter said.

26

EMMA SAT IN THE TENT FOR THE DAILY DOWN- pour. She hoped the rains helped dilute her scent on the trail. She hadn't heard the baying for half a day. She kept her own rifle close. The time might come when she'd meet the men and dogs face-to-face. She'd have to fire first.

Sumner lay next to her, breathing softly. While he was weak, he wasn't feverish. Although he still didn't say much, he never withdrew as far as he had in the beginning, when Emma thought he'd looked a little deranged. His maggot guests had all left for greener pastures. Emma had cleaned out the slice, which was pink and healthy, and replaced the gauze.

"Thank God" was all Sumner said when she was finished.

"Now all we need are some leeches. They will hold the wound together so the skin will heal without a scar," Emma said.

Sumner turned white. "Oh, God, no."

Emma chuckled. "Relax, I'm kidding."

"Remind me to get you for that when I'm feeling better." He slipped back into sleep.

The rain pounded so hard on the roof that Emma thought she'd go mad with the noise. Even though Sumner was next to her, they couldn't hold a conversation during these storms, the hammering rain was so loud. Within minutes the ground turned to mud, creating deep rivulets that would grow to a flash flood. Emma tried to anticipate the showers, but more often than not they caught her by surprise.

This storm produced a deluge, and she and Sumner had taken care to set the tent up on a plateau jutting from the slope. Two trees formed a living wall that provided cover from above and broke up the rushing water from the side.

Lightning cracked above them, and thunder boomed seconds later. Water flowed around the tent, turning the ground underneath them soft. Emma felt the water saturate the tent's nylon floor. She and Sumner had pulled leaves off a palm to stack in a makeshift base that they'd hoped would keep the tent's floor dry, but it hadn't worked. Water was everywhere, and the palms, and then the tent floor, became soaked within ten minutes. After half an hour, the rain trickled to a drizzle.

Emma toyed with one of the rifles and listened to the water patter on the tent. Her stomach growled. The remaining tray of airline food was so rancid that she'd tossed it. They'd eaten only cattails and some berries that they'd found on a bush. Their need to stay on the move and the driving rain killed any chance they might have had to hunt for more food. Emma resigned herself to being hungry.

She picked up the rifle to test its heft. It was heavy. The right side had letters in a strange language etched next to a sliding switch. Two poles attached underneath opened to create a bipod. When not in use, they retracted to lie flat against the gun's stock. She opened the bipod and balanced the gun on the ground. She lay down on her stomach and pretended to sight a target through the mesh opening on the tent.

"The safety's on," Sumner said.

Emma jumped. "You're awake. How do you feel?"

He shrugged but didn't move from his prone position next to her. "Better than before, but weak as hell."

"You know about guns?" Emma said.

"I do."

"What are these markings? They look like letters, but I can't figure out the language." She tilted the gun toward him so that he could see the letters.

"Hebrew. That gun's a Galil assault rifle. Israeli made. The toggle switch is the safety and the fire selector. When you move the switch down, it's in autofire; down farther still and you're in single fire."

Emma tried the switch. It was surprisingly difficult to move. There was an audible click when she did.

"Noisy," she said.

"Yes. Not a stealth gun. You don't want to switch modes when hidden in the bushes with an enemy standing over you. But these guys aren't what I would call finesse shooters anyway."

"How did an Israeli assault rifle end up in Colombia?"

"Israeli army unloaded them when they adopted the M-16. South America is a huge dumping ground for old technology."

Emma slid the safety back on and reached for another rifle.

"What about this one?"

Sumner moved his head to look at the next rifle.

"Kalashnikov AK-47. Russian made. The tank of weapons. Thing will shoot after being dragged in the mud or hauled through water. Same basic function as the Galil."

Emma hefted the gun to her shoulder. "Heavy."

"Actually, it's considered a medium-weight weapon."

"What's this gun attached to the bottom?" She showed Sumner the underside of the rifle. A small pistol with a wide mouth was hooked to the bottom of the gun, in firing position. The pistol had its own trigger.

"That's a grenade launcher."

Emma looked at Sumner. "These people aren't kidding, are they?"

"I'm afraid not."

Emma analyzed the AK-47. "How do I want to shoot it? Single shot or automatic?"

"Can you shoot?"

"Not at all. I found the pistols in the debris from the crash. I only brought them along for effect."

"They're mine. I was supposed to give a report and then teach target shooting."

"Did you know the jet would be hijacked?"

Sumner shook his head. "No. There was some online chatter to the effect that terrorist action would occur, but we assumed that they were talking about London. I only got worried when I saw the copilot arrive. Something about him seemed shifty, but I couldn't put my finger on it."

Emma put the AK-47 to her shoulder and pretended to sight the far side of the tent.

"If you can't hit a target, your best bet is auto, but be prepared for the gun to buck like crazy on the recoil. You want to cover the area with shot and hope that one lands. Unless *I'm* in the area you're spraying. Then I request that you switch to single shot and do your best to target only the bad guys."

"I'll try to remember that."

"How did you know about the traveler's palm and the water?"

"I'm a chemist for a laboratory that invents skin products for the cosmetic market. I'm constantly scouring the world for plants that may have an antiaging or antioxidant effect. I learned about the traveler's palm during an excursion to the British West Indies."

"Have you discovered the plant that will reverse aging?"

Emma laughed. "Not yet." She wagged a finger at him. "But don't kid yourself. The chemist who unlocks the secret to skin renewal will make billions."

"Any plants that are contenders?"

Emma nodded. "We're working with a few now. Licorice reduces brown spots and evens out skin tone, feverfew has some benefit, but it's allergenic to many, so it's not ideal, and there are always the classics, like rose water."

"My mother uses something outrageously expensive. Sea kelp or some such thing."

"Crème de la Mer. Very pricey."

Emma nestled the gun back against her cheek, pictured herself targeting Rodrigo, then pulled away. Her stomach turned. Sumner noticed her discomfort.

"What's on your mind?"

"Rodrigo won't stop until he finds us, you know that," she said.

"I know. That reptilian brain of his will not forget an insult."

"I look forward to killing him," Emma said. She thought of Patrick. "God kills the good ones and leaves the bad," she added.

Sumner raised an eyebrow.

Emma felt the need to clarify. "I've been in a running argument with God for the past year."

"Arguing with a force more powerful than you is always a mistake."

"Now you tell me." Emma gave him a small smile.

"I always thought that death was the ultimate equal-opportunity experience."

"Well, then, Rodrigo is about to get his opportunity."

Sumner shifted but remained quiet.

"Go ahead, say what you're thinking."

"I'm thinking that it's one thing to kill in self-defense, but it's an entirely different thing to kill in cold blood. Snipers have to be trained, because such killing doesn't come naturally to most people. If you get into such a situation, I think you'll be surprised at how hard it is."

"Have you killed in cold blood?"

"Yes," he said.

Emma wasn't surprised. His preternatural calm led her to believe that he could do whatever he deemed to be just, should the need arise. She had no doubt that it would be just, though. He wouldn't kill for bloodlust.

"Was it awful?"

Sumner took a deep breath. "It was necessary." He reached out and touched her cheek. "I don't recommend it, though." He sighed. "I'm tired again. Wake me when the rain is over." Emma continued to play with the guns while Sumner slipped back into a fitful sleep.

The next day they walked into a small village. Four huts stood in a semicircle, a fire pit in the middle. About ten women loitered there. One rotated the carcass of a pig on a spit over a fire, her lank hair pulled back into a ponytail. Two more argued in the doorway of one of the huts while four or five others stood in the remaining doorways watching the bickering. They wore pea-green army fatigues and sweat-stained gray T-shirts.

The entire crew spun around to look at Emma and Sumner as they stepped into the camp. The smell of the pig on the spit set Emma's mouth watering. They'd found some more berries this morning, but that was all. She was light-headed with hunger.

The village women fell silent and stared at the newcomers. They exuded hostility and curiosity in equal measure.

One of the women barked a name, and a tall, dark-haired Amazon emerged from the nearest hut. Her long shining hair swung as she walked. She wore the same fatigues as the other women, but on her they looked like haute couture. A gun hung in a shoulder holster, its butt under her armpit. She sauntered up to Emma and Sumner, casually removing the gun as she did.

Emma heard two clicks as Sumner pulled the safety on the rifle.

Semi, Emma thought. He stood a few steps behind her, and when he raised the rifle the tip of the weapon entered her peripheral vision.

"You are a long way from home," the woman said in English, directing her comment to Sumner.

Predictably, he said nothing.

"We are lost," Emma said. Her voice cracked on the word *lost*.

The two bickering women snickered.

"You are from the jet, no?" the tall woman said.

Emma didn't reply.

"Then you are a very long way from home." The woman stretched her mouth into a cobra's smile and waved toward the huts. "Come, please. Make yourself comfortable. Our home is your home."

The women tittered again.

"My name is Mathilde." She pointed to Sumner's rifle. "But that must be put down now. You wouldn't hurt a woman, would you?" Mathilde smiled at him from under her lashes.

Emma could have told her not to waste her time flirting with Sumner. Her beauty wouldn't sway him in the least. Sumner stood still, a grim look in his eye. The rifle didn't move.

"I said put the gun down, señor." Now Mathilde sounded testy.

Sumner didn't budge.

Mathilde moved toward him, and he responded by stepping into her. Now the rifle tip hovered only four feet away and remained aimed at her chest. Mathilde's slash smile fled. She turned to Emma.

"Is he a moron, your lover?"

This comment set the bickering women to laughing out loud.

"He is unbalanced," Emma said. "I found him in the forest, eating the arm of a dead guerrilla."

Emma watched in satisfaction as the women stopped laughing, fear in their eyes. The woman turning the pig froze, a look of horror in hers. Two other women in the circle crossed themselves. Even Mathilde seemed to hold her breath.

"Perhaps he was *your* lover?" Emma said.

The smell of charred flesh wafted through the air. Emma waved at the woman working the spit. "The pig is burning, señora."

The woman jerked out of her stunned state and resumed turning the spit. Emma strolled up to Mathilde and didn't stop. She got within one foot before the other woman stepped back. Emma counted the retreat as a psychological victory.

"Thank you for your hospitality," Emma said. "I think I will accept it. I will need a phone or radio to call the American embassy in Bogotá. I need to radio for help."

"We will never help you," Mathilde said.

"It's not for me. You see, my crazy friend here chopped the arms off all of the guerrillas he could find, and he left them there to die. They need help quickly, or they will bleed to death."

A woman to the far right of Emma squeaked. Mathilde waved a hand in the air for silence. Her eyes narrowed.

"Perhaps you take us to these *freedom fighters,* and we will see to their wounds."

"Of course. Please remove all of your guns and ammunition first and place them in a pile. We wouldn't want the rifles to discharge by mistake." Emma smiled her own snake-oil smile. She heard the chopping sound of a helicopter's rotors, somewhere in the distance, growing louder. She wanted to scan the sky, to see if friend or foe approached, but she didn't think it wise to take her eyes off Mathilde.

"Put down our guns? Never," Mathilde said.

It appeared they were at a standoff.

Sumner settled it. He pointed the rifle at Mathilde's feet and pulled the trigger. The sound exploded in Emma's ears. Dirt flew up at Mathilde's face. The bullet left a crater in the ground, two inches from her toes, and ricocheted into the forest. Mathilde jumped, but recovered so fast that it was impossible not to feel a grudging respect for her. When the dust settled, Emma looked around. The woman at the spit was gone, and the bickering women emerged from a hut with guns drawn.

Then all hell broke loose.

The *huff huff* of the helicopter overhead grew louder. Mathilde glanced up and blanched. The tops of the trees bent with the force of the propellers, and dust kicked up all around them. The helicopter came into view, looking like a large spider. It hovered over the clearing, engaged its guns, and blew away the hut and the bickering women with it.

"Down!" Sumner yelled.

Emma threw herself to the ground as the bullets strafed the clearing. They drew a dotted line in the dirt, and the explosions rang in her ears. She ate dust as she screamed into the dirt. Sumner pulled her up by her hair and dragged her to the trees just as the helicopter made a turn and aimed for them. The machine-gun blasts rattled again and Emma heard a woman howl.

They ran toward the tree line near the pig on the spit. Sumner never let go of her hair. He propelled her forward by pushing his fist against her skull. The helicopter swooped past and turned again toward them.

It made another pass, the bullets ripping up the dust and hammering into the bodies already there. It hovered in one place for a moment, then began to swing its tail from side to side, spraying bullets the entire time. It shot past Sumner and Emma before turning and facing them.

Sumner changed direction so fast that Emma felt he would pull her hair out of her head. They turned and ran perpendicular to the helicopter. As they did, Emma saw the man sitting in the open door toss something out.

Sumner pushed her the final steps into the trees. He didn't follow her. Instead he turned to aim at the helicopter. Emma heard its guns begin their staccato noise and looked back to see the bullets crack into the dirt in a line toward Sumner. Emma watched as he raised the rifle to shoot, taking care to aim even as the bullets ran toward him.

He fired the grenade launcher.

The helicopter exploded, spewing metal shards everywhere. A fireball rose into the air, and pieces of burning helicopter landed in the clearing. The copter flung itself sideways as one of its propellers broke off. It flew to the side, all the while losing speed. After sixty seconds, it turned, runners up, and then dropped like a stone. It landed in the forest and exploded on impact. A second explosion released another fireball into the air, and the tops of the trees went up in flames.

Sumner watched the treetops burn for a second before he bent to help Emma. She stood up, and her legs wobbled with fear. She turned on him.

"They were saving us! Why did you shoot them down?" Emma could feel the cords in her neck as she raged.

Sumner shook his head. "They weren't saving us, they were killing them." He waved at the clearing. Emma looked around, still unable to believe what had happened. The women were all dead, lying in their own blood. Mathilde was not among them.

"That was a drug runners' copter," Sumner said. "The guerrillas must be nearby."

"How can you be sure that wasn't the military sent to find the jet?" Emma still shook with her anger at the missed opportunity to get out of this jungle hellhole.

"Caldridge, they shot at us."

"Because they thought we were part of the camp. You can't be sure that they weren't the good guys."

"I'm sure," Sumner said, a grim note in his voice. "They left a calling card." He waved at the thing thrown from the helicopter. At first Emma thought it was a bomb that hadn't exploded. She moved toward it to get a closer look.

It was a human head.

Emma stared at the thing in horror. "Oh my God." Her voice was a whisper.

"Let's get out of here." Sumner reached down to grab Emma's arm. She jerked out of his grip and stalked to the spit. She shook with an all-encompassing anger. Anger at Sumner, anger at the killers in the helicopter, even anger at the women who lay dead all around them. She took the pig off the fire and placed it on a piece of wood.

"Come help me cut this thing up," she said. "This may be the last food we see for a while."

She ignored the dead women all around her as she opened

a bag that sat next to the spit. She pulled out carving knives and tongs, as well as several dishes. Sumner made an impatient sound and strode over to her. He grabbed the bag, turned it over, and dumped its entire contents into the dirt. He picked the pig up and shoved it in, whole. He threw the knives in, stood up, slung the bag over his shoulder, and pointed to the jungle.

"I liked you better when you had a fever," Emma snapped at him.

Sumner headed back into the forest.

Emma followed, still simmering with anger and frustration. It didn't take long for the second helicopter to arrive. This one sank below the tree line and shot along the stream. Sumner and Emma ran into the growth along the banks, crouched behind a bush, and watched as the helicopter flew by. Emma stared hard at its sides. It didn't bear any markings. A man in jeans and a black polo shirt sat in an open door with a rifle in his hands. Another sat in the passenger side and scanned the area with binoculars. They shot past Emma and Sumner's hiding spot and disappeared around a corner. Emma slid the backpack and tent off her shoulders and let them drop to the ground. She rubbed at her sore shoulders.

"Just give me a minute. This thing is heavy," she said.

Sumner just stood next to her, waiting.

Emma pulled the pack back up. "Let's go."

Sumner took it away from her.

"How's your wound?" she asked. "The strap will rest right along it and might inflame it again. Frankly, I can't afford to have you fall back into a fever."

"And yet that's when you like me so well," Sumner shot back.

He slung the backpack over his shoulder; she hauled the bag with the pig onto her back, and they continued downstream.

THEIR PROGRESS WAS RIDICULOUSLY SLOW. IT WAS
over eighty degrees and the humidity made it feel as though
they were walking through fog. The banks of the stream
consisted mainly of mud, and it sucked at their shoes. Every
so often Emma would see a snake slither past. One was
black with orange bands in a geometric pattern. None of the
wildlife seemed inclined to attack them, but she kept her
distance nonetheless.

Clouds of bugs hovered in the air. Emma and Sumner
waved at them with their hands, but there were too many.
They flew into Emma's eyes and ears and clung to the edges
of her lips. One crawled up her nose and she snorted like
crazy to get it out.

"God, that's disgusting," she said.

Sumner looked at her and nodded as he smacked at the
black buzzing veil of bugs.

They pitched camp. This time they built a fire and
warmed the pig. Sumner shaved pieces off the side and
handed them to Emma. She pulled out the small bottle of
red wine from the pack.

Sumner burst into laughter.

"You're like Mary Poppins. Always pulling something good out of that bag." A smile creased his face and real delight shone in his eyes. Emma was stunned by the reaction, but recovered enough to grin back at him.

"Fresh meat deserves a fine wine." She held the bottle out like a sommelier at the Ritz. "Sir. Bolla, Valpolicella, vintage yesterday. Our finest offering." She twisted off the screw top and took a sip, rolled it around in her mouth, and swallowed. "Excellent." She gave it to Sumner and he swallowed his own large gulp. They ripped into the pork.

"God, this is great." The pork fell apart in Emma's mouth and tasted like heaven. Sumner nodded and carved some more for her.

They ate in silence. Sumner retreated into himself and his private thoughts. It was as if the burst of laughter had never occurred. After eating, Emma shoved a small steel bowl she'd pilfered back at Mathilde's checkpoint into her backpack and used it as a pillow. She stared at Sumner, thinking about his shot at the helicopter.

"Where did you learn to shoot like that?"

"My father."

"Where did you grow up?"

"Minnesota. Guns came with the territory."

"What do you do for the Southern Hemisphere Drug Defense?"

"I monitor unidentified planes flying under radar in and out of Miami."

"Ah. So that explains your extensive knowledge of the habits of drug runners and your excellent Spanish."

Sumner shrugged and stayed silent.

"How many languages do you speak?" she said.

"Four."

Emma was impressed. "I speak two. Well, three, really. English, German, and Latin. As a scientist, Latin is the language I probably use the most, which is odd because it's a dead language. Is German one of the four you speak?"

Sumner nodded. She wanted to press him for more personal information but decided that further interrogation wasn't necessary. Besides, his one-syllable answers made for slow going. They had plenty of time to get acquainted, and the mosquitoes were out and eating her alive.

"I'm headed to the tent. I've had enough of bugs for one day," she said.

Sumner nodded again and continued to eat the pork. Emma scrambled into the tent, smashing two mosquitoes that had found their way in behind her. She rolled onto her side, but rather than sleep she found herself waiting for Sumner to join her. There was something reassuring about his quiet presence. She liked that he rarely spoke unless it was required, and that he hadn't been swayed by Mathilde's beauty into relaxing his caution. Emma had dealt with intense people before. Many of her ultramarathon friends had the same quiet intensity, and she herself could not be described as a social butterfly, far from it.

She also liked that he seemed at ease with the isolation. In Emma's experience, few people were so content with themselves as to spend long periods of time alone, and the ones who were tended to be damaged in some way. She had the feeling that this man might be one of the few who could handle both isolation and society with aplomb.

Sumner pushed aside the netting door and crawled into the tent, taking care not to touch her. Emma pretended to sleep while he arranged himself against the far wall. He lay down on his side, facing her. The nights were so dark that Emma couldn't see anything, least of all Sumner's face, but she had the distinct impression that he was awake and staring in her direction. She stayed still, and after fifteen minutes more, she heard him sigh. She fell asleep.

28

EMMA CALDRIDGE LIVED IN A CONDOMINIUM complex in the South Pointe area of Miami Beach. The complex occupied an entire block on Second Avenue. Close enough to walk to the beach, but far enough to allow for some peace. Stromeyer stood in front of Emma's door while she watched Miriam Steinberg, the chairman of Emma's condo association, put a key into the lock. Mrs. Steinberg wore cotton sweatpants with a matching cotton top and spangled flip-flops, and carried a huge straw tote bag as a purse.

"I don't know what to think, what with you coming with a warrant and all," Mrs. Steinberg said. Stromeyer sought to put her at ease.

"It's nothing to be alarmed about. I'm in charge of looking into the victims' lives in order to get background on them. You needn't worry." Mrs. Steinberg shook her head.

"The poor girl. Such a tragedy." The door swung open. "There. Just close it behind you. It'll lock. I'll come by later and throw the dead bolt."

Stromeyer stepped into a small living room lined with windows. Sunlight streamed in through open curtains. The room was decorated in browns and greens with a mixture of modern furniture pieces and a few antiques thrown in to break up the minimalism. Tall palm plants in large planters occupied the corners, near sliding French doors that opened onto a small terrace. A flat-screen television sat on a modern wood credenza. Next to it was a Bose Wave stereo. To the right of the living room was a narrow hallway with two doors. To the left, in an L shape, was a small dining area, and farther left, behind the wall that held the television, was a small, square kitchen.

The kitchen was spotless. Stromeyer walked to the dishwasher. The display read CLEAN. As if Emma had started it before she left.

Stromeyer chided herself for calling Ms. Caldridge Emma, even in her mind. The more she learned about the woman, the more she wanted her to be a victim in this disaster, not a player, as Banner had called her, but Stromeyer needed to keep her objectivity. What she wanted and what was real might not match.

A telephone mounted on the wall docked in an answering-machine base. The machine blinked the number three in a pulsing LED display. Stromeyer pushed the message button. The machine whirred, and a woman's voice poured out of the speaker.

"Emma, it's Cindy, please call me. I heard about the crash and we're all worried about you here." Cindy was Caldridge's secretary at Pure Chemistry. The second message was Cindy again, sounding even more worried. On the third, Stromeyer hit pay dirt. A man's voice poured out of the machine.

"Honey, I know you said not to call, but I'm worried. Please send me a message that you're all right."

Stromeyer grabbed the receiver. A button allowed the owner to scroll through the caller identification list for the phone. The phone numbers of the last ten calls were there, neatly recorded, except the last. The last read PRIVATE CALLER.

"Damn," Stromeyer said. She heard a key in the lock. She placed the phone into the dock without making a sound and moved to the corner of the kitchen. She peered around the wall at the front door. It swung open, and a man stepped into the living room. He hesitated a moment before turning to close the front door with a quiet push. Tall, tan, with silver hair cropped close to his head, he looked to be about sixty-five. He wore tailored khakis and a yellow polo shirt. He moved toward the kitchen, giving Stromeyer a full view of his face. It was George Caldridge. The resemblance to his daughter was unmistakable. Stromeyer stepped out of the kitchen.

"You must be George Caldridge," she said.

The man gave a violent start. He pulled a small gun out of his pocket and pointed it at her.

"Who are you and what are you doing here?"

The gun surprised the hell out of Stromeyer. It was as unexpected as his visit. It was also obvious that Mr. Caldridge didn't know how to use a gun. Stromeyer put up a hand to calm the man.

"I'm Major Carol Stromeyer. I work with a company in conjunction with the Department of Defense. I'm here investigating the hijacking of Flight 689. Please put the gun down."

The gun stayed pointed at her. George Caldridge gave her a grim look.

"Haven't you people done enough?" he said.

Now Stromeyer was confused. "What in the world are you talking about?"

Mr. Caldridge waved Stromeyer out of the kitchen. "Come out of there."

She did, moving slowly, keeping her hands in sight so he could see that she wasn't armed.

"You know what I mean. First you try to confiscate my

daughter's research, then you threaten her with treason should she not cooperate with your plan. She's a scientist, not a traitor. She came upon the formula completely by accident, and you and your people knew it."

"Mr. Caldridge, I swear to you, I have no idea what you're talking about. I work for Darkview, a security consultant firm contracted by the DOD. No one has informed me about any of this. What formula?"

Mr. Caldridge stared at Stromeyer hard for a moment. He sighed and lowered the gun.

"I don't know what formula. Emma wouldn't tell me. All she said was that she'd discovered something by accident. She said someone claiming to be from the DOD got wind of her discovery and wanted her to license the formula to them. When she refused, they started harassing her. Threatening to charge her with treason. Tapping her phone."

"Did she give you a name?"

He shook his head. "No. She told me she had a plan that would end the harassment, though. She warned me to leave Florida for a while. She said she'd call when it was all clear. I knew that she'd intended to fly to Colombia. When I heard that the plane went down . . ." Mr. Caldridge's voice cracked. Tears filled his eyes. He shook his head.

Stromeyer put her hands down. "Mr. Caldridge, she's still alive, as far as we know. When the plane first went down she sent a text message to her boss at Pure Chemistry. And since then our search-and-rescue team found her luggage with yet another note from her tucked inside."

Relief flowed over Mr. Caldridge's face. "Oh, thank God. I'd heard about the toll-free number to call for information about the passengers, but I was afraid to turn on my cell. Emma insisted that I keep it off until she returned. She said they could use the signal to track it. She was afraid they'd use me to pressure her."

Stromeyer had to agree with Emma. If whoever was harassing her had engineered the hijacking, then they were not afraid to employ any method to achieve their aims. Now Emma's text message to her boss made sense. She had been afraid to send something to her father for fear of its being tracked.

Stromeyer waved at Mr. Caldridge. "You'd better come with me."

"Where?" Mr. Caldridge's voice was loaded with mistrust.

"Don't worry, not to the DOD. I'm taking you to Darkview's temporary offices. I need you to tell this story again to my partner."

Mr. Caldridge put the gun in his pocket. "I'm sorry about the gun. I wouldn't have shot you."

Stromeyer nodded. "I knew that."

Mr. Caldridge looked surprised. "How?"

Stromeyer opened the door for him. "The safety was on."

29

ALVARADO CAME TO AND SAT UP IN A GROGGY haze. It was black as pitch. His head throbbed something awful, and his vision was blurred. Walking anywhere was out of the question. He lay back down and fell asleep.

The next morning he walked into a tense camp. The passengers huddled next to one another on one side, the guerrillas on the other. Both groups eyed Luis with dread. He was busy beating a male passenger with his bare fists. The passenger lay on the ground, his body curled into a tight ball and his arms over his head to protect himself from the blows. Luis grew tired of punching and graduated to kicking the passenger with his steel-toed boots. It sounded like he was kicking a side of beef.

Alvarado sighed at this display of Luis's usual inability to control himself. Luis looked up and spotted him. He stopped kicking.

"Where the hell have you been? And where are Jorge and Gordo?"

"They deserted," Alvarado said.

"What? That's not possible." Luis was shocked. His best men.

"Leave off the passenger and let's go in your tent. We need to talk."

Luis delivered one more blow to the groaning man and stormed into his tent. Alvarado followed at a slower pace. Once in the tent, he delivered the news as quickly as he could.

"The diabetic man is dead, but the tall man escaped with the help of an English-speaking woman. I believe she was the one tracking us, not El Chupacabra. Jorge and Gordo were afraid to tell you this, so they attacked me and ran off."

Luis stood, unmoving. The only sign that showed he'd heard Alvarado was the twitching in his left cheekbone.

"I will track that man down myself and kill him. Only after he is dead will my luck change."

Alvarado wanted to pull his hair out at Luis's ridiculous statement. The only thing that stopped him from doing so was the fact that Luis was partially correct. His luck on this venture had been bad, and it was getting worse by the day. Nevertheless, Alvarado reached for a way to placate Luis. In point of fact, things were not at a total loss, and they were so deep in the shit now, going deeper was the only alternative.

"He is one gringo and they were three men who cannot call themselves soldiers. Surely things are not that bad, Luis. We have the hostages still, and we have lost only two to the mines instead of the ten or fifteen that we expected."

Luis looked at Alvarado, and for the first time Alvarado saw what might have been fear in his eyes.

"The Americans have dispatched a troop of special forces to find the passengers."

Alvarado felt a cold chill run down his spine. He shook it off. "So? You said yourself that they will never find us. We know these mountains well. Not the gringos."

"And I can't raise Mathilde. I've tried several times, but she doesn't respond."

"What happened to them?"

Luis exploded. "How the hell do I know? I am pounding on the radio all night while you slept in the forest!"

"I was attacked, Luis. Perhaps you call our contact at the cartel. Maybe they have heard something."

"I did."

"Ah, good. And what did they say?"

"They say the Cartone cartel becomes nervous. The Americans are furious at the hijacking. They say that unless the passengers are released in twenty-four hours, aid to Colombia will stop and the American government will demand extradition of all cartel and paramilitary leaders."

"Cartone is in jail, is he not? Didn't he agree to lay down his arms under a nonextradition deal?"

Luis paced the length of the tent. "He did. His second in command says that he will never allow Cartone to be extradited. Now the other cartels are worried that the hijacking will force the president to offer up the rest of the leaders to the Americans as a peace offering. They have teamed up with the paramilitary groups to the west against us."

"What are they planning?"

"To kill us! What the hell do you think?" Luis screamed.

Alvarado stood up. "If this is so, Luis, then we are on our own. We cannot fight them all."

"We will fight them all, Alvarado. We have no choice. Don't forget, we have the FFOC on our side. Or do you question their, and my, ability?" Luis's mood had shifted in an instant.

Alvarado took a deep breath and tried to step lightly. "Of course not, Luis."

"Then it does not matter that the other groups are angry. They are fools for believing the president and his offers of light sentences and no extradition."

"But Maria, Mathilde. We must go there and see if they survived."

Alvarado dated Maria but wanted Mathilde, who was

Luis's woman. He could live without Maria but would mourn the loss of Mathilde.

"Mathilde cannot be killed. That woman is a cat with nine lives."

"So what do we do?"

"We go back and take the secondary trail to Mathilde's watch post. After we check on them, we continue to the ransom point. But forget the trucks. We cut a path through the mountains. If we stay on the trail, Cartone's helicopters will find us."

"And the American special forces?"

"They are the least of our problems." Luis dismissed them without further thought.

Alvarado left the tent, his mind whirring with plans. He would follow Luis until the checkpoint, where he would see how much money would be collected on the first ransoms. He wouldn't leave the checkpoint with the group. After he got his money, he would find Mathilde and get the hell out of Colombia.

30

LUIS, HIS MEN, AND THE PASSENGERS STRAGGLED
into Mathilde's base camp at three o'clock in the afternoon.
The stench was unbearable. Bodies, most of them bloated
from the gases released inside their skin, littered the clearing. On seeing this, one passenger screamed over and over
until a guerrilla slapped her.

The base camp contained six huts arranged in a circle
and one watchtower made of wood that rose two stories into
the air. To reach the second floor, one needed to walk up
a ladder built into its sides. The first level stood eight feet
off the ground and had a narrow walkway built around the
perimeter. From this landing, a sentry could view the immediate vicinity, but not see over the treetops.

The ladder continued up to a second level, a crow's nest at
the top. It was open air, with a three-foot-high railing running around the edge. From this location a sentry could see
over the trees and down the road about two hundred fifty
meters before the jungle swallowed the view. A gun on a
tripod filled the top floor, and ammunition belts were kept in
a small wooden chest in the corner.

Two huts were reduced to cinders. Luis poked around in
the burned wood and found some bodies. They were burned

beyond recognition, but neither looked tall enough to be Mathilde. He continued searching the clearing.

Three-quarters of the way around, he came upon the severed head. It stank like overripened fruit, and crawled with flies and maggots. Luis waved away the flies and looked at it.

"Alvarado, get over here!" He roared his anger.

Alvarado jogged to the grisly find. He bent down to take a look.

"Jesus, it's Jorge." Alvarado breathed the name. He looked a little closer and saw a piece of paper stuffed in the head's mouth. He found a stick and used it to poke at the head, dislodging the note, which fluttered to the ground. Alvarado spread it out.

We're coming for you.

"What does it say?" Luis asked. He'd grown up on a remote farm in the Putumayo district of Colombia. He'd learned rudimentary English from listening to the Christian missionaries his father traded with, but he had never learned to read or write in any language.

Alvarado read the note out loud.

Luis sucked in his breath. "It's from the Cartone cartel."

Alvarado nodded. The Cartone cartel controlled the drug trade in Cali and was known for its grisly calling cards. Jorge had family in Cali, so it made sense for him to have gone there. The fact that he'd been captured and killed told Alvarado just how bad their situation was, because normally a man with friendly connections among the cartels would not have been killed in such a fashion.

"We're in deep shit, Luis."

Luis shrugged. "Jorge has killed how many people? Thirty? Forty? He must have pissed off someone in the cartel. It has nothing to do with us. Besides, we have the FFOC behind us."

Alvarado stared at Luis. That he would be so blasé about an

open threat from such a powerful cartel was insane. Alvarado didn't know what to say. He stood up and took a deep breath.

"Let's keep looking for Maria and Mathilde."

Alvarado edged around the tree line. He found Maria's body lying facedown. He recognized a small bracelet that he'd given her on her twenty-fifth birthday. She'd been thrilled beyond belief. Her life had been spent in the slums of Bogotá. No one had ever given her a gift of that value. Alvarado had not loved her, but he couldn't help but feel sadness for her now.

Mathilde's body was not among the dead. Luis reported this fact with satisfaction.

"That woman makes the snake in the Garden of Eden look like a saint," he said.

They put the passengers to work collecting the dead. By now, most walked through the day with a sense of resignation. Luis liked it like that. Each day they presented less and less of a problem to him. He kept to his daily beatings, nonetheless. No sense letting them get any ideas.

That evening, during dinner, Mathilde strolled into camp. Alvarado jumped up from his position at the fire and watched as the light played over her sweat-soaked T-shirt. She looked tired but none the worse for her near miss with the Cartone cartel.

Luis watched her amble up to him. "So you live, Mathilde. I knew you would."

Mathilde shrugged. Her beautiful brown hair rippled over her shoulders, and Alvarado felt an almost physical reaction at the sight of her.

"I was talking to the two escaped passengers when the helicopter came."

Luis's head snapped up. "What two passengers?"

"A man with brown hair and a woman. They wanted to use the radio to call the American embassy."

"You let them go?" Luis's voice took on a quiet, menacing sound. If his show of menace bothered Mathilde, she didn't show it.

"I had no choice, now, did I, Rodrigo? The copter, he came and killed them all. There was no time for capturing."

Luis grabbed Mathilde's arm. "Did the tall man get away?"

Mathilde snatched her arm back. "Don't touch me like that, Rodrigo, if you know what's good for you. I will tell my father, and he'll have your liver for lunch."

Mathilde's father ran the Putumayo division of the FFOC. He had several children by various women in different districts. He'd paid for Mathilde to attend school and even paid for her to learn English. Nevertheless, his parenting skills left something to be desired, because he'd seen her only a few times during her life.

Mathilde's threat set Luis back on his heels, because her father was perfectly capable of killing him and his entire crew before breakfast. Tales of the man's vicious exploits ran rampant in Colombia, and Luis wasn't entirely sure he wouldn't fry a human liver and eat it. He let go of Mathilde and made a show of his nonchalance.

"It is just that the tall man is a thorn in my side, and I would like to have him and the woman returned to me."

"Then you shouldn't have let them go, eh, Luis?" Mathilde's voice was taunting.

Luis reddened. "Jorge let them go. But he has paid for his stupidity." Luis waved an arm at the head still sitting on the edge of the camp.

Mathilde's eyes widened at the sight. "Who did that?"

"The Cartone cartel. It is a warning about the hostages. But tell me, which way did the tall man go?"

Mathilde waved at a small path. "To the stream. You will find them there, Rodrigo."

Rodrigo nodded. "Tomorrow I will call to the FFOC and

have them send a helicopter. I need to find the tall man, or my luck will not change."

"And I want the woman dead, Rodrigo. She insulted me." Mathilde put on a pout.

"We can't have that, now can we?" Rodrigo said.

No, we can't, Alvarado thought.

BANNER AND WHITTER SAT AT A SMALL CAFÉ IN
the Little Havana area of Miami drinking after-dinner café
cubanos. The ever-present sound of electronic dance music
filtered to them through the traffic noise. It seemed that
wherever Banner went in Miami, salsa, Latin, or electronic
music blared nearby. Banner's rolled sleeves and missing tie
were his only concessions to being "off duty." Whitter wore
a green neon-colored polo shirt and khakis. Banner thought
the combination unfortunate, but by no means the worst the
man had worn.

It was Whitter who suggested they have dinner away from
Southcom's headquarters, and Banner had agreed whole-
heartedly. He needed a break. They'd been eating for an
hour and during that time Whitter kept the conversation
light, but Banner suspected he had some private information
he wanted to pass on. As did Banner.

"We have information that the first transaction for a passenger occurred sometime today," Banner said.

Whitter looked pained. "What? Who?"

Banner shook his head. "We can't confirm it, but a family
of one of the victims told Stromeyer that their insurance
company paid out on a kidnap policy. The passenger was

an oil-company executive. The transfer took place using a private recovery company."

Whitter turned to Banner. "Perhaps your company arranged the deal?"

Banner refused to take the bait. "Darkview doesn't currently provide that type of service. Although we may in the near future."

"You'd be creating a whole industry based upon kidnap and ransom," Whitter said.

Banner snorted. "The insurance companies have already capitalized on that industry. Why else would they write kidnap insurance?"

"Still," Whitter said, "most of the passengers are regular citizens. They don't have kidnap coverage on their home owners' policies."

"Which is why we will get them out of there. And why you need to authorize movement of those five hundred special forces soldiers currently on the pipeline."

Whitter shook his head. "We keep going around and around on this one. But something's happened that will make that impossible. The Colombian president responded to Margate's ultimatum with one of his own. He insisted that all American forces leave Colombia immediately."

"I didn't see any press conference to that effect," Banner said.

"It was a private call between the Colombian president and Margate."

Banner felt his anger growing. What had Margate expected? "Does the withdrawal include the five hundred on the pipeline?"

Whitter nodded. "He mentioned them specifically."

Banner sipped the hot coffee laced with so much cream that it tasted thick.

"Does the Colombian president realize that he's biting off his nose to spite his face? The paramilitary guys won't back down just because he makes a show of annoyance. They'll go on a rampage over the extradition demand alone."

Whitter sighed. "I know, it's just his ego talking, but it's important to him not to appear weak. If he allows the U.S. to interfere in local matters, then it will seem as though he's our lapdog."

"What did Margate say in response?"

"Nothing. But the word got out somehow and Oriental's oil executives descended on him in a fury. Seems they think they'll be slaughtered if the special forces leave. Margate's arranging emergency evacuation for them and their families prior to troop withdrawal."

"And Miguel and his little band?" Banner said.

"They have to leave as well."

Banner put his cup down so fast that it smacked into the saucer with a clanging sound. "So Margate just leaves the passengers high and dry?"

"He's demanding their release in return for no extradition."

Banner snorted. "But what's he going to do if the para-military guys don't play ball? How does he intend to hunt them down and extradite them?"

Whitter gave Banner a sly look. "I imagine a covert operation will be one likely scenario."

Banner shook his head. "He hasn't contacted me. Besides, I don't know that I'd take the project. The Colombian president will expect some sort of covert action, and he'll put the border forces on notice. Plus, there are an estimated twenty thousand paramilitary and cartel guys running around Colombia. I'd need a small army to run a decent operation. Sending in less would mean certain death for them."

"It appears as though we'll end up with sixty-eight more

American hostages held in Colombia," Whitter said. Banner reached for the check that lay between them and started counting out his money.

"Has Margate issued withdrawal orders yet?"

Whitter shook his head. "Not formally, no, but plans have already been set in motion."

"Keep the change," Banner said to the waitress. He downed the coffee and pushed from the table.

"Banner, where are you going?" Whitter said.

"Whitter, just keep in contact with Stromeyer. She can handle anything I can."

"You're not going to confront Margate, are you? Banner, that's a bad idea." Whitter sounded strained.

"Calm down. I know better than to butt heads with the secretary of defense, for God's sake."

"You do not. I was there when you did exactly that not twenty-four hours ago. Then you said his suit was bad." Whitter sounded panicked.

"His suit *was* bad, but what can you expect from a man who has the body of a dumpling and the brains to match?" Banner strode out of the café with Whitter at his heels.

"I have a bad feeling about this."

"About what? I'm just headed back to my hotel room." Banner patted Whitter on the arm. "You should head back, too. This whole affair has got to be taking its toll on you."

"I may not have known you long, Banner, but I've known you long enough to realize when you're headed for trouble. Remember what Montoya from the embassy said. The Colombian special forces are good at recovering hostages."

"Like they recovered those bank executives?" Banner said.

"But this situation is completely different." Banner stopped walking so fast that Whitter bumped into him.

"Listen to me. The only thing different about this situation is that there are more hostages at risk. The best chance those passengers have to survive is right now, when there are special forces in the area searching for them. Once those forces evacuate, you can kiss those hostages good-bye."

Whitter rubbed a weary hand across his forehead. "I agree, but what do you expect us to do? Defy the Colombian president?"

"Tell Margate to withdraw his ultimatum. The Colombian president will withdraw his, and we can proceed to find and free those passengers."

"The secretary of defense is not a man who likes to lose face or reverse position," Whitter said.

"And what about you, Whitter? Do you believe that the ultimatum is a good idea?"

Whitter paused. "I do not."

"Then tell Margate."

Banner left Whitter standing alone on the sidewalk, with the pulsing music of Miami in the background.

THAT EVENING EMMA AND SUMNER ATE THE LAST of the pig and stared at each other. Emma didn't want to state the obvious, but she couldn't help it.

"We're out of food."

"So it would seem," Sumner said.

"Do you think you could shoot an animal if we came across one?"

Sumner nodded. "I could certainly try."

Emma sighed. "My concern is that we'd alert the guerrillas to our location."

"We're on borrowed time as it is. If we stay along the stream, they will surely catch us on one of their pass-bys. If we go to the interior, we risk the land mines. If we stay where we are, we risk growing old in these mountains."

"Better than dying. How many land mines?"

"Colombia is one of the top five countries in the world with regard to land mines. We estimated that at least a thousand people are injured or die each year."

Emma was aghast. "Who is planting them?"

"The paramilitary groups. They control their perimeters with the mines."

"Is there no rule of law in Colombia?" She didn't bother to hide her disgust.

"In Bogotá, yes. When dealing with the cartels? Only the rule of survival of the fittest."

Emma grabbed the tent and popped it open. "Mr. Sumner, if that's true, then I expect to survive. Because I am the fittest, not those goddamned criminals."

Sumner raised an eyebrow but didn't comment.

Two hours later, they woke to the sound of a helicopter overhead. The blades chopped and whirred, sounding as though the machine would land right on top of them. Sumner and Emma stuck their heads outside the tent.

The night sky glowed in the north.

"They have a landing strip there." Sumner stared at the sky.

"That's close. Maybe two miles away, no more." Emma watched the glow as well, straining to see if she could make out the shape of the copter. She popped her head back in the tent and grabbed her shoes and socks. "Let's go."

"Go where, there?" Sumner pointed toward the night sky.

"Yep. There."

"And what do you intend to do once we get there? Introduce yourself to the guerrillas?"

Emma handed him his shoes. "You can fly a copter, can't you?"

"Of course, but what's your point?"

"Then let's go steal one, shall we?" She grinned at him. After a few seconds, he shook his head.

"And I thought scientists weren't risk takers."

"You thought wrong." Emma crawled out of the tent.

TWENTY MINUTES LATER, Emma and Sumner were flat on their stomachs, staring at a helicopter squatting on a dark landing strip, looking like a dragonfly that was resting. Fifty yards away, a group of men crouched by a fire, talking in low tones.

"How long would it take to get that thing off the ground?" Emma said.

"Too long. They'll reach us while the damn thing is still winding up."

"We need a distraction," she said. "How about if I pop up at the perimeter and taunt them? Then when they chase me, you can jump in the copter and rev it up."

Sumner shook his head. "And what will that prove? I'll be in the copter and they'll have you hostage."

"I'll run in far enough to get them away," Emma said. "After a few minutes, I'll double back to the runway. They'll never catch me. At least not on foot."

Sumner shook his head. "And if I have to leave quickly? It's too risky, Caldridge."

Emma snorted. "Riskier than what? Staying in these mountains and getting killed? Dying of starvation? Sumner, we don't even know which direction to head to save ourselves. I run like the wind. They won't catch me."

Emma and Sumner glared at each other. The sound of the men's laughter floated across to them. Sumner gazed at the men again, assessing them.

"They're playing craps," he said.

"And drinking. If we let them go a little longer, they'll be too impaired to catch me."

"These guys are like cockroaches. They don't die, they just mutate."

"Do you have a better idea?"

After a long moment, Sumner shook his head. "Actually, I don't."

"I'll work around to their right. When you hear them yell, run to the copter. Give me enough time to lure them into the trees, then get that piece of machinery moving."

"And if I have to leave quickly?"

"Fly along the stream. I'll be there."

Emma put the backpack on her back. She'd left the tent behind. If they got out of there they wouldn't need it, and if they didn't, they could go back and retrieve it. She prepared to move. Sumner grabbed her arm.

"Be careful," he said.

Emma nodded once, and then she was gone.

Three minutes later, one of the men in the craps game sent up a yell.

"You bastard! Why you throwing rocks?" He pushed at his neighbor.

"I didn't!"

The two men squared off.

A rock flew into the circle and hit one on the back of the head.

The men exploded into action, grabbing their guns off the ground.

"In there. See it moving?" One man swung his rifle up and shot.

"Get it! Come on!"

The three ran into the tree line.

Sumner jogged, bent over, to the copter. He swung under the nose and crawled into the pilot's seat.

The copter was an ancient Blackhawk. The backseats were ripped out. A couple of battered coolers were strapped to the floor on the right, held in place with bungee cords. A magazine picture of a buxom blonde in a tiny bathing suit was taped on the wall over the coolers. Someone had drawn a mustache on her.

Sumner turned his attention back to the control panel. He kicked the thing to life. The engine turned over and the blades started a slow rotation.

"Come on, come on," he muttered. The blades whirred faster, but not fast enough to take off.

More gunshots cracked through the night.

The helicopter blades began to create their characteristic chopping sound. Sumner couldn't hear anything over the copter's din. He glanced back just in time to see two of the men plunge out of the trees. They fired rounds at the copter. Sumner didn't hear the shots, but he saw the muzzle flashes. He turned on the helo light and yanked the collective. The helicopter rose into the air, rocking back and forth like a lazy fly. Bullets flew past him, flashing in the helicopter's light like silver sparkles.

"Come on, you fat beast, move faster!" Sumner yelled at the dashboard, wishing that his will alone would make the copter respond. He couldn't stay and wait for Emma. Bullets hammered at the helicopter's skin. He rose even higher, trying to rock the copter back and forth to make it a more difficult target for the men to hit.

"Goddammit, Caldridge, where are you?" Sumner said. He rose three stories up before taking another quick look back.

He saw Emma burst from the trees to the left of the runway. Her arms and legs were pumping in a smooth, coordinated rhythm. She ran fast and efficiently, whipping down the side of the airstrip, chewing up the pavement. A man was chasing her, but it was clear he couldn't hold on. Sumner watched the man stagger sideways, bend over, and put his hand on his knees, his chest heaving.

The helicopter's radio crackled, and a voice barked at him in Spanish.

"This is Officer Lopez of Air Tunnel Denial, Colombia. Your aircraft is unregistered and has been deemed to be of suspicious origin. Please identify yourself."

Sumner grabbed at the radio. "Officer Lopez? It's me, Cameron Sumner. I've hijacked a para's copter and I'm under fire."

"Señor Sumner? You live!"

Bullets hammered into the copter's skids. Sumner yanked the copter to the other side.

"Not for long if I don't get out of here. Where the hell am I?"

"You are east of Cartagena along the Venezuelan border."

"Report my coordinates to the guys in Key West."

Sumner swung the chopper around and flew back the other way. He circled the runway and lined up. He flew the copter straight down the runway, nose down and tail up, remaining fifteen feet off the ground. He headed right for the men, who screamed and leaped sideways as the copter flew into them. Sumner slowed a bit, but as he came even with Emma, he watched her grab the copter's landing skids. She wrapped her arms around them.

The copter tilted sharply left with the added weight, but Sumner corrected and continued forward. They were twenty feet from the tree line, heading for it, when the rocket-propelled grenade took out the tail.

33

LUIS WATCHED AS TWO MEMBERS OF THE FFOC dragged the tall man and a woman into camp. They were tied at the wrists and lashed together with ropes. Scratches covered the left side of the tall man's face, and the pinkie finger on his left hand jutted out at an unnatural angle. His left arm bore a gruesome road rash, as if he'd been dragged across gravel. All of the scratches and gouges bled freely. Despite it all, he still walked with his characteristic efficiency of motion. The man scanned the camp, his eyes coming to rest on Jorge's head, which had been placed on a stick at the edge of the forest, near the passengers. Luis had put it there as a warning to them. He liked the way it focused their fear.

The woman with the tall man looked like a wild creature. Mud covered her skin and her hair hung in thick oily clumps that resembled long snakes. Even filthy and covered with mud, Luis could tell that she was beautiful. Her eyes were cat-shaped and a vibrant green, and they sparked with anger while she scanned the camp. Luis knew that if she smiled she would show the straight white teeth that he thought of as the hallmark of an American. She wore cargo pants and running shoes of an indeterminate color, and on her back was a grimy backpack.

She stood as straight and unbending as the tall man, and moved just as easily. Her gaze came to rest on Jorge's head and skittered away. Luis noted that she didn't appear surprised to see the head, and also appeared not as afraid of it as he would have liked.

He walked up to them. As he did he kept an eye on the woman, waiting to see if she would shrink in fear at his commanding presence. She looked at him in a straightforward way, showing no particular fear of him, and no respect. It was then that Luis decided to break her.

"So, we finally find the woman responsible for stabbing two of my men and causing many more to desert," Luis said.

The woman locked eyes with him, as if she were his equal.

He slapped her with an open hand. The sound of his palm hitting her cheekbone cracked through the camp. She staggered sideways. She regained her balance and looked at him again. This time anger shone in her eyes, but still no fear.

He hit her again.

She staggered sideways again, this time leaning into the tall man, who braced himself and managed to keep her standing. She raised her eyes again to Luis. She still showed no fear, just anger. It was as if the anger was a waterfall, flowing out of her. Something about it bothered Luis. The anger seemed unrelated to him. As if it came from a deep place inside of her and had nothing to do with the present.

Luis was a superstitious man. While he never believed in the El Chupacabra nonsense that his men babbled about, he did believe in demons, ghosts, bad luck, and evil portents. Something about this woman, and her proximity to the tall man, made a feeling of inevitability wash over him. It was an emotion that he did not like. He refused to label it. If he were a lesser man, he would have ended this operation two days ago, when he'd learned that the Cartone cartel was after him. But Luis was not weak. He refused to bend. He would see this operation to a successful conclusion in spite of these two worthless gringos. He would kill them both, after breaking them. He would triumph over it all.

Alvarado touched his arm. Luis snapped out of his reverie.

"What do you want?"

"The FFOC soldiers have news. They want to meet with you."

"Tie him to that tree." Luis indicated a tree in the middle of the camp. "We'll have some fun with her later, eh?"

The men laughed as they dragged the prisoners away.

When they reached the main tent, Alvarado delivered the bad news. "The FFOC want you to bring the hostages south, Luis, especially the woman."

Luis felt his blood pressure rise. The lying, cheating bastards wanted to take his prisoners away.

"I won't do it." Luis's voice was flat.

"You must do it. They have sent thirty of their best men here to find and kill you if you don't."

"They will try to kill me either way, Alvarado, you know that. And why the woman, eh? What's so special about her? I refuse to give them my only bargaining chip. Never! The deal was I march them north, guard them, and get twenty percent of the ransom money. If they are so afraid of the gringos, then they should never have pinched their tail in the first place."

"It's not just the gringos that come, Luis. The Cartone cartel and the other paramilitary groups have taken back their weapons and are coming for us also. None of them wants to be extradited to the United States. The army comes, too. They want the aid from the United States restored. Without it, they do not get paid. We need to get the passengers out of here. It's safer in the south."

"And how do they intend to move them? Seventy people? It's taken us days to get this far."

"They are sending the planes. Interrupting their own business. This tells you how serious they are."

"Planes! Are they crazy? They'll be shot down in a matter of minutes."

"Time is short. They say the others are arming and already have three helos in the air."

Luis paced back and forth. He pointed a finger at Alvarado. "We stay here tonight. I'll kill the tall man, and tomorrow morning we march to Panama, to the sea. We are not far now. We will sell the hostages there."

Luis stalked out of the tent.

MIGUEL KNEW HE'D HIT THE FIRST CHECKPOINT
when the trail ended at a dirt road covered with tire tracks.
They had been hiking for almost three days. He gave the men
a rest and picked up his field phone. To his surprise, he had
a message from Banner as well as Señor Lopez at the Air
Tunnel Denial station. He called the Air Tunnel man first.

"Major Miguel? We had a suspicious aircraft sighting in
your area. We believed it was a helicopter, flying low. When
we attempted to establish contact, Mr. Sumner spoke back
to us."

"Cameron Sumner, in a helicopter? What did he say?"
Miguel felt an adrenaline surge. It was about time they had
a break.

"He had stolen the helicopter and was under fire. Within
seconds, all contact was broken."

Miguel's mood crashed. "Was he able to give you any idea
of where he was?"

"I have the actual coordinates. May I give them to you?"

Miguel's mood rose again. "Have I said what an excellent
program the Air Tunnel people run?"

A chuckle came over the line. "We do our best, Major
Miguel. We do our best."

Miguel called Banner at Darkview and waited while the receptionist routed the call elsewhere. When Banner finally came on the line, his news was not as uplifting as Lopez's.

"Margate pulled the plug on aid to Colombia until the passengers are returned safely. He's demanding extradition."

"There goes the deal," Miguel said.

"Right."

"Any news on the paras' response?"

"The Cartone cartel is hunting Rodrigo to kill him, the other paramilitary guys are hunting the Cartone cartel, Rodrigo, and the FFOC to kill *them,* and the Colombian military has orders to shoot on sight. They're all converging on your area."

"And the passengers?"

"Caught in the middle. These guys kill. None of them has any experience in actually *saving* people. I wouldn't count on any passengers surviving the shit storm that's coming your way. So get the hell out of there. It's going to be raining fire in your area in the next twenty-four hours."

"You want me to pack up and go? Just like that?" Miguel was astonished.

"*I* don't want it, the Colombian government does. When Margate pulled the plug on aid, the Colombian president demanded an immediate withdrawal of all U.S. military personnel in Colombia. He said that any further search and rescue will be conducted by the Colombian army."

"You said I have twenty-four hours. If that's all I get, then I need more backup. I need a guy, a leader, who can do what it takes without me being there to hold his hand. The guys I have here are good, but too young to be of help."

"Margate refused any additional assistance. I can't overrule him, and even if I could, I'm not sure I want to. I'd be putting whatever poor slob I picked into a death trap."

"Banner?"

"Yes?"

"Where are you? How do you feel about coming back into the field?"

The silence on the end of the line was almost palpable.

"I'll get back to you," Banner said. Then he hung up.

Miguel mapped out the coordinates. "He's ten miles away, due north."

"Did Sumner say if Ms. Caldridge was with him?" Kohl hated the idea of leaving the path and heading up the road. He was sure Ms. Caldridge had continued through the jungle.

"He did not." Miguel sat back on his heels. "I know this landing strip. It's on the Air Tunnel map." He hauled out the ATD's map showing the known landing strips. "There's a second near an abandoned training center for Colombian military."

"Maybe it's not abandoned now. Maybe it's filled with passengers," Kohl said.

"Maybe. The good news is that I think I know how to get there. The bad news is that it's back down the path. It's a switchback that cuts in about five miles from here."

Kohl groaned. "Five miles on that path will take us another day."

Miguel hit him on the shoulder. "We have a direction, Kohl."

"What about Ms. Caldridge?"

"The human race car? Don't worry about her. She's probably run all the way to Cartagena by now."

EMMA SAT NEXT TO SUMNER, WHO WAS TIED
against the tree, and watched the sentry walk around the
wooden watchtower. Every so often the man took a hit off
a flask he kept in his boot. He'd swallow the liquid, smack
his lips, and spit down to the ground. Once it got dark, he
put his rifle on the parapet and jumped down. He put the
liquor bottle next to four others that sat open in a row on
the ground. He waved at Emma, giving a guttural order in
Spanish.

"He wants you to help build a fire," Sumner translated.

Emma rose wearily and assisted three male passengers
to start a fire. The passengers' clothes were soaking wet.
One coughed while he shoved dried sticks under a collection
of wood, some of it still wet. While the passengers worked
stacking the wood in a large pyramid, Emma walked to the
edge of the camp collecting dried weeds. She'd pull a few,
then push them under the sticks for kindling. She concentrated her weed-searching efforts close to the open bottles
of *aguardiente*. Each time she returned to the bottles, she
pulled a seed pod from her cargo pants' pockets, hit it with
a stone to break it open, and dropped it in the liquor. By the

time the bonfire was burning, Emma had managed to fill the bottles undetected. The flames lit the night sky. She would have enjoyed her first dry heat in days if it wasn't for her fear of being thrown on it in some awful sacrificial manner. She didn't trust Rodrigo.

"He's insane, isn't he?" Emma whispered to Sumner when she returned to sit next to him.

"I think so, yes." Sumner's voice was bleak.

"He isn't the leader, you know. Smoking Man in the shirt-sleeves at the airstrip was."

"Rodrigo couldn't lead his way out of a paper bag."

Mathilde sauntered over. She stopped in front of Sumner, tossed her hair, and struck a pose.

Sumner ignored her.

She sneered at Emma. "So, you and your lover meet mine, eh? He is one of the best leaders in the north. When this mission is done, all of Colombia will know his name."

Mathilde eyed her fingernails as she spoke. Emma had the distinct impression that she didn't give a damn about Rodrigo. All she cared about was his upward mobility.

"I feel sorry for you, Mathilde. A woman with your intelligence and looks stuck in this hellhole of a jungle. You deserve better." Emma accompanied these words with a sigh, as if Mathilde's situation was truly tragic to her.

Mathilde bristled. "I don't need your"—she appeared to search for the right word in English—"sorry."

"You have the opportunity to change your situation right now. But"—Emma shrugged—"if you like the jungle so much . . ."

"What opportunity do I have?"

Emma narrowed her eyes. "Perhaps you would like to trade, eh?"

Mathilde looked at Emma in surprise. "What do you mean? You have nothing to trade."

Emma leaned forward in what she hoped appeared to be a friendly, conspiratorial way, like two girlfriends, chatting.

"I'll trade my lover for yours. It is not an even trade, because mine is much more valuable to you, but yours has me prisoner, so right now he has some value to me."

Mathilde looked at Emma as though she'd gone mad. Sumner raised an eyebrow at Emma as if to say, *What the hell?* Emma acted as though the conversation was routine.

"My lover works with the Air Tunnel Denial program. If you free him, it will be a sign of your good faith. He could pull strings to get you a deal under the disarmament, with no extradition. You could get out of here for good."

Sumner shot an appalled glance at Emma. Emma kept her eyes on Mathilde.

Mathilde gave a toss of her head. "The disarmament deal is not offered to Rodrigo, only to the far right."

"Sumner could speak to his superiors here and in the United States. Get them to make an exception for you. After all, you weren't really involved in the hijacking with Rodrigo. Why should you suffer for his mistakes?"

Mathilde turned to Sumner. "What do you say to this?"

Sumner said nothing, but it appeared that this time staying silent was taking a huge toll on him. He looked as though he was gritting his teeth.

"Ah, yes, I remember. He is mute, this man of yours."

"Isn't that the best type of man?" Emma shot back.

Mathilde laughed out loud. Then she caught herself. "It won't work. He would whine to the authorities that he'd been forced to make the deal, and they would extradite me."

"Not if I'm part of the deal," Emma said.

"What do you mean?" Mathilde seemed curious, in spite of herself.

"He agrees to get you a no-extradition deal and make it stick; and you free him and lead him out of the jungle."

"Do you think I'm a fool? He would kill me and leave."

"Not if I stay here. He knows Rodrigo would kill me in retaliation."

Mathilde leaned forward. "Rodrigo will kill you either way."

"Then I will only agree to get you a no-extradition deal if you agree to free Emma during the night," Sumner said. "Once she is free, I will leave with you and speak to the authorities." He spoke soft and low, but both women jerked in surprise.

Mathilde straightened and stared at Sumner. Emma could almost see the gears turning in the woman's head. Before Mathilde could reply, Rodrigo stormed out of a nearby tent. Alvarado and the other guerrillas followed at a slower pace.

Rodrigo's face shone with sweat, and his eyes were crazier than normal. Emma didn't think it possible for the man to look even more psychopathic than he already had, but there he stood, breaking new ground.

Rodrigo waved at his men and spoke in Spanish. Emma felt Sumner's body jerk next to her.

"What did he say?" Emma watched as the guerrillas untied Sumner.

"He said to move me from the tree. He needs a clear shot."

Before Emma could react, Rodrigo marched up to her and kicked her in the leg.

"Why do the gringos want you so much?"

"I don't know what you're talking about." Emma tried to keep her voice from cracking.

"Liar." Luis smiled, his lips stretching so far as to show his gums, the edges blackened from rot. The light from the fire flickered, turning his eye sockets into black holes. Emma didn't have a lot of experience dealing with Rodrigo, but she knew that what made him smile was not good.

Sumner sat next to her, watching the proceedings with a

grim look. Emma watched his eyes flick over the crowd as if he, too, was reaching for options, trying to plan a way out of the camp.

"Tell me, or I'll shoot your friend and leave him to bleed to death in front of you." Rodrigo raised a gun in Sumner's direction. He pointed the gun at Sumner's temple. Sumner stilled.

The guerrillas passed around the bottles of *aguardiente* and started murmuring, chanting something in Spanish over and over again. It wasn't hard for Emma to figure out that they were saying "kill him."

"Why do the gringos want you!" Rodrigo shrieked.

"Shoot him and I'll never tell you." Emma was surprised to hear that her voice didn't shake, belying the actual fear roiling in her stomach. She wouldn't, couldn't, watch Sumner die. She had never felt such fear, never dreamed such a bottomless pit of terror could exist inside a human being. She struggled to keep focused, keep thinking of options, but even her logical, trained mind could not shove the primal fear that gurgled up from her stomach, rendering her mind blank.

Rodrigo screamed in rage, flipped the gun around, and slammed the butt of his rifle into Sumner's neck. He hit Sumner low, at the point where his neck met his shoulder. The force of the hit knocked Sumner sideways. He landed on his bad shoulder. He winced and Emma saw blood start to seep through his shirt at the location of the still-healing machete wound.

Sumner planted both palms on the ground and rose back into a kneeling position. Then he uncurled and began to rise. Rodrigo followed his movement with his rifle, pointing it at him, tracing an arc in the air as Sumner straightened. At six foot three, Sumner towered over Rodrigo. He glared down at the little man. The assembled guerrillas stopped their howling and seemed to suck in their breath, all at once. The entire camp fell silent. Alvarado took a swig of the *aguardiente* and stepped closer to Rodrigo, as if he wanted a better view of the action.

"Watch him die," Rodrigo said.

Emma did the only thing she could. She lurched to her feet, catapulting herself between Sumner and Rodrigo. She faced Rodrigo but started walking backward, pushing Sumner with her, using her body as a block between hers and Sumner's, and she started talking.

"He works for the United States government. A branch of the Drug Enforcement Agency. You kill him and the U.S. will hunt you down. And if you kill me, the Smoking Man at the airstrip won't stop until he kills you."

Emma watched Rodrigo freeze at her words. And then the entire camp went mad, guerrilla by guerrilla.

"El Chupacabra! He's here." A guerrilla started screaming. He clawed at his face, backing up in terror.

Luis spun around.

Another guerrilla started twitching. He fell to the ground, writhing. A third went to help him, then staggered and fell. A fourth screamed in terror and jumped in the air, keeping his feet moving in a dance, as if he was trying to avoid something on the ground. He kept howling the same sentence.

"What's he saying?" Emma spoke to Sumner in German.

"He's saying that the turtles are coming to kill him."

"Turtles?" Then, feeling the need to be sure, she said, "Turtles?" again in English. She glanced up and back at Sumner.

"Yes." A look of admiration came over his face. "You put something in their *aguardiente,* didn't you?"

"Scopolamine. From jimsonweed."

"Devil's breath," Sumner said.

"That would be the Colombian street term for it. Keep going back, slowly. We need to get to that machine gun, the one the sentry left on the watchtower parapet."

"How long will it last?" Sumner took a cautious step back, moving in unison with Emma. She kept her eyes on Luis, who held his rifle and watched in stunned silence as his men started seizing.

"Depends on the concentration each one drank. Hard to tell with these guys. But I used the seeds, the strongest part."

Another guerrilla jumped up, foaming at the mouth and yelling.

"He's seeing snakes," Sumner said.

They took another step closer to the tower.

Alvarado stood still. His eyes were glazed, and he appeared stuck to the spot.

Luis said something sharp to him in Spanish. Alvarado didn't react.

"Look at Alvarado." Sumner spoke in low tones. "That's why the street dealers call it the 'zombie' drug. It makes people lose their will and become completely suggestible."

They were three feet from the watchtower and still moving. Emma kept her focus on Luis, who remained with his back to them.

"I've always considered the zombie stories to be a myth. I think some people just get a paralytic reaction to it," she said.

"Paralysis is good. We're under the strap."

Emma glanced out of the corners of her eyes, trying to move as little as possible to avoid drawing any attention their way.

"Can you reach it?"

"No. Too high."

"Let's go to the ladder." The ladder was at least twelve feet away.

"No time. When I say 'now,' I'm going to come around the front of you, pick you up, and hold you against the wall. It'll be a stretch, but I think you'll be able to reach the gun."

"And then?"

"Aim it at them while I lower you back down. Be ready to use it if you have to."

Another guerrilla started walking in jerky movements, like a robot. The majority of the guerrillas were affected now, but Emma counted at least ten who were not. Mathilde had worked her way around the group to stand next to Luis. She held a rifle as well. She prodded Alvarado with the tip while she yelled at him. Alvarado turned his attention to her, but there was no recognition on his face as he stared.

The passengers huddled in the circle drew closer together. One of the affected guerrillas fell into the center. He writhed and screamed on the ground.

"Get ready," Sumner said. "Now."

Sumner stepped in front of her. He grabbed under her arms, lifted her in the air, and held her against the watchtower wall. His muscles bunched as he held her up.

Emma grabbed the parapet edge with her hands. Now she hung from the parapet, but if she let go to grab at the strap, she'd fall to the ground. She needed to brace herself and to stay high enough to reach the strap. She wrapped her legs around Sumner's waist.

She gripped him tighter with her legs while she pushed herself higher against the wall. Her head struck the underside of the wooden parapet. She crooked her neck to allow her arm to reach up and over. She moved one hand farther onto the parapet. The angle forced her to bend her arm, elbow forward. She swept her hand along the shelf, feeling for the gun.

One of the drugged guerrillas started screaming "Rat, rat, rat," and let loose a volley of gunfire at a beast only he could see. His bullets bounced off the ground. Emma glanced forward. She saw Luis turn to look behind him. He locked eyes with her.

Emma's fingers closed over the machine gun's strap.

36

EMMA BROUGHT THE MACHINE GUN DOWN AND
aimed it over Sumner's left shoulder just as Luis yelled an
order to the remaining sober guerrillas and swung his rifle
into position. She squeezed the trigger. The gun vibrated in
her hand and gunfire exploded in her ears. She swept the gun
to the left, spraying bullets in a semicircle. The gun bucked
like a wild animal, hitching upward with each recoil. She
watched the men rear up and plunge into the trees. Some
made it to safety, but most went down, blood catapulting out
of their bodies.

She swung the gun back, showering them with shot,
trying to control the weapon long enough to aim for Luis.
The bloodlust rose in her. She wanted Luis dead. She saw
the back of him disappear behind a tree and she aimed that
way. Bullets hammered into the tree, sending bits of bark
flying. She concentrated on the tree and the area around it
before swinging the gun back the other way. She heard high-
pitched screams from the circle of passengers. They scattered and ran straight into the woods.

Emma continued to empty the gun. She couldn't stop. It
was as if she were possessed. She heard her name, repeated
over and over, but the voice was far in the distance. The

shooting stopped only when the gun was empty. She heard a long series of hollow, clicking sounds.

"Caldridge, stop!" Sumner said.

He still braced her against the wall with his body. Emma tore her eyes away from Luis's tree and looked down at Sumner. She tried to open her mouth, but she couldn't speak. He put a hand on the side of her face. She felt the warmth of his palm, and it helped to calm her.

"The gun is empty. I'm going to lower you down. We need to run. Can you run?"

Emma didn't move. She wanted to nod but couldn't. Sumner let go of her. For some reason, she stayed where she was. Her legs remained locked around Sumner's waist in a vise grip.

"You need to release your legs." The urgent sound in Sumner's voice got through to her. It took all her willpower to relax her leg muscles and release her grip on him. The minute she did, Sumner crouched low and jogged to the fallen men. He rooted around the corpses until he found one with a machete in a sheath attached to his belt. He took it off, belt and all, and wrapped it around his waist while he reached for a machine gun. He collected the gun with the grenade launcher and pulled rounds of ammunition out of a pile. He slung the rounds over his shoulder, grabbed several more, and returned to Emma.

Emma stood there, shivering in the heat. Sumner laid the rounds down and jogged back to the main tent. He disappeared inside for a few seconds. When he emerged he was wearing a new, clean T-shirt. He carried a second shirt in his hand as well as her backpack.

"Yours," he said.

Emma still held the gun. Now she was having a hard time getting her fingers to release their grip on the gun so she could take the shirt. She took a deep breath and reached out.

She slid the shirt into the backpack, and then accepted the ammunition rounds Sumner held for her. She put the rounds across her body, over her shoulders. She put the backpack on last.

"Let's get the hell out of here," Sumner said.

Emma looked around the encampment before she turned to Sumner. "Not until after we burn this place to the ground."

"We don't have the time."

"I don't care."

"Let it go." Sumner sounded aggravated.

"No."

Sumner made an irritated motion with his hand.

"God knows you're stubborn. Let's not stand here in the open longer than we have to. You get the fire and I'll move toward the tree line and give you cover." He jogged away.

Emma went to the bonfire and pulled at the end of a stick protruding out of it. As she headed back to the watchtower she snagged a bottle of liquor lying abandoned on the ground. She sloshed the alcohol over the watchtower's supports before applying the fire. The old wood lit up with a satisfying whoosh.

The sound of gunfire erupted from the trees, somewhere near Sumner's hiding spot.

She heard Sumner yell, "Caldridge, run!"

Emma flung the stick away and ran. Her arms and legs pumped as her feet flew. She ignored the sounds of gunfire behind her. She ran out of the clearing onto the path, paying no attention to the rocky, narrow, and at times slick surface. She scanned the ground only long enough to avoid the obvious obstacles. She avoided the rest by using her peripheral vision. Her feet flew and her heart pumped. The path curved upward and she powered into the rise, the exact opposite of what she would do on an endurance run. She wasn't aiming for endurance, she was aiming for speed. A branch lay across the path ahead, creating a natural fence. Emma hurdled it like a pro, leaping into the air, front foot extended out in front of her. She landed on the other side and kept moving, not missing a stride. She lowered her head and forced her muscles to bring on another burst of speed. Her arms and legs pistoned in a precise rhythm.

She ran even faster. She careened through the jungle and shortened her stride, trying to add even more speed to her already blazing pace. She heard Sumner's grenade launcher fire, the distinctive thud overpowering the lesser sounds. The noise faded into the distance as she chewed up the miles.

MIGUEL, KOHL, AND THE REST OF THE TEAM STARED
into the night sky. It glowed dark red in the north.

"Little early for sunrise," Kohl said.

"It's them. They've burned the old army base," Miguel
said.

"Ms. Caldridge? Sumner? Who? Why do you say that?"
Kohl looked astonished.

Miguel barked an order to the team to prepare to march
to the fire.

"You asked me what I'd do if I were in their shoes? Well,
I'd burn something to indicate my position."

"They're indicating their position to the guerrillas, too,"
Kohl pointed out.

"Something tells me they've got them on the run. We're
deep in their territory. Even guerrillas don't burn their own
homes. That fire is a sign that something disastrous happened."

Miguel whistled to Boris. "Hope that nose works just as
well in the dark as it does in the day, boy."

Within fifteen minutes, Miguel and his troops were on the
move. Boris trotted in front, his head swinging from side to
side. Miguel estimated the fire to be five miles ahead. The

path currently ran in a straight line, with only a slight rise. If the path stayed straight, and there were no switchbacks, Miguel hoped to reach the burn site in an hour and a half.

The exhausted men fanned out behind. They were used to pushing through exhaustion, and none complained, but Miguel would have to allow them to rest soon.

Forty minutes into their march, a man stumbled out of the bushes and onto the path.

Boris barked once, and the soldiers dropped to the path and took aim.

Miguel saw the man's tattered civilian clothes. "Hold your fire!" he shouted. He walked up to the man, who swayed in place, and then fell to his knees.

"Do you speak English?" the man said.

"Major Miguel Gonzalez, United States Special Forces. Who are you?"

The man burst into tears.

They helped him to a nearby tree stump and gave him some water. He gulped it down and wiped his eyes.

"Sorry. I never thought I'd hear English again. I'm James Barkett, from Flight 689."

"Where are the rest?" Miguel said.

"Scattered in the jungle. When the woman started shooting, we all ran for our lives."

"What woman, and how did she get a gun?"

Barkett shook his head. "I don't know her name. She was captured later, with Mr. Sumner." He described Emma and told Miguel about Rodrigo threatening to kill Sumner unless she told him what he wanted to know.

"Jesus." Kohl breathed the word.

Miguel's face hardened. "Do you know which way Rodrigo went?"

"No. I don't think he's far, though. It's even possible that she grazed him."

"What about Sumner and the woman? Do you know which way they ran?"

Again, Barkett shook his head. "I don't, I'm sorry. When she started shooting, I dove for cover and then ran like hell. I assume they started the fire, though. That's the watchtower burning."

"Any idea where the other passengers are?"

Barkett waved at the jungle. "Behind me. We should see them in a few minutes. It takes time to get down the path because of the land mines. There are lines strung all over that path."

"Any idea how many lines and at what levels?" Miguel said.

"They seemed to run in patterns. Mostly low, but some higher up."

"Five to one, I'll bet."

"I beg your pardon?" Barkett looked confused.

"Five low lines, then one higher. It's a good rule of thumb when stringing land mines."

Barkett stared at Miguel. "I'm a manager of a small office-supply store, so I'll have to take your word on that."

Miguel smiled. "You're making jokes. Guess you're feeling better."

"Oh, yeah. Now that I'm with you guys, I'm feeling a whole lot better."

Miguel used the field phone to call for helicopter backup.

"I expect to have most of the passengers here with me soon, but at least two are still out there. Cameron Sumner and Emma Caldridge."

"Mission's over. We've already dispatched two copters to extract you. We'll load up and that's it," a soldier with the Southern Command, and Miguel's liaison, said.

"Banner said I had twenty-four hours. These two managed

to free the passengers, and they're close. They deserve to be rescued."

"I don't think you understand what's happening. The cartels and the guerrillas are blanketing your area. Our helos have been fired on twice already. Frankly, they're going to set down fast, load up, and get the hell out of there. I suggest that you do the same."

"And the two?"

"The Colombian special forces are on their way."

"Are these the good ones, or the bad ones?" Miguel didn't bother to keep the sarcasm out of his voice.

"I hear your frustration, Major, but there isn't much we can do. The army has been ordered out of Colombia. We're not wanted here."

"I want to talk to Banner. He's in charge of this operation."

"His jurisdiction extends only as long as the Department of Defense wants it to."

"Has the DOD pulled the plug?" Miguel said.

There was a short silence. Then the phone crackled. "Not yet, but we expect it to very soon. They've been negotiating with the pipeline executives. Apparently the executives believe that they will be summarily executed by the guerrillas once the special ops guys are pulled off the detail. The DOD agreed to evacuate them first out of the pipeline area."

"I need to speak to Banner."

"He's not available."

"Then get Carol Stromeyer from Darkview on the phone and call me back when you have her."

Miguel snapped the phone shut.

He turned to look at the passengers huddled together on the path. Kohl stood next to Boris, patting him on the head. Miguel waved him over.

"We leaving without her, sir?" Kohl said.

"Washington pulled the plug on Colombian aid, and Colombia pulled the plug on our mission. Helos are on the way to pick us up. I want you to load everyone on and stay with them until they are out of this godforsaken country."

"What about you?" Kohl said.

"I'm waiting for a call from a very important woman."

Kohl stared at him for a moment. "If you stay, I stay."

Miguel shook his head. "You can't stay. It would be in defiance of a direct order from Southcom."

"Isn't that what you're doing?" Kohl said.

"I'm falling back on a technicality. I'm operating under different orders issued by Edward Banner under a joint operation between the DOD and his private security company."

"I don't see how that changes anything," Kohl said.

"I haven't been ordered out by Banner yet." At least that's what Miguel would argue if and when he would be dragged in front of the powers that be. He was pretty sure Banner would cover his ass.

"I'm not leaving," Kohl said.

Miguel sighed. "Don't get stubborn on me. I'm old enough to get out without much flak. You're too young to mess up your career."

"I'm not leaving until we find Ms. Caldridge, sir!" Kohl snapped to attention and stared forward.

The phone rang, sparing Miguel from having to respond.

"Let me guess, you want to stay until the party's over." Carol Stromeyer's voice poured out from the field phone.

"Yes, ma'am, I do," Miguel said.

"Don't you ma'am me."

Miguel grinned at the phone. "Banner led me to believe that I have some more time. Do I?"

"Hold on a sec." There was a clicking noise in the background as Stromeyer typed on her keyboard.

"Technically, the order to suspend your rescue operation has not come down."

"Excellent," Miguel said.

"*But* I can't assure you of any further support from Southcom once those extraction helos leave. That's the bad news."

"What's the good news?"

Miguel heard some more clicking noises from Stromeyer's keyboard. "Under a general order issued to Darkview as an authorized contractor, Banner has the authority to man and run a covert operation and two helicopters into any listed hot area in cases of an emergency."

"Is Colombia listed as a hot area?"

"It is."

"Great! Can you send them in to get me in, say, twenty hours?"

"The bad news—"

"Wait, you already gave me the bad news."

"The *other* bad news is that the helicopters can be manned only by Darkview personnel. No regular army."

"Just a private company running a private operation, huh?"

"You got it. No chance of the host nation getting their panties in a bunch over what might be viewed as unauthorized U.S. military involvement."

"Any Darkview personnel available to run the operation?" Miguel heard the *whap whap* sound of a helicopter's propellers in the distance.

"Plenty, but Banner gave me strict orders not to let any of them go. He said he wouldn't be responsible for their deaths."

Miguel sighed. "Can I speak to Banner? Do you think he'll change his mind if I tell him I'm not leaving?"

"I'll ask him. When I do, I'll get back to you." Stromeyer rang off.

Over the next hour the passengers straggled into the clearing. Each one cried when they saw the soldiers. A short reconnaissance revealed ten more wandering in the jungle, all still with their arms tied in front of them. It was as if they had no energy to free themselves. Twenty minutes later, eight others appeared on the path. All of them greeted Miguel and his men with a tired elation. Two women started crying in relief. The entire group acted as though the ordeal was as good as over.

Miguel didn't have the heart to tell them that the firepower of a small army was headed their way.

38

LUIS STOOD IN THE JUNGLE AND WATCHED THE
watchtower burn, pinpointing their location like a huge
torch. Mathilde and a somewhat recovered Alvarado stood
next to him.

"Now the Cartone cartel comes, eh?" Mathilde said.

"Time for us to go get our ace in the hole," Luis said.

Alvarado hid his dismay at Luis's comment. His "ace in
the hole" was an asset that he'd sworn he wouldn't use until
things were dire indeed.

"That is a drastic measure, Luis. Do you think it is necessary?" Alvarado said.

"You tell me, Alvarado," Luis said. He pointed to the sky.
In the distance, just emerging from the dawn mist, flew a
Blackhawk helicopter.

"The Americans," Mathilde said.

"So soon they found us?" Alvarado was shocked. "Luis,
you said they would never track us."

Luis gave Alvarado a measured look. "Are you afraid, Alvarado?"

Mathilde eyed Alvarado.

Alvarado watched Luis finger the hilt of the knife he kept
attached to his belt.

"Let's go get your ace in the hole, Luis."

"And when we are done, Luis, we find that gringo woman," Mathilde said. "She must be killed, Luis. I hate her."

"Yes, Mathilde, we will kill her *and* the man."

Alvarado sucked in his breath. "Luis, think. We can't kill her. She's worth too much."

"I want her dead, Luis," Mathilde said.

Alvarado started to protest.

Luis put up a hand to quiet him. "We find the woman, get the Americans that want her to come with the money, and when they do, we ambush them and kill them all, including the woman. Is this sufficient for you, Alvarado?"

"Yes. But we kill the man, too."

Mathilde's eyes shifted to the side, and she said nothing. Rodrigo didn't notice her reaction, but Alvarado did. His stomach twisted with jealousy.

"We should kill the man, too. Shouldn't we, Mathilde?" Alvarado prodded her.

Mathilde shrugged. "It is no concern of mine."

Alvarado lit a cigarette and watched the sky.

BANNER LISTENED TO MR. CALDRIDGE'S STORY
from beginning to end without interruption. Stromeyer had
produced a cup of the strongest coffee he'd ever had outside
of Europe and sat in a nearby chair while the story unfolded.
Banner said nothing for a few minutes after Mr. Caldridge
was finished. Stromeyer let him think, not speaking. It was
just one of the things that made her invaluable to him—her
ability to gauge what he needed at just the right time.

"Where have you been staying?" Banner said to Mr.
Caldridge.

"Here and there. I took a drive up the East Coast. I was
headed to Jacksonville when I heard about the plane going
down."

Banner nodded. "Why don't you continue that way. Stay
out of sight."

"What about my daughter? What do you intend to do?"

Banner stood up to escort the man to the door. "I intend to
get her out of there."

Mr. Caldridge gave Banner a frank, assessing look. "Then
I guess I can't ask for more. You strike me as the kind of
man who does what he says he will. But just remember, she's
as smart as they come and stubborn as hell. She won't quit

until she's completed whatever she went down there to do. And she won't let anyone control her. Those DOD men made a mistake when they messed with her."

Banner smiled. "Spoken like a father who knows his daughter."

Mr. Caldridge nodded. "She's special. Bring her home."

When Mr. Caldridge was gone, Banner turned to Stromeyer.

"I have to wonder about Margate's order to pull everyone out of Colombia, including Miguel and his troops. He knows that Caldridge and Sumner are still stuck down there, but he doesn't seem to care."

"It's one way to isolate her. Gets us out of the way so he can track her down," Stromeyer said. "And now a comment made by Caldridge's boss keeps circling through my head. He said that the Mondrian Chemical Company was looking to license her new plant-altering technology."

Banner finished the coffee and reached for the carafe sitting on the table. At least he thought it was a carafe. It looked like a piece of modern art.

"Wasn't Margate a member of the Mondrian board of directors before he took his political post?" Banner said. He tried to pour the carafe, but nothing came out. "Damn, is the coffee gone? That was the best pot I've had in days."

Stromeyer reached over and unscrewed the cap two turns. "You have to open it first. How is it you can pilot anything that flies, shoot every weapon invented, and kick the shit out of most men, but you can't operate a coffee carafe?" She picked up the pot and refilled Banner's cup. "And yes, Margate was a member of Mondrian's board."

"I can't open the carafe because it's a ridiculous design." He took a sip of the coffee. "I don't like the connection between Margate and Mondrian. It stinks, doesn't it?"

Stromeyer nodded. "Yes, it does. But the real question is, what are we going to do about it?"

Banner downed the cup. "Can you keep our contract alive for a few more days? Slow the withdrawal order somehow?"

He watched Stromeyer ponder his question. "I used to date a man who's now the undersecretary to the Office of Diplomatic Security. Its jurisdiction runs to contracted security forces in foreign nations. If the DOD pulls our contract, he could issue one of his own. I'll call him."

Banner frowned. "I don't want to put you in an awkward position."

Stromeyer grinned. "Not at all. He's a nice man."

Banner felt annoyed. "Fine. Just don't let him blackmail you into anything." He put the coffee cup down with just a little more force than was necessary. Stromeyer raised an eyebrow at him, but said nothing. Amusement danced in her eyes. Which annoyed him more. He tamped down the emotion.

"I'll get ready to head out." He'd made it to the door, when Stromeyer called to him.

"Banner."

He turned.

She looked grim. "Be careful down there."

All his annoyance melted away. "I will. Thanks."

40

EMMA RAN UNTIL SHE SAW A HUT. ITS TIN ROOF
shone in the sun. The house sat at the end of a field of coca.

"Great. Another coca farmer," she muttered. She didn't
hear the footsteps behind her until it was too late.

It was a woman, one of the indigenous peoples. She wore
rough-hewn clothes that appeared homemade, and she carried a cloth bag slung over her shoulder. Her brown hair
flowed down her back, like a young woman's, but her eyes
held the sad, somber look of a much older person. She stared
at Emma, a wary look on her face. She glanced at the gun
slung over Emma's back.

"I'm from the U.S. I need to talk to the police," Emma
said.

The woman said nothing.

Emma's Spanish was nonexistent. When she'd moved
to Miami, she had intended to take a language course, but
somehow life had gotten in the way and she never found the
time for it. Now she wished she had.

"Do you have any food?" She mimed eating.

The woman nodded and waved Emma toward her. She
turned and headed into the jungle, following a small foot-
path no wider than her shoulders.

Emma followed the woman for half an hour, before she came upon a small village. Several children, also in homespun clothes, ran around in circles, barefoot in the dirt. Six huts, all in a semicircle, formed a small encampment. A fire burned merrily in the center. It was all Emma could do not to run to it and drop before it. Despite the heat of the jungle, she felt chilled to the bone. The woman watched her, a curious look on her face. Two children ran up to her, one about six and the other four. The woman seemed too young to have children that age or that many. She might have been twenty years old. The camp was devoid of men or any other women.

"Are the men out planting?" Emma said. She pretended to rake the soil.

The woman nodded.

The children stopped playing and surrounded Emma.

"Candee! Candee!" they said. They held out their hands.

Emma laughed. "The universal child's word, eh?"

She plunged a hand in the pockets of her cargo pants. Luis and his men had taken her wallet, passport, and cell phone. They'd left the lipstick testers, two packets of gum, and a roll of mints.

She gave the mints to the kids.

They shrieked in happiness and ran off.

The woman didn't smile.

Such sadness, Emma thought.

"Do you have any food I can eat?" She crossed her fingers. She was once again starving.

The woman nodded. She disappeared into a hut, then reappeared with what looked like some type of meat and rice. Emma sat cross-legged before the fire and tasted the meat.

"*Pollo?*" she said to the woman.

The woman nodded, with just a hint of a smile at Emma's attempt at Spanish.

Emma wolfed the food. The woman watched her with con-sternation. When Emma was done, the woman took the plate and scrubbed it clean with some sand from a wooden tub.

She returned to stand before Emma. The children came back, too, jostling one another as they gathered around the woman.

"*Gracias*," Emma said. "I know food must be scarce and you shared yours with me."

The woman nodded, but it was clear she understood only the one word Emma said in Spanish.

Emma wished there was a way she could properly thank the young woman.

"Wait. I have something I know you'll like." She reached into her cargo pants pocket and pulled out one of the lipstick tubes.

The woman's gaze locked on the tube.

Emma held it before her. "Lipstick. From one of the best cosmetic companies in the world." She swiveled the tube and the red color emerged.

The woman sucked in her breath. Her eyes widened.

"I developed the red. Do you like it?"

The woman just stared at the lipstick.

"I'll take that as a yes," Emma said.

Emma handed it to the woman. "It's yours. Try it. You will be one of the first women in the whole world to wear the color. I designed it to last all day, and it won't dry out your lips."

The woman looked at Emma in awe. She seemed almost afraid to touch the tube.

"Here." Emma moved the tube closer to the woman. "It's yours. *Gracias por pollo.*" She knew she'd murdered the sentence in Spanish, but the words did the trick. The woman reached and took the tube from her.

She ran over to a bucket that held some water. She stared into it, using the water as a mirror. She applied the lipstick and turned to Emma.

"Oooh," the children said in unison.

Emma sucked in her breath. The color looked perfect. It complemented the woman's coloring and made her appear more youthful, even happier somehow.

"You make my color look beautiful. *Gracias*." Emma whispered the words:

The woman broke into a shy smile. "*Gracias*," she said.

Emma nodded. "I must go now. I don't want to be here when the men return."

The woman looked somber again. She waved Emma to the door of a nearby hut. Emma had noticed the hut when she first entered the camp, mostly due to its difference from the others. It was set off from the main circle of buildings. There were no windows, and instead of a cloth covering an opening, this hut had a real wooden door, bolted into the frame, with a bar that hung across it.

As Emma walked over to the hut, she noticed that the children all had fallen silent. Their eyes were huge in their heads, and for the first time Emma felt they were looking at her in fear. Emma didn't want to open the door. Yet she felt compelled to see what was inside. She lifted the wooden bar. The door swung outward. It creaked on rusty hinges. The noise was loud and grating in the quiet clearing.

The inside was so dark that it took Emma a minute to adjust to what she was seeing. Only tiny shafts of light glowed through the occasional crack in the boards. The floor was dirt. Larger stones ringed the sides. The center of the floor contained a deep hole, so deep that she couldn't see into it.

Emma glanced back at the young woman. The woman

wasn't looking at her, she was staring at the hole. Emma didn't think it was possible for the woman to look any sadder than when she had first met her, but she did. Her eyes were dark pools of despair.

Emma took two steps into the hut and stared into the hole.

It was nearly ten feet deep and three feet wide. At the very bottom was a person. It looked to be a woman. Long hair tangled around her body. Her arms were like sticks. Her bones were clearly visible under skin so thin it seemed translucent. Heavy leg irons were wrapped around her ankles. She was lying on her side with her knees drawn to her chest in a fetal position. Her eyes were closed.

"Oh God, no," Emma said.

The prisoner opened her eyes and looked at Emma.

Emma felt her head swim. Tears came so quickly that it left her feeling light-headed. She took a deep breath and forced herself to calm.

"Can you speak English?" she said.

"I can." The woman's voice was reed thin and soft. She spoke English with only a slight French accent.

"How long have you been here?" Emma said.

"I think two years."

Emma knelt at the side of the hole. "Can you walk?"

The woman nodded. "They lower a ladder every day and I walk to the jungle to go to the bathroom."

Emma looked around. She saw the ladder lying on the far side of the hut.

"I'll get it," she said.

Emma shouldered the ladder, swaying with the ungainly size of it. She felt it steady. She looked up to see the young woman holding the far end. Now she looked more determined than sad.

They lowered the ladder into the hole. The woman below crawled up it with surprising agility. The leg irons clanked against the wooden slats. Emma grabbed her hand and helped her climb the last four steps. They stepped out into the sunlight.

The woman was tall, taller than Emma's five foot eight. Her clothes hung on her frame and her face was hollowed out. Her hair was matted and her fingernails caked with dirt. She stared around her, blinking in the sunlight.

"What is your name?" Emma said.

The prisoner turned her head slowly at Emma's question. She stared at Emma, but it appeared as though she was trying to remember her name. She took a deep breath that she exhaled on a sigh.

"The sun is beautiful," she said.

Emma nodded.

"And the air is warm. So nice. There were times that I thought I would never be dry again."

"Your name?" Emma prodded gently.

"Vivian Callenoute. I'm the daughter of a Colombian, raised in France. I was visiting relatives in Colombia to celebrate my twenty-first birthday. They kidnapped me at an espresso bar in Bogotá. I insisted that I would only be a minute, and urged my driver to wait in the car. For the past two years I have regretted that cup of coffee." She covered her face with her hands.

The sun shone, the trees swayed in a soft breeze, and the birds sang. Emma looked at the woman crying in front of her and wondered at the contrasting beauty and devastation that was Colombia. She reached out and touched Vivian's arm.

"I'm Emma Caldridge. I don't want to sound paranoid, but we need to get out of here. Now. I'm being chased by a paramilitary group. I need to find my friend and get the hell out of Colombia."

Emma turned to the young village woman. "Can you unlock the leg irons?"

The young woman turned to Vivian, who spoke to her in rapid Spanish.

The young woman snapped an order to a young boy, about eleven. He took off running.

Vivian turned back. "She sent Oliver to get the key to the leg irons."

"What is her name?" Emma said.

"Maria," Vivian said.

"Where are the other women and the men?"

Vivian spoke to Maria again. Maria gave a short explanation.

"The village is small. The men are on a three-day trip to the fields to gather the coca. The women are with them. They help with the camp and collect seeds and herbs. Maria was left behind to watch the children."

Emma turned to Maria. "Do you and the children want to come with us? Will you be in trouble when the men return and find their captive gone?"

Once again, Vivian translated. The two talked back and forth. Emma waited, but grew increasingly nervous. Finally they finished, and Vivian turned to Emma.

"She says she will be fine. She believes that the man who kidnapped me was killed yesterday by the Cartone cartel. She said she saw the watchtower at his camp burning. He terrorized the village, but if he is truly dead, then she will be free."

"What was his name?" Emma said.

"Luis Rodrigo."

Emma went cold. "Does he come here often?"

Vivian translated. Maria shook her head and chattered in Spanish.

"She says he comes every month, on a Friday, for one night. He checks on me, then he leaves," Vivian said.

"What day is it?" Emma said.

"I apologize, I don't know."

Vivian asked Maria the question before turning back to Emma.

"I am sorry to say, today is Friday."

41

IT WAS DAWN WHEN MIGUEL LED THE PASSENGERS
down the path to the location where the extraction helicopters would land. Boris went first, Miguel second, and Kohl and the rest fanned out behind.

They didn't see the ambush until it was too late.

One minute Boris was loping down the path, the next he was on the ground, growling.

"Down!" Miguel dropped and rolled. His quick thinking was the only thing that saved him. Bullets hammered into the ground in front of him.

Boris took off into the jungle. The soldiers scattered, throwing themselves into the foliage, some dragging passengers with them. The passengers flowed into the trees in all directions, making it impossible for the soldiers to return fire for fear of hitting one.

Twenty men appeared out of the jungle, guns drawn. Each was dressed in military fatigues, and each held a passenger in front of him, using them as human shields.

"Come out of your hiding place!" A guerrilla in filthy pants and a black shirt put a gun to the head of the passenger held by the man next to him. "If you don't, I kill the first hostage!"

The passenger was about eighty, with white hair and

watery blue eyes. His back curved in a hunch, but anger blazed from him. His clothes were stained and dirty.

"Ignore them, whoever you are! They are scum and will kill us anyway." The man spoke in Spanish. He turned to the guerrilla and looked into the muzzle of the gun, now pointed four inches from his face. "I am Colombian! You are an abomination!"

The guerrilla started to squeeze the trigger. Miguel watched, helpless. He couldn't risk firing and revealing his location as long as there was a chance, however small, of saving the rest of the passengers.

A gunshot rang out, somewhere to the front and right of Miguel. Blood spurted out of the guerrilla's neck. The shot was a real feat. Whoever did it had found a three-inch space between the old man's head and the guerrilla's neck. The guerrilla fell in place, taking the old man down with him. The other guerrillas scrambled off the path, dragging their human shields with them.

Silence again reigned in the jungle.

"Was that you, sir?" Miguel heard Kohl whisper somewhere behind him.

"Not me. One of ours?"

"I think they're all dead." Kohl's voice broke on the word *dead*.

"Then stay hidden. Whoever did that is one hell of a shot."

"I sure am glad he's on our side, whoever he is."

"Don't be too sure. Just because he's against them doesn't mean he's for us."

Miguel stared into the jungle. He couldn't see a thing. He strained his ears to listen for the telltale rustling of leaves. He heard the wind moving through, making a continuous, soothing noise, but nothing that sounded like a footfall.

"Let's move to the right. I want to outflank them," Miguel said.

He pulled himself backward, one tiny inch at a time. His elbows sank in the soft earth below him. His real concern was that he would be outflanked before he could achieve a location of relative safety. The guerrillas knew this jungle as only a native could. Miguel and his men were at a huge disadvantage, and this problem was compounded by the existence of the unknown sniper. Miguel figured that the sniper was moving through the jungle as well. The question was: which way? Miguel had no desire to meet the man who could shoot like that on any other terms than his own.

Miguel kept his eyes glued on the far side of the path while he crawled. After ten feet, his view was blocked, so he moved sideways. He heard Kohl behind him. Kohl was doing a good job moving in stealth, but there was a certain amount of rustling that couldn't be avoided.

The noise of a helicopter drowned out any sound Kohl could have made. Miguel looked up to see it hovering over the path. He got a mental picture of the flying monkeys from *The Wizard of Oz*. As a child they had scared the hell out of him, and this helicopter was doing the same. He watched while a man perched in the open door and fired round after round into the forest below.

Miguel heard men screaming. The helicopter flew low. Guns mounted on the side rained fire down on the hapless soldiers and anyone else in their path.

Another helicopter joined in the fray, this one filled with guerrillas. Miguel watched as one pulled the pin on a grenade. Miguel took aim and shot him. The man died instantly, but the grenade fell out of his hand anyway, dropping to the path below and exploding. Miguel heard more screams and watched as a gun flew ten feet into the air.

Return fire erupted from a location ten feet forward of the sniper's previous location. The sniper didn't waste bullets by laying down sweeping fire. Instead, he shot repeatedly into the area revealed by the fire bursts.

The helicopters hovered over them. The rotor's downwash bent the trees and forced the leaves aside, leaving the guerrillas in the open as they knelt on the passengers' backs. The nearest guerrilla tried to rise, but before he could, the sniper shot him right in the center of his forehead. He dropped like a stone.

Damn, that man can shoot, Miguel thought. He used the opportunity afforded by the helicopters' downwash to take out another guerrilla who'd had the bad luck to be exposed by the swaying vegetation. He heard Kohl's gun discharge to his right and watched yet another guerrilla fall backward.

The sniper shot twice more. Miguel wanted to see the result in order to assess the remaining force, but assistance came from an unexpected place when the men in the helicopter leveled the playing field and started firing on the guerrillas.

I'm in a gang war in the middle of the jungle, Miguel thought. He watched the helicopter fire into the vegetation below.

Now the tables had turned and the kneeling guerrillas were acting as human shields for the passengers below them. They took the brunt of the helicopter fire that rained down from above. Screams joined the cacophony. Some guerrillas were quick enough to jump up and run into the bush, leaving their hostages behind in their desire to save themselves.

The sniper fired a grenade at one of the helicopters. It flew into the open door and exploded. Bits of metal and chunks of fire fell into the jungle while the copter pitched sideways. It flew horizontally for a few seconds before landing in the jungle below. The second veered off, following the retreating guerrillas, peppering them with shot as it did.

42

"FORWARD," MIGUEL SAID TO KOHL, WHO AP-
peared at his side. They laid fire as they walked toward the
path. A passenger, still dazed from the horrific scene and
disoriented, staggered in front of them.

"Get back down! Now!" Miguel yelled at him. The man
dropped and froze. Miguel snorted in exasperation. The fool
was lying directly in the center of the path. If a stray guerrilla didn't shoot him, the sniper might. Miguel continued
sweeping the area with shot. He aimed high, hoping to spare
any other passengers who thought to get up and walk around.
When he reached the man on the path, he knelt down, still
firing, and tapped on his shoulder.

"Crawl past me into the bushes behind and stay there until
I tell you to move," he said. The man nodded and scrambled
across the path and into the bushes. When the sniper didn't
fire on him, Miguel decided to take the risk and send more
passengers that way.

The next two were young, in their twenties, and moved
with lightning speed. Miguel reached the far end of the path
and knelt next to the old man who had shouted his defiance.
He was still, his eyes closed, the dead guerrilla on top of
him. When Miguel touched his back, he opened his eyes.

"I'm faking death. Is it safe to move?" the man said.

"Only if you can move as fast as those two just did," Miguel whispered to him in Spanish.

"They are youngsters with flexible bones. I will wait until you tell me to move." The man closed his eyes again.

By the time Miguel reached the far side of the path, silence once again greeted him. Silence was not a friendly sound in the jungle. It occurred only when a predator, either four-legged or two-legged, roamed.

He rooted around, looking for his soldiers. He found two, dead. Two others lay in the bush, wounded, but not critically. He pantomimed to them to stay put. Four were missing. Miguel suspected they were hiding, and he hoped they continued to stay concealed. The guerrillas had retreated toward them. Now was not the time to move.

Miguel continued to collect the passengers and sent them crawling. The sniper stayed hidden and allowed them to pass. Kohl sat in a depression next to a verdant palm and waved the passengers into a group behind him as they crossed to him. After they were settled, Miguel went back and got the old man.

"Time to move, sir," he said.

"And here I was just planning a catnap."

Miguel admired the old man's attempt at humor. "Plenty of time to nap on the other side of the path."

"And the shooter in the trees? The one who is silent now?"

"He's had plenty of opportunity to hit us, but hasn't. I don't think he's a risk to us."

The old man rose and straightened his back with a wince.

After the passengers, Miguel turned his attention to the wounded men. One had a bullet in his thigh, the other in his right arm. He pointed to the one with the injured leg.

"Did you get a look at the sniper? He must be in those trees on the far side." Miguel couldn't remember the soldier's name. He was a black man, about twenty-one, from the hills of Tennessee. This was his first special forces assignment. Miguel liked him, and was glad to see he'd survived the gunfight.

The man shook his head. "I could see his muzzle fire, but not him. He's in the trees, about even with that twisted palm." The man pointed to a palm at the side of the path and about twenty yards away. Vines covered every branch, pulling the palm sideways. "He has a perfect view of the path, not that he needs it. Jesus! That dude could shoot, couldn't he? Did you see that grenade go right over those guys' heads into the copter?"

Miguel nodded. "Not a man to mess with."

"Who is he?"

"I have no idea. Problem is, he could be a cartel junkie not happy with the guerrillas infiltrating his neighborhood, a northern paramilitary guy, also unhappy, or a member of the secret police."

"If he's police, why don't he come out and introduce himself?"

Miguel shook his head. "There's a rumor that some have contacts with the paramilitary groups. He could be moonlighting for them and may not want us to know who he is in case we meet him during his 'day' job."

"Ain't nothing easy here, is there?" the man said.

"Not a thing," Miguel replied.

43

EMMA LOOKED AT THE SKY. "I'D SAY IT'S ABOUT
four o'clock. Ask Maria if Rodrigo comes in the night, and
does he come alone."

Vivian nodded. "He comes only at night, and usually with
his lieutenant, a man called Alvarado. They check on me,
and sleep in that hut." She pointed to a hut located dead
center in the semicircle.

"Tell Maria that Rodrigo is injured, but I don't think he
is dead."

Vivian translated.

Maria sucked in her breath. She spoke to Vivian in rapid
Spanish, punctuating her words with arm gestures. Her agitation was clear.

"Maria says that if the man is not dead, then the village is
in danger. The man threatened to kill all the children unless
we cooperated. She asks that you find the man who injured
Rodrigo and ask that he kill him."

"I am the one who injured Rodrigo. Believe me, I was
trying to kill him, but I had thirty other guerrillas to deal
with, and Rodrigo managed to slip through my fingers."

Vivian stared at Emma. "You fought thirty guerrillas?"

"Vivian, I had a gun. It wasn't like we were in hand-to-hand combat."

"Forgive me for saying this, but I always heard that Americans were a violent lot."

This from a Colombian? Emma thought. She shook her head. "We can debate the relative merits of our two societies later. Tell Maria that I won't leave the children to be injured. She should take them into the jungle while I wait for Rodrigo."

"And when he comes?" Vivian said.

"I injured him. I'll kill him."

Vivian blinked.

Emma looked at Maria. "When do the village men return?"

Vivian translated and Maria spoke in rapid Spanish. She kept shaking her head.

"She says we cannot depend on them to save us. They are so afraid of Rodrigo that she doubts they would help us attack him."

"So we're on our own. Fine. Let's get moving. We need to set a trap."

"What do you have in mind?'

Emma reached the fringes of the jungle and started picking through the foliage. She found several sticks sturdy enough to do the trick. She handed four to Vivian.

"Please ask Maria for two knives. She needs to help us turn the end of these sticks into points."

Two hours later, Vivian, Maria, and Emma stood around the pit in the center of the hut. They'd placed the sticks in the ground at the bottom, points up.

"I tell you, before now I never gave a thought to a sharp stick. Now I seem to be the queen of them," Emma said.

"It is a classic trap, is it not?" Vivian said.

"Yes, it is. But"—Emma turned to look at the entrance

to the hut—"we need to make this door open inward." She analyzed the door frame.

Vivian looked at the deepening shadows all around them.

"Emma, I don't think it's possible to do this in the time we have remaining. We would need to rehang the entire door."

Emma looked at it with a critical eye. She had to concede Vivian's point.

"What are you trying to do?" Vivian said. "Is the trap not enough?"

Emma shook her head. "There is no way he will just step into that hole. Someone has to wait until he gets close and then push him into it. That means that someone must be hidden inside. If the door swung inward, you could hide behind it."

Vivian gave a worried look around the clearing. "Emma, I think you worry too much. You have the rifle. You will shoot him as he steps into camp." She snapped her fingers. "Poof! End of problem."

Emma gnawed on a hangnail. "I only have four rounds *and* I'm an awful shot. You say you are worse, and Maria refuses to touch a gun. This is a backup plan if the shooting goes south."

Vivian patted Emma on the back. "Then it will not go south, eh? Because I tell you, if you do not get him, *I* will. Even if I have to rip him apart with my bare hands."

Emma rolled her shoulders, where an ache was forming. "Maria told the children to hide? Did she tell them what to do if we all end up dead?"

"We will not end up dead, Emma." Vivian sounded determined.

Maria said something to Vivian, who laughed grimly.

"Maria says that if I do not kill him, and you do not kill him, she will ask God to kill him."

Vivian and Emma looked at each other.

"She's going to end up in heaven, and we're going . . ." Emma didn't want to finish the sentence.

"To hell," Vivian said.

"Bad place to be. He'll be there," Emma said.

"But I'll be with you, and together we will be his worst nightmare."

Emma laughed for the first time in days. After a few seconds, Vivian joined her.

Their laughter ended when Alvarado stepped into the camp. He stopped cold when he saw Vivian, Maria, and Emma. His paralysis didn't last for long. He pulled his gun off his shoulder. Emma's gun sat in the center of the village, next to the fire pit. There was no way she could reach it in time to save them.

"Run!" Vivian shrieked the word. Emma spun backward to head to the woods. Out of the corner of her eye she saw Vivian and Maria dodge into the prison hut. Alvarado sprinted straight for the hut. He charged into it at full speed. Emma heard a howl, cut short.

MIGUEL RAN, LEADING THE SMALL GROUP IN THE
sprint of their lives. He heard the report of the still-firing
helicopters and the occasional explosion of a grenade.

Miguel held the soldier with the injured leg over his shoulder. The man groaned.

"Shit, Major, that hurts like a bitch," he said.

Miguel ignored him. His goal was to save the man's life,
not necessarily his leg. The man moaned as his injured leg
bobbed against Miguel with each step. The soldier felt like a
lead weight on Miguel's back. The group spread out accord-
ing to their ability to continue the pace on the slick path.

When Miguel had first ordered the passengers to run, the
old man had said, "Is running required?" When told that it
was, he had sighed.

Now Miguel was surprised to see that the old man was
not the slowest by far. He outpaced one much younger man
and two women.

They ran quietly, most too exhausted to even grumble
about being driven to and fro on the path. By eight o'clock,
the sun had burned off the mist and the heat had risen to
over eighty degrees.

Kohl carried Drake, another soldier, and jogged next to

one named Washington, who had jerry-rigged a splint for his leg that allowed him to move with enough speed to keep up. They turned a corner in the path.

"Well, look at that." Kohl pointed. A can of Coke, dented and rusted, sat on the dirt. He pulled his leg back to kick it.

"Stop!" Miguel said.

Kohl froze, his toe mere inches from the can.

A man stepped out of the jungle, twenty feet in front of Kohl. In one hand he carried an AK-47 with an attached grenade launcher, and the other was wrapped around Boris's collar. Miguel raised his rifle, but the old man reached over and placed a hand on his arm.

"Don't shoot, it's Señor Sumner!"

Sumner looked at Kohl, still poised over the can. "I recommend you listen to your commander over there and avoid moving that can."

"Why?"

"Because it's the trigger for a pressure-sensitive land mine."

A passenger gasped and several moved away from the can.

"How do you know?" Kohl said.

"I devised it."

"Works for me," Kohl said. He lowered his foot and stepped carefully away. He hefted Drake higher on his shoulder. "I'm Private Gabriel Kohl. Why the can as a trigger?"

"You ever walk by a can you didn't want to kick?"

Kohl looked sheepish. "I guess not." Then he brightened. "Hey, Boris. You okay, boy?"

Boris wagged his tail.

Sumner watched Boris and raised an eyebrow at Kohl. "You know this dog?"

"He's a land-mine-sniffing dog we borrowed from the Colombian military."

"That explains a lot. He's saved my hide three times in the past few hours."

Sumner sauntered over to Miguel and stuck out his hand.

"Cameron Sumner, Air Tunnel Denial program."

"Major Miguel Gonzalez, special operations."

Sumner waved a hand at the Coke-can mine. "How'd you clock it?"

"I've seen the technique used during an operation in Lebanon."

Kohl stepped up to Sumner. "Is Ms. Caldridge with you? Is she okay?"

Sumner went still. "How do you know about her?"

"We . . ."

Miguel waved at Kohl to silence him. He saw the emotion that rippled over Sumner's face at the mere mention of Ms. Caldridge. He didn't want Kohl's enthusiasm for her to rub Sumner the wrong way. The last thing he needed was a man as skilled as Sumner pissed off.

"She sent a text message after the flight went down. Then we found another note hidden in her suitcase, and the passengers told us what happened at the watchtower."

Sumner seemed to accept this explanation. "I don't know where she is. After we burned the watchtower, helicopters came. I used the grenade launcher while she ran."

"Was she okay?" Kohl said.

Sumner gave Kohl a measured look. "She was angry. Very angry."

"How angry?" Miguel said.

"Rodrigo escaped. Instead of getting the hell out the area for her own safety, she insisted on burning down his checkpoint."

"Do you blame her?" Kohl said.

"I don't blame her, but I tried to talk her out of it. She has no time to waste on revenge if she wants to survive this mess. And if she gets her wish and has an opportunity to kill him in cold blood, it will haunt her the rest of her life."

"Maybe not. Maybe it will free her. I mean, maybe it will be . . . what's the word?" Kohl said.

"Cathartic?" Miguel supplied.

Kohl snapped his fingers. "Yeah, that."

"It won't," Sumner said.

"How do you know?" Kohl said.

"Because I've done it."

45

"WERE YOU THE ONE SNIPING AT THE HELICOPTERS?"
Miguel pointed at Sumner's rifle with the attached grenade launcher.

"I was."

"That was some shootin', mister," Washington piped up from his seat at the edge of the path.

"Thank you."

"How many were left when you were done?" Miguel eyed the sky, as if he thought the copters would suddenly reappear.

"Two, but there'll be more. Those were Cartone cartel guys, along with some guerrillas. Those groups never get along, but here they were actually cooperating. Do you have any idea why?"

"Do you know anything about this area?"

Sumner nodded. "We're fairly close to the pipeline now. Once we get within five miles of it, this jungle is going to be swarming with guerrillas of every shape and size. Their soldiers are good, but they're high on drugs most of the time, so don't expect anything like rational behavior. What about the special forces there? Are they still guarding the pipeline?"

Miguel shook his head. "Not likely. Last I heard the Colombian government asked them to leave."

"Asked them to leave? Why?"

"When your plane was hijacked, the U.S. suspended aid to Colombia unless the Colombian president agreed to extradition."

Sumner got an enlightened look on his face. "So that explains the fighting. The Cartone cartel and the paramilitary groups hope to put an end to the crisis and restore their sweet deal with the Colombian president?"

Miguel nodded. "Something like that. The FFOC and Rodrigo's group are fighting back."

"And we're stuck in the middle," Sumner said.

"Hopefully not for long. I expect some more rescue helicopters in three hours."

The group marched forward. Boris loped between Sumner and Miguel. Sumner spelled the passenger and carried the injured soldier. Miguel carried Drake.

"This guy's leg looks bad," Sumner said.

"He's not the worst. Drake here is. He hasn't woken up at all." In the distance came the drone of helicopters.

Miguel looked at his watch. "Shit, we're late." He stepped onto the path and waved the flagging passengers forward. "Let's go. That's our ride!"

Washington hobbled forward. "We gotta run. I am *not* missing that train."

A Blackhawk extraction helicopter appeared above the path. Miguel's phone crackled to life.

"Major Gonzalez?" The man spoke in a thick southern accent.

"I'm here. Come on down and pick up these civilians."

"There's a clearing one hundred yards north on the path. We'll put down there. But you better make it quick. There are three enemy copters behind us, and they're all headed this way. These guys are better armed than most military bases."

"Most of it's ours. We sell it to Colombia and they steal it."

"In Arkansas we call that free enterprise."

They reached the pickup location just as the first helicopter came into view. It touched down and took on the injured soldiers. The old man and several women followed. The pilot waved several more on. The second copter landed and loaded more passengers. This pilot took on extras as well.

Then the third touched down. It was the pilot from Arkansas.

"Come on in! We're short on birds, so I'm gonna fly heavy. You got six enemy copters coming your way, each packed to the brim with guerrillas, drug guys, and I don't know who all."

"How far?"

"Thirty minutes away, no more." The pilot watched as the passengers packed into the helicopter. "Where the hell you get all these people?"

"The guerrillas walked them right to us," Miguel said.

"I can't fit you all."

"Take the civilians. I'll take care of myself."

"That's a death wish."

"You got any better ideas?" Miguel said.

The pilot shook his head. "No, but I do hate to leave you here, and that's for sure."

"Don't worry about me," Miguel said, with more confidence than he felt. The copter soon was filled to the brim and beyond. Miguel watched as Boris got his turn to load. Kohl waved him into the copter.

The dog refused to move. He swung his head back and looked at Miguel.

"Come on, Boris, up," Kohl said.

Boris sat down.

Kohl put his hands in the air.

Miguel walked over and waved at Boris. "Come on, get in the copter, Boris." He patted the copter's doorway. "Up."

Boris whined.

"He doesn't want to go either, sir," Kohl said.

"I can see that. Boris. Up. Now," Miguel said.

Boris lay down.

"Now, *that's* a well-trained dog," the pilot yelled over the rotor noise.

Miguel gave up. "Put the other shepherd in the copter." Miguel stepped away to allow Natasha to load. Boris followed Miguel, his tail wagging behind him like a flag.

Miguel, Kohl, and Sumner were left.

"Room for one more." The pilot yelled over the noise of his rotors.

The men all looked at one another.

"You're the civilian, Sumner. Get on," Miguel said.

Sumner shook his head. "I don't leave without Caldridge. I'm going back in to find her."

Miguel eyed Sumner. He had no real authority over the man, and he knew it. He sighed and turned to Kohl.

"I ain't leaving without her, either," Kohl said.

"I'm giving you a direct order, Private," Miguel said.

"Sir, I gotta stay!"

Miguel pointed to the open field. Kohl turned to look, and Miguel punched him in the head. Kohl dropped like a stone. Sumner looked as surprised as hell.

"Put him in," Miguel said.

Sumner shook with laughter as he grabbed the unconscious Kohl under the arms. Miguel took the legs, and they heaved him into the copter.

"When we get there you want him sent to the brig for insubordination?" the pilot asked.

Miguel shook his head. "That was a heat seizure you saw. I never touched him and there was no insubordination."

The pilot grinned. "Got it." He reached back into the copter and grabbed a small pack. "Woman named Stromeyer from Darkview said to tell you that Banner is out of communication. And she sent you this." He threw field rations to Miguel, and more to Sumner. "And this is from me." The pilot handed him a pocket cigar humidor. "They ain't Cuban, but they're great. There's one in there for him, too."

Miguel nodded to the pilot. "Thanks."

The pilot got a grim look on his face. He saluted both men before returning to the controls. The helicopter rose slowly into the air and flew away.

46

BANNER SAT IN A GRIMY ROADSIDE BAR IN A PARA-military-controlled town near the border of Venezuela. He drank sips of coffee so thick that the grounds formed a silt pile at the bottom. They slid into his mouth. He swallowed without blinking and scratched absentmindedly at his day's growth of beard.

He'd taken steps to alter his looks. His hair was dyed black and he wore dark contact lenses to dim his blue eyes. The measures were only half successful. Two women who loitered at the bar had already marked him as a wealthy outsider. They'd approached him, twining their arms around his neck, telling him how handsome he was, and whispering the things they would do to him. For a price, of course. Their bodies were warm and full and he'd enjoyed the brief contact. He'd thanked them for the offer, bought them both coffees, and sent them on their way.

Ten minutes later, his good friend Raul Perez sauntered into the bar. Perez nodded at the bartender, ordered an espresso, and took a seat at the bar stool next to Banner.

"Hello, amigo, you don't like our girls?" Perez said.

Banner shrugged. "I like them just fine, but my interest is elsewhere."

Perez gave him a shrewd look. "And how is Major Stromeyer?"

Banner eyed Perez over the rim of his coffee cup. "Still my employee."

Perez chuckled. "And therefore untouchable. You know, for a covert operator, you sure do follow the rules."

Banner smiled. "I'm a business owner now. I haven't a choice. And you? How is your business? I brought you some medicine for the clinic."

Perez rubbed his hands together. "IV bags? Needles?"

"And six boxes of vaccines."

Perez slapped him on the back. "Excellent." The bartender pushed an espresso cup in Perez's direction. "Hey, Juan," Perez said, "bring your little girl to the clinic tomorrow. Vaccines for everyone compliments of my friend here."

Juan the bartender smiled but said nothing.

Perez downed the coffee in one gulp. "Come on, Banner. I have someone I think you should meet."

Banner shoved some money under his saucer and stepped away from the bar. Juan reached over, picked up the coffee cup, and pushed the money back at him.

"Thank you for the vaccines, señor."

Banner took the money and stuffed it in the tip jar. "For the niños."

Juan nodded his thanks.

Perez drove his battered jeep down the dirt road to the outskirts of town. Educated at a medical school in Grenada before President Reagan decided to "free" it, he'd met Banner during the evacuation. Perez had practiced in hospitals in Miami before returning to this border town. He'd started his clinic to help the local people. Ten years ago, when a paramilitary group threatened to bomb the clinic unless he agreed to pay protection, he'd called Banner in a panic. Banner managed to convince the guerrillas that harassing the only doctor in town was a very bad idea. The convincing took a while. Every day for three straight weeks, Perez's clinic treated the broken arms and noses of a stream of guerrillas. The same ones who had demanded protection from him were now forced to accept his care. He'd done it quietly and without question. At the end, the guerrillas not only viewed Perez as an untouchable entity but as a friend. Now they routinely brought their own families to him to treat.

The clinic consisted of a series of connected cinder-block buildings in an L shape. Paint peeled from the walls, and the last building's second floor remained unfinished. Long pieces of rusted rebar jutted out from the roof.

"Still haven't completed that wing?" Banner said.

Perez sighed. "Every time I try, something arises that requires the funds go elsewhere. Like the person I'm taking you to meet."

Banner stepped into the cool hallway of the inpatient wing. It smelled like astringent antiseptic and ammonia. A ceiling fan with one broken blade turned slowly overhead. The piece creaked as it completed each turn. Perez waved Banner into a room on the right.

A large woman with tightly curled gray hair and tubes running out of her arm sat up in the room's only bed. She looked to be in her late sixties. Her skin was gray, but her eyes were bright with intelligence. She wore a hospital gown that tied at the back. Banner could see the strings poking out from behind her neck. The gown had a bizarre, faded pattern of blue flowers intermixed with pictures of teddy bears. The bears wore little blue diapers. Banner gazed at it in fascination. Perez broke his reverie.

"I've brought someone for you to meet," Perez said to the woman. He spoke in a hearty voice, his usual good humor moving up a notch.

"Does he have a cigarette for me?" the woman said, a sly look on her face.

Banner tore his eyes from the diapered bears and laughed.

Perez put on a frown. "Gladys, those are coffin nails."

Gladys waved a hand in the air. "But it's my coffin, now, isn't it, Dr. Perez?" Perez shrugged, giving up.

Gladys peered at Banner. "I'm Gladys Sullivan."

Banner reached out and shook her hand. "Edward Banner."

"What's wrong with your eyes?" Gladys said.

Banner heard Perez suppress a laugh.

"Why do you ask?" Banner said.

"They look surreal. Like liquid tar."

"I'm wearing colored contact lenses. But I'm surprised you've noticed. Most people wouldn't be able to tell."

"What's their real color?" Gladys said.

"Blue." Banner saw no reason to lie to the woman. He'd liked her on sight, and her request for a cigarette in spite of her obvious dire health condition indicated a woman who knew what she wanted.

Gladys gave a satisfied nod. "That's better. I like it when a man tells the truth." She gave him a critical look. "I have to say, each man I see on this journey is better looking than the last. You, mister, are a stunner."

Banner didn't know what to say. He was used to women flirting with him in the sideways manner women had, but rarely had a woman so blatantly placed her thoughts on the table. He did his best to ignore Perez, who grinned at him from the corner of the room.

"Thank you, Ms. Sullivan." It was all Banner could think of to say. He didn't think Perez had brought him to Ms. Sullivan so that they could have an extended discussion of his looks. To his relief, the doctor changed the subject.

"Gladys has a story to tell you, Banner." Perez ambled to the door. "While she does, I'll just arrange to unload the booty you brought." He left Banner and Gladys staring at each other.

"I'm from Flight 689," Gladys said.

Banner started. A chrome chair with a torn red vinyl seat cushion sat in the corner. He snagged it, placed it next to her bed, and sat down.

"Perez told me about you. He said you were working with the government on the hijacking."

Banner nodded. "I am, in a manner of speaking. I'm here to collect a helicopter."

Gladys heaved a relieved sigh. "I think I'm the last person to see Emma Caldridge. She saved my life. And I'd like you to save hers," she said.

An hour later, Banner stood next to Perez's jeep. "Will she live?"

Perez rocked his hand back and forth. "Hard to say. She needs a triple bypass and to stop smoking. She also needs helicopter transport to a major city. I had one lined up through a relief organization, but she ceded her spot to a child with meningitis. Now she has to wait at least three more weeks."

"If it hasn't happened by the time I get back, I'll try to arrange transport."

"What'd she say?" Perez said.

"She rode with a band of cartel flunkies out of the hijack area. While on the ride, she saw a caravan of trucks carrying what sounds like Dragunov semiautomatic rifles with telescopic sights."

Perez gave a low whistle. "Cartels arming for a fight?"

Banner shook his head. "Apparently not. She said they were headed to the ocean to be smuggled into Miami. She said some American businessmen were assisting in the transport. She knew this because she'd seen them earlier at a checkpoint location." He yanked open the jeep's door. "But that whole story isn't what worries me. What worries me is that these gunrunning Americans were focused on finding one particular passenger."

"What's so special about this passenger? Didn't most die in the crash? And the rest taken hostage?"

Banner nodded. "The only people that know this passenger is alive are with the Department of Defense. Looks like our hijacking friends have some help from inside the States."

Perez's mouth dropped open.

EMMA RAN INTO THE SMALL PRISON HUT AND
stumbled over Maria, who was hovering just inside the doorway. Vivian crouched at the edge of the pit, staring downward. Alvarado hung there, his body impaled on the sticks. One went straight through him and came out his back. His arms were stuck out at ninety-degree angles from his body. He looked like he'd been crucified. Blood was everywhere.

"Did you push him?" Emma said.

Vivian shook her head. "No. He slipped when he reached the edge and fell straight forward."

"I know he deserved it, but it looks awful."

"He would come here every week and taunt me. He called me Rodrigo's 'ace in the hole' and then he'd laugh. Once he took one of the men, brought him to the edge of the hole, and shot him in the head. The body fell on me and he made me carry it out and bury it. I hated him."

Maria said something in Spanish.

"Maria says that God let him fall."

"Maria has much more faith in God's sense of fair play than I do," Emma said.

All three women were silent, staring at the body.

Maria spoke up. She chattered at Vivian and waved her arms around in the air.

"Maria says we must move the body. She says the children should not know what occurred here."

Emma nodded, but she shivered. All three women fell silent again. They stared at the dead man.

"Let's go," Emma said.

They lowered the ladder down the hole. Maria handed Emma one end of a rope. Emma grimaced as she wrapped the rope around Alvarado's chest and tied it into a slipknot. She climbed out and waved to Vivian.

They heaved on the rope. The body slid off the sticks and slammed into the side of the hole with a sickening thud. They walked back, dragging it up onto the ground.

"Now we bury him," Emma said.

Two hours later, they stood in the jungle and patted dirt over the grave site. Maria held a burning torch. No one said anything. Emma thought it was the worst moment of her life so far.

"You need to hide in the jungle again. The village is not safe," Emma said.

"Maria is leaving with the children. She will not return until she is given a sign that Rodrigo is dead."

Emma glanced up. "What type of sign? We may not be able to return for a long time."

Maria patted Emma's arm while she spoke to Vivian.

"Maria says that God will give her a sign. She is sure that Rodrigo will meet his end soon. She thanks you for freeing her and the children."

Emma shook her head. "Vivian, does she understand that I am a terrible shot? That this plan could fail?"

Vivian translated for Maria, who smiled as she replied.

"She says that God will guide your hand. Things are in

motion now that will call the end to Rodrigo. She says you set those things in motion, and she thanks you for it."

Emma wished she could have such faith in God. As it was, she thought that their situation was worse than before. Rodrigo and Alvarado were a team. When Alvarado failed to return, Rodrigo was bound to wonder what happened and come looking.

"What do you think, Vivian?" she said.

Vivian hesitated a moment. Then she shook her head.

"I do not share Maria's faith. I think we need to kill him or he will kill the children, as he once threatened to do."

"I agree with you, but you aren't staying here. Two years in that hellhole is enough. You're free now. Go with Maria and don't return to the village until you hear that Rodrigo is dead. I'll try to get the news to you somehow."

Vivian hesitated. "I don't want to leave you here alone."

Emma gave her a little push. "Go with Maria." Vivian left to join Maria and the children hiding in the jungle, taking her torch with her.

Emma sat in the bushes at the edge of the little camp and thought about Sumner. She closed her eyes and tried to feel him. Tried to discern if he still lived and worried about her. She remembered watching a television show about miracles in ordinary life. The show's host interviewed person after person, all of whom told incredible stories of impossible phenomena. Stories about speaking to people after they were dead, having premonitions of both good and evil before events occurred, and of returning to life after near-death experiences.

Emma hadn't scoffed at the stories exactly, it was clear that the people were in deep pain and soothing themselves in any way they could, but she didn't believe them, either. She believed that many such premonitions were nothing more than animal instinct. The subconscious mind made connections based upon actual occurrences, and it put the puzzle pieces together in a way that felt surreal but was not. Yet now she sat in the bushes and tried to conjure up some of the same feelings. She wanted Sumner to be alive.

Twenty minutes later, Emma watched Rodrigo and Mathilde walk into the small village. She picked up the rifle and sighted Rodrigo's back.

And then she froze.

The image of Patrick on his deathbed, clutching his rosary, bloomed in her mind. She shoved the image away and refocused on Rodrigo's back.

"Maria!" Rodrigo bellowed the name.

Emma inhaled deeply and started to squeeze the trigger. Then she froze again.

"Don't think, just shoot him. He's not even looking this way." Emma talked to herself as she tried to motivate her finger to depress the trigger. Still, her hand stayed frozen.

Have you ever killed a man in cold blood? Sumner's words ran through her head.

Not only in cold blood, Sumner, in the back, too, she thought.

She sighted Rodrigo's spine dead center, between the shoulder blades, her vision focused on just that spot. She hovered there for a second, trying to conjure up her rage from the watchtower. She felt the anger still, but the awful image of Alvarado dead on the sticks kept intruding, sending waves of revulsion through her. The finality of death weighed on her.

Emma lowered the gun.

Two pickup trucks and a black SUV roared into the village. The pickups had the word DAIHATSU painted on their hatches. Each one was filled with boxes marked BANANAS— PRODUCT OF COLOMBIA. The top banana box on one truck was open. Instead of carrying bananas, it was loaded with long thin rifles. Each rifle had a telescope at the top. Emma watched as a soldier backed one of the pickups deeper into the foliage.

Smoking Man emerged from one of the pickups, followed by his bodyguards. He marched toward Rodrigo. At one foot away, he hauled off and punched him square in the face. Rodrigo staggered but swung at Smoking Man. His offensive move was short-lived. The two bodyguards grabbed his arms and pinned his hands behind him.

Smoking Man struck Rodrigo in the stomach. He wound up to punch Rodrigo again, when the roaring sound of diesel engines echoed through the air. Two large army trucks, the type used to transport personnel, barreled into the small village. A Range Rover followed. The vehicles stopped in a cloud of dust. The doors on the Range Rover swung open, and two men dressed in businessman's attire stepped out. They marched up to Smoking Man.

A long conversation ensued. Soon the men were yelling at one another. Emma gasped when she heard the lead businessman address Smoking Man in clear American-accented English.

"You had her in your hands and lost her. Not only her, but the hostages as well. You told me this loser"—the man stabbed a finger at Rodrigo—"could handle the job. Well, we're not depending on you or your men anymore. See those soldiers?" The man waved at the trucks filled with paramilitary soldiers. "They're here to take over after you and your men recover that woman. You *will* listen to them."

Smoking Man took a drag off his cigarette and spit on the ground in the direction of the new set of guerrillas. His show of defiance spurred the American man to yell even louder.

"I don't give a damn what you think of them. I'm going to get the bloodhounds back on her trail." The man stalked back to the cab, reached in, grabbed a briefcase, and threw it at Smoking Man. "We're leaving. Either you find her or there will be no more." He turned to his men. "Make sure they get it right and then drive those trucks to the beach." He pointed at the two Daihatsus.

Four soldiers jumped out of the transport vehicles and trained guns on Rodrigo and Smoking Man. The lead American stormed into his Range Rover. The second followed more slowly. He avoided looking at Rodrigo or Smoking Man. The Range Rover started with a roar and drove away.

Smoking Man threw a gun at Rodrigo before spinning around to head back to his car. He made a great show of nonchalance as he sauntered past the four soldiers. They kept a rifle trained on him but let him pass. He slammed into the SUV and disappeared in his own cloud of dust. An expectant silence settled over the village.

Emma could focus on only one thing, the hounds. If the men brought back the dogs, the chances were high that they'd catch her this time. She couldn't afford that until she completed what she came to Colombia to do. The only way to evade the dogs was to be far away when they came, and to get away in a vehicle, leaving no trace of her scent.

She turned her attention away from Rodrigo to the Daihatsu trucks.

SUMNER, MIGUEL, AND BORIS SLOGGED THROUGH the jungle in the general direction that Sumner believed Emma had run. Miguel held a compass out in front of him and warned Sumner when they deviated the least bit from it. They kept a straight line, allowing the dog to jog in the front. They'd managed to avoid two land mines, thanks to Boris. To Miguel, the jungle held a quiet, waiting feeling. The sky glowed amber, the way it did twenty minutes before a tornado hit. Miguel had experienced a tornado in Oklahoma, and he never forgot that amber sky and the feeling of peace right before all hell broke loose. He'd never really understood the term *calm before the storm* until that day. Now he knew the phenomenon existed.

Sumner was a man on a mission. Miguel liked working with him. He rarely spoke, except for essential things, and he moved with a stealth that Miguel admired. He didn't seem overly desperate to find Ms. Caldridge, more like quietly determined. Miguel felt as though he would not stop until he did.

Rodrigo should be worried. He is no match for this man, Miguel thought.

They broke through a stand of palm and stumbled onto a trail.

"Does this look familiar at all?" Miguel said.

Sumner shook his head. "Whole damn jungle looks the same to me, I'm afraid. Feels the same, too. Hot, wet, and dangerous."

Miguel nodded. "Maybe this is a good place to take a little break. Boris could use some water."

Miguel poured a small amount of water into a tin cup. Boris lapped it and looked for more when it was empty. They started again. They had walked fifty paces when Sumner gave a low chuckle. He pointed to a tree with a crude *X* scraped into the trunk.

"She thought ahead," Miguel said.

"She always does."

An explosion ripped through the air. They smelled the smoke before they saw the fire. A large plume of black smoke rose into the sky.

"Now what?" Miguel said in exasperation. They headed toward the smoke. It took an hour for them to reach the plume's location.

They stood there, struck dumb by the devastation. It was the pipeline. The large metal tube was an ugly metallic blight on the green landscape. Metal tripods held it off the ground. Dark smoke roiled from where the guerrillas had bombed it. Oil spilled everywhere, oozing across the grass and stones, turning the green field to black. Miguel gagged at the stench. His feet slipped on the slick grass. Someone had set makeshift oil drums under the gaping hole to collect what they could.

A small tin shack sat at the end of the field. It leaned sideways, looking like a poor man's version of the Leaning Tower of Pisa.

"Let's canvass it first," Sumner said. He worked his way around the shed in a large semicircle. Miguel followed behind, trying not to slip on the oil. They reached the back of the structure.

"No windows. Anyone could be inside," Miguel whispered.

Sumner nodded. He reached out and pulled on the wooden door. It was spattered with oil, and opened with a smooth swing. The dark interior smelled like burning tar—the kind of smell that roofers make with their tar-melting vats. Sumner's eyes stung from the fumes.

The hut had ragged wooden walls and a dirt floor. A blackened kerosene stove sat in the corner. The rest of the hut was bare except for a small wooden desk made of plywood. It hugged the far wall, with a matching chair pushed in front of it. On top of the desk sat a briefcase, open. Around it, stacked in piles, was more money than Sumner had ever seen outside of a bank. He reached over and lifted a small packet off the stack. He fanned the bills, watching them flutter in order.

"Ten-dollar bills," he said, "and they're still crisp. New money. Payoffs?"

Miguel peered at Sumner in the gloom. "Didn't work. They bombed the pipeline anyway."

"Maybe the payoff was to make the guard look away so they could bomb the pipeline," Sumner said.

"If so, why leave it here? Let's get the hell out of here."

Sumner grabbed a handful of bills and shoved them into his pants' pockets. He gave another handful to Miguel.

"Put these in your cargo pockets. We may need this to bargain our way out of a tough spot."

Miguel counted the stacks, then snorted. "I can carry a grand total of six thousand dollars. If that buys me anything, I'd be surprised."

Sumner shrugged. "It's something."

"That it is," Miguel said.

They stashed as much cash as they could and headed back outside. The stench in the air surrounded them. Miguel pulled out a compass and waved toward the broken pipeline.

"That way is the sea. We should be close now. We'll have to work our way to the other side and head down that hill."

They jogged to the pipeline, angling under it. Miguel swung his head from side to side, looking for movement or any sign of an enemy. Sumner waved toward a tree. They slipped behind it.

"It's too quiet," Sumner said in a whisper.

"I agree. Do you see anything?" Miguel said.

"No, but the hair is standing up on my neck. Not a good sign."

"You know what to do in case of an explosion, right?" Miguel whispered.

"Run like hell?" Sumner said.

"No. Drop to the ground and open your mouth. That way the shock waves will flow through your body instead of blasting it apart."

Sumner looked at Miguel a long moment. "Thanks for the tip," he said.

Miguel smiled. "Let's move, shall we? Flush these losers out of hiding. I'll be damned if I can spot them, and I can't tell you how badly I want to get to that beach. I'll go first, you watch for snipers."

Miguel left the tree line and ran in the direction of the beach. He felt Sumner's eyes on his back. He also felt a presence to his right. Whoever had targeted them was sitting in the trees. Miguel estimated the sniper was fifty feet ahead of Sumner's position. He would draw even with him in ten seconds. He prepared to drop and fire.

The explosion came out of nowhere. It blew apart a section of the pipeline five hundred yards from Miguel's position. Miguel hit the deck and opened his mouth. He watched Sumner out of the corner of his eye. Sumner dropped and turned his head toward the blast. The shock wave hammered through Miguel. It rattled his bones and he felt his tongue suck backward into his mouth.

A second explosion came on the heels of the first. A huge plume of fire shot skyward, fed at the base by the oil pumping out of the pipeline. Black smoke roiled into the sky. An inky sludge seeped downward, starting a slow spread across the grass.

The sniper stepped out of the trees, on Miguel's right. Miguel clocked him with his peripheral vision only. His body felt like a thousand fists had hammered into him, making the simple act of turning his head seem too difficult a maneuver. It was only after the sniper snapped his rifle into firing position and Miguel felt the adrenaline dump into his system that he was able to move. He lurched upward. He saw the sniper's muzzle flash. Felt the bullet thud into him. It knocked him sideways, but he did a funny two-step with his feet, which allowed him to stay upright for a brief moment. He didn't feel any real pain. A detached side of his mind registered the lack of pain in an almost clinical way. He dropped to his knees and hung there, unable to stand, but unwilling to fall to the ground. The sniper took a step forward, farther into the field. Miguel heard a shot from behind him, and he watched the sniper's chest explode in a red flume. He wanted to congratulate Sumner on the shot, but now the pain was upon him. It was a violent, terrible, clawing agony that snatched his breath away.

Boris ran up to him and started licking his face. Miguel felt someone grab him from behind. He started to struggle, but stopped when he heard Sumner speak.

"Get up, Miguel, the beach is on that far side of the hill. You said you wanted to get to the beach, didn't you?" His voice held a cajoling note. Miguel tried to laugh, but pain shot through his side as he took a breath.

"The wound must be bad, Sumner, because that's the longest sentence I've ever heard you say."

Sumner's grin was strained. "I'll look at it when we get to that boat."

Miguel let Sumner help him up. Boris danced in front of them, running forward, tail up like a flag, and then circling back to run alongside. Miguel leaned on Sumner and they limped down the beach. A cabin cruiser floated in the water, anchored twenty feet out into the water.

"That thing isn't a boat, it's a small yacht." Miguel could barely get the words out.

"Looks like we're about to steal a cartel leader's pleasure ride," Sumner said.

Miguel wanted to respond but found that he couldn't. Stars danced before his eyes and his side hurt like a bitch. They reached the beach and Sumner continued forward, plunging knee-deep into the water and dragging Miguel with him.

"Canvass it first," Miguel said. His voice was so weak that it came out like a whisper.

"No time," Sumner said.

"You've got that right," a man's voice said behind them. Sumner turned to look into the face of the man at the airstrip with the two bodyguards.

BANNER TOUCHED HIS HELICOPTER DOWN TO RE-
fuel at an airstrip, where the signing of paperwork ensued.
While he stood at the dirty counter in the tiny airstrip, his
phone rang with the ring tone he reserved for Stromeyer.

"Tell me some good news," he said without preamble.

"Everyone's pounding down my door to speak to you, and
none of them believe that I can't reach you."

Banner smiled at the phone. "Your reputation for knowing everything precedes you. Now you're reaping the re-
sults, eh?"   .

He heard Stromeyer's snort from five thousand miles away
and down the phone line. "Margate is losing it. Word just
came that the pipeline was blown and two U.S. soldiers were
captured seconds later. The implication is that they deliberately blew the pipeline in retaliation for the hostage situation
and order to evacuate."

"What soldiers?" Banner shifted the phone to his left
hand to allow him to sign yet another piece of paper that a
hangar employee shoved under his nose. "None of ours is
anywhere near it, and I thought Margate gave the order to
extract the rest."

"Miguel is one and Sumner is the other."

Banner stopped writing. "Who captured them?"

"A high-ranking member of the FFOC."

Banner slammed out of the small office. The sun hit him full force. He shoved on a pair of wraparound sunglasses. Almost smiled at the instant relief they gave him.

"Where are they being held?" He strode quickly toward his helicopter.

"Don't know. I think at the pipeline. But word is that Miguel is injured."

"Get me the coordinates for the pipeline. I need to know where to find them."

"I'll send them in an attachment to your phone. I'm also going to route Margate to you."

"Can't you hold him off a little longer? I don't feel like dealing with the man."

"Honestly, I'm afraid if he doesn't speak to you soon, he'll give an order that will just make everything harder."

Banner couldn't argue with her logic. "Fine. Send him through."

Within seconds, Banner heard the beeping sound that indicated another call was coming through.

"What did you do, have him on hold?"

"You bet," Stromeyer said in a sweet voice. "Banner?" Now she sounded serious.

"Yes?"

"I still don't trust him completely."

"I know. I'll tread carefully."

Banner heard her click off the line before he could respond.

"Banner, explain to me how two of your soldiers got near the pipeline hours after the last soldiers had already been evacuated." Margate's anger burned through the line. Banner swung into his helicopter before answering.

"When did Major Gonzalez become mine?" he asked.

"The moment he disobeyed a direct order to evacuate. I'm arranging the paperwork to have him arrested the moment he steps back into the States."

Banner took a deep breath to avoid snapping at Margate. The man pissed him off to no end, but he needed to keep his cool if he was to save Miguel's career. "Major Gonzalez operated under a joint order of the DOD and my organization. I have not received the paperwork to withdraw my people, and so he did not leave."

There was a short silence on the line. "What people? I understood that the only soldiers in the area were regular military special forces," Margate said.

"General Corvan signed a memo naming my organization as part of the rescue mission. He had to in order for me to be present at the initial meeting." What Banner said was a technicality only, but he was more than willing to stand behind it to protect Miguel's decision to overstay his welcome. Now it sounded like Miguel and Sumner were being set up to take the fall for a bombing.

"If he's under your umbrella, you'd better be prepared to answer to the Colombian government regarding this bombing. I don't expect them to offer any leniency." Margate was already working an angle, Banner could tell. But he didn't care. He'd figure out the details later. Now he needed to get to the pipeline and pull Sumner and Miguel out of whatever nightmare they'd encountered.

"Margate, I doubt they're responsible for the bombing," Banner said. "What possible motive could they have?"

"The oldest one in the book, Banner. Money. Colombian government says their pockets were loaded with cash and an entire briefcase of the stuff was nearby."

Banner stopped fiddling with the helicopter while he absorbed this information. He thought about Gladys's claim that American businessmen were involved in arms trafficking. He was tempted to tell Margate, but reason prevailed. Time enough to figure out what was going on after he'd located everyone he needed to find.

"I'm sure there's a good explanation, Margate."

"Glad you're so convinced."

"Where did the Colombian government get their information about the cash?"

Margate coughed over the line. "The FFOC. They're demanding two million in ransom and safe passage back to their enclave in the south."

Banner couldn't believe his ears. "Wait a minute! This accusation comes from the FFOC and you and the Colombian government believe them? Have you lost your mind? Why would you believe anything a bunch of paramilitary killers tell you?"

"I am inclined to believe them because this Gonzalez seems to have gone off half-cocked. He should have evacuated with the rest. When he disobeyed a direct order, it tends to make me wonder why."

"Your last extraction helicopter was full, so he never had a chance to evacuate. Plus, he's helping Sumner find Emma Caldridge."

"I hope you're right, Banner. If not, then I intend to hang the guy high. The passengers are freed, the military evacuated, and the mission accomplished. As far as I'm concerned, this hijacking has been brought to a successful conclusion. The last thing I need is a couple of rogue soldiers wreaking havoc on our political allies. They're on their own."

"And Ms. Caldridge? She's still stuck out there."

"She's a casualty of the situation. I think you'll agree that losing only one of the survivors is a very acceptable outcome."

Banner had to clamp his teeth together to stop himself from raining insults on Margate. "I don't agree at all. I intend to do my best to bring all three of these people back to the States alive."

"You are free to try, Banner, but we won't pay Darkview's expenses from this moment forward, and if you are captured, expect us to deny that you even exist."

"I'm a contracted security force, Margate. When was the last time you guys acknowledged our existence under any circumstances?" Banner shut off the phone before he felt compelled to tell Margate what he really thought of him.

50

EMMA MOVED TOWARD THE WAITING TRUCKS. THREE
of the four soldiers milled around near the first truck, leaving the one truck closest to the trees shrouded in shadows.
She couldn't see the fourth soldier.

She checked on Rodrigo. He stood in the village center, as
if waiting. I wonder where Mathilde is, Emma thought. Just
then Mathilde stepped into the village. It was as if Emma's
thoughts had conjured her.

Emma crept closer to the truck. She heard a footfall behind
her. She spun around to see the fourth soldier pointing a rifle
at her chest. It was the boy she'd helped escape from the
truck at the airstrip almost a lifetime ago. His eyes widened
as he recognized her. They stood that way, facing each other,
for what felt like an eternity. Emma saw a bead of sweat run
down the boy's face. It dripped into the bandanna he wore
around his neck. His lips were parted and he breathed rapidly in and out, as if he'd just completed a run. Emma felt as
if she could see his thoughts racing through his head.

Rodrigo's voice as he spoke to Mathilde echoed through
the clearing.

The boy started. He jerked his head toward the truck in

the trees. In two short strides he was at its side. He waved
at her impatiently. Emma jogged over. Put her foot on the
bumper. The boy reached out and supported her arm to help
her swing her leg into the truck bed. It was a strangely chiv-
alrous gesture under the circumstances, but it told Emma
more about the boy's character than any words could have.
She insinuated herself between the boxes of rifles, moving
them gently aside. They were stacked three high. When she
was able to lie down, she lowered herself onto her back. She
stared up at the sky. The boy hovered over her, worry in
his dark eyes. He moved the boxes on top closer together,
until a shadow fell over Emma. She could see the boy's face
through the remaining shaft of light shining between the
boxes. The boy caught her eye. He gave a curt nod. She felt
the truck bounce as he jumped off.

The tangy smell of metal was all around. The flatbed's
steel bottom felt cold against the backs of her arms. She
would have given anything at that moment to be able to see
what Rodrigo and the others were doing, but she dared not
lift her head. Her hands were down by her legs, palms flat
against them, straight. She touched the cargo pocket of her
pants. Felt the lumpy stones of the rosary. She slid her fingers in the pocket. Wrapped them around the rosary, tight.
She thought of Gladys. She pressed the stones into her palm,
took a deep breath, and waited.

After what seemed like forever, but must have only been
minutes, she heard a man walking next to the truck. His feet
crunched on the stone ground. She felt the truck cant to one
side as someone stepped onto the wheel well. A shadow fell
across her face. She looked up and locked eyes with Rodrigo.

"So, lady, there you are."

He shoved the boxes aside, grabbed her arm, and hauled
her upright. He yelled to Mathilde as he dragged Emma

across the back of the truck to one of the huts. He dumped her on the ground. Mathilde sauntered up and kicked dirt at Emma. The bits of earth landed in Emma's eyes.

Rodrigo gave an order. One soldier stepped forward, uncoiling a rope in his hand as he did. In seconds he had Emma's hands and feet tied. Rodrigo motioned the soldiers away. They all nodded and shuffled to their vehicles. The young boy soldier moved the slowest. He cast Emma a look full of sadness and apology as he walked by. The soldiers climbed into their vehicles and drove out of the village. Only a few of Rodrigo's guerrillas remained. They hovered forty feet away, on the edge of the jungle. Rodrigo motioned Mathilde into the hut.

Emma wasn't alone for long. Mathilde reappeared. She strolled to Emma.

"Rodrigo called the Americans. They come. We will be paid a lot of money for you, but why they think you are worth it, I don't know." She yanked Emma's backpack off her back.

"You won't need this anymore," she said. She tore into Emma's backpack and rummaged through the contents, throwing the various items in the dirt. Emma watched her empty the small side pocket. She pulled out the remaining tube of Engine Red. Swiveled it open.

"Nice color," she said.

"It's mine. Don't use it."

Mathilde analyzed the lipstick. "It's new. I shall try it."

"No," Emma said.

Mathilde raised an eyebrow. "You don't tell me what to do." She went back into the hut. After a few moments, she returned. In her hand was a small round mirror. She smirked at Emma and brought the Engine Red to her lips. Emma lurched to her feet. The ropes around her ankles hobbled her, and she fell to her knees.

"Don't! It's poison. It will kill you." Emma infused the warning with all the intensity she could.

Mathilde flipped her hair. "I will look beautiful while I watch you die."

"I'm telling you, it's poison. Do not touch it." Emma pleaded with her.

Mathilde ignored her. She prepared to apply the lipstick.

"Mathilde, don't!" Emma was frantic. "You'll kill us all."

"Liar," Mathilde said. "I saw Maria in the forest. She wears it. You gave it to her." She leaned forward. "We will deal with her later." Her gaze returned to the mirror, and she rubbed the stick across her lips, leaned back to look at her image. The color complemented her olive skin and dark hair. She threw Emma a superior look.

Within seconds, she started to sway. The blood left her face in a rush, rendering her skin pasty white. She started to cough. She clawed at her neck and made gagging sounds. Panic rose in her eyes. She staggered to the hut's door, holding her throat, just as Rodrigo stepped out. She dropped to the ground, writhing. Rodrigo asked her a question in Spanish, but all she did was show him the lipstick still clutched in her hand before she pointed to Emma.

Rodrigo rounded on Emma. "What have you done?"

Emma wanted to cry. She shook her head. "I told her not to touch the lipstick. It's poison."

Mathilde began foaming at the mouth. Rodrigo stepped back in revulsion. He stormed over to Emma, his machete drawn. He grabbed her by the hair. Placed the machete at her throat.

"Poison. Is it true?"

Emma nodded. "It's true. It's a weapons-grade nervous system disrupter."

"Who made it?"

Emma sighed. "I did."

"Will she live?" Rodrigo jutted his chin at Mathilde's prone body.

Emma sighed again. "No."

"Is there a cure?"

"I can make a liquid that will halt the poison. An antidote. But it would be for us. She is lost."

"What do you mean, for us?"

"The molecules release into the air, like a miasma. It works as a nervous system disrupter and paralytic."

Rodrigo pressed the machete closer. "I don't understand these English words!"

"Think of rabies—you know the word *rabies*?"

Rodrigo nodded.

"The lipstick kills on contact, but it also kills through secondhand exposure. When the stick is rubbed on warm skin the molecules release into the air like a cloud, affecting anyone in a ten-foot radius. For those of us subject to secondhand contact, death is delayed. We have twelve hours."

Rodrigo started breathing faster. "Make the cure."

"I need to get to the Lost City. The only plant that will reverse the effects grows there. I destroyed all the others in my lab, because the same plant can create the weapon."

"I don't believe you."

Emma waved her bound hands at Mathilde. "What's not to believe?"

"I mean about us. We have not touched the poison."

"I told you, it's in the air. You just can't see it. And don't tell me that you don't believe. You were there when the Americans came looking through the hostages. You wanted to know why it was so important that they find me? Well, now you do. They're arms traders. They're looking for the poison to sell on the black market." Emma watched comprehension dawn in Rodrigo's eyes. He thought a moment.

"The Lost City is a six-hour walk from here. We cannot get there and back in twelve hours."

"We only have to get there, not back. I'll make the antidote once we arrive."

"I tell you, we can't go there. The path runs through Cartone cartel territory." Rodrigo shrieked the words into Emma's ear.

Mathilde started convulsing. Rodrigo shot a look at her, jerking on the ground. He was sweating. Emma could smell his fear. She sought a way to calm him down, to reassure him before he exploded.

"You're wrong," she said in a patient voice. "We *can* go there. We'll pay the protection money. That's what the tourists do. That's what I did when I went there last year."

"I told you, I can't go there. It's Cartone cartel territory. They'll kill me on sight."

Now Emma understood. "But I can go there. I *have* gone there."

"The cure. Now." Rodrigo pushed the machete again. Emma felt a sting. A line of warm blood ran down her neck.

"What you are demanding is impossible. I told you, I need to go to the Lost City. You can stay here. Send one of your men with me. They weren't close enough to be affected. Have one walk with me and another one waiting on the path. The fresh man can run the antidote back to you in time. Or come with me. Perhaps the Cartone foot soldiers will not see you."

"The soldiers line the path to the Lost City. You will not see them, but they will see you, and for sure will know me," Rodrigo said.

"Then you must send someone with me to run the antidote back. Decide now, Rodrigo. You need to release me, quickly."

Rodrigo stayed still, breathing hard. After a moment, he lowered the machete, cut through the ropes binding Emma's arms, and stepped back.

"So. Go. But do not double-cross me. You have eight hours. I'll find your friend, and each hour you are late, he will lose a piece. First his left arm, then his right." Emma didn't doubt that Rodrigo would track Sumner.

"First you put down your weapons, order your men to do the same, and lay face-first on the ground."

"No!" The cords stood out on Rodrigo's neck. Mathilde made a groaning sound. Her eyes rolled back into her head as her throat convulsed.

Emma pointed at Mathilde. "You'll look like her in twelve hours, Rodrigo. Put down your weapons. If you don't, you're a dead man, because I refuse to go."

"You will die, too, if you don't make it."

"If you don't put down your weapons, then I know you will track my friend the minute I leave here. Either you put down your weapons or I don't go. It's that simple. But decide quickly, Rodrigo. We're wasting time."

The remaining guerrillas gathered around Mathilde, wide-eyed and silent. Rodrigo gave a sharp order.

The men looked at one another, confused. Emma assumed that their confusion stemmed from the nature of the order. Rodrigo bellowed the same order. This time the men jumped to obey. Their guns rattled as they were dropped, one on top of another, in a pile. They unbuckled their ammunition belts and removed the weapons strapped to their ankles. They lowered themselves to the ground, face-first.

Emma turned to Rodrigo. "Now you."

His face was red, his lips pressed tight. He tossed his machete at her feet, so close that she had to jump back to avoid being cut. He lowered himself to the ground.

Emma recovered Rodrigo's machete. She went to the pile

of weapons. Unloaded each one and took the three ammunition belts.

Emma retrieved her backpack next to the fallen Mathilde. The woman no longer convulsed. She was dead.

Emma pried the lipstick tube out of her clenched hand. She tied up each man. Rodrigo was last. He glared his hate at her. Emma didn't flinch. As she tied him, she bent closer. Her face was only inches from his.

"The next time you mess with me, you die. You've been in over your head this entire time, Rodrigo, deeper than your small brain can comprehend." She stood. Waved at the man they called Manzillo.

"Let's go. We don't have much time."

"Manzillo!" Rodrigo shouted to the farmer, who stepped forward. He spoke in Spanish so the American lady wouldn't understand him. "Show her the way to the Lost City. Get back here as fast as you can. After she gives you the cure—kill her."

51

THE PATH TO THE LOST CITY WAS STEEP AND
rocky, but at least it was clear. Emma didn't need a machete
to navigate it. She ran in long strides, working her way up
the mountain. She settled into a race pace, but she knew she
wouldn't sustain it for twelve hours. She was too hungry,
thirsty, and tired. Manzillo ran next to her, huffing and puff-
ing. In the distance came the baying of hounds. Louisiana
State was back with his bloodhounds. She remembered Mathilde saying that Rodrigo had called the Americans. They
must have discovered him bound and tied and were mount-
ing a search for her.

After an hour of running, she came to a fork in the path.
Manzillo stopped.

"Which one goes to the Lost City?" Emma said.

Manzillo pointed to the left. "There. But I no longer come
with you."

"What about Rodrigo? Who will take him the antidote?"

Manzillo shifted his gun higher on his shoulder. "I don't
care. He is the devil. I will not help him live only to watch
him kill again. If you want his life on your shoulders, then
you take him the cure. But know this, lady, if you save him,

then many more people will die. This is the way it is with Rodrigo. You will have these other people's death on you."

"Kill one to save many?" Emma said.

Manzillo nodded. He pointed to the path. "Go that way. There are no more forks." He turned and trudged away.

Emma took a swig of the liter bottle in her backpack and resumed running. As she ran, she racked her brain to try to remember how many water crossings remained between her and the Lost City. When she'd made the hike the year before, she had started from a different location. Now she estimated that she was more than halfway there, much closer than the six hours Rodrigo had estimated. During the initial trek she thought she navigated seven or eight water crossings. At this height she might have two left; one would be waist-deep. Perhaps a water crossing would dilute her scent enough to make the dogs unable to track her, but she doubted it. Besides, it wouldn't take much for her trackers to figure out that she was using an existing trail. They had to realize she was headed to the city. If they knew enough to hunt her, then they knew why she was in Colombia.

The rains came, turning the track to mud. She sank ankle-deep, pulling each foot out with a loud sucking sound. The run became a slog at a sloth's pace. The mud forced her to exert more energy than straight running, because of the strength needed to free each foot from the mire. The rain created its usual drumbeat noise, canceling out the howling dogs. This drove Emma's adrenaline higher. She hated not knowing how far they were behind her. The rains subsided. Emma strained her ears to listen for the howls. They were there, in the distance. Softer. The rains must have slowed them down, too.

Emma turned a corner and came upon an indigenous village. Round huts with conical, pointed thatch roofs sat in a semicircle. Several women cooked over an open fire while two children played in the dirt near them. All stopped and stared at Emma. One woman gave a sharp command to a child of about ten. He took off, running. He entered a hut on the far side of the village.

Within seconds, Emma was surrounded by men and women. She remembered the village from her trek the year before. She was close now. Close to the place that these people held sacred.

A wizened man stepped out of the farthest hut. Long white hair hung down his back. He held a large staff as a walking stick. He wore the trousers of the same burlap material that all the villagers wore, with a rope belt. The villagers parted to allow the man to walk toward Emma. When he reached her, he stared at her, saying nothing. His dark eyes held concern and the wizened look of a man with the knowledge that comes only from many years of living.

"I'm in trouble. I need your help." She put her hand in her pocket. Fingered the rosary there. She pulled it out and started worrying the beads between her fingers while she watched the old man. He said nothing. Far off in the distance came the baying of the hounds. Emma worried the beads faster.

"They want the poison I can make from the special plant I found in the Lost City. The one with the black berries. I made it by accident and refused to give it to them. Now they are hunting me."

The man said nothing.

"I must reach the Lost City. But I don't know if I can make it. I haven't eaten and my legs are weak."

The old man gave an order. A younger man, dressed in the burlap pants of the indigenous but sporting expensive black Wellington boots, stepped forward. From a pocket he dug out a woven pouch. He handed it to the old man. The old man upended it. Several coca leaves fell into his palm. He waved at another young man, who stepped forward with a gourd. The young man opened the top of the gourd and used a stick to pour powder onto the leaves. The old man rolled the leaves between his palms. He held the resulting roll out to her.

For the indigenous people, coca was sacred. It figured in their religious rituals as well as their daily lives. They also used it to maintain energy. While chewing coca, they were able to work long hours without stopping or eating.

Emma knew that the man believed he was offering her a gift of great value, greater than food. She didn't want to insult him by refusing, but she was wary of going near it. During her trip the year before, she'd been careful to avoid any contact with it.

Emma knew exactly how it worked its magic. How it changed exhaustion to exhilaration, suppressed appetite, and helped control altitude sickness. What areas of the brain it affected to alter its chemistry. How its effects then dissipated, leaving the person who used it feeling bereft, depressed, and drained. How those people who were unlucky enough to get addicted started on an endless cycle of lesser and lesser highs, with deeper and deeper lows, until they felt trapped in a soul-depleting hell. Like the man who'd driven his car into Patrick's. The autopsy revealed that the man had both alcohol and cocaine in his system. He'd been drinking the alcohol to "unwind" after a long night fueled by coke.

As a chemist, Emma had access to pure cocaine, as well as any other controlled substance she might have needed for her research. This access made her cautious. She had never tried cocaine.

She knew what the man held in his hand was fresh and

unprocessed. This was coca in its pure form. If she chewed the leaves, it would release its energy-elevating power for hours, much longer than any food she could eat.

The old man held it out to her as an offering. Emma stood there, her breath heaving. She needed the immediate boost it would give her. She wasn't sure how it would interact with the poison that she knew was filling her system, but she assumed the chemical reaction wouldn't be good. It would likely accelerate the poison's effects as it juiced her bodily functions. She didn't know how much more quickly it would allow the poison to kill her, but she knew she wouldn't get to the Lost City without it. And if she didn't get to the Lost City in time, she was dead anyway.

"What do I do?"

The young man took another set of leaves from the pouch, added the alkali, and put the leaves in his mouth. He chewed, opening his mouth wide and closing it, exaggerating the motion to show her what he was doing.

She reached out, put the leaves in her mouth, and chewed. The coca had a pleasant, pungent taste. Her mouth became numb in seconds. She swallowed and her saliva tasted bitter. She coughed, choking on the acrid liquid. Emma felt the drug's effects almost immediately. She could feel her body start a low hum. She nodded to the old man.

"Thank you," she said.

The old man stepped forward. He reached out and touched Emma's hand holding the rosary. His hand felt rough but warm as it closed over hers. She stopped her fingers' compulsive movements on the beads. He held her hand in his palm, stroked her fingers open, and removed the rosary. He placed it over her head like a necklace. When he was finished, he stepped back, nodded once, and waved her toward the trail.

She took the hint and started running once more.

Emma reached the Lost City late in the afternoon. Clouds hovered over the site. A heavy mist blanketed the area. She heard thunder in the distance.

The entrance to the city began with twelve hundred stone steps. To the left, another flat stone had a crude map etched into it. Emma started her climb, moving as fast as she dared on the slippery stairway.

Her heart raced. Blood coursed through her veins at an alarming rate. She could hear it pulsing in her ears. She felt short-winded. She knew it wasn't from the run, despite its grueling nature. She'd run much farther and faster before under worse conditions. It was the cocaine combining with natural adrenaline produced by the run that was overloading her system. Her nose started to bleed. Large dollops of blood fell onto the stones. She used the bottom of her shirt to wipe it away. She was halfway up the steps when the poison started to kick in.

It began with small convulsive movements in her leg muscles. Her right thigh began to twitch. Just a little at first. Within minutes, the entire length of her leg began to spasm. She struggled to control the leg in order to place it in front of her. She lost her footing on the slick stone. She tumbled four steps down. She rose again, fighting her convulsing leg in order to move forward.

She no longer heard the hounds howling behind her. But within seconds of having that thought came the beating sound of a helicopter's rotors. She didn't have to speculate as to its destination. She knew it was after her.

She made it to the top of the stairs and collapsed on the plateau. The Lost City lay before her. It consisted of several flat stones raised from the ground in staggered progression, each one covered in green moss. They looked like individual stages. Mist shrouded the area, clinging to the trees and drifting through the open spaces. She needed to find the leaves growing around the third platform.

She limped across the flat plateau. Her leg continued to spasm, flailing out of her control. She hopped on the remaining leg to the platform and the prize.

The plant was there. Several grew at the platform's base. It looked like a common weed, with the exception of the small black berries sprouting from the top, like flowers. She fell to her knees. Her bad leg refused to bend, so she sat down, leaving it straight. Her leg bounced on the dirt as she sat there. Like it had a mind of its own. Emma did her best to ignore it.

She ripped two plants out of the ground, shook off the dirt from the roots, and shoved the plants into the tin bowl from her backpack. She hobbled over to the trees to find firewood. Her right arm started shivering, her biceps twitching. She used her left hand to collect the wood. The helicopter sounds grew louder, but whether they were close or still far, Emma couldn't tell.

By the time she'd collected enough wood to build a fire, her entire right side was convulsing. Hopping on the left leg was no longer an option. She started to crawl back to her backpack and her pot, dragging her twitching leg in the dirt. Thunder boomed above her, the noise echoing through the trees. She fought down the panic that accompanied the sound. She needed to start a fire and make the antidote before the rains came and doused everything.

She piled wood in a small pyramid. It was damp, but so old and sun-dried that Emma didn't think burning it would be a problem. She pulled dry grass from the base of the platform and tucked it around the wood. She fumbled in her backpack to find her silver lighter. She flicked the top open, but had a hard time focusing on the roller piece long enough to light it. After a couple of tries she managed to start a flame. Emma sat there twitching, watching the fire ignite. Shooting pains started in her right leg. Her right arm jerked up and down, and now her left thigh started to spasm. Only her left arm remained calm. She used it to pull her liter bottle of water from the pack, filled the pot with water, placed it on the fire, and sat down to wait.

By the time the water was near boiling, Emma's entire body was jerking. She was sure she looked like a victim of St. Vitus' dance. She focused on removing the pot from the fire to allow the liquid to cool. In her disintegrating state, this simple act became so difficult as to be impossible. She clenched her jaw to stop her teeth from chattering. After taking long, deep breaths, she managed to knock the pot off the fire without spilling its precious contents.

The thunder crashed above her now, interspersed with flashes of lightning. Fat raindrops began to fall. Through the noise she heard the helicopter approaching. Emma decided to drink the liquid hot. Once the muscles in her throat began to spasm, she wouldn't be able to swallow. She put the scalding rim to her lips and drank. It burned all the way down. She drank half the pot. It took all her strength to hold it steady. When she was done she lowered it to the ground like it was fine china. She lay down by the still-burning fire while the rain fell and the thunder crashed.

The helicopter heaved into view, flying high above her head. A searchlight on the front raked over the Lost City. Emma curled as close to the platform as she could.

The helicopter began its descent. Although she still shook from the poison, Emma forced herself to rise. She didn't have much time to accomplish what she'd come to Colombia to do. She shoved a hand in her backpack to remove the lipstick Mathilde had used. She swiveled it open and dropped it into the pot of antidote, neutralizing it.

Next she began to pull up the plants, throwing each into the fire. As far as she knew, these were the only plants like this in existence. Once they were gone, the ingredients for the formula would be extinct. No one would ever be able to make the weapon she had again. She pulled the last plant from the ground and threw it into the fire when the helicopter began settling onto a cleared space about two hundred yards from her.

52

EMMA WATCHED THE HELICOPTER TOUCH DOWN.
Her muscles still twitched, but the left thigh was already
still. By no means could she walk, but she wasn't getting any
worse, either. Three men stepped out of the copter. Smoking
Man, his bodyguard, and Gerald White, Emma's boss.

Emma felt as though someone had kicked her. All the
pieces began to fall into place. White was the one she'd told
when she'd noticed the plant's unusual qualities, White was
the one she'd gone to when the strange man claiming to be
from the Department of Defense came to demand the formula, and White was the one she'd consulted when she was
deciding to fly back to Bogotá.

He ran to Emma. The still-beating helicopter rotors and
crashing thunder drowned out any sound of his approach.
When he reached her, he picked up a stick and used it to fish
the still-burning plants from the fire. He managed to rescue
a few scorched leaves and stems. When he was finished, he
turned on her.

"Are you insane? Killing the plants! Do you have any idea
what these are worth?" He looked at the fire. "You burned
them all, didn't you?"

Emma just stared at the man she'd grown to respect. "You told Mondrian about the poison."

"Of course," he yelled at her. "How the hell else do you think they learned of it? You were too stupid to see the value in what you'd discovered. Do you have any idea what it's cost me to track you down?" White picked up the tin pot and fished out the lipstick. He shoved it under her nose. "Does it still work?"

Emma shook her head. He kicked her in the thigh before tossing the lipstick into the fire. He grabbed the pot, turned it over, pouring the liquid onto the ground. He flung the pot away.

"That was the antidote," Emma said.

"Do you think I care?" White's face turned a dark red as he raged at her. "Do you know how much a weapon like this will garner on the arms market? Hundreds of millions. And the uses! A female terrorist could be sent into Parliament or Congress, and with one application of lipstick wipe out an entire room. No bombs to carry. No chance to be caught at security."

"She'd die on contact."

"And the autopsy would show nothing."

"Did you bring the plane down just to get to me?"

White snorted. "Don't flatter yourself. I could have gotten to you every time you walked into the lab." White leaned in close to her face. "I already have a buyer for this weapon. They were working up the hijacking for their own purposes. When you said you were going to Bogotá, we decided to kill two birds with one stone. It was an opportunity too good to pass up." White blew on one of the still-smoldering plants.

"My buyers want some modifications. They want to punch up the residual effect, have the molecules travel much farther than ten feet, and to delay the direct effect on the user to give her time to slip away. I told them if anyone could do it, you could."

Emma's right arm stopped twitching. Her leg continued to bounce.

"It's over now. I've burned the plants," she said.

White laughed like a hyena. "You can't possibly think that. You, of all people."

Emma said nothing.

He leaned in to her. "I guess you'll just have to make new ones."

Emma shook her head. "How in the world would I make new ones without the original?"

"With your artificial chromosome technology, of course."

Emma went cold. "With what? I don't have the original plant's chromosomes. The technology won't work without them."

White picked up some of the scorched plants. "With these."

White waved over Smoking Man's bodyguard. He turned back to her. "They don't have the ability to reproduce, that's true, but they'll suffice as chromosome donors. You'll just have to insert their chromosomes into a roomful of plants that *can* reproduce."

"I won't do it," Emma said.

White stared at her. "Oh, I think you will. I promised these buyers a weapon, and if I don't deliver, they'll kill me. We have your Mr. Sumner. Rodrigo's there. He's twitching like hell, but he'll live long enough to administer his unique form of torture. You're going to watch. When he's done, we'll start on you. Don't worry, we won't kill you, we'll just give you that added incentive to do what needs to be done." He turned to the bodyguard. "Put her on the helicopter."

The bodyguard hauled Emma to her feet, wrapped her arm around his neck, and dragged her to the copter. Her right leg still jerked out of control as it plowed through the mud. He hauled her into the copter, placing her in the back where the seats, if there ever were any, had been removed. He handcuffed her hands with plastic tie cuffs. White and Smoking Man took seats near the pilot. White buckled up, but Smoking Man didn't bother. He crossed his legs.

They rose into the air. The lightning sparked all around them, followed by crashing thunder. The rain came harder, pounding on the helicopter's windshield. Within minutes, it became a deluge. The rain hammered the sides of the copter while the wind buffeted the machine. They pitched and rolled through the night.

"Can we make it back?" White yelled to the pilot, who responded in Spanish.

"What'd he say?" White asked Smoking Man.

"The storm is bad. One hit from the lightning and down we fall." Smoking Man removed a cigarette from his shirt pocket. He flicked on a lighter. Emma saw his grin by the lighter's flame.

"You don't seem worried," White said.

Smoking Man just shrugged.

The rolling worsened. One flash of lightning lit the entire cabin. Emma thought she could hear the sizzling as it streaked by. The pilot swore in Spanish.

Smoking Man's bodyguard clutched his stomach, groaning. The lightning illuminated the interior of the helicopter like a strobe light. Emma could see White clutching the sides of his seat. His knuckles went white. Smoking Man smoked. The tip of his cigarette glowed brighter with each pull.

Emma used her legs to brace herself against the metal side of the helicopter. Her left leg had ceased its twitching some time ago. Each time the machine bucked, her back slammed into a steel support. She could feel bruised spots along every inch of her spine. She wished with all her might that she was back on her swollen, blistered feet and working her ruined shins. Those aches and pains were more welcome than this. She railed at God in her head: You spare me from the plane crash and Rodrigo and poison only to kill me now? Some benevolent being You are. If God heard her, the only response was another boom from the heavens.

Lightning struck the helicopter halfway through their descent. One minute they were lowering in a controlled fashion, and the next they were plummeting downward. The pilot yelled an oath. Emma lost her grip on the floor. She skittered sideways until she slammed into the back of Smoking Man's seat. The bodyguard muttered something that might have been a prayer, and White gave an incoherent yell. Only Smoking Man remained silent.

They landed with a bang, catapulting into the tree line. Emma heard the branches splintering as they plowed through them. The windshield cracked. The helicopter ground to a halt.

Emma lay against the sidewall, catching her breath. She watched the pilot shake his head. White slumped in his chair, breathing heavily. Smoking Man unfolded from his seat. He patted the pilot on the back. The rain poured down the sides of the helicopter, like a waterfall. Smoking Man leaned into White.

"You want to bring her now?"

"I want to get the hell out of this helicopter," White yelled over the noise of the rain. "We'll deal with her in the morning."

Smoking Man gave an order to the bodyguard, who looked pale as death. The bodyguard staggered toward Emma. He pulled her back to a sitting position against the sidewall before handcuffing her ankles together with another plastic tie cuff. He followed White, the pilot, and Smoking Man out into the downpour.

Emma sat in the dark, dank helicopter thinking of Sumner. She pictured Rodrigo torturing him in front of her. The thought was unbearable. She tried to think of options. She could sabotage the artificial chromosome procedure. Deliberately arrange it so it would fail. White was a scientist, true, but only she knew how to insert the chromosomes. The process was tricky and prone to failure, even when she'd done it. White wouldn't know she'd sabotaged the trials until the formula failed to work. At least she would have bought a little time to make an escape plan.

One thing Emma was sure of; she wouldn't make the weapon again. If she and Sumner died for her refusal, then so be it.

EMMA STARTED AWAKE HOURS LATER. THE LIGHT-
ning lit the interior of the helicopter, throwing eerie shadows. The thunder still boomed, but long after each flash.
The storm was losing its force. The rain pattered on the helicopter's side rather than buffeting it like before. She heard
irregular footfalls outside. She listened as someone's steps
crunched toward her, making a strange lurching sound. The
rhythm was step, drag, step. She felt a stab of fear.

The helicopter shook. Rodrigo hauled himself into the
cabin. He clutched a bottle of whiskey in his left hand and
his ever-present machete in his right. The lightning illuminated him. His right side twitched and jerked with a palsy,
his right leg bounced back and forth. He tried to raise the
bottle to his lips. His hand shook like an alcoholic with
withdrawal symptoms. He prevailed and managed to drink a
huge swallow. He began moving toward her, his lips twisted
in a snarl. The helicopter lit with a huge crash of lightning,
then plunged into darkness so deep that Emma couldn't see
Rodrigo. She struggled sideways, pushing herself with her
legs while she scooted along the wall. Her panic rose with
each second that she couldn't see him.

The lightning flashed again. Rodrigo was on his hands and knees now, only a few feet away from her. The machete flashed as he used the hand that held it to crawl forward. His entire body convulsed as the poison took over.

"You spilled the antidote. The gringo told me," he said. He spoke in a jerky fashion, as if he couldn't control his vocal cords. The helicopter went dark. Emma pushed harder with her legs. Her shoulder hit the end of the cabin. There was nowhere left to go.

The lightning sparked, illuminating the helicopter's interior like a strobe light. Rodrigo loomed over her, frothing at the mouth. He raised the machete, gasping as his throat convulsed. The helicopter went black. Emma screamed and scrabbled against the floor. She felt her foot hit Rodrigo. He fell on top of her, convulsed once, then stilled.

Emma pushed at his body with her bound hands. She was in a complete panic at just the thought of Rodrigo so close. She managed to move most of him off her. His body pinned her legs to the floor.

She sat that way for a long time. She tried to take deep breaths to slow her racing heart, but each time the helicopter interior lit up, all she saw was Rodrigo's face, contorted in a death mask. After what felt like forever, the rain stopped and the sky took on a transparent color. Birds started twittering in the trees. She felt the helicopter lurch sideways again. The boy soldier stepped in. He shot worried looks all around, his gaze coming to rest on Rodrigo's body lying across her legs.

His eyes widened. He pulled Rodrigo's body the rest of the way off her. He slid his own machete out of a beaded sheath and started sawing at the plastic cuffs around her ankles. When he was finished, he indicated she should turn around to allow him to work on the handcuffs. He had those cut in seconds. He operated in complete silence.

Emma heard a man call a name, somewhere in the distance. The boy's head shot up. He nodded once to her before leaping out the side door. She was free. Emma didn't hesitate. She crawled out of the helicopter, which was embedded in the trees. The ground was still wet from the downpour, but the heat was already rising, even though the sun was a good hour away.

She slunk around the copter's tail. To her right was a dirt road that sloped gently down into the water, forming a boat landing. A long sleek yacht floated in the water not fifty feet from the landing. It bobbed gently in the swells. Its windows were bright spots in the gloom. A deck light shone on the water.

The Daihatsu pickup trucks were lined up at the edge of the landing. They still carried their cargo. Emma could see the boxes labeled BANANAS arranged in neat rows in the pickup's bed.

She craned her neck the other way. The waning moon broke through the clouds, bathing the area in light. The road opened onto a grassy field that sloped upward and was lined on one side by trees, the other side by the ugly, metallic pipeline. The pipeline sat on four-foot-high tripods, running like a large snake along the trees. In the distance, Emma saw the tip of a column of flame. The pipeline burned steadily.

She returned her attention to the yacht. They were going to off-load the guns onto it for transport. She was certain. And she was just as certain that not every weapon would make it to the boat. She needed one if she was going to survive.

Time to move, she thought.

Emma jogged to the pickups, keeping low, watching for the soldiers to return. When she got to the first pickup, she reached into an open box and pulled out one of the rifles. It was close to the same design as the AK-47, but even Emma, with her lack of experience with weapons, could see that it was a technological leap forward. It was sleek and felt powerful in a way the AK-47 wasn't. The high-tech scope on the top looked like the weapon had been designed for a marksman or a sniper. Someone who would hide in cover and had the expertise to shoot the enemy at a distance and with skill. Someone like Sumner. No one like Rodrigo and his band of losers. She thought of the damage that even one shooter with such a weapon could do from a hidden position in a high-rise building. She fiddled with the rifle a moment, checking to see if it was loaded. It wasn't. Emma wanted to spit, she was so disappointed. She climbed into the truck to rummage through the boxes. The open box contained some spare ammunition. She grabbed it, jumped off the truck, and retreated a hundred feet into the trees. She squatted down next to one to analyze her new weapon.

Despite its advanced design, or perhaps because of it, the gun was easy to load. There was no denying that it was a step up from her other weapon. She peered through the scope. It gave her an excellent view of any target, but adjusting to it felt awkward. Up to this point she'd shot at someone only in the heat of the moment, and failed miserably when she'd had the time to think. This gun required the calm of a professional.

She jogged up the hill, toward the leaping flame, away from the boat landing. She wanted to get her bearings, to see what she was up against. She ran through the soft darkness. Her feet made very little sound. Her shin flared with each step, but she ignored it. She was just thankful that it didn't spasm anymore. She'd felt much worse at the end of a hundred-mile run. She knew she could handle the pain. She reached the point where the pipeline had been exploded open. Its twisted metal dripped oil into a large oil drum that was filling rapidly. Her feet slipped in the oily grass.

Light shone from a small hut that sat one hundred yards

away. Emma could hear the soft murmur of voices. She inched along in the darkness toward the hut. There were no windows, but the door hung open. A triangle of light poured out from it. Emma stepped into position opposite the door. She used the scope to see into the hut. She gasped.

Sumner and a soldier sat on the floor against the far wall. Blood covered the soldier's shirt, and he slumped sideways onto Sumner's shoulder. The soldier's face was contorted in pain. He kept his eyes closed.

Sumner looked unhurt, but grim. His eyes were red-rimmed and his beard more pronounced. He leaned against the leg of a desk or table while he supported the soldier and stared at something, or someone, just out of Emma's vision. Both men had their hands tied and resting on their laps.

Smoking Man came into view. He yelled something in Spanish at Sumner, who answered in one short sentence.

So, one at least to eliminate, Emma thought. But where Smoking Man was, so were his bodyguards. Two more somewhere very close by, perhaps in the hut itself, and one was an excellent shot. She remembered that from the way he'd targeted the capybara at the airstrip.

A black Range Rover came barreling up. White slammed out of it and headed to the hut. One of Smoking Man's bodyguards followed at a slower pace. Emma lowered her weapon. The odds had just changed for the worse. It was eight against two: Smoking Man, two bodyguards, four soldiers, and White. This impressive array of might against Emma, Sumner, and an injured soldier who looked as though shooting a gun was well beyond his capabilities just then.

Ridiculous odds, Emma thought. There was no way they'd survive in a shoot-out. She'd have to come up with something else.

She needed to find the four soldiers in order to determine

their location. She jogged back along the stinking pipeline toward the beach, keeping low and in the shadows. When she reached the Daihatsu trucks, what she saw made her spirits plunge. The soldiers were busy stacking the boxes of rifles onto a small dinghy floating at the edge of the boat landing. When the dinghy was full, three of the soldiers hopped in and fired up the engine. They motored out to the cruiser, where Emma could just make out the features of the boy soldier. He stood on the deck, waiting.

One truck was empty, and the second nearly empty. Emma ran toward the last truck and clambered onto it. She needed at least two more rifles. She clawed at one of the remaining boxes. The lid came loose with a tearing noise that nearly stopped her heart. She crouched next to the pickup's side-wall. The only sound that greeted her was the soft lapping of the waves against the shore. She hauled the rifles over her shoulder before running her hand around the box's bottom to search for ammunition. She found two belts, a carton of cartridges, and a small rectangular box that contained long sticks of dynamite. She gathered it all up and shot off the truck just as she heard the dinghy's engine fire up again.

Emma dragged her own weapon by its strap as she moved farther into cover. She dumped it onto the ground while she focused her attention on loading the new rifles. When she was finished she grabbed all of them and returned to her position outside the hut's entrance. Soon one of Smoking Man's bodyguards stepped into view. He held an assault weapon at his side while he took a long drag off a cigarette, blew the smoke out, and scanned around the hut.

Emma left the extra rifles in a pile behind a tree and proceeded to canvass the area, moving in a wide semicircle. Halfway around, she found a well-worn trail. She took it, moving as quietly as she could.

After four hundred yards, the path ended at a clearing. A long, low gazebo with a thatch roof but no walls ran the length of it. Long wooden tables with trestle benches sat under the roof. Plastic five-gallon cans and heaps of rubber tubing were piled all around, along with a huge mound of coca leaves. Glass beakers rested on the table. A wooden pallet at the end of the table was stacked high with plastic-wrapped bricks of white powder cocaine.

Emma wandered around the table, checking the items with a scientist's eye. Several cans with pour spouts were lined up against one side of the gazebo. The first had the word ACETONE written on it in crude black marker. The second said PEROXIDE and the third PETROL. Emma knew that gasoline and acetone were often used to distill coca leaves into cocaine paste, but the peroxide threw her. She couldn't figure out how it would be used in refining coca. She bounced the three components around in her mind, trying to find a link among them. Then it came to her. The peroxide could have a very lethal use.

Emma walked the length of the gazebo a second time, reading the labels on all the cans and glass beakers, looking for a specific ingredient. Sure enough, there it was, sitting at the farthest end of the table: sulfuric acid.

They were making bombs.

The synthesis of acetone peroxide carried with it so much risk that Emma was surprised the guerrillas would attempt it. The substance was volatile and unstable. When the two liquids were mixed, they could create enough force to blow off fingers. Add a blasting cap, and one could create a decent-size bomb.

Problem was, there was no telling when the mixture would explode. The only way to be safe was to cool the liquid to low temperatures. Acetone peroxide achieved a level of stability when cold. Emma couldn't imagine where they'd cool the mixture. They would need a refrigerator or freezer, because the jungle environment would warm it far too fast.

She once again walked the length of the gazebo, this time looking for anything that could contain ice or dry ice. Nothing.

Perhaps they're storing it farther away for safety in case it blows, Emma thought. She widened her search area. She found two coolers twenty-five yards into the trees. She knelt down and very gently removed the lid. There, nestled in a glass container labeled AP, sat the dried granules of acetone peroxide. Ice filled the remaining space. She opened the second cooler. This one was stacked with silver metal plates just like the ones she'd watched the guerrillas use to mine the road back at the airstrip. They, too, were covered with ice. Several rolls of duct tape lay all about.

An idea bloomed in Emma's mind: AP explodes when jarred or pressed. She could use the AP to create her own pressure-sensitive mine. If she could bury it outside the hut's entrance, the first person who stepped on it would be blown up. Her biggest challenge would be to add only the amount of AP needed to affect the individual stepping on the mine. She didn't want it to destroy the hut, and Sumner and the soldier, with it. The other question was, How would she ensure that Sumner or the wounded soldier didn't step on the mine first?

Emma shook off her indecision. It was the only idea she'd had so far. She'd solve these problems when she came to them. She got to work creating her mine. She took the AP out of the cooler, being careful not to jar the glass. She sprinkled it over a flat metal disk. Then, very slowly, she lowered a second disk over the first. She was impressed that the guerrillas thought to cool the metal disks as well. When held together with the tape, they would help keep the AP stable for a bit longer. She bound the ends of the disks together.

She made a second mine as quickly as possible. The outside temperature was rising steadily. When the disks warmed to above ten degrees Celsius, the AP would once again become unstable.

Emma carried her two mines back down the path. She moved with as much grace as she could muster so as not to jar them. She reached the spot outside the hut where she'd hidden the rifles and lowered the mines to the ground.

The situation at the hut seemed to have taken a turn for the worse since White had arrived. He paced back and forth in front of Sumner in agitation. Sumner watched White with his characteristic lack of emotion. White crouched down and spat directly into Sumner's face. Sumner's eyes remained blank. He gazed at White's face, only inches from his own, with a level stare.

"Who the hell are you?" Sumner's voice floated to Emma. She strained to hear White's response.

"I'm your worst enemy, you just don't know me," White said. "Caldridge owes me the formula, and with your help, I'm going to make sure she delivers."

Sumner frowned. Emma could see him trying to make sense of what White said. Before he could say anything, White backhanded him, hitting him in the face. Sumner pitched to the side but managed to catch himself before he fell on the wounded soldier. Emma felt her anger begin to bubble under the surface. She reached up and fingered the cross hanging around her neck. Worried the beads with her fingers. She calmed almost immediately. She took a deep breath.

Focus, she thought. The soldier leaning against Sumner looked unconscious, but for a second she thought she saw a flash of awareness in his body language. He was not as bad off as he wanted everyone to believe. She was right to have brought him a weapon.

It took an effort for Emma to divert her attention from the unfolding scene. She analyzed the dirt around the hut, trying to get a handle on the most likely traffic pattern. The grass was beaten to dust in a line outside the door that curved to the left. Twenty feet away sat a large, flat boulder. The path curved around it and continued down toward the ocean. Halfway down the trail, Emma saw the glow of a cigarette tip moving toward the beach. The second bodyguard was headed toward the water's edge.

Emma lifted both disks off the ground, took a deep breath, and carried them to the path, taking care to stay out of direct line of sight from the hut. She placed the disks back on the ground before clawing at the dirt. She was sweating and in a state of near panic. The sun was rising and along with it came the heat. The AP would soon be too warm to handle.

While she worked, she heard White talking to Smoking Man, outlining a plan.

"Burning the plants set us back at least six weeks. It will take that long for her to grow new ones that can be infused with the chromosomes we need."

She finished burying the first disk. She turned to the second. Her panic was taking over now. She didn't want to remain out in the open any longer. The second bodyguard could return at any time. White's Range Rover was parked next to the line in the dirt. She maneuvered the second disk through the open passenger-side window and lowered it onto the seat. The minute she let go of the mine she hightailed it back toward her hiding spot. Once in the trees, she used the scope on the rifle to look down the path. The second body-guard was strolling toward the hut, still pulling on the cigarette in his mouth. Emma held her breath as he approached the buried mine. He walked past it, missing it by only a few inches before heading into the hut.

"Get started on him," she heard White say. He waved at the bodyguard. "Go get her. She needs to watch." Smoking Man repeated the order in Spanish. The guard loped off, once again missing the mine by inches.

Emma's panic spiked even higher. The guard would discover that she was gone and raise the alarm. Whatever she was going to do, she'd better do it now.

The remaining bodyguard grabbed Sumner by the shirt. The wounded soldier rolled off him onto the hut's dirt floor. The bodyguard dragged Sumner out of the hut straight toward the mine.

Oh, no, Emma thought. She targeted the bodyguard, preparing to shoot him in order to stop him before he dragged Sumner right over the mine. Six feet from the spot he veered off and headed to the flat boulder ten feet farther away. Emma lowered her gun.

Smoking Man snapped out an order in Spanish. Sumner said nothing, but Emma could see that he had gritted his teeth to prepare himself. For what, Emma couldn't tell. She didn't know what was going on, but Smoking Man, his second bodyguard, and White all stood around with an expectant air, so whatever they were preparing to do, it wasn't going to be good. Her fingers returned to worrying the rosary stones.

There was a yell from the bodyguard who had been ordered to get her.

"He saying she's escaped," Smoking Man said.

White's eyes bugged. "What?" Emma watched his face grow red with his rage. "Are you kidding me?"

The bodyguard ran up to Smoking Man, babbling in Spanish.

"She's gone," Smoking Man said.

White rounded on him. "Find her. Now. Tell him to get the pilot to use the helicopter to search from above."

Smoking Man spoke in rapid Spanish. The second guard nodded and ran back down the path.

He didn't come close to the buried mine.

White rubbed at his eyes with his beefy hands. For a brief moment, Emma relished watching him panic.

"She can't be far," White said.

Smoking Man pulled a cigarette out of a pack and lit it. He stared at White, a speculative look in his eyes.

"Did you take her away? Have your soldiers bring her to the buyers while we were up here?"

White looked indignant. "Why would I do that?"

"To keep the money for yourself. Cut me out of the deal."

White drew himself up. "I wouldn't cut you out. Besides, where would I hide her while I negotiated with the buyers? You're the one with the network down here, not me. You'd find her in a heartbeat."

Smoking Man just pulled on the cigarette, watching White with his hard, dead eyes.

"You want to see what we do to those who betray us?" He jutted his chin at Sumner, still held against the boulder. "Continue."

The bodyguard stubbed out his own cigarette. He untied Sumner's hands, grabbed Sumner's right arm, and yanked it flat across the boulder, holding it in place. He dropped his weapon on the ground. He pulled a machete out of a holster attached to his belt. Smoking Man and White watched with anticipation for the bodyguard's next move. He raised the machete high.

Emma realized in that instant what he intended to do. She let go of the rosary, flattened again onto her stomach, pulled the rifle into position, flicked it into automatic mode, placed the crosshairs on the spot where she'd buried the mine, and started firing. Bullets hammered into the ground above the device.

It exploded.

The force of the blast knocked both White and the bodyguard backward. The machete flew out of the bodyguard's hand. White landed hard, but regained his feet and ran behind the hut. The bodyguard rolled to his stomach and crawled into the trees, dragging a bloody leg.

Emma wasted no time in sighting her second target, Smoking Man. She flicked the gun back to semiautomatic. She'd wasted only six seconds between blowing the mine and turning to her next shot, but they were enough to save Smoking Man. He dove downward. Emma's single shot flew harmlessly over him, hitting the trunk of a tree growing thirty yards behind him. In a flash Smoking Man was on his feet. He dove behind the hut. Emma heard the ominous sound of helicopter rotors thumping in the dawn light, growing louder. The pilot was beginning his search for her.

At the sound of the shots, and the minute the bodyguard fell, Sumner was up and running toward the hut. Emma looked for White. She saw the driver's-side door of the Range Rover open. Sunlight reflected off the moving window. White's head and shoulders appeared above the metal door. Emma watched as he bent to put a key in the ignition. The Range Rover's engine roared to life. The vehicle's wheels spun on the dirt, kicking up a huge cloud of dust as White threw it in gear. He drove past the hut, headed away. The car bounced over the ruts in the dirt trail. Emma could hear the suspension squeak in protest. The car fell into yet another rut and the right side tilted at an angle.

The car exploded. Emma watched it burn with a strange mixture of elation and disgust. She dragged her attention away. She didn't want to let herself feel anything over

White's death. She needed to keep her emotions in check until she got herself to safety.

Emma heard shouting from the soldiers at the boat. She couldn't see them, but she knew they were coming. Added to the sound of the soldier's yelling came the ever-increasing noise of the approaching helicopter.

54

EMMA HAULED THE REMAINING TWO RIFLES OVER
her shoulder and headed for the hut to deliver them to
Sumner and the wounded soldier. Sumner was there, bend-
ing over the soldier, when gunfire exploded through the hut's
back wall. The bullets punched through the wood, creating
a dotted line behind Sumner's head. He hit the deck, pulling
the seated soldier flat. Emma threw herself down. The bullets winged over her head.

Sumner wrapped his arms under the soldier's to drag him
across the hut's dirt floor. He kept low, crawling on one knee
as he dragged. His crouch saved him. Emma watched as
bullets continued to shatter the wood, this time even lower.
Either Smoking Man or the injured bodyguard was behind
the hut, shooting directly into it in an attempt to kill anyone
left inside. Emma needed to get around the structure to see
who it was.

The helicopter appeared overhead. Emma looked up and
saw the cracked windshield.

"Sumner, stay where you are!" she screamed over the din.
Sumner reached the hut's entrance but stopped. The bullet
holes appeared behind him. The helicopter hovered above
him. Emma recognized the pilot and Smoking Man's second

bodyguard. The guard held an automatic rifle in his right hand. He yelled something at the pilot, and the helo swung around and began descending. While it did, the guerrilla began firing down, over the hut's roof. Smoking Man continued to punch holes into the back of the hut, each set lower than the last, while the hovering helicopter rained fire at the hut's entrance. Sumner and the soldier were caught in the middle.

Emma pulled her own weapon. Her angle was all wrong, it was unlikely that she'd hit the man hovering over Sumner. She fired anyway. She targeted the pilot's window. Her first shot hit the helicopter's body and pinged off harmlessly. The second cracked through the glass. She heard a yell and the helicopter reversed course, shooting up and away from the hut.

Emma grabbed the rifles and ran to the hut. Once she cleared the trees, she looked to her right. She could see the soldiers pulling the dinghy onto the beach. The helicopter spun around and turned back to face her. She continued running to the hut, the rifles banging on her shoulder.

MIGUEL REMAINED IN A HAZE of pain. He felt Sumner hauling him across the hut's floor. He could see the bullets flying through the back wall, but he couldn't bring himself to help Sumner by taking over and crawling on his own. It was as if his legs belonged to someone else, they didn't move at his command.

The rising sun hit his eyes when his head was two feet from the hut's entrance. Sumner was dragging him along on his back, so he got a wonderful view of the helicopter hovering over the hut and the man inside preparing to blow them away. Miguel was too weak even to yell a warning, but he thought he heard someone scream at Sumner to stay put.

Sumner reversed direction and shoved Miguel back inside the hut.

Seconds later, Miguel saw the helicopter veer off. He took a look outside to see what had scared it away. He was astonished to see a wild woman running toward him. Her skin was caked with dried mud and her hair hung past her shoulders in dreadlocklike clumps. She grimaced, revealing white teeth that glowed against her blackened face. She wore a dirty gray T-shirt torn at the neck. She was thin and tall, and moved in long, fluid strides. While she did, she removed a gun off her shoulder and catapulted it into the air like a spear. Sumner reached up and caught it in one hand. She threw another that sailed over them. It landed on the hut's floor and skittered across to the far wall. She disappeared around the corner.

Miguel wasn't leaving that weapon behind. "Sumner, let go of me. I need that rifle," he said.

EMMA CRAWLED ON HER ELBOWS and knees, her weapon held in her hands, around the hut. She stopped at the corner and peered around it. Smoking Man was busy reloading. He stood up to deliver another volley. Before he could, the hut's wall coughed up splinters of wood as someone from inside shot through it. Two of the bullets hit Smoking Man. One in his thigh, the other in his arm. He staggered away.

Emma was up in a flash and ran back around to the hut's entrance. The wounded soldier was conscious and aimed a rifle at the back wall. He'd shot Smoking Man. Recognition flashed across his face when he saw her.

"You're Ms. Caldridge," he said.

Emma didn't bother to ask him how he knew her name. Sumner was checking the back of the hut. He swung around at the soldier's voice. Some strong emotion rippled across his face at the sight of her. She directed her attention to the soldier.

"We've got to move. The helicopter is still out there as well as a small platoon of soldiers."

"How many?" Sumner moved to stand behind the open door to survey the area.

"Four. One is a young boy. Do your best not to kill him. He helped me escape."

"Where are they?"

"Near the beach. There's a cabin cruiser floating about fifty yards out in the water. If we can get to it, we can use it to get away."

Sumner hauled the wounded soldier upright. "Come on, Miguel. We're going on a cruise."

The soldier turned sheet white for a moment, as if the act of standing made all the blood in his body head south. He wrapped one arm around Sumner's shoulders.

"The rifle. I'm not leaving without it," he said.

Emma slung the strap over Miguel's other shoulder. "I'll cover you both."

Sumner grabbed Emma by the shirt and pulled her toward him. He kissed her, openmouthed and urgent. He broke away to look at her.

"In case we don't make it," he said to her.

All Emma could think to do was nod.

Sumner hitched Miguel higher on his shoulder. "On three!" he said, and began to count.

They burst out of the hut. The sun was up and the heat rising. It reflected off the pipeline's metal and bounced off the oil-slicked grass, making the area stink even more than before. Sumner started a slow jog. He pulled on Miguel, who managed to move his feet only every few steps, forcing Sumner to half drag him along. Emma scanned the field, looking for the soldiers. They were at the base of the hill, next to the pipeline, moving in a crouch formation toward the hut.

The helicopter was back. It swooped over them. The shadow it cast covered Emma, blocking out the sun. She peppered it with bullets. It shot upward again and spun in a circle.

She ran sideways down the hill in order to watch the approaching soldiers. She fired a random shot in their direction. They scattered and ran for cover. Emma continued behind Sumner and Miguel. They passed the spot where she'd hidden in the trees. The box of dynamite was still there. Emma diverted sideways to snatch the box off the ground. She ripped it open while she continued moving. The helicopter flew somewhere to her right. She heard the sound of a second growing louder. If there were two, then they were doomed. She did her best to ignore it and focus on the job at hand.

The soldiers were huddled under the pipeline. They hid behind the narrow tripod legs, waiting for their chance. Sumner had dragged Miguel to the far left, using the trees as cover. The trees might help with the helicopter, but Emma expected the soldiers to fire on the men as they drew parallel. Plus, a huge German shepherd shot out of the wooded area, running full tilt at Sumner. Emma didn't know if it was going to attack, but whatever it was going to do, Sumner was going to have to deal with it. She didn't have the time to put it down.

Emma refocused on the immediate threats. She ran next to the oil barrel parked below the pipeline's gash. Oil still poured into the can. She ran past it, then stopped dead as an idea came to her. She jogged back to the can, pulled two sticks of dynamite out of the box, and rammed them into the hole in the pipeline, fuses out. She pulled out the silver lighter, flicked it on, and lit the fuses. They sparked like

Fourth of July sparklers on steroids. Emma sprinted like hell across the field toward where she'd last seen Sumner.

The helicopter was back and bearing down on her. The second helicopter roared out of the trees, rising up to Emma's right. This helicopter had guns mounted on the front. Emma gazed into the telescope and put her crosshairs on the second helicopter's pilot. She gasped. It was an American man in army fatigues. An American flag was stitched on the front of his shirt. Emma hesitated in the face of that flag. He bent forward to touch a switch, and the helicopter's guns started firing on the guerrilla.

A huge explosion rocked the field. It blew Emma off her feet. Metal shrapnel landed all around her. One piece pierced her arm near the biceps. Her fingers lost all feeling. She regained her feet, only to be knocked down by a second explosion. Another piece of shrapnel hammered into her head. She saw stars dance before her eyes. A huge fireball flew out of what was left of the hemorrhaging pipeline. A line of fire surged from the metal in a solid wall of flame fed continuously by the still-pumping fuel.

She forced herself back up on her feet. The soldiers were gone. The portion of the pipeline they were hiding under was reduced to twisted metal. The helicopters were high in the sky and still battling it out. Emma saw Sumner swimming in the water, dragging Miguel, ten feet from the cabin cruiser. The dog swam behind them, also headed for the boat. The boy soldier was there, standing on the deck, holding a gun.

"Oh, God, don't let him shoot them. We've gotten this far." Emma said the prayer out loud. "Please, God, I don't deserve this favor, but let them live. Make the boy understand." She continued running down the hill. She made the beach and splashed into the water, never taking her eyes off the boy on the boat.

Sumner made it to the ladder. He was yelling something at Miguel, who grabbed the rungs and started to climb. When he was halfway up, the boy reached down to help him, pulling Miguel up while Sumner pushed from below. Miguel flopped over the railing. Sumner turned, grabbed the dog by the ruff, and pulled him up with him on the ladder. He threw the dog over the railing. He leaped lightly onto the deck, slapped the boy on the shoulder in thanks, and took the gun from him. The boy nodded and stepped back. Sumner checked the weapon and turned to the beach. She knew he was looking for her. She began her own swim to the boat. She turned her attention to the helicopters. The American in the helicopter fired again, and the guerrillas' helicopter exploded into a thousand little pieces.

Within a minute, peace descended.

55

EMMA WATCHED SUMNER AS SHE SPLASHED DEEPER into the water. He lowered the gun, put a hand to his eyes, and watched the remaining helicopter as it lowered to the beach. Emma followed its progress as well. It settled on the ground and grew quiet as the pilot cut the engine.

The helicopter door opened and a devastatingly handsome man with hair cropped close to his head and dark, almost black eyes stepped out. A thick stubble of beard gave him a slightly disreputable look, as did the AK-47 slung over his shoulder. He wore spotlessly clean jungle fatigues with high lace boots. His eyes swept the field and then locked on Emma. He smiled a dazzling smile.

"Ms. Caldridge, we meet at last," he said.

Emma knew that her mouth hung open in shock, both at the unlikely appearance of such a beautiful man in this jungle hell, and at his use of her name. She snapped her mouth shut and swallowed once.

"How do you know my name?"

The man smiled. His teeth were straight and pearly white.

"I'm Edward Banner, special consultant to the Department of Defense. We received your text message after the crash. I had twenty special forces personnel searching for you and the passengers, as well as three helicopters prepared to extract you once we found you."

"Had?" Emma said.

Banner nodded. "The Colombian government asked them to withdraw." He consulted his watch. "By now most have been extracted. I was searching for two that I'm told stayed behind—Major Miguel Gonzalez and Cameron Sumner." He waved an arm at the boat in the water. "Is that them?"

Emma nodded.

Banner scanned the beach. "You'd best get in the helicopter. We may only have a short window to get out of here before reinforcements show up."

Emma shook her head. "Not me. I've had enough flying for a while. I'll go on the boat with Sumner. The soldier with him is injured. Can you use the helicopter to take him to the hospital?"

"I have a doctor I know who will fix him up, no questions asked. I'll get him in the copter and deliver him to you. I should warn you, the authorities in the U.S. are asking quite a few questions about Miguel's and Sumner's roles in the bombing of the pipeline. I may not bring them in until I can assess the mood over there."

Emma snorted. "The pipeline's all they can think about?"

"Guns and oil. For some, they make the world go 'round."

"Then let them know that the soldier and Sumner just helped me stop a much bigger deal. My former boss wanted to force me to make an entirely new stealth weapon that he intended to sell on the black market to terrorists. I destroyed the weapon and its ingredients."

Banner took a step closer to her, a concerned look on his face. "Where is this boss of yours?"

Emma pointed up the beach. "Back there. In that burning car."

She watched Banner turn to look at the Range Rover, still burning in the distance.

"Do you know who his buyers were?"

Emma shook her head. "He claimed some shadowy figure from the Department of Defense wanted it, but he was a first-class liar, so there's no way of telling." She wanted to ask Banner for something, but hesitated.

He picked up on her hesitation. "Go ahead. Say what you're thinking."

Emma sloshed back to the beach and walked up to him. "Do you have a compass?"

56

STROMEYER SAT AT A CONFERENCE TABLE IN THE
Southcom headquarters pounding on the keys of a laptop
computer. The memo to suspend operations in Colombia
was drafted, but not yet signed by Margate. Stromeyer was
composing an e-mail to the bureaucratic heads of various
obscure offices in the Department of Defense asking for further input on the memo's language. She wrote, *A decision
of such import should be analyzed and approved by more
than three branches of the Department of Defense. Protocol
requires that these offices review and offer input. Darkview
suggests that a committee be formed to determine the best
approach to suspending the operation.*

She hit send and sat back, satisfied. A committee would
take days to appoint, convene, and inform. She hoped the e-
mail would slow Margate's signature even longer and allow
Banner the time he needed to get the hell out of Colombia. Just then Margate himself slammed into the conference
room, followed by Whitter and an assistant secretary.

"I just got word that the Oriental pipeline's been bombed.
The entire length of it is on fire. The third largest source of
oil for this country destroyed in an instant. Where the hell

is Banner?" Margate's voice was low and held a thread of anger that Stromeyer had never heard before.

"I don't know," she said.

She watched Margate's face suffuse with red. "I don't believe you. Word is that you know everything, Major Stromeyer."

"I'm flattered," she said.

Before Margate could respond, there was a knock at the door.

Stromeyer was relieved at the interruption. "Come."

Private Campbell, a female soldier newly recruited at Southcom, entered the room, followed by a man in his mid-forties. Private Campbell was charged to assist Stromeyer in debriefing the passengers. She was a quiet woman in her early twenties. Stromeyer found her to be efficient and friendly, two qualities she needed right now.

Campbell shot a worried glance at Margate before turning to Stromeyer. "The passengers are waiting to be debriefed. You'll find the rest in conference room B. This man is Mr. James Barkett."

Stromeyer shook hands with Mr. Barkett while Margate stood still. Barkett must have felt the hostility emanating from Margate, because he looked almost afraid to shake his hand. Stromeyer watched Margate's face relax into a smile.

"Glad you're back home, Mr. Barkett," Margate spoke in an overly hearty voice and managed to make the sentence sound threatening rather than friendly. Barkett nodded, a wary look on his face. Stromeyer was impressed by the man's caution. He was right to be careful around Margate. Barkett turned to Stromeyer.

"I wanted to meet you right away to tell you what I heard down there."

Stromeyer raised an eyebrow. "All right."

"One night, after we stopped for the day, three men came into the camp. They were obviously Americans. I overheard one talking to the man named Rodrigo." Barkett hesitated.

"Go ahead, please." Stromeyer urged him on.

"He said that the Department of Defense wouldn't pay anything until Emma Caldridge was found. He said they were sending dogs."

"Dogs?" Stromeyer said.

Barkett nodded. "Tracking hounds. At the time I didn't know who Emma Caldridge was, but later I saw her at the watchtower."

"Why are you telling us this, Mr. Barkett?" Margate's voice was still threaded with anger.

Barkett pulled himself up and stared at Margate. "Because I thought it was strange that Americans from the Department of Defense were negotiating with our captors. They obviously saw us sitting there, held hostage, but acted as though they didn't care."

Stromeyer felt her own anger rising. "Do you know anything about this, *Secretary* Margate?"

Margate snorted. "I do not." He pointed a finger at Barkett. "What makes you think these people were telling the truth?"

Barkett hesitated. He shook his head. "I can't be sure of anything they said. I'm just telling you what happened."

Margate took Barkett's arm and steered him toward the conference room door. "Thank you for that information. Rest assured that we will do everything in our power to determine if what those criminals said was true. Also, be assured that at no time before your actual rescue did we know how to find you. If we had, we wouldn't have failed to act." He ushered Barkett through the door and closed it behind him. He turned to Stromeyer. "Quite a story."

"One that I intend to follow up on," she said.

Margate gave Stromeyer one of his fake smiles. "Of course you must. But I'm pulling the plug on this operation and I want everyone out of Colombia now. You will not conduct your investigation from inside that country, is that understood? And Banner had better not be there."

Before Stromeyer could respond, her BlackBerry started beeping with an incoming text message. She watched it scroll across the screen.

"Is that Banner?" Margate indicated the buzzing device.

Stromeyer nodded. "He said to tell you that Emma Caldridge has been rescued. That she claims to have destroyed a terrorist cell operating out of the States that was intent on getting her to create a new weapon for use against Americans." She continued to read the unfolding message. "Ms. Caldridge says the ringleader of the group was her former boss. He was preparing to sell the weapon to an unidentified member of the Department of Defense."

Stromeyer watched Margate and Whitter closely as they digested this information. Whitter looked shocked, Margate, not so shocked.

"Did she say who the person was who was attempting to buy it?"

Stromeyer shook her head. "We'll debrief her when she gets back." Stromeyer thought she detected speculation in Margate's eyes, like he was running names through his head.

"That's a serious claim," he said.

"So was Barkett's."

Margate turned to Whitter. "Sit in on the debriefing. I want to hear everything this woman knows. I won't have a turncoat in my operation."

Stromeyer disliked Margate, but at that moment she almost admired him.

"What is this weapon she can make? Maybe she can make it for her own government?" Margate looked intrigued.

Stromeyer's brief moment of warmth toward Margate was extinguished. His obvious desire for a new weapon of death was more like the man she'd come to know and dislike. She read the text. "Banner doesn't describe it, but he says she destroyed the ingredients for it. No one can make it anymore."

Margate shook his head. "That's a shame."

"Guess it's lucky that she was able to avoid such an outcome, despite the damage to the pipeline." Stromeyer couldn't help but stick it to Margate a little. She could see the gears in his head turning as he considered the new information from all angles.

"It's still tough, losing the pipeline like that. Repairing it will cost hundreds of millions," he said, but now he sounded like he was already trying to backpedal from his earlier outrage.

"Shall I write a memo describing how the DOD and Darkview successfully thwarted a major terrorist arms purchase?"

Margate gave her a look that told her he knew exactly where she was headed. "You do that." He left the conference room, trailed by his assistants and a thoughtful Whitter.

57

EMMA SAT ON A DECK CHAIR, WATCHING SUMNER fish over the side of the boat. Miguel slept beside her on a deck lounger. The attached canopy protected him from the sun. Boris dozed on the deck next to him. The dog was never far from Miguel's side. Miguel slept the day away. His injuries didn't allow for much else.

Emma watched through slit eyes as Sumner sat in the fishing chair and played out the line of his fishing rod. The boy, a fourteen-year-old orphan whose name was Enrico, sat next to him in the jump seat, also watching. Enrico was well on his way to idolizing Sumner. He didn't say much, and they didn't ask him too many questions.

Sumner fished every day without fail, and he always managed to catch something good to eat. The cruiser was well stocked, but not with the type of food required for their long journey. It was jammed with alcohol, high-end vodkas and whiskeys, cigars from Cuba and the Dominican Republic, as well as some of the finest armament that money could buy. The tinned food was adequate, but Sumner's daily catch inevitably made dinner something special.

They'd been cruising for a week, informing no one of their location or their destination. Only they knew that they were in the Caribbean Sea, headed to Key West by way of Puerto Rico. The radio crackled, starting Emma from her reverie. She grabbed the receiver.

"Banner?" she said.

"Yes. Everything all right there?" Banner's smooth voice came over the line. A few days before, Emma had used the radio to call him and ask for a favor. Now he was reporting in.

"Fine. All clear."

"Good. How's Miguel?"

"Sleeping. The wound is healing and the pain seems to be receding. Tell Perez thanks for the assistance. It's not every day that a doctor makes a cartel cruise-ship house call."

"I will. And I have some news for you. Gladys Sullivan says hello. She's in Bogotá recovering from bypass surgery. She told me to tell you that she still prays for you every day, in between cigarettes."

"What! They're allowing her to smoke?"

Emma heard Banner's chuckle over the line. "I doubt it. Her brand of humor, is all. Vivian's doing well also. She's no longer in Colombia, but reunited with her family."

"And Maria? Were you able to find her?"

"I was. She asked to be moved to another location. I arranged for her and the children to be relocated to the Christian ministry formerly run by Gladys's sister. They didn't know what to make of Maria at the mission."

"Why is that? Maria is a wonderful woman, and very pious."

"They said that she is the first indigenous woman they've ever met who wears red lipstick."

Emma laughed out loud. "My Engine Red."

"I assumed you had something to do with it. Rest assured, you have a convert. Maria wears it every day. I have to say, it suits her."

"I'm glad I could give her something."

"Maria says that she always knew that God would protect all of you. Between Gladys's prayers and Maria's faith, you seem to be well protected by the powers that be."

"I'll take any protection I can get," Emma said.

"And you? Are the headaches and nightmares getting any better?" Banner's voice was concerned.

Emma was suddenly uncomfortable. She'd been having debilitating headaches along with recurring nightmares. The dreams revolved around Rodrigo. He'd walk toward her. His head was cut off, and he cradled it in his arms. When the head saw her, it turned into White and it would scream at her. Emma would start awake, sweating. In the last seven days, she'd had the dream four times.

"Still there, I'm afraid."

"It's post-traumatic stress. When you reach the States, if they haven't resolved, I'll arrange for you to attend some therapy sessions. Southcom holds them weekly for soldiers returning from Iraq."

"Thanks, I'll consider it." To Emma's great relief, Banner changed the subject.

"I've arranged for a crew to relieve you of the weapons before you hit United States territory. Until then, you may need them. We've been unable to pinpoint who the American businessmen were that you saw, but they've got to be furious at the loss of their cargo."

"What about this yacht? Perhaps it is registered in their name?"

"No. It's actually owned by one Miguel Estanga della Petroya, known throughout Colombia as 'Estanga 60.' The most notorious drug cartel leader in Colombia. Word is he was shot twice and his boat stolen in a siege orchestrated by the United States' DEA."

"Smoking Man," Emma said.

Emma heard Sumner chuckle from his seat. "A siege? Mr. Della Petroya is embarrassed to admit that two men and a woman shot him and stole his yacht?"

"That you, Sumner?" Banner asked.

"It is."

"Well, both of you, listen up. I was wondering if you would care to ditch your day jobs and join Darkview. The pay's good and the excitement just about nonstop."

"Banner, I was just relishing the lack of excitement," Emma said.

Banner laughed. "Well, give it some thought. You don't have to decide now. I'd better ring off. Don't want anyone tracking you guys. Emma, you turned off that gps wristwatch I gave you?"

"It's off. But I thank you for it. I'll never go anywhere without a compass again."

"Keep it. I'll get another one."

Emma hung up. She settled down on the deck chair to think about Banner's offer and to watch Sumner fish. Despite her ordeal and the lingering effects, she had a feeling of lightness that she hadn't felt in years, perhaps not ever. She knew it was because she had faced the worst that life had to offer, and the ordeal had given her a greater appreciation of the best. And that moment, sitting on the sunny deck, in a cool breeze, on the gently rolling boat, and watching the sun reflect off the undulating sea, was definitely one of the better times. She smiled.

AUTHOR'S NOTE

Emma Caldridge's story is, of course, fiction, but many of the various plants and techniques she uses exist. Thankfully, the key item, the weapon with the ingenious disguise, is a figment of my imagination.

I especially love the medicinal maggots. I'd read about their use in sores that appear intractable. My thanks to Ronald A. Sherman, MD, MSc, DTM&H, Department of Pathology, University of California, Irvine, for his assistance in explaining the collection and application of these amazing creatures.

Emma's use of scopolamine, or "devil's breath," its Colombian street name, is based in fact. Scopolamine is a chemical that contains antinausea properties and in commercial use is a favorite of scuba divers. It's derived from the datura plant, a member of the nightshade family commonly called jimsonweed. All parts of the plant are toxic. When ground to a fine powder and blown in the face of the victim, it is said to create hallucinations and a "zombie" effect that renders the victim completely suggestible. While the hallucinatory effects are well documented, and the drug can cause the victim to fall into a stupor, I have my own personal doubts about the zombie reports. My cynical trial attorney's antenna started vibrating after I read the claims of a politician who denied responsibility for stealing cash by claiming that he did so only while in a zombie state after thieves used devil's breath on him. Be that as it may, jimsonweed is no joke, and it can kill.

The leaves and branches of the neem tree are used the world over as an antiseptic, and the indigenous people of Colombia chew coca leaves to settle an upset stomach and as a tonic to impart energy. Coca tea is sold legally in some countries in South America.

The traveler's palm exists, though it is not indigenous to Colombia, and one can drink from it as described. My thanks to the Landscapers at the CuisinArt Resort in Anguilla, British West Indies, for teaching me how to drink from theirs, showing me the neem tree, and describing the many other edible plants growing on the acreage under their management.

Cameron Sumner's job is fictional, but is loosely based upon a former joint program between the United States and Colombia called the Air Bridge Denial program. For an in-depth look at how the real program worked, read the study issued in 2005 by the United States Government Accountability Office (GAO) at www.gao.gov. In fact, read anything listed on the GAO's site. I am continually impressed by the quality of the reports that I find there. My thanks to Jess T. Ford, director, International Affairs and Trade, for his update on the report.

The Lost City exists, but the elusive plant that Emma destroys does not. The city, discovered thirty years ago by grave robbers, continues to be a six-day hike through paramilitary-controlled coca fields, past indigenous villages, and into areas that even a donkey cannot navigate. A group trekking to the Lost City was kidnapped in 2003, but I could find no other reports after that date.

Kidnappings in Colombia have settled down quite a bit in

recent years thanks to the Uribe administration's crackdown on the paramilitary organizations. The arrests have reached into the highest echelons of Colombian society and include some officials considered to be Uribe's allies, as well as a cousin. However, FARC, Colombia's best-known paramilitary organization, has vowed to once again increase its efforts. One can only hope FARC changes its stance, because Colombians are some of the nicest people I have ever met. My thanks to all who assisted me with this book.

Somali pirates have just attacked a cruise liner in the Gulf of Aden. But the ship may carry more than just wealthy passengers—it could also hold a new weapon of unknown origin. Edward Banner, head of the security company Darkview, enlists the help of brilliant biochemist Emma Caldridge and special agent Cameron Sumner—who is secretly aboard the ship—on a mission located in one of the most dangerous areas of the world.

Don't miss the pulse-pounding sequel to
Running from the Devil

RUNNING DARK

Coming July 2010 in hardcover from

wm

WILLIAM MORROW

An Imprint of HarperCollins*Publishers*

EMMA CALDRIDGE PASSED MILE THIRTY-SIX OF THE fifty-five-mile Comrades ultra marathon in South Africa when a roadside car bomb exploded. The force of the explosion blew her out of her shoes and catapulted her into the air ten feet before hammering her into the dirt at the side of the road. The detonated car burned, flames leaping out of the shattered windows. She lay in the clay-colored dust with the hot sun beating down, blinding her. She moaned, turned her head away from the sun's glare, closed her eyes, and lay still, trying to gather her wits about her. A shadow fell over her face. She opened her eyes without moving her head and saw the blurry image of a man's legs from the knees down. The limbs appeared to shimmer in the heat waves thrown by the burning vehicle. He wore running shoes, like everyone else that day. The shoes stopped next to her and rose to their toes as the person crouched down. A silver necklace in the shape of an antelope head swung into her line of vision. The amulet hung on a black rawhide cord. Emma tried to ask for help, but her dry mouth wouldn't form the words.

The man's dark hand came into view, holding a white plastic injector, similar to an EpiPen carried by people with allergies. In the next instant, the hand jammed the tip into

Emma's forearm, right above the wrist. She felt the prick of a needle and the rush of medication pulsing into her skin. Before she even had a chance to make a sound, he jerked the point out of her arm. The shoes flattened onto the dust and walked away with a crunching noise.

KHALIL IBRAHIM Y MUNGABE'S NICKNAME was "the Bone-picker," because he began his career stealing the left-over shreds of offal found on the commercial fishing boats that trawled the seas off the coast of Somalia. It was said that Mungabe liked nothing and no one, but that wasn't exactly true. He tolerated his wives well enough, and his children occasionally did something to make him laugh, even if he didn't know their names and so could not praise them. He called them "that one" or "this one" and left it there.

He sat in Dubai and shivered in the snow. Dubai's temperature that day was a blistering thirty degrees Celsius and rising higher, but inside the mall where he sat it was snowing fake snow. Mungabe thought the affectation ridiculous. To him, it just highlighted how the Saudis had bowed their heads to the European oppressors. He sat in the food court and waited for his contact, fingering the silver ring he wore in the shape of an antelope head.

Mungabe's power was on the verge of exploding, and he was taking the next logical step to ensure his future in this life and beyond. The man he was to meet had the power to bridge Mungabe's world and the European world, and Mungabe planned on exploiting him and then killing him, in that order.

The man strolled up, tall and thin, like Mungabe himself, but wearing an expensive suit purchased in London. He had the hard, pointed face that Mungabe thought was the mark of a European. The man's nickname was "the Vulture" because he'd risen to power by driving his rivals into crisis through any means necessary. When the distressed companies began selling their assets one by one in their frantic attempts to save their floundering businesses, the Vulture would swoop down to snatch up the bones.

The Vulture took a seat across from Mungabe, looking unaffected by the freezing air, which Mungabe thought might be real rather than false bravado. Likely he was far more accustomed to such temperatures than Mungabe.

"How do you like the snow? I thought you'd want to experience it," the Vulture said.

Mungabe clamped his teeth together to stop their clattering. He hated the snow, and he suspected the Vulture knew it. It was all calculated to put him at a disadvantage. Mungabe couldn't wait to complete their joint mission and then finish the man off. He'd do it in Somalia and leave his carcass in the sun to rot. Wonder how he'd feel then? Mungabe thought. He shifted in his seat and got right down to business.

"Tell me what you require. I haven't much time. My ship leaves from the port today. Did my associate in South Africa perform well for you?"

The Vulture raised an eyebrow. "You look cold. Perhaps we take a seat in the restaurant." The Vulture smiled a fake smile and waved Mungabe to the nearby bistro. Once inside, the Vulture crossed his legs and leaned back in the wooden chair. A waiter came by to hand them two menus. Mungabe took one and was somewhat relieved to see pictures next to the names of the dishes offered, which made ordering much easier. The Vulture waited for the server to leave before continuing.

"Your associate worked fine. But I have another request of you. There's a large ship off the coast of Somalia that I want you to intercept."

Mungabe's ears perked up. He excelled at stealing ships.

He supervised a large crew of Somali pirates, and in the last years his enterprise had grown exponentially. He'd expanded his fleet, and just this quarter had purchased night vision goggles, GPS radar scanning equipment, and new weaponry. All so his pirates could troll farther out and net bigger fish. As a result of his investment, he was having an outstanding year so far. He'd taken fifty ships to date, with eight hundred hostages, usually crewmen, and netted twenty million in ransom paid. His spectacular successes included an oil tanker worth ninety million and two commercial tuna fishing boats worth twenty million each. One of the boats was currently docked in the village of Eyl, where it was slowly sinking into the ocean as a result of a hole shot in the hull by one of his crew. He often warned them to shoot above the water line so that the boat, once boarded, could be piloted back to shore for salvaging, but that particular ship had put up a fight and the only way to take it was to disable it and kill everyone onboard.

But now several freighters had hired Darkview, an American security company, to protect their ships that used the Gulf of Aden trade route. In the last two months, Darkview personnel managed to sink four of Mungabe's boats. In one incident, the security company continued to chase his crew two hundred miles, not even stopping when they came within Somali territorial waters, as they were supposed to do. Darkview captured the pirates and dragged them into Hargeisa to be tried. Mungabe paid a princely sum to ensure their acquittal—it would not do to have any of his men sit in prison. Prison tested a man's loyalties, and Mungabe wanted no one to turn traitor on him. It was during the trial that Mungabe decided to launch his own offensive against the company that plagued him so.

"What type of ship do you want me to steal?" Mungabe said.

The waiter was back to take their order. Mungabe pointed to a fish dish, while the Vulture ordered in French. When the waiter left, the Vulture leaned into him.

"A cruise ship. The finest in the world. It embarked on its virgin cruise from Dubai to the Seychelles Islands a few days ago."

Mungabe settled back in his chair while he thought about what the Vulture said. He didn't read papers, didn't care about world news, and had little interest in the politics of the West, but even he could see that taking the finest ship in the world would reflect well on him. Still, he frowned.

"The cruise lines don't come near Somali waters. Victoria is two thousand kilometers away. Too far. We've only taken ships at six hundred."

The Vulture raised an eyebrow. "Are you saying you can't do it?"

Mungabe felt a flash of anger. He could do anything. "I can but for a very large price. What will you pay?"

The Vulture shook his head. "I pay nothing. You do this for the ship and its hostages—your usual take."

Mungabe laughed. This Vulture was joking. "I don't need a cruise ship. I need a fishing ship! They are at least useful after. What do you think my crews do when they are not pirating, huh? They fish. They use the hijacked commercial boats to do it. They do it for Somalia. Without my assistance, Somalia's waters would be emptied by the rest of the world. They sneak into our territorial boundaries where the tuna lives, steal our fish by the tons, and leave nothing for us. We stop this plundering by the rich and give to the poor."

The Vulture smirked. "Spare me the Robin Hood story. You don't give anything to the poor. You keep it all for yourself."

Mungabe shook his head. "Still, I don't do this for the boat. You must pay."

The Vulture shifted. "I will pay you then, but in that case, it is understood that I get both the ship and its cargo."

"Cargo? What cargo?"

The Vulture shrugged. "Pharmaceutical products. Not important for you, but I would like to have them."

The waiter returned with the meals. As he lowered the Vulture's in front of him, Mungabe thought he would retch. On the plate was a large lobster, its black legs, hard cara-pace, and beaded eyes were revolting, as was the heavy, oily smell of the drawn butter that sat in a cup next to it. The sight and smell of it repelled Mungabe. Like most Somalis, he would never eat a lobster, which he considered the equiva-lent of a sea cockroach. It was a bottom feeder, eating the fecal remains of the rest of the ocean's creatures.

The Vulture sliced the beast in half with one deft cut from a long, wicked-looking knife. He twisted off a leg, put it to his lips, and sucked on it. He did all of this while gazing at Mungabe. Mungabe feared no man, but in that minute he wondered if he was dealing with a demon. He shook off the thought.

"I want two million dollars, and as I told you last month, I want the American security company called Darkview put out of business. For that price, I will hijack the ship. You get the carcass and cargo. I get any money onboard and its pas-sengers to ransom as I see fit."

"One million. No more. Plus you pay all expenses."

"And Darkview?"

The Vulture waved a languid hand in the air. "It is already begun."

CAMERON SUMNER STOOD next to a lounge chair on the deck of the *Kaiser Franz* cruise liner and stared at the hori-zon, waiting. The chair was one in a long row of chairs, all occupied by passengers clad in swimsuits, baking in the sun. The woman to Sumner's right, noticing his preoccupation with the horizon, did her best to capture his attention.

"I see you watch the ocean every day after your workout. It's beautiful, isn't it?" the woman, an American, said. Sumner eyed her. She wore a string bikini on a figure with full hips, fake breasts, and striking, artfully streaked hair. Her lips were painted a bright coral, and her forehead didn't move when she spoke. Her husband, a good ol' boy from Mississippi who owned a string of car dealerships, spent his days in the ship's casino drinking gin and playing blackjack. His wife spent her days watching Sumner swim laps in the pool or run on the track. The woman's question was the first time she'd worked up enough nerve to speak to him.

"It is beautiful," he said. He grabbed a towel and dried his dripping body, while the American woman eyed him with bright, avid eyes.

"So what brings you on a cruise ship alone?"

"I work for the company that owns the *Kaiser Franz*." Sumner kept his answers short to discourage more conversation.

"How *interesting*." The woman breathed the words.

Sumner did his best to contain his annoyance. His patience ran thin these days. He slipped on a pair of track pants, sunk into a nearby lounge chair, and thought about Caldridge. He'd been having dreams of her, some so vivid that he thought he might be able to touch her, some so frightening that when he would reach her after a slow-motion chase, he would find himself to be too late and his anguish at her death would overwhelm him. He pulled up a mental picture of her: light brown hair a little past her shoulders, green eyes, a straight nose with no upturn, and a lithe, athletic runner's body. He sighed and kept his eyes on the water.

The ship's sundeck ran the width of the foredeck. In the

center was the rectangular lap pool. Lounge chairs, each with bright blue cushions, filled the rest of the available space. A small walkway ran along the railings. Sumner spent much of his time on the sundeck, because it allowed him to view both sides of the vessel.

The ship itself was smaller, more intimate, and much more luxurious than the larger cruise lines out of Miami. It boasted mahogany-lined staterooms with flat-screen televisions, marble bathrooms, and thick Persian carpets. Each room had a private butler assigned to it. They'd embarked from Dubai, passed through the Arabian Sea, and were deep into the Indian Ocean on their way to the Seychelles Islands. It was ten in the morning. Only half the sundeck chairs were taken.

The woman shifted in her chair to lean toward him. Her blond, highlighted hair and overly manicured nails were the antithesis of what Sumner liked in a woman. He said nothing as he finished drying off. He grabbed a pair of Ray-Ban sunglasses and stretched out on the lounge chair. He basked in the sun while he continued to keep watch.

"Are you working on this trip?" said the woman, interrupting his reverie. It was all Sumner could do not to sigh out loud.

"I'm headed to the Seychelles to check on our land-based operations."

"How *interesting*," the woman said again.

Sumner continued to scan the area, his eyes hidden behind his sunglasses. The ocean swelled in calm, regular waves. A waiter worked his way through the lounge chairs, handing out complimentary juices to the sunbathers. Another employee followed, offering a spritz of mineral water to cool them.

The German family walked along the deck rail toward Sumner. He felt a prickle of awareness shoot down his

spine. Sumner worked for the Southern Hemisphere Drug
Defense Agency and had been hired out to the *Kaiser Franz*
in response to a vague piece of intelligence that suggested
trouble sailed with the ship. The trouble was thought to be
drug-related, but nothing in the communiqué detailed the
precise nature of the problem. An assignment off the coast
of Africa carried the added benefit of getting Sumner as far
away from the Southern Hemisphere as possible. Sumner's
last assignment disrupted a major drug cartel in Colombia.
His employers feared retaliation.

Sumner reviewed the ship's manifest and had settled on
three potential groups of passengers as the ones he would
watch. One Russian traveling with his mistress, a French-
man traveling with two other businessmen, and this family.
Two parents with their grown daughter. The father, a businessman in his late fifties, had the build of a steelworker.
His large stomach hung over his expensive pants, throwing
a shadow over his black loafers. His face bore the bright red
hue of a man whose skin was unaccustomed to the outdoors.
He held the *Frankfurter Algemeine* newspaper in his hands
and looked surly.

His wife, also somewhat north of fifty, was as thin as he
was wide. Her blond hair, her natural color and none of it
highlighted, ended at her ears in a blunt cut. Her blue eyes
and cool, superior attitude telegraphed that she was from
Hamburg, where blond hair and cool eyes abounded. Her
manner telegraphed her dislike for her husband.

The daughter, a shy beauty, with blond hair and a fresh,
almost translucent complexion, was twenty-four. Six years
younger than Sumner and light years more innocent, she
too, would cast glances at him whenever their paths crossed,
but she hadn't yet worked up enough nerve to speak to him.

The father turned his head to gaze at the horizon. The
woman next to him was speaking again.

"Harry says we don't need to travel anywhere, that there's nothing to learn. But I think you should always see how the other half lives, don't you?"

Sumner refrained from commenting on the fact that she was unlikely to see "the other half" while sailing on the sea in a yacht with massive suites and private butlers, but he assumed the woman meant well. Before Sumner could respond, Harry himself walked up to his wife.

"Whatcha doin', sweetheart?" He boomed the question at his wife, towering over her lounge chair. He thrust his hand out at Sumner.

"Harry Block. Pleased to meet you."

"Cameron Sumner."

Sumner rose to shake Block's hand. Based on his own six-foot-two-inch height and weight of one hundred seventy-five, Sumner estimated that Block stood a full two inches taller and weighed an easy three hundred pounds. He was built like a linebacker, with a big, doughy face, hair just starting to gray at the temples, and shrewd eyes, despite his easygoing exterior. Sumner watched Block size him up.

"No need to stand up. Didn't mean to bother you." Block shook Sumner's hand in a vise grip.

Sumner squeezed back with some amusement. Block's wife sat up.

"This is Harry, my husband, and I'm Cindy. Harry, hon, he works for *Kaiser Franz*."

"You a cabin boy?" Block hollered at Sumner.

"Harry!" Cindy hit Block on the arm.

"What's wrong with that? It's honest enough work, ain't it?" Block turned innocent eyes on Sumner. Sumner hid his amusement.

"I'm not a cabin boy, no," he said.

The German family was upon them, walking along the rail. Sumner felt the father's presence at his right, then behind him. He heard the wife speak to the daughter in German. Sumner spoke fluent German, so eavesdropping came easy.

"Americans are so loud," she said. Sumner kept his eyes on Block while he strained to hear the German girl's response.

"But friendly, I think so, Mother." She spoke in low tones.

Don't be fooled by Harry, Sumner thought.

The father stepped past Sumner. Out of the corner of his eye, Sumner could see that he continued to stare at the ocean. Sumner redirected his attention to Block, who was speaking.

"What's the point of all this 'cultural differences' mumbo jumbo? Folks from Africa to Mexico count their money the same as us, is what I say. So what do you do for *Kaiser Franz*?"

Sumner glanced back at the water. He saw the dot, speeding toward them. He felt a surge of adrenaline. It made his scalp tighten and his fingertips tingle.

He slipped a black T-shirt over his head. The dot grew larger every second. Soon it was joined by another. Sumner heard the distant roar of the cigarette boats' engines. The crafts hurtled toward them at an impressive speed.

"Block, get Cindy and the others off the deck. Tell the waiters to move everyone below."

Block looked shocked. "What?"

"Mr. Block, do it. Now."

"Well I never been ordered around like that," Block said.

Sumner didn't stay to see if Block obeyed. He sprinted across the deck to the stairs that led to the bridge, clambered up, and burst onto the small walkway that surrounded it, just as Captain Joshua Wainwright stepped out.

"Pirates," he said.

Sumner nodded. "Coming fast. Use the LRAD."

Wainwright, a competent, friendly man in his early forties, snapped an order to his second in command. They pointed a large gun in the direction of the cigarette boats, now well within a mile of them.

"Hit it," Wainwright said.

The long-range acoustic device released a beam of high-pitched sound at the boats. Over one hundred and fifty decibels of concentrated noise blasted through the air, like a sonic boom. Sumner winced as the sound assaulted his eardrums. He saw the driver of the lead cigarette boat clap a hand over one ear.

They continued to hurtle toward the *Kaiser Franz*.

"Again," Wainwright said. He watched the cigarette boats through binoculars.

The LRAD blared again. When the sound faded, Sumner could hear the tourists screaming on the deck. Still, the cigarette boats kept coming. Sumner grabbed a second set of binoculars. The pirates looked like Somalis, dark-skinned and thin. They stared at the cruise ship with undisguised greed in their eyes. He watched one of them hoist a large gun to his shoulder.

"They've got RPGs," he said.

"What the hell is that?" Harry Block's loud voice echoed on the bridge.

"Sir, you don't belong here. Please get below deck." Wainwright waved at an underling, who stepped up next to Block.

Block shook off the crew member's grip on his arm like a horse shaking off a fly. "I said, 'what the hell are RPGs'?"

Sumner lowered the binoculars to glance at Block. "Rocket-propelled grenades."

"Holy shit," Block said.